Bridget,

Happy Reading!
All the best —

For Internal Use Only

Cari Kamm

Cari Kamm

S0-AHL-390

Copyright © 2012 **Cari Kamm**

All rights reserved.

ISBN: **1479220493**

ISBN -13: **978-1479220496**

Library of Congress Control Number: **2012916421**

LCCN Imprint Name: **CreateSpace Independent Publishing Platform, North Charleston, South Carolina**

Disclaimer

This is a work of fiction. Names, characters, places and incidents are either the product of the author's imagination or are used fictitiously. Any resemblance to actual persons, living or dead, events, is entirely coincidental.

No part of this book may be reproduced or transmitted in any form or by any means, electronic or mechanical, including photocopying, recording, or by any information storage and retrieval system, without permission in writing from the author.

Dedication

For Holly, Chloe, and Heidi.
A sparkling example of unconditional love.

Acknowledgments

I would like to thank my Grandma Jo for her bits of wisdom throughout my life. Her words fueled this fire within me while growing up and for my need to devour the world up like a bowl of cereal. Cookie Crisp to be exact! No matter where I am in the world, her words travel with me. Always. Especially . . . "Don't worry about that mule going blind, just keep loading the wagon." Translation: Dream big. Never stop. Just keep going. It's an honor to be named after you. To my father and brother, thank you for constantly pushing my buttons and being there in your own way. Your sarcasm is my lifesaver. To my Aunt Aimee, my free shrink, the person on the other end of the phone who's always there. I love you. A huge appreciation to a group of women who were my first *For Internal Use Only* readers. Thank you for sparing your time to read the entire novel & send me feedback within a week! Much gratitude to my friends for your support over the years. I must give a big shout out to Chris & Idil O'Connor. I could not have written the Hamptons scenes without your presence or champagne supply. You are wonderful friends.

I must give credit to the following people who assisted me with taking *For Internal Use Only* to the novel that I hoped it to be. Thank you to my editors Liza French and Heather Hummel for helping me shape the novel into the story I wanted to tell! Also, my brilliant cover designers for creating this fabulous cover. Alan and Ian at BookDesigners.com were a dream to work with. To the Envision

Multimedia team for producing the edgy trailer I imagined. You guys rock! Also, I'm grateful to all of the great relationships I've developed with talented authors, passionate reviewers and book clubs on social media. It's a pleasure chatting with you daily. Thank you to Amy Bromberg for booking the best blog tour ever!

I feel absolutely blessed for having my fiancé RF & our mutt Schmutz in my life. For showing me love through your light and that true love does exist. I'm living my fairy tale.

Lastly, thank you to all my readers and Facebook fans for your love, support, and being a part of my journey. Even when it's eating cupcakes or me posting pictures of my dog. I'm thrilled to release *For Internal Use Only* on my 35th birthday and Valentine's Day. It means the world to me.

xo

Cari

Part One

Chapter 1

And there it was. What I had been looking for the past fifteen minutes, my sign—to The Brooklyn Bridge. I had officially been a New Yorker since I hit my ten-year mark. But shamefully enough, I had never made the effort to walk across this New York landmark. My reason for not doing this sooner was that Brooklyn was simply outside the center of my universe. Manhattan was my sanctuary, even when its asphalt attitude challenged me. However, crossing the bridge today would not only be to support my dear friend, Emma, but it would distract me from my recent habit of stalking.

So when Emma West pushed the invitation to join her at the hottest new book club in the Brooklyn neighborhood of DUMBO (Down Under the Manhattan Bridge Overpass), she suckered me in with the *be a supportive friend* title and teased with my *bridge inexperience*. Emma and I had been buddies from playing with Barbie dolls to chasing boys, and we'd moved to Manhattan in a team approach. Well, more for her, since she required a tag-along for almost everything.

"Brooklyn?" I asked hesitating. "I'm sure we have clubs in the city."

"Chloe, open your *New York Magazine* to page fifteen, now." I sensed her teeth clenching through the phone.

"I don't have one," I said, attempting to change the subject.

"Chloe Kassidy, get it now. I know how you keep tabs on gallery openings by your subscription," she alleged more sternly than ever. I knew better than to get sucked into another one of her missions, but damn, she didn't take no for an answer. Saying yes was painless compared to the alternative of her whining.

"Did we already forget what happened with your last soul mate?" I asked.

"I remember the wedding, Chloe," she laughed. "It was a memorable day for me."

"Ha! It wasn't exactly your special day," I reminded her. "It was Stephanie's wedding day."

Emma had caught more than the bouquet at Stephanie and Alexander Cudneys' nuptials. Always in search of her soul mate, she had fallen heels over head, a less-than-Southern-belle approach, for one of the groomsmen.

"I swear the signs were there!" she continued. She had convinced herself this groomsman had *soul mate* stamped across his head like a piece of prime meat approved by the U.S.D.A. Emma had caught Stephanie's lily bouquet, advanced to bed, grew a bump, and now had beautiful baby, Lily.

"I'm on page fifteen, lunatic."

"He's my one, Chloe." She sounded even more relieved than the previous soul mate. "Little Lily is fifteen months, and when I opened the magazine it was on that page!"

"Emm—"

"He's the guy I saw several months ago at Pastis eating breakfast and reading his iPad. I told you about him, remember?" I knew she smiled immensely. I felt her expression. "It's a sign!" she shrieked.

The article announced a new event created and hosted by an extremely handsome Columbia University professor. His name was Thomas and he resembled a Calvin Klein model, not a book club host.

"Houston, we have a problem. The One? Sweetie, you mean The Ninth?"

"You're doing it again," she said, now clearing her throat.

"What's that, Cinderella?"

"Chloe, stop with the judgment. I know it might be hard to believe, but love doesn't always work so effortlessly like your methodical closet that resembles a J. Crew catalogue."

"But you always compliment me on my outfits," I laughed.

No matter my expertise and technique, I was unable to edit and change the outcome of some of Emma's choices. Equal to having a baby, heartbreak couldn't be retouched.

"When it comes to the heart, you can't order A, B, and C. Sometimes you gotta grab life and make an actual choice rather than having Corporate America tell you how things are paired."

"Aiming for the jugular, I see." I felt attacked, but proud of her. I mean we need to fight for something. It was her fairy tale and Emma's choice. She followed her universal signs. I had my online personal shopper.

So what if J. Crew was one of my obsessions? It was classic, smart, and my *rational hat* worked with every piece. It allowed me an organized and well-paired outfit minus the doubt. I was too busy being focused and following my head to have daily dress rehearsals and wardrobe dilemmas. Since moving to New York City, being a risk taker when it came to fashion wasn't on my To-Do list. Maybe, I was a bit of a control freak, but I believed it to be, frankly, smart.

"Our two spots are confirmed," she said, "and this is an opportunity for you to snap some famous structures from a different perspective, which wouldn't kill you."

"What's that supposed to mean?"

"You can work, then meet me on the other side of the pond," she continued. Emma's last soul mate was British and, even though he was no longer around, his vocabulary made an appearance occasionally. "They say to be a better writer, you must be an avid reader. I'm sure somehow that applies to photography."

"Who are *they* exactly?"

So, yes . . . I admit that crossing the bridge today would distract me from stalking the mailman for the letter that could change my life forever.

"See you at four-thirty at the DUMBO General Store cafe. Get there early, since his handsomeness will bring out the weirdoes."

"Obviously," I mumbled, wondering if she were that mental to consider herself a member of the latter. Early I would be, as keeping Emma stable with a decent seat was a necessity for my own safety. I was her buffer guest for book club.

I wanted her to be happy, to find her other half. I couldn't stand in the way of her soul mate theories or ever live with an *I told you so*. I admired her careless ways, even though I had a more rational approach to being hopeless and a romantic.

After my own much-needed sign, I was at the Manhattan entrance of the Brooklyn Bridge, staring at the one-hour estimated cross time ahead. I removed the Canon from its protective shell and headed towards the light. Surprisingly, this was a bit more of a dangerous shoot than expected. I had to multi-task with finding those angles and staying within the lines. The lines delineate where to walk between the bike lane and the edge of the bridge, as there was noticeably no speed limit for bikers and bladers. *Christ.*

My Canon 5D Mark III was a massive upgrade from the fancy cardboard Kodak when I was a child. I purchased my first Canon in college as a prize, even though it was a gift from me to me. My parents couldn't afford the purchase. As my father always noted, the hefty price tag was equal to his tax return. I believe my overcompensation for my lack of new equipment was what made me less focused on technical photography. I concentrated my training on composition. Composition was what told the story. My shooting essentials were my camera and the rest of the world. That was all I needed. Events in my life developed similarly to the exact photographs I created, requiring multiple retouches, several solutions, a rainbow of color, and sometimes essential cropping, always resulting in my desired picture-perfect memory.

Strolling and dodging along, I unexpectedly turned *point and shoot* mad with landscape shots of gleaming panoramic Manhattan skylines, with the American flag waving to the beat of the day's breeze. Finally, to up-close shots of the nuts, bolts, and twisted metal strings that suspend into the sky, holding each pound of this bridge, a man-made creation, together as one. My camera, an intelligently crafted piece of hardware, allowed me to transform light and explore the world through its lens. Today's light was holding up and expected showers appeared to be holding back with a teasing drop here or there while I shot the Woolworth Building, Empire State Building, and a distant Lady Liberty. *Click. Click. Click.*

The most fascinating part of photography is before the camera rests on my eye. I see this whole world in front of me, which might be many things: bright or dark, beautiful or dirty, gentle or sharp, thought-provoking or relaxing. When the camera is lifted to my eye, I have the privilege of making that frame, whatever it may be, my own. I can focus on one tiny fragment of the scene before me and find light in the shade or beauty in the midst of what might be overlooked. To me, nothing is more productive than finding a gem, and even though it may be tunnel vision and not practical, viewing the final print is the reward. A photographer has the power of choice, to hold within each image what we want others to see.

The opportunity to reveal work in one of Chelsea's hippest galleries had come up and was occupying my mind. This was my chance to break into the art world and display my work to the public under a reputable gallery's name. This was my chance to make a name for myself. Most of all, the exhibition would boost my confidence as a real artist. The event offered prestige and my chance to take love from my hard drive and hang it on a gallery wall.

Realizing I still had the second half of the bridge to go, I hustled. Time allowed thirty minutes to get to the other side, pop into Barnes & Noble to snatch the first book for tonight, and meet Emma outside the cafe.

The forecast for today suggested possible showers, but suddenly drops turned into a downpour. Protecting the Canon and securing it under my shirt, I did what any sane person would do. I started running for its life.

I will not fall.

I reached the finish line, running over the metal plate marked *DUMBO*. I exited the bridge, down a couple of steps onto spacious, cobblestone streets with a hop, skip, and a jump right into a Barnes

& Noble. It was an industrial neighborhood brushed with an artistic touch.

I shook off, I would have to worry about my appearance later since I had to find the book and make it in twelve minutes to the cafe. I found a computer for a quick search; I carefully slid out the now-damp note neatly folded in my pocket. *The Reader*, by Bernard Schlink.

God, I'm a complete mess.

"Excuse me, Miss, do you need help?" A techie-looking man practically on his tiptoes interrupted me while I wiped off my fingertips.

"No, thank you." I typed in my search and turned my attention to him.

"Sure, Miss Portman," he added with a chuckle and left.

Yes, there was an insane resemblance between Natalie Portman and me that usually sparked a chain reaction of staring.

Ten minutes.

Search field: Barnes & Noble

Results: Not Found

Search field: Barnes

Results: Julian Barnes, *Love etc.* Description: best-selling author of six novels. Mr. Barnes is known to write under a pseudonym, a pen name.

I didn't understand why anyone would want to write under a fake name.

Wait. Barnes?

I had searched by the name of the store I was dripping in and not the task at hand. I was losing minutes learning about this pseudonym writer.

Eight minutes.

I turned around quickly; I spotted my fan of the day, who hadn't gone terribly far.

"Excuse me, I'm starting a new book club today, and I'm late. I need you."

"Anything, Miss Portman." His smile quickly turned into a blush.

"I need *The Reader.*"

"Of course, by Schlink. Step in line and I'll meet you at the register."

"Perfect! Please call me Nat," I whispered and winked. It's confirmed; when in DUMBO, be a dumbo.

Six minutes.

"Do you have a membership card?" He circled behind the counter.

"Can you please look it up for me?"

"Your e-mail address?"

"C-h-l-o-e underscore K-a-s-s-i-d-y at Gmail," I whispered. "A pseudonym of course." I winked again.

I hurried out of the store back into the monsoon, book in hand and saw the Southern Belle down the block waiting for me in front of the cafe. One of Emma's most noticeable features, besides her luminous baby blues, was her tousled honey hair accentuating her wide shoulders from years of college volleyball. As I walked towards her, I couldn't believe I was attending a book club so she could meet this guy. I imagined our friends simultaneously stating the obvious: "You only have yourself to blame, Chloe."

Our friend Kate Watts, a.k.a. Kit Kat, preferred to be solo, breaking off the male pieces that attached to her. The word *soul mate* almost made her nauseous. Stephanie and Alexander, who met and married with fairy tale love, but didn't want to see me sucked into

Emma's soul mate scenarios. I reminded myself of the history Emma and I shared as I proceeded in her direction.

We had traded in the Big Peach for the Big Apple after graduating from Oglethorpe University in Georgia. And although Emma was a philosophy major and I focused on studio art, one thing was for sure: we were both eager to explore love in the city. Well, mine in my work and Emma in finding her soul mate. Most philosophy majors I knew were nuts.

This guy better be her one.

The newly renovated historic building where the meeting took place was charming, and the elevator emptied into a large loft space with people mingling by a refreshment table of wines, teas and a Jenga looking cheese tray.

"What a marvelous space," Emma said.

"God, this would make a bad-ass apartment," I said, distracted by the black stained wood floors and exposed brick wall I estimated had been painted too many times by the dried globs of white paint. A big circle of foldout chairs waited at the room's center, and people were selecting their spots. I quickly slipped out my camera and stole a couple shots.

"There aren't two seats together," Emma whined.

"We'll just have to sit across from each other. Don't worry, I don't think anyone will bite over books." I poked her.

A roster was passed around, collecting names and e-mail addresses. While waiting my turn, I counted twenty book lovers, one crazy Emma, and one hostage—me.

The mid thirty-ish Tom Selleck look-alike positioned himself in the middle of the circle.

"Welcome to The Readers' Circle. My name is Thomas." He spoke with hints of an Australian accent. He wore beige pants, a three-button crisp white shirt, and camel leather shoes. "I'm glad to see a diverse group of people join the club this evening. At any time, please help yourself to the refreshments in the back." I wondered if I should grab wine immediately to ease the boredom. His thick brown leather watchband didn't go unnoticed when he brushed his messy hair away from his shaven face and adjusted his glasses. "This isn't just a book club, but a social club. Each week we'll review a book with open discussion," Thomas said.

Studying his frames, I considered Emma's rose-colored glasses that led her along this imaginative and fanciful path for affection. Who wouldn't want the fairy tale after listening to them each night throughout our childhood, generation after generation, before we slipped into our dreams? Then there was Disney World where all of these characters were born. As a child, with chestnut locks, I wanted to be the princess, fit into the glass slipper, and find my prince. Not the girl with the seven dwarfs. Observing Emma with her feelings constantly overriding her common sense made my decisions seem safer. I grew up and found love from behind my lens. No poisonous apples involved.

The roster went counter clockwise, as the man beside me skipped himself, passing it directly to me. "Is our contact information optional?" I whispered.

"You should give it to stay in touch with the group." He smiled. "I've got to attend each month." He rolled his eyes. "Thomas is my husband," he revealed, and I thought, *of course he is,* while I filled out the form.

The host took his seat. "Does anyone have questions before we start?"

I glanced at Emma; I noticed that sparkle in her eyes. She had no idea Thomas was in love with his happily-ever-after next to me.

When Thomas turned his attention to a raised hand, I slid out my phone and urgently typed a text to Emma so she could cross number nine off her *match made in heaven* inventory.

It's a no go with the glass slipper. He has a husband!

Chapter 2

My love for photography had led me down an unimaginable career path. Most currently, it led me to anxiously sitting on a stoop outside the New York City mid-rise building that contained my overpriced one-room apartment. I closed my eyes, allowing the morning light to calm me while I took in the delightful bird chirps and excruciating taxi beeps of the East Village, ignoring the slight smell of urine that accosted my senses.

I started my afternoon again with stalking. I eagerly awaited the mailman's arrival between 1:06 and 1:13 p.m., while he transported paper fate, sporting his pale blue polyester trousers, tucked in long-sleeve shirt pressed, and Converse sneakers.

We lived and loved through technology, so I was frustrated that my fate was arriving via snail mail and the timing matched every part of the description. Technology was the trusted source of banking transactions, meeting your husband, ordering your groceries, making restaurant reservations and even spying on your pets through a kennel cam while sunburning on a beach. But today, this life-altering letter crawled its way to me by a government official, a man I rarely saw, and never exchanged words with. I was waiting to hear if my dream would come true, and dreading it would never be.

"Good afternoon," I said, with a smile, merely able to stare at the navy stripe that lined his pant leg. The clock showed that it was 1:11 p.m. I made a wish.

"What a surprise," he muttered, while he manhandled the heavy stack wrapped with a thick, green rubber band and passed by me. I studied him meticulously stocking the empty boxes, one by one, approaching my slot.

"Do you mind if I just grab the mail for three-C, please?" I interrupted.

"If that's what it'll take," he moaned.

Between my J. Crew catalogue and my electric bill was a fancy rectangle of heavy stock ivory paper with gold trim. I squeezed the four-by-six response card. Contained in this saliva-sealed envelope were the words that would inevitably change my life. The weight of those words was heavy in my fingers and I was hesitant to open it. Without the answer the card contained, I still was able to hold onto hope.

My destiny was in my lap with the warmth of the sun counteracting the fresh chill October presented while I flipped from sweating to freezing like an on/off switch. I reassured myself it was only rejection. I had my health and photography. Whether it was amateur or professional, it was still my first love. Even if it was a two-letter response, I would remember my love for art, and how every time I shot I searched for the immense beauty that existed within the balance, tone, and temperature of my tiny frame. Having an image worth a thousand words was never my intention. I wanted to capture one word to describe each photograph. One word can define everything, *love* being a true example. There is something compelling about visualizing a picture and capturing it. There is nothing compelling about the words, *We regret to inform you.*

My fingers trembled and taking a couple photographs would be soothing. Photography to me was the perfect cocktail: one part heart, one part head, a dose of imagination, with a splash of patience.

The tearing of the envelope felt like scratches on my heart. I proceeded with caution, hoping this document wouldn't be only a keepsake to remind me *what if.*

Inch by inch, I slid out the card to reveal the twelve-point Apple Chancery font and held it to the light, observing the maker's name in the watermark. Rubbing my index finger over the engraved symbol, I was impressed. The brand, Smythson of Bond Street stationery, supplied paper to the British royal family. I was holding the same stationery as the Queen.

Dear Miss Kassidy,

We write to inform you of your acceptance into the exclusive Bruce Smith Gallery as part of our exhibit for emerging artists, hosted by curator Grayson Gates. You will be receiving your review and luncheon date via e-mail. Please be prepared to present your theme for the Love Through Light exhibit within the deadline. You will be required to exhibit three pieces.

Opening Night & Reception
Friday, February 7, 8:00 p.m.
Bruce Smith Gallery
504 West 22nd Street

I read *your acceptance* at least ten times, intoxicated with excitement and then *Love Through Light* offered a swift sobering sense of reality. I began to panic. I couldn't deny the exhibit theme made me uncomfortable.

The *Love Through Light* exhibit was inspired by the word *photography* itself and its Greek meaning, *writing with light*. As the emerging artists in Grayson Gates's exhibit, we were to create stories of love. Instead of ink, we would be writing with our three photographs.

I composed a text to Stephanie, Kate, and Emma, my inner circle. *I'm in!*

Our bonds from beginnings to endings were unbendable. Each our own elements, but together our friendship made a rare metal.

As I headed upstairs to my apartment, sane and with my wall secured, I noticed the postman staring at me. "I'm accepted!" I screamed and flashed him the invitation.

He shook his head and mumbled, "Strange."

I pinned the acceptance over my computer next to the image I've cherished since childhood. Today it meant more to me than ever before. I still had the photograph, in which I wore a white lace blouse tucked into my navy blue skirt, and rain boots, plus the tacky gold bow my mother had fastened to my ponytail.

When I was ten years old, I had attended the Atlanta Preparatory Academy. For a week during one summer, the school had taken a field trip to New York City. I was a fourth-grader going on twelfth grade, my mother would say. I had begged her to cancel the family vacation to Disney World for the opportunity. I clearly remember this defining moment, on the bus sitting alone by the window, three rows back from the driver, watching the thunderstorm while the blurry Manhattan skyline blew by. I had begun to sweat like the Welch's grape juice box I was gripping and wasn't sure if it was a result of the downpour or that my heart fluttered while we approached the Big Apple.

I had slid my cardboard Kodak camera (my first camera ever) out of my purple backpack. While no one looked, I had turned the lens towards myself, double-checking the flash was off, and snapped a shot. As a child, I had hoped to be a famous photographer one day, maybe even paparazzi. I had wanted to shoot the New Kids On The Block or even the Olsen Twins, the exact celebrities I often wrote letters to in hopes of becoming their pen pal.

I loved ambient light, natural light that already existed in a scene. It didn't even matter if I had my Kodak in hand. While my friends were on the playground, I was always assessing the light. I would join my thumbs together in a kiss and hold my hands like goalposts, always picturing what my subject would look like in it.

At that moment, moving to New York City when I grew up became a priority on my list of life goals. The list had included getting an A on every math test, making the Girl Scout cookie quota, becoming faster at the stop, drop, and roll move etched in my brain for events involving fire, avoiding the school bully, Sally Caudwell, and one day having a fairy tale like Cinderella.

Chapter 3

I woke up melancholic to an overcast Sunday morning offering a cool forty-two degrees and greeted by an e-mail from an unfamiliar sender.

From: Mary Polt
To: Chloe Kassidy
Subject: Introduction
Date: October 11, 9:59 a.m.

Hi Chloe,
I know this is a bit unusual, but I was at book club last night. You only live once, right? I saw you and instantly thought of my dear friend! You guys would be perfect together. He's going to kill me, but my intuition never steers me wrong. I feel like a secretary (LOL!), but I had to reach out to you. His name is Christoph. I attached a photo of him. I would love to set you guys up.
Mary

Immediately pushing my index finger into the invasive lens on top of my computer screen, I looked around my apartment, insuring my privacy. This had to be a joke. Would Emma do something this absurd to get back at me for going a bit overboard about her defective gay-dar? Were the girls teasing me for participating in these soul mate scavenger hunts? Which of them would even consider this mischievous? Actually, I could hear Emma pointing out to me, *One more thing about you, Miss Aquarius, you freak out when someone comes too close.*

How did she even get my e-mail address? The sign-in sheet! Opening the attachment to take a peek at the mystery man . . . *Hail Mary, full of sexiness!*

Predicted showers turned monsoon, running to save my Canon's life, and sitting through another one of Emma's sagas possibly were all well worth the introduction to the man staring back at me. His glassy eyes pulled my attention further into my screen suchlike a crystal ball, causing my heart to flip inside out. His dark hair, distinctive facial features and five-o'clock shadow made me assume a European background.

This had to be a prank, although neither of the girls had called me yet to tease me endlessly with one of their *LOL* rampages. Maybe it was SPAM! The other day I had scrambled trying to close a penis-enlargement ad to *Get Your Hard On*, but accidentally opened it. My friends or a spammer couldn't know by 10:00 a.m. that I had been at the book club the night before. Maybe this was real. Even if this was, who was Mary? I'm not sure which was worse, having a woman organizing our introduction or online dating. There would be no Internet love for me. How can you control what you can't see? Actually, his having a secretary was worse, as those online dating services had millions of members.

Was her feeling so intense about us that she would put herself out there to contact a complete stranger? I mean, should I at least respond to say, no, thank you? Even if I was absurdly intrigued, did Mary Polt have an exit strategy, or would she be involved in all communications? They might be a couple of swingers. I had just watched a *Dateline* episode on that actual issue. I swore on my Canon, as my blood rose to a boil, if this were a cruel joke, I would have no choice but to unleash the Kassidy wrath. A bad photo could follow one forever.

While the afternoon arrived, I was still playing detective. I had lived in the city for a decade. I was a smart, creative, and effortlessly stylish thanks to *Jenna's Picks* and *Instant Gratification* on J. Crew. com. This was how I might potentially meet a man? A secretary who snatched my e-mail address while Emma stalked the gay man of her dreams?

Immediately, the Portman fan from the bookstore became a possible candidate, considering that I gave him my e-mail for my membership. Saving ten percent was not worth this hassle. What if he were pretending to be a she named Mary from the book club just to talk to Natalie Portman? What if Mary was real and wanted to introduce me to her gorgeous friend Christoph?

Hypothetically, let's say I replied back, *Hello*. What happens then? Would my friends laugh in my face for playing along? Would his secretary send me his e-mail? I would never make the first move. Would her move count as the first move? So *my* emailing *him* would actually be the second move.

Let's say I emailed him. He emailed back. I emailed him again. He made me smile and giggle. He emailed back. I obviously made him smile. I emailed him. I can't believe I'm doing this. He emailed back. This is where he should have his friend ask for my phone number, or perhaps he should simply ask me. Should I give it to him? *Hmm*.

I imagined our first date. We're enjoying a spicy Malbec at the Monday Room. He is wearing a dark blue suit, chocolate-colored leather shoes and belt, a purple tie. He has just finished work. He looks a little tired, yet has a stupid smile on his face every time I bring up how we met. I'm wearing a more casual outfit of skinny jeans, a perfectly pressed white button-down shirt, and ballet flats and clutch. I'm trying not to smile too much, but I can't help it.

This was a bigger sign than I had bargained for, as the bridge not only connected Manhattan and Brooklyn, but two strangers. A bridge, a location, a friend, the book, the emails, and the future memories . . . nope, I should hold back and take a while to respond to her. Then again, is a true connection up for games? *Snap out of it.*

It was official. I was in a black and white frame of mind. Going into my walk-in, color-coded closet, I grabbed the page-twelve ensemble I had recently purchased. Today was fit for my dark denim matchstick jeans and a carbon color merino oversized sweater that exposed the white-ribbed tank across my left shoulder. I slid on my tall black leather boots and grabbed my black pea coat. My entire pre-picked attire was simplicity at its best, and I indeed mirrored the dim mood of New York this morning. Getting ready in fewer than ten minutes and looking put together as a homemade pie was a silent victory for me compared to Emma's one-hour episodes of never having anything to wear. The amount of time I saved on dressing I spent photographing. Verizon didn't have a thing on me with their minute-saving plans.

I had seven blocks to go until the faceoff at the West 22nd Street gallery, and only four months to decorate my wall. The paperweight on my head had shifted to a boulder. This gallery had been the hot spot on an artist's map since 2001, since his expansion to both contemporary and historically talented photographers. Bruce Smith's mission was to discover innovative and influential artists, and I needed to be his next significant discovery.

The Smith Photography Annual (SPA) was a yearly invitational exhibition and displayed ten emerging artists, selected by the guidance of a prominent curator.

Fortunately, Mr. Grayson Gates, the curator of the Bruce Smith gallery, had discovered me at last year's Art Basel in Miami Beach. My Portman identity crisis had caused commotion. This attention usually became my crisis. Once it was confirmed that I wasn't the Hollywood starlet, Grayson Gates had realized who I truly was. Two months earlier, *New York Magazine* had featured a two-page spread on a campaign created by Bright Images, Inc. The article had happened to include my name and picture, praising the creative director for its success. My boss had been outraged with my free press since he was Milton Bright, the face of the company. In all honesty, he was a total press whore.

I had envied Grayson Gates's man purse that evening, a classic leather satchel that strapped his chest like a seatbelt over his flashy tailored suit, which had presented him to be much shorter than his five-foot-eight stocky frame. Although his greasy black full-bodied mane had given him a good inch and a half extra. It wasn't until the topic of art had turned into his history of female pop tarts that I'd recognized he was a womanizer. Each ex-girlfriend, *sweet little things*, had resembled a particular actress or model he had relations with. He was known for his talking, tanning, and Tic Tacs. You heard the man coming miles away while the tiny mints shuffled in his pocket from stride to stride before your senses overdosed on his cologne. His scent had its own ego.

Today, past my reflection, was the *Love Through Light* gallery walls sleeping as a blank canvas. For now, I preferred looking from the outside in at the bigger picture. While I stared through the oversized glass-plate door lined with its industrial metal frame, I adored the minimalist space more each visit. It was raw, a clean palate. I closed my eyes and imagining my work hanging above the slate flooring, flashing from the pristine white walls, made me feel warm. I opened my eyes to the foggy spot where my breath hit the glass; I scribbled *Chloe Kassidy*. I took a step back, a deep breath, and a mental snapshot. That felt pretty damn good to process.

I had no meetings scheduled. I stuck my inspiration key in the ignition and accelerated full speed ahead towards the Museum of Modern Art. After taking in a view of where I wanted to be, I craved quality time with my three boyfriends—Warhol, Picasso, and Matisse. The MoMA membership was affordable, and included a ten percent discount at the sophisticated-yet-bustling restaurant located inside, The Modern. My men, membership card, and a modern meal were my preferred method of recharging my own batteries. One reason I adored New York, dining alone was acceptable and comfortable. It was quiet time for my inner self and ego to have a play date, resolving any issues and allowing creativity to take its course.

Today's ominous weather caused me to crave comfort foods created by the chef. Appreciating food as art entirely came with the territory of being an artist, a code to be respected. The saffron tagliatelle with cider-braised rabbit, wild mushrooms, and baby zucchini, served in a quiet space overlooking the sculpture garden, sounded medicinal.

Turning the corner on West 53rd Street and heading towards Sixth Avenue, my eyes zoned in on a billboard for the NBC show,

The Office. I didn't have time to think about Mary's e-mail, his *secretary*. A tingly sensation hit my butt, and then traveled upward along my spine. My Blackberry signaled for my attention. *Jesus, could it be her?*

Text from Stephanie: *Meet us at the Boat House for lunch, 1:30 p.m.? East 72nd Street and Park Drive North entrance. xoxo.*

Stephanie and Alexander oddly complimented each other equal to those *Dancing with the Stars* duos. She, a petite, porcelain, ex-ballerina, from the Midwest, with a warming soul similar to the comfort of my grandmother's stew. He, a towering, tan, ex-surfer from California, who spoke more tongue-in-cheek. They both required the country, she to gallop on her Quarter Horses and he to play eighteen holes outside the city.

They had met in Corporate America, both on their first day at work, and it was love at first sight. They were engaged months later. Their two-year anniversary had been a couple weeks ago and we knew it was two going on sixty for The Cudneys. Within our inner circle, Stephanie was my mentor and the one I exposed myself to the most. She gave me honest advice, never the easiest, and I cherished her for it. It must have been the constructive criticism in her plié days.

It was approaching noon and having lunch with the lovebirds was always a pleasure. I replied, *See you soon!*

The mall in Central Park, specifically Literary Walk, was another reason I loved New York. The Mall was the only straight walkway in Central Park lined with American elm trees, some of the last remaining in North America, which formed a cathedral-like canopy over the wide pathway. The trees were living legends, with their own stories and circles of life. I always felt spiritually connected there, as if I were standing in any place of worship. This wide pathway reminded me of the aisles in the churches I had photographed throughout my travels. I pictured the greenery that would leisurely dance to the invisible beat of a spring day's breeze. Standing at the south end of the mall, I was at Literary Walk and simply intoxicated by the warm romanticized view the fall offered.

Gently slipping out my Canon, I switched the mode to monochrome. Today was the day for shooting RAW. I was surrounded by a low-contrast situation from the overcast sky. The color was vague and unable to lead me. Only a well-trained eye still captured the shapes, tones, and texture within the frame and revealed the different features among the shadows and highlights. This was a test to see how far I could make this happen and would be excellent training for retouching. Following each click, I checked the three-inch display, noticing a grand competition for attention between the highlights and dark tones.

Black and white photography was classic, elegant, and most suitable for this dreamy scene. Even though there were no fireworks of color exploding or tulips blooming, it was an opportunity to learn. My eye wouldn't be distracted by color, and the subject or scene's individuality could be more easily recognized. Some may have seen winter approaching as nature's end, but I aimed to see life through the lens and beauty in the most unexpected places.

I captured the angles of the historic bronze statues including Robert Burns and Sir Walter Scott, and as I walked north, Fitz-Greene Halleck, all prominent writers and all adding to Literary Walk. Just like these men defined one of the places I loved in New York, Stephanie and Alexander defined true love for me. I would never forget the evening before their wedding when Stephanie shared with me *Alexander* was the one word that defined *true love* for her.

I continued to point and shoot at the bare intertwined branches hugging each other tightly while the shadowy sky peeked through. The backs of bikers passing by, a woman sipping a Starbucks Tazo tea and reading *Anna Karenina*. *Click.* I captured a sixty-ish man in a gray pin-striped suit and cashmere pea coat reading the Cindy Adams section of the *NY Post*, while keeping an eye on the pigeons above him that lined a single branch, contemplating what to drop on next. *Click.* A desperate vendor offering ice cream in this unfriendly weather with no takers. *Click. Click.* A striking French woman holding her husband's fingers, looking up, down, and around, "Le parc est stupéfiant" (the park is breathtaking). *One second. Almost. Click.* The smooth to rough flakey ridges of the elm's gray and dark brown bark showing winter symptoms. *Click.*

Approaching the Bethesda Fountain marked the end of this journey. It was 1:18 p.m. and I was on time for my lunch dates.

Stephanie and Alexander were already seated inside by the window overlooking Turtle Pond and sipping what looked like a Riesling from the yellowish tones of the glass.

"Hello there!" I called out approaching their table.

"Chloe!" They responded in unison.

"You look great even when you're casual. I hate you," Stephanie joked, flashing her pouting face and giving me a hug.

"Thanks. Page twelve."

"Jenna's Picks?" she asked.

"Who's Jenna?" Alexander interrupted.

"Nope, believe it or not, 'Instant Gratification.' Each piece under a hundred bucks." I winked.

Stephanie rolled her eyes. "Sweetie, Jenna is Chloe's personal style guru."

Alexander quickly scanned me. "Hmm. She does an excellent job." He returned his nose to the food selections. I didn't explain Jenna was an online persona created by J. Crew.

"How's the exhibit coming along?" Stephanie asked.

"Everything's coming along beautifully," I implied, trying to sound confident. Each day felt like a paperweight on my creativity, getting closer and closer to the exhibit deadline. I needed to focus. Now my passion had deadlines, and occasionally I found my index finger and me on different pages. I feared developing shooter's block. I had to prove I was wall-worthy and Mr. Gates had chosen wisely.

"Excuse me, sir, can we get another glass for our friend?" Alexander interrupted, grabbing the server's attention. "Is Sauvignon Blanc okay, Chloe?"

"Perfect." I nodded. *Damn, I was off on the shade of his wine.*

"I stopped by the gallery this morning," I continued. The walk across the Brooklyn Bridge is an experience." I took a sip. "My index finger and camera have kissed and reconnected."

"What are you exhibiting?" Alexander asked.

"It's my choice. I can create new work or tailor my theme by pulling pieces from my archives," I said. I had time to research, but exploring a solid theme on love for the three sixteen-by-twenty prints generated an emotional block. "I'm searching for the one concept, the one to stand out from the rest," I admitted. The truth was this same search was occurring in my love life. I was thirty and waiting for the one who would rationalize the risk and define a love I had never known. A genuine feeling, that shaped my needs for a man because I loved him.

Alexander raised his glass. "To Miss Kassidy's debut." He made a reach to pretend-clink our glasses.

"I love you," Stephanie said to him as they kindly kissed, resembling the cutest couple ever. I'm sure they held hands under the table.

Sometimes I felt like their adoptive child, even though we were all thirty years old. They had this wisdom belying a couple so young. I felt a responsibility to never disappoint them since they had invested so much advice in me. I'm sure Stephanie had a running mental tab for her hours served.

"Speaking of the bridge, Emma convinced you to go to a book club for another soul mate?" Stephanie's brow arched.

I knew Emma had good intentions, but she had played the game too often, passing 'Go' too many times and collecting too many souls. She abused her *Get out of Jail* privileges.

"How was the first book-club meeting? What's the novel?" Alexander asked, postponing a possible Emma debate. It always led back to Emma's soul mate incident at their wedding, leaving her now not just a single woman, but this time a single mother.

"I'm saying you have a great deal to concentrate on . . . don't get distracted by her wild man chases," Stephanie interrupted. "Emma shared with me this month's gay soul mate. I couldn't get a word out of Kate." She tipped the corners of her mouth downward. I rolled my eyes, not surprised. Ever since Kate's breakup, her bumping heads moved from occasional to routine. The easiness and effortless way of the Cudneys' life aggravated Kate's core and created a grudge. She resented how Stephanie's marriage worked so painlessly.

"We should still introduce Emma to our single friends," Alexander added.

"Emma would see a setup as settling. She wants the exceptional connection, that Big Bang story where the universe brings two people together and their worlds collide . . ."

"Sounds like a Snow Patrol song," Alexander joked.

"Besides, after taking your day and making it her special day, do you want to get involved with Emma's love life again?" I asked. We took a significant sip of our wines and sighed. "It annoys your wifey to share her beloved wedding date with the day Emma throws Lily's annual 'I got prego' party," I giggled.

"Well, I want you to worry about your needs, Chloe. Don't be scared to show the world what you've got," Stephanie provoked me with the shake of her fist. "Don't worry if the sky feels like it's going to fall on your head and all of a sudden you'll be vulnerable. Exhibit or not, it doesn't change the fact you're an extraordinarily strong and talented woman." Stephanie glanced at Alexander for confirmation. *A matching pair.*

"Well, the book-club host might be gay, but he was gorgeous," I laughed. "I did want to get your impression on what love is to the both of you. I need all the inspiration I can get."

"True love can turn you around and next thing you know you're face-to-face with it." Alexander glanced at Stephanie. "I'll never forget that day she walked into my office—a person I would eventually come to know, befriend, date, and marry."

Stephanie leaned in and kissed his smooth-shaven cheek. "I admitted to him that I saw my future in him when he brushed by me. It was something I couldn't imagine or was ready for."

"What do you mean ready for?" I asked.

"I had just moved to the city and it was my first day at the company. It wasn't ideal timing," Stephanie said. She reached over and pinched Alexander's right ear. "You can't be afraid of something like that."

"It's something we all dream about," Alexander added, finishing his wine.

While he paid the check, I silenced my vibrating Blackberry. The red icon was above my personal Gmail account. *Open.* Immediately my mouth became dry, my fingers stiff, and my core tight.

From: G. Gates
To: Chloe Kassidy
Re: Appointment Confirmation
Date: October 13, 3:33 p.m.

Dear Miss Kassidy,
I'm writing to confirm your lunch appointment with the gallery board and myself for Friday, October 21, 12:00 p.m. at Cookshop restaurant, located on the corner of Twentieth Street and Tenth Avenue. Please bring your proposal for the theme you will be exhibiting.
Grayson Gates

I had to acknowledge Grayson Gates was more than his Tic Tac walking and ex-talking man with a messenger bag. He considered his emerging artists the only risk for his career to crash and burn since he was already a celebrated success. New York embraced him for his flair in finding breakout artists. He had curated shows since the age of nineteen.

"You look terrified," Stephanie said. "Are you all right?"

"Yep, I'm fine." I shoved my phone into my bag. "It's just an e-mail confirming my lunch with Grayson Gates. I'm confident but second-guessing myself a bit with creating my theme."

"It's love," Alexander said reassuring. "Why are you uncomfortable? Haven't you been in love?" he asked.

"I'm a huge hopeless romantic." I reassured them as much as myself and avoided the question, since the topic of this conversation caused my chest to tighten. "Thank you for a yummy lunch." We collected our belongings to leave.

"Let's share a cab," Stephanie suggested and flung her arm to hail one.

"Duty calls me to finish work in the park," I said, hoping I didn't appear rude. I wanted to make it to the museum.

Chapter 4

Thinking of the essentials concerning love for both my exhibit
and myself, I must admit, frightened me. Failure in both scenarios
wasn't an option. I had to stay focused since my insecurities
behaved similarly to ankle weights, making it even more intense to
move forward. This was my downfall with my previous attempts at
opening myself to a guy. That was the catch with the relationship
environment. It was much easier to control the outcome in
photography. Heartbreak couldn't be retouched. Watching Kate suffer
through hers didn't improve my worries.

We had coined her nickname Kit Kat for two deserving reasons.
One, she loved to remind us how staying single is healthier than
compromising and sharing a piece of yourself. She always broke
up and off with every other *piece* in her life since her candy bar
had crumbled. This was also known as the *Ian incident*. Also, Kate
became Kit Kat for our own victory, since referring to her as the

processed candy annoyed the ex-fat-kid-turned-devoted-well-being guru to her core. Or, center, as she would constantly remind us.

Hours later, my stomach was killing me from sucking down several coffees while reading Grayson Gates's e-mail three times, scrolling through my shots from the park and touring the exhibits at the MoMA. I'm pretty sure the feeling of butterflies in your stomach was supposed to feel more whimsical, but the artistically winged creatures were gnawing at my insides. The tightness in my chest was still present as once again my heart flipped inside out, cramped and tried to work its way back to its natural position. The stress was proving to be a strenuous workout for this muscle.

I tried uploading my shoot from the afternoon for retouching, but was getting nowhere. My fingers were swollen and tight from the walking in the cold weather. I lay back on my bed to regulate my breathing and suffocate my nervousness.

Just close your eyes. Get a grip.

The ceiling was white and blank, identical to the gallery walls where I was going to be showing my art, my voice, and my perspective on *Love Through Light*. I would be hanging my heart on the wall. I believed in my work and I wanted others to believe in me as well. Photography built me up, but at the same time, made me insecure, as the thought of rejection and disappointment was unbearable. Love to me was a blank canvas that put the artist at risk. You began with the best intentions, but might end up being the only one seeing a masterpiece. The heart was a life-sustaining organ and I protected mine as such.

The sheer panic tightened my posture at its core, when I realized I had completely forgotten to respond to the curator's lunch confirmation. I had gone and lost my head.

From: Chloe Kassidy

To: Grayson Gates

Re: Appointment Confirmation

Date: October 13, 5:33 p.m.

Dear Mr. Gates,

I'm confirming my appointment. Thank you in advance and for this opportunity.

Chloe Kassidy

I unpinned the fancy exhibit invitation from above my workstation to read it a couple more times, boosting my optimism in creating this required theme. I was sure Grayson Gates would be pleased with my proposal.

While the images were uploading, my search for my portfolio case was interrupted when the phone rang. It was my mother.

"Hi, Mom," I answered.

"Can you talk? Are you busy?" she asked.

The familiar tone of her voice spiked my pulse. "For a few minutes. I'm working."

"You're still at the office? It's late."

It wasn't late. My mother was a teacher and to her 3:00 p.m. was end of day. "I'm home retouching," I confirmed, attempting to recall my thought before her call.

"Oh . . . I thought you meant your job," she said.

Prior to the acceptance, my work had primarily focused on hiring professional photographers and incorporating their work for stock photography. I helped our clients create brands for their companies to memorable moments they wouldn't have captured without our guidance. Telling their stories through our ideas was rewarding.

Well, a close second to claiming space at the Bruce Smith gallery in Chelsea. Bright Images, Inc. created inspiring work, but I wanted to be on the other side with the photographers.

The 350-employee company afforded me my Manhattan studio apartment, the use of their top-notch technology at my personal disposal and a creative environment with views of the Hudson River.

"Mom, photography is my job. In fact, I received life-changing news the other day." Irritation rasped my voice. "I was accepted into the exhibition in February," I announced.

"Good for you." She paused. "I just hope you don't compromise your real job."

Oh God. "Mother, this is a chance of a lifetime to become a professional." I covered my eyes with the palm of my hand and took a new breath. "You know my childhood dream. Can't you understand?"

"I guess not, Chloe. I've had a long day. I've been awake since five-thirty this morning and my classroom behaved badly the entire afternoon," she ranted. "I don't think you understand what it's like."

No matter what day it was, it was a bad day for my mother. I couldn't recall the last time she had ever been excited about anything or when she had possessed a spectacular moment. Instead, her life was hard-hitting, overwhelming, and intense. Her day ended at what could be considered a late lunch break. She had three months vacation during summer, and she started her workday by the set time of the alarm clock; doing her hair took forever. Taking two hours to prep for preschool was her prerogative. Teaching was one of the most honorable professions, a vital and fundamental career, but she carried the title as if it were a cross on her back. *The preschool martyr.*

"I'm facing hours of work ahead of me, Mom. Just tell Dad the good news for me," I fumed, abruptly ending the conversation. My mother was no mood-booster. Her moaning replaced her obligation of motherly support.

They say there is an inevitable moment in every child's life when subconsciously we cut the umbilical cord from our family and start building our life in a stage of rebellion and independence. Although my parents didn't consider taking pictures a professional career, with my mother a teacher and father an accountant, I was indeed the sum of their expertise. Their flaws and immaturities, their stumbling, their invincibility, their high and low moments, their dreams and fears, were a part of me. However, taking photographs belonged all to me.

My mother's lack of full support didn't matter since I had a curator now standing behind me. Even though the acceptance was confidence boosting, it was also a relief the exhibition was a flock of artists including photographers, painters, and sculptors. I had nightmares on catching my first significant break, exposing myself, and failing to impress a swanky crowded room full of hipsters who carried attitudes not so casual as their clothes.

The next morning I headed into Bright Images, Inc. to wrap up a few client projects. After I received my exhibit acceptance, my new daily goal was to get in and get out of the office as soon as possible to work on my theme and to prove my mother wrong. Her doubts fueled my ambition to succeed even more. I depended on this opportunity to pluck me out of my routine life and place me into a passionate one. I exited the elevator into the office with candy-colored painted walls. The morning had officially begun with the sounds of the ping-pong table in full action. The aroma of exploding popcorn kernels stung my senses and complimented the casual jeans-wearing staff.

At my desk, I gave the mouse a swirl, ignoring my instant messenger flashing. I was sure it was my boss following up on potential clients in the works. He smelled fresh blood entering the office, which was his signal to go into an aggressive thirty-second sales speech, to make us ravenous. Even though he considered himself a young Steve Jobs, he was more like Chef Gordon Ramsey with a touch of Bob Barker.

From: Mary Polt
To: Chloe Kassidy
Subject: Checking in
Date: October 14, 10:18 a.m.

Hi Chloe!
I hope you're having a fantastic morning. Again, I know this is a bit awkward and you have no idea who I am, but I really have the desire to connect you two. You guys would be great together. I've already told Christoph about you and the gut feeling when I saw you with *The Reader*. He is now hoping you'll respond as well. He doesn't want to intrude on your privacy and contact you without your permission.
Just checking in . . .
Mary

Her e-mail completely sidetracked me. I couldn't afford wasting minutes as my creative process and deadline wouldn't be forgiving. I had to rule out my friends since they would have come clean by now. Maybe the bookstore guy still thought I was the starlet and was following my pseudonym procedure by calling himself *The Secretary*. Or, perhaps the universe really was conspiring to bring

Christoph and me together? My rational hat said *Delete the e-mail*, but tiny signals escaped from the middle of my chest that poems, stories, and quotations referenced *Follow your heart*. My heart kept murmuring, *What if?*

I quickly processed my court's opinions on how to proceed. Emma would say it was fate. Stephanie would suggest simply emailing back, but being careful. Kate would remind me how being single is safer, to stay off the Internet, and suggest a juice, maybe wheatgrass.

From: Chloe Kassidy
To: Mary Polt
Subject: Re: Checking in
Date: October 14, 10:28 a.m.

Hello Mary,
Thank you for your e-mail and checking in. To be honest, I'm not sure how to respond. This is a bit odd, writing to a stranger about your friend, a man I know nothing about. Saying that, it's fine for you to pass my e-mail to him. I guess there is no harm in that.
All the best,
Chloe

Mixed emotions ran through me and in manifold. I was smiling, but pensive. I was panicky, but enthusiastic. I thought I might vomit. I felt reluctant with a pang of naiveté. Thankfully, I hadn't mentioned this to anyone and would be the only witness to my silliness. The cropping would be less tedious when it blew up in my face.

"Chloe! Where are we on new clients for next month?" came an abrasive voice through my speakerphone. It was the demon attempting to drag me to Hell. *Back to reality.*

The first three words that come to mind when I think of my boss, Milton Bright, were insecure, narcissistic and inappropriate. The forty-eight-year-old resembled a Toby Maguire and possibly wore a Spiderman suit under his daily wardrobe of jeans, checkered button-up shirts and bowties. He lacked superhero potential. The superhero status lived only in the chaos between his ears. To him, he was extremely well-liked and the best-looking guy around town. Milton's existence was this company. Bright Images, Inc. was his family and the employees his only friends. We'd heard the story how the ex-chiropractor had taken a trip to Peru twelve years ago and returned home, creating a completely new identity. No one knew what truly happened in South America, but it hadn't been a peaceful effect like someone might assume a retreat would offer.

Milton returned obsessed with empowering himself and controlling others. He memorized and referenced daily every sales-driven, how-to-control and *take power away from others* self-help book he could find. His assistant revealed to us she had spotted his secret stash of these books while organizing his office.

The men at this company had it far worse than us ladies. Stomaching Milton's inappropriate-bordering-on-sexual-harassment remarks were nothing compared to his competitiveness with testosterone. He compared himself to mankind, sizing them up to conclude he was the handsomest of them all. In my opinion, he would have found true happiness and a happy ending if he'd just come out of the closet.

"Come into my office!" he screamed once more. "We need to have a meeting!"

I reminded myself I had few choices here and took a deep breath. If the opening was a success, I would no longer be dealing with this jerk. I would be my own boss. *Don't let him get a rise out of you, Chloe.* I had learned to manage him over the years by allowing him to think he was the mastermind behind our creative projects. His feeling of complete control pacified him similarly to an infant's binky.

"Milton." I knocked three times on his office door before entering.

"Yes!" he yelled with the recurring sounds of his rope slapping the wooden floors.

I guessed our crucial meeting would be accompanied by his jump-rope workout. He was always training, but never competed in anything.

"Our sales are slipping this month! What's going on around here? We need to launch major cross-promotional and branding campaigns . . . Now!"

His bowtie was coming undone. It was a shame it was too short to trip him. "Mr. Bright, three promotional campaigns are starting tomorrow and another next week. As far as the rejuvenated branding ideas, we're still waiting on your response. I've followed up twice by e-mail with you. Are they approved?" This was his way of reassuring himself he was the authority who led our sales to its steep incline month after month. Sales were higher than the previous two years for October. In all honesty, Milton was amazing at his job. He inspired sheer panic, created chaos, and brilliantly spread a lack of self-worth around all of us. Somehow, he still found time for daily self-promotion and to change his wardrobe twice without ever leaving the office. We were one big happy Bright family.

"And I spoke to the Fletcher client. He's not overly impressed with you. Are you slacking on your responsibilities?" Milton asked.

"I assure you that I give every client 200%," I said. "I will try harder."

While I returned to my office, I laughed at Milton's attempt to undermine my work. He was unaware that the Fletcher client had called me yesterday to personally thank me for a job well done. I closed the door behind me to stare at my computer screen and pixel count. This eased my frustration and appeared to work with Milton leaving me alone. I prayed for the day I would no longer call this space my office.

Chapter 5

I hailed a cab home. Mr. Attachment may have caused my heart to whisper, but my images and exhibit boulder were crushing my mind to bits and pieces.

Cozy on my bed, pulling the top of my MacBook open, and balancing my espresso on *The Reader*, I began to take a look at my most-recent images, blocking out the mental ones of the sexy man. *Tingle. Tingle. Tingle.* I felt the phone vibration.

Please don't let it be a response! I felt reckless for letting my guard down. *How could I respond, seriously?*

The black device was pushing my buttons with its aggressive little red light.

Flash. Pathetic. Flash. Dumb ass.

Deep breath, Kassidy. I had to open my eyes to read the message.

From: Christoph Kostas
To: Chloe Kassidy
Subject: Good Evening
Date: October 14, 5:32 p.m.

Hello Chloe,

Well, I'm a bit reluctant, but I'm glad my 'secretary' was eager in connecting us. That didn't come without a price, of course, since she's coming from Brooklyn into Manhattan on Saturday and wants dinner and drinks as a gesture of 'gratitude' on my part. It is wonderful to meet you, well in a sense, since we're merely two strangers emailing one another this evening.

A little bit about me . . . I'm Swiss (from Geneva), half elitist and half traditional, French-speaking, Swiss-speaking, and English as you can see, half reserved and half open. It's a challenge, but hey, all writers need a muse in every moment and every small or big occurrence. Yes, I'm a writer and you're reading *The Reader*, one of my favorites.

About two years ago, I quit a career at the foreign office of Switzerland to move to Italy to just be on my own and write. When I got myself back together—after finishing my 'soul mate theory' manuscript, I took a break from writing and created two programs that promote the rights of minorities. I moved to NY last June to try and bring the European values to the Blackberry obsessed and rather fast-track-dating Americans. I hope to publish my book one day.

And this is the title on my business card but it does require decoding: Committee of Legal Advisers HUDOC

Expert consultant of the ICC (Ts)

Delegations Official

p.s. I hope to hear from you. Worse comes to worst, we'll have a funny story to tell over coffee.

Christoph Kostas

His hesitation created comfort, since Mary had pushed him as well. I was in a MasterCard commercial. New first date outfit, $150. Therapy session if all goes to shit, $200. Painkillers, $50. Finding true love, priceless. I held my chest to alleviate the uneasiness while my heart flipped inside-out once again.

What would a simple reply hurt? He had weekend plans with Mary, so touching base wouldn't cause me any harm or risk of self-destructing from humiliation. He was correct. His business card was the Da Vinci Code, but his boisterous telling of himself was a bit of a put-off. Even so, he intrigued me with endearing his use of postscripts.

According to Google, the ICC (Ts) was *an independent, permanent court that tries individuals accused of genocide, war crimes, and crimes against humanity. The Rome Statute, signed by 106 nations, established the ICC in 1998*. I didn't understand HUDOC and it didn't seem like Google could either. I had to know more. I began my extensive research and *Christoph Kostas* turned up no results with the exception of a couple Facebook profiles. None resembled the attached picture in her e-mail. My rational hat was tightly fitted to my head with the pressure squeezing me into a migraine. I couldn't penalize him for not being a social media fanatic, and I sensed a rather sophisticated and traditional demeanor about him.

From: Chloe Kassidy
To: Christoph Kostas
Subject: Re: Good Evening
Date: October 14, 6:17 p.m.

Hello Christoph,

I must admit I've never met another stranger by another stranger. It's nice to meet you as well. I'm American, a bit too traditional at times, quite reserved, only English speaking and a photographer. My passion is my work and has been since I was a little girl. I quickly learned that rather than pretending to be a princess posing, I wanted to be in the action behind the lens.

What a coincidence you're from Geneva. I traded in my Switzerland art internship for one in New York when one of my best friends suggested we move to the city after graduation. I'm glad to meet another artist. What kind of writer are you? Speaking of *The Reader*, I do need to start reading so my fellow book-club members don't shun me. Although, I guess I should be thankful for their selection. Chloe

Turning down Switzerland for New York City had left me with no regrets. My cousins from New Jersey had seemed experienced and more independent than me, when we were kids. Perhaps it was upbringing, but I had a hunch it was the direct train service to Penn Station that made them worldly. I was right.

Returning to the task at hand, an instant messenger chat invitation popped up, covering my photograph in progress. It was from *Kostas_Christoph*. I accepted, even though it seemed slightly aggressive for my taste.

IM from Christoph: *Hi there . . . Thought instant messenger would be easier to continue our chat.*

IM from Chloe: *You're a writer, a painter, and a man working to save the world? Do you prefer Mr. Diplomat or is Christoph sufficient?*

IM from Christoph: *Christoph will do. Being a diplomat pays the bills, but writing is my true passion. That trip to Venice sparked my painting days. Have you been there?*

IM from Chloe: *I've traveled to Venice. It fueled my passion for photography and to fight for the artist I want to be. Similar to your painting, I occasionally sell my pieces through word of mouth, and to clients at work, a job that pays the bills. I had never considered myself a professional until I landed a wall in an upcoming exhibit.*

IM from Christoph: *Congratulations! How did that happen?*

IM from Chloe: *I was in the right place at the right time! I hopped a flight to Miami last minute to attend Art Basel and bumped into a curator.*

IM from Christoph: *I could say the same with Mary being at book club . . . When is your birthday?*

IM from Chloe: *Although I'm not aggressively saving the world, my goal is to inspire people to love, create, and feel by their own imagination . . . I suppose. p.s. January 29*

IM from Christoph: *Your birthday is 1/29? That's my mum's birthday! You're intelligent and playful . . . just like her, an Aquarius. She's my favorite woman in this world and a true Aquarian. My birthday is March 29. I'm a stubborn, adventurous, complicated, yet simple Aries. This is where you should have thought . . . 'that made me smile, for he has taken time to see deeper than my surface.'*

IM from *Chloe: It seems that I'll need to read up on the astrological signs! You just admitted that an Aries is complicated!*

IM from Christoph: *Perhaps, we could chat if you're comfortable giving me your numerical code? I'll use your number if you want me to. Speaking of which . . . you've been a disaster to my working abilities today. Hey, but I'm a hopeless romantic and do adore tragedies.*

I took a moment watching the cursor blink. My head, heart and even gut didn't warn me with an *insane* signal. I had a green light.

IM from Chloe: *Well, I've never been referred to as a tragedy before . . . blame your friend Mary. You already know plenty of information—full name, birthday, sign and occupation. Are you going to ask for my fingerprints or social security number next? Maybe this is the time to mention my run-in with the law? LOL.*

IM from Christoph: *And now I can't work because I'm sitting here thinking whether I offended you by amusingly calling you a tragedy. Wait, what? That makes you indeed one! All right, Miss Kassidy, we'll do this properly: take out your planner and let's see how your evening looks for me to call.*

IM from Chloe: *Anytime after 9:00 p.m. My number is 917.555.4409.*

Managing stress always twisted my stomach, leaving behind an ill sensation. These symptoms required TLC with comfort food designated for sick days. I dialed a diner serving Ukrainian soul food, ordering their soup of the day with toasted challah bread.

Forty-five minutes later and at the same time, I received my food delivery and a new chat popped up, blocking me once again from my retouched image.

IM from Christoph: *To be honest, I'm completely distracted from my legal reports. Describe to me your setting.*

When I looked around and caught a glimpse of reflection in my flat screen, it wasn't pretty. My J. Crew ensemble had been replaced with sweats, a T-shirt, and my polish needed a touch up from my recent nail biting meltdown. Even though it was tiny, I adored my apartment. The non-working Louis XIV marble fireplace was what seduced me when the broker pitched the monthly rent for the 500 square foot steal. It brought me back to the French Revolution with its ornate and elegant style. With a limited decorating budget and space, I had pulled it off, thanks to Overstock.com and Sundays at the flea market. You could capture the apartment in one glimpse with my king-size soft yellow duvet-covered bed with matching lamps, while pictures of New York's cherry blossoms hung above it for the bedroom. The cream cushioned Antoine reading chair with exposed hardwood frames and intricate carving sat by the window, looking out onto the fire escape, a perfect spot for reading. Although I couldn't recall the last time I read a book there. The other side of the room was my living room area slash dining room. I ate dinner on my couch, and my workspace included an L-shaped white wooden desk the home for my iMac, Post-it note mess, and a million Sugar Daddy candy wrappers. The toughness on my teeth distracted me from my worries. The wall art was an enlarged photograph of Stephanie I had taken one night by placing my lens and shooting through her empty scotch glass. Her shadow was a kaleidoscope of light and darkness with shades of orange, yellow and black. It was my personal Alice in Wonderland *Through the Looking Glass* shot. Also strategically hung were my photographs from years of shooting and that one and only self-portrait on the bus when I had been a kid. Ironically, I had been camera shy.

An eleven-by-fourteen oriental plush rug designed of gold, pink, and turquoise tones covered the hardwood floor to each corner. My life could be whisked away on a magic carpet ride.

I imagined him sitting in his office, with a serious suit and tie combination, flipping through legal documents while signing away with a fancy Mont Blanc pen.

How could I taint our beginning with my current appearance?

IM from Chloe: *I'm in a tiny-but-cozy French cafe downtown, obviously on the computer, flipping through images from a recent shoot. Just finished a large cup of coffee and am trying to ignore the man beside me devouring what seems to be a ham & avocado crunchy baguette. He doesn't have nice table manners and is a bit distracting.*

Immediately, my phone rang displaying a blocked number. I clicked ignore.

IM from Christoph: *I just tried to call you, but I forgot to mention my work phone shows an unavailable number, the elitist manner of diplomats. I know it wasn't ideal to call you for the first time while you were in a cafe with the echo of a man eating a noisy sandwich, but I wanted to prove a Nalickian point: 'In my head, your voice it's got all that I need.'*

IM from Christoph: *I'll call you this evening after 9:00 p.m.*

Google: Nalickian. No results.
Google: Nalick. Results for singer Anna Nalick popped up.

I adored this artist and the lyrics of her songs such as *Breathe (2 a.m.), Forever Love,* and *In my Head.* It didn't cross my mind he had been referring to the singer. The flesh-eating moths had reinvaded my stomach, accompanied by a fiery throbbing in my head. My rational hat was attempting to squeeze my brain through my ears.

Chapter 6

I was nervous waiting for his phone call, like it was the doctor calling with test results, and the anticipation was nauseating. The Nalick comment, "In my head, your voice it's got all that I need," bothered me. Now I had the pressure of having a pleasing voice since we had already come this far with our alphabetical chemistry through our keyboard exchanges. How on earth was I going to naturally answer a scheduled call with a blocked number? I knew it would be him and he knew as well.

The phone rang at 9:02 p.m. and sent me straight into a cannon-ball position while I sat on my bed and tucked my head into my knees, as if my Blackberry were a bomb about to blow me up.

Answer it, you pill.

"Hello?" I answered with my busy voice.

"Hi, Chloe, it's Christoph." He spoke with the sexiest, most soothing accent ever.

Gorgeous. Charming. Humanitarian. Writer. Witty. I'm totally screwed.

"Did you get your work done?" he asked. "I don't want to interrupt you."

"Yep. I was pretty productive today." I wondered if my voice was pleasing enough to pass his test.

"Ah. Is that Jack Johnson I hear?"

"You can hear my music?" I asked. It was low and now I worried if he could hear my thoughts. "Yes, it's him. This is my playlist with my favorites when I work. If the music doesn't help, it's straight to red wine."

"Music or Merlot, that's an interesting approach," he laughed. "That's actually my favorite song, Miss Kassidy. Can you guess my favorite line?"

Cocoon was my favorite song. "Hmm . . . your favorite line?"

"Yes, I'm waiting," he joked.

I knew my favorite line, but was hesitant to respond, as I didn't want to screw up the dots we had been connecting. I repeated my chosen lyric. "And I don't want to be your regret. I'd rather be your cocoon?"

Please let me be right!

In his soft deep voice, "You're exactly right," he said. "I was thinking . . . what's our story going to be?"

"Our story?" I wondered if I would have to Google everything we talked about.

"Well, we obviously are connecting. I couldn't stop talking to you today, let alone stop thinking about wanting to call you. It's making me feel like a silly little boy," he laughed. "Are you okay with my friend stealing your e-mail address?"

The notion of switching out the bookstore employee for Christoph came to mind. The attached picture had character, words, a voice I now knew accompanied flesh and bones. This was happening. He was indeed real.

"We met at Barnes & Noble. You couldn't help but approach me when I caught your eye," I said.

"I like your confidence," he said. "Please go on."

"I was soaked, an absolute mess," I laughed. "You asked what book I was looking for and when I said *The Reader,* we hit it off from there." I waited for my *Bravo.*

Do not share your hypothetical first-date scenario and that he wore a purple tie, you complete psycho.

"That's our story then. Just for the record, I wouldn't care what others thought of how we met. I'm glad Mary connected us."

I felt a squeeze from my rational hat again. *This is moving a bit fast.*

I realized my jaw was aching from holding a smile like a yoga pose. Thank God for living alone, as roommates would be witnesses and I didn't have a hook-up in the mafia.

"Well. Well. Well . . ." he said.

"What is it?" I asked, opening my MacBook to Google just in case.

"Mary just emailed me. She's upset that, after I received your contact info, I left her outside."

"Do you mean you left her out in the cold?"

"Oh, these American expressions." He caused us both to laugh.

"I'll have to thank her this weekend with dinner and drinks."

"That's nice of you."

"Well, look what she did. I'm incredibly lucky. I mean if we pass the coffee test, meeting you will be the best Christmas gift ever."

"It's right around the wall," I said. *It was October.*

"You mean corner?" he laughed. "I know that one, Chloe!"

His Swiss accent was delicious and his giggle charming. It was like eating dessert. Each bite was sweeter and sweeter, but I'm not sure I could ever get sick of it, and getting chubby was a side effect maybe worth the risk.

"If I may ask, Chloe, when are you free to grab a drink?"

I had to get through the week and prepare for my lunch with Grayson Gates Friday afternoon. "How about Friday evening?" I asked.

"Friday it is. We can have our own discussion on *The Reader*."

"The pressure," I joked. "I haven't made much progress. It would be embarrassing to be kicked out of the club the second meeting."

"Let's start it," he suggested.

"What?" I asked, not following.

"Grab your copy and open it to page one. Hold on, I'll be right back." I could tell he had put the phone down.

"Okay, I'm back. Are you comfy?"

"Are you really going to read to me?"

"Why would I not? I have my favorite book and my new buddy has a deadline. Now shush. It's book-club time."

While he cleared his throat, the rain started to tap dance on my bedroom window. "Chapter One. When I was fifteen, I got hepatitis . . ." he read.

Entering Chapter 8, he stopped. "Are you okay, Chloe? Are you enjoying the book?"

"Yeah, of course. I'm captured with his writing style."

"And the . . . voice reading it?" he asked a bit cautiously.

"Yes, I think that's my favorite part." The sting of embarrassment pinched me. That was out of character, but I felt this different part of me within myself unsure where the new me headed. "I can't believe we've been on the phone for three hours."

"That's quite telling for our first conversation," he said.

"I appreciate the help on this book-club assignment."

"I don't understand why you're in a club. You should ditch the group and we can start our own. Come on, admit you enjoy being here rather than there, Chloe."

I froze.

"Hello?"

"I'll consider it." He was right, but come on. He needed to work for it a bit more.

"Geez. I just read to you over the phone. I didn't mean to make you uncomfortable."

"I'm not," I responded. It was too early for me to freak him out as well.

"I enjoyed tonight. I definitely owe Mary for taking the initiative to introduce us," he said. "Since I've been among these overwhelming and crowded city streets in the US, it's nice to come across you."

"Please buy her a thank-you drink on my behalf. The best champagne in the house." I laughed.

"May I ask what you're up to this weekend while I'm entertaining and thanking our secretary?"

Our.

"I'll be working this weekend on the exhibit."

"Working over the weekend? I'm acquainted with that experience," he sighed.

"It's not really work to me. I adore the entire process, but I'll admit the exhibit has added pressure." Saying it out loud caused goose bumps.

"Hey, you have a wall in a New York City gallery!"

"Maybe you can pinch me when we grab that coffee."

"I'm looking forward to this Friday evening."

"Me too. I'll probably need an espresso after pitching my theme to the curator," I replied with less hesitation than normal, which jolted me a bit.

"Espresso is quick. Are you trying to get rid of me already?" he joked.

"Okay, make it a double," I teased.

"Would six-thirty that evening work for you?"

"Perfect," I said. "Do you have a spot in mind?"

"There is a wonderful Italian cafe on MacDougal Street, Cafe Dante. Do you know it?"

"Yes, it's one of my favorites." I blushed.

"It's a date, Chloe. Well . . . good luck with your meeting."

"Sounds lovely and thank you."

"I know you have a lot to prepare for, but if you have a chance feel free to say hello."

"I will. Until then," I said.

"Goodnight, Miss Chloe Kassidy. Sweetest dreams."

"Goodnight Mr. Christoph Kostas." We laughed.

I was tickled and tucked in under my covers as my eyelashes touched. There was no denying Christoph intrigued me. I hoped my dreams would compete with our talk tonight.

Chapter 7

Everyday this week felt the same. My daily routine had been a reciting of identical actions creating the portfolio I would present to Grayson Gates today at our lunch appointment. In between the rapid eating of a meal and sleeping was time spent tediously retouching and composing my theme. I was certain the curator would be impressed once again with me and remain confident with my images taking up real estate inside his gallery.

My mind felt clear and my heart was warmed. I believed it had something to do with Christoph pushing me a bit out of my comfort zone. In our spare time, we found moments to quickly call to say hello or send a spontaneous text. I was emotionally stimulated and my senses were heightened, so I was seeing the unfamiliar in my familiar sights, sounds and smells of what had been my previous surroundings.

Moving forward, Friday, October 21, would be coined National Swiss day. Today was our date. I couldn't believe I'd booked a coffee test with him on the same day as my exhibit lunch. My portfolio was composed, but I couldn't say the same about myself.

A pep talk from Stephanie was just what I needed to battle these nerves.

"Good Morning!" I screeched.

"How did you sleep? Are you ready? You've been waiting for this day since you were a kid!" She sounded just as excited as me.

"Yes!" I answered. I wanted to tell her about Christoph, but she reminded me today was about G-A-T-E-S the Great.

"Today is about making your dream come true and winning over the curator! Concentrate on just that, okay?"

"I am. He's like my fairy godfather," I joked. "Yes, Grayson Gates, the fairy godfather. Maybe his messenger man purse was full of magical fairy dust."

Stephanie laughed. "Chloe, believe anything is possible."

She always pulled my head out of the clouds just enough to see how far my feet were floating above ground. It helped me prioritize in my 911 moments.

"Please call me as soon as you're finished," she said.

I immediately checked my emails to see if Christoph had sent a good morning.

From: Christoph Kostas
To: Chloe Kassidy
Subject: A bit of inspiration for your Good Morning
Date: October 21, 8:27 a.m.

The heart is a voice of its own, the very end of dreamland, and the beginning of forever.
p.s. Good luck today!

When I approached the cozy greenmarket-inspired restaurant, I spotted Grayson Gates alone by the window. Our first encounter in Miami still made me smile from my spontaneous trip for Art Basel.

"Well, there she is," he said, opening his arms. It was awkward, considering we'd met once. Smiling, I stretched for a distant hug, as the thought of my breasts touching him was an experience I wanted to live without.

"We're having an emergency at the gallery today, my staff is putting out the fire. I have time to grab only a drink," he said and returned to his seat. "I wanted to check in with you and see how your theme is developing."

I had overestimated the formality of the luncheon and felt ridiculous for the excess stress that had been abusing me lately.

"Thank you for your time. A drink is fine." A glass of red wine would offer me the liquid courage I needed to get through this one-on-one.

The server took our order and stepped away. "Wow, doesn't she look like Demi Moore?" Grayson Gates asked while he watched her ass walk away.

"Who?" I asked, knowing exactly what he was infamous for. Our server's appearance just won me a Moore monologue.

"About six years ago, I dated a woman who looked just like Demi Moore. It was hot and heavy until I found out she returned to her ex-husband. He was a retired banker. Obviously, a gallery curator was too sophisticated for her," he noted. He pulled out various gadgets, but no fairy dust.

"Let's hear it, Chloe."

I took it as my cue to pitch.

I placed my black leather portfolio in front of him along with a copy of my one-page proposal, trying not to stare at the exorbitant amount of chest hair sticking out from his opened shirt. *Free me!*

"Chloe?"

"Oh yes." Getting back to my task at hand, I described images both recent and past that contained circular symbols. "Love in these moments displays commitment. I'm exploring the idea of one true love, specifically focusing on the bond inspired by the Egyptians and the wedding band." I sipped my wine slowly. Even as Grayson Gates examined my portfolio, I had to admit how lovely the shots looked while he flipped the pages. The cropping was precisely focused on the circular shapes, pulling me into the familiar shots. I immediately glanced at my own bare finger, the hand that always held a camera, but no sign of a vow.

The expression on his face was matched to my blank wall. "No, Chloe." He shut my book while shaking his head. "Love is an invisible mentor that, if you allow, will guide you to beauty. It will lead you to your dreams . . . This theme of yours won't."

"Okay . . ." My thoughts attempted to form the sentence that I was trying to communicate. I was undergoing a full-blown case of perfectionist paralysis.

"Got me?" he asked.

"Yes . . . I'm—"

"Are you ready for this?" He turned his attention to his scotch on the rocks with a splash of water. *That must put hair on his chest.*

"How do you feel about love, Chloe? I mean . . . what's your story?"

"My story?" I gulped.

"Are you in love? Do you have a boyfriend? I mean surely you can pull inspiration to create something from your life experiences," he wondered while searching for the answer in my facial expression.

"Of course, Mr. Gates," I trembled trying to avoid an answer. The truth was I had never allowed myself to fall into love. I couldn't convince myself the risk of heartbreak was worthy of the feeling. Love is this one word, this emotion so powerful it sparks numerous debates of its true definition. One thing was for sure, whether it was considered rational or irrational, a fictional fairy tale or a daily part of reality, love itself was capable of pulling people out of their depth, making the weak stronger and the strong weaker. Love was an enormous promise.

"Chloe, you'll know without a doubt when you capture it. Tell your story, not the story you think others want to hear. Tell the story people need to be reminded of. I need you to go deeper instead of tiptoeing around with these empty overused platitudes. Got me?"

"Yes. Mr. Gates," my voice squeaked. I could only put together those three words. I was in shock. I couldn't think straight from the tremors that shot from my toes, rattling my concentration. I heard my mother's voice: "Don't quit your day job."

"Opening night is going to be beyond belief. Completely press-worthy and a night Manhattan will remember. Now, each of the exhibitors will be sent individually to Miami for a week to be under the direction of one of my self-discovered mentors," he explained.

"I'm going back to Miami?" I asked.

"You'll get to observe our latest exhibit opening . . . You can see the results of hard work. My team will get back to you with your travel itinerary." He threw back the remaining scotch, with the ice slamming against his teeth and then crashing back into the empty glass. "Hmm. I think it'd be beneficial for you to contact Reed Scott, an associate of mine. He's just what you need, Chloe."

"I need?" I took a gulp of wine to catch up to him. "I'm not familiar with Mr. Scott, but if you feel the intro—"

"Reed is a close friend and excellent with themes. He'll be attending the opening in February. His company in Miami is flying in to shoot a documentary on The Smith Gallery." He signaled for the check. "He's a native New Yorker who lives in Miami now, and has been in the art industry since he was a kid. Here's his number . . . I suggest you consult with him sooner than later."

I received the curator's text immediately displaying a name, number, and my only hope. "Will do. Thank you." I tried not to sound overly impressed and desperate from being pulverized. "I'll give my love and attention to my pieces," I promised while my body bounced back to a more confident position.

The check arrived as he counted out his cash.

Straightaway, my mind traveled to Christoph and my dedication felt like a slight lie. The timing of Christoph Kostas coming into my life was a major distraction. I didn't have time for this relationship, for Emma dragging me to Brooklyn on harebrained soul mate chases and for Grayson Gates chatting about his exes. These outside distractions made it impossible for me to create anything impressive.

As we parted ways, I noticed the man purse, such an unflattering accessory on a man whose life created exquisiteness. I bet it held the souls he stole for his afternoon snack time. I had to admit, I was officially in bitch mode. I clenched my fist, wanting to rip out his unruly chest mane.

While heading home, the devastation began to manifest while my hopes of winning over the curator shattered. It was a rare occurrence, but I heard or saw nothing of the city during the fifteen-minute walk. His critique had been numbing. *How didn't he recognize an ounce of my passion for finding love in my work?* This was embarrassing and I couldn't admit it to anyone. I felt like a fraud, a wishful amateur who had fooled herself into thinking she had an honest shot.

Then again, *how challenging might this be?* I respected love. I treasured the sentiment. I also had an incredible group of trusted friends whose personal love lives could be dissected. I had four months until opening night to get my heart together.

Turning the keys to open my front door, I felt my cell vibrate. It was either Stephanie seeking a lunch update or Christoph confirming a spot to meet tonight. Disgrace wasn't the ideal first-date accessory.

I dropped my portfolio on the floor, rushed to my workstation and switched the screen to dark. Grabbing the robe from the back of the bathroom door, I avoided my reflection and felt soothed by the cashmere's softness against my body while I slipped it on. I required a glass of wine before contacting the Swiss man. Curled on the couch, I sent him a brief e-mail explaining my lunch, an apology, and a rain-check request for tonight's date.

The phone buzzed, before my next sip.

"Are you okay, Chloe?" he asked.

"Rough day is an understatement," I confided.

"I've got a solution," he responded with a promising tone. "Get comfy, something to eat, and grab the book. I'll call you in twenty minutes when I'm home and read to you."

"I'm sorry for canceling like this."

"Don't worry. Either way, I get to spend the evening with you."

Hours had passed when he came to the end of the book. My thoughts had already left the story he read and were chasing the sound of his words. Christoph's voice was a story on its own. It was strong yet velvety, while it impaired my ability to pay attention to the book. It was intoxicating and, unlike my wine, came without a health warning. I prayed it wouldn't be harmful when operating my common sense.

"What else should I know about you?" I asked while finishing the remainder of wine.

"Ask me anything," he said.

Although this was my idea, I wasn't prepared to lead with the questions. "What's your favorite alcoholic beverage?" I asked saddened by the sight of the empty bottle.

"You're quite interesting," he laughed. "Wine. Second best would be a dry martini . . . the winter second best would be Baileys on the rocks. Next?"

I searched around my apartment for the next question. "Are you a credit or cash person?" I asked realizing the lackluster value of it.

"Cash. I'm insecure with holding just credit. Please continue," he pushed.

"Favorite TV show?"

"You're not allowed to share this with anyone. *Grey's Anatomy*." I didn't admit

to never watching the show.

"Favorite vacation ever?"

"Mytilene. It was a summer filled with sun, water, fresh fish and books. Good one, Kassidy."

"Okay, let's get a bit deeper. Are you a half-full or half-empty kind of person?"

"Half-full, of course," he answered with no doubt. I'm sure it was one of many noble characteristics for a man who worked to save the world.

I entered the kitchen in search of more wine. The only thing in my refrigerator was one Corona Light. "How about your favorite beer?"

"Sol, a beer from Mexico. I'm charmed with your interview system," he said with obvious sarcasm.

"Just trying to keep you on your toes," I said. "I'm sure this is comparable to your UN interview. No?" I joked. We laughed.

"Stop distracting me," I demanded. The sip of the iced cold beer was energizing as I lay on my bed staring at the pillow wall built on the left side. "What side of the bed do you sleep on?"

"I usually sleep on the left." I was enjoying my casual interrogation and relieved if it came to the point, we wouldn't be fighting for my right side of the bed.

"What's your preference with movie theater seating?"

"Cinema seats? Always closer to the back than closer to the front."

"And flights?" I asked now not knowing where I was going with this.

"Plane seats would be aisle, aisle and aisle," he said. "I'm not a tiny man."

From the picture emailed, his stature was impossible to miss. To be completely honest, I'm not sure a poet could capture what oozed from the screen. Finishing the last drop of beer, I headed back into the kitchen for water. Risk of dehydration or a defeating hangover wasn't an option.

"And what water do you prefer?" I asked. My creativity was becoming less impressionable.

"Perrier with ice and lemon."

"And would you say you're a sweet or salty person?"

"I'll take cheese pie over chocolate mousse any day," he answered. "You're making me hungry!"

"Favorite season?"

"If I had to choose one season out of four, I'd go with autumn."

"Favorite coffee?"

"Espresso."

"Favorite tea?"

"Green, and cinnamon."

"Favorite accessories?"

"Hmm . . . a noteworthy question. I would say pens, ties and watches."

"Favorite time of day?"

"Too late or too early, when everyone else is still sleeping."

"Favorite sport?"

"Tennis. I'm a huge Federer fan."

"Righty or lefty?"

"Left-handed and always write with black ink."

"Religion?"

"I believe in God and fate," without a doubt.

"Anything else I should know about you?" I asked, wrapping up my Q&A and completely ignoring the one I wouldn't dare ask . . . *Number of sexual partners?*

"I love words, mainly because they express feelings, feelings people sometimes aren't ready to reveal unless hidden in fiction or poetry or biography. If I had to choose one city in the entire world to go and wander round for a few hours in my attempt to be inspired, I'd go for New York," he added.

"The good news is I think after this full investigation, I've determined we'll have a successful coffee date," I laughed, pulling the gap in my robe closed. Our long conversations without seeing him face to face were risqué enough.

"Now it's my turn, Miss Photographer," he said.

"Ask away," I said, giving him permission.

"No questions for you. I want a picture. Your eyes will tell me all I need to know," he admitted. "I know Mary sent you one of me."

"Seriously?" I asked. I quickly did a 360-degree spin in my studio. My framed memories included friends, family, and snapshots of objects that had caught my eye like an antique chandelier, a New

York moment or an exotic flower. "I'll send you one before I go to bed. Deal?" I needed to buy more time.

"I better have a surprise in my inbox tomorrow morning," he laughed.

We exchanged goodnights after five hours on the phone. He was going to sleep and I was getting to work. Scrolling through folders for recent shots, I didn't have one picture of me or one to crop myself out and create. The truth was I wasn't a fan of being the subject of any camera, only the shooter. It was 10:30 p.m. and I was setting up to shoot a self-portrait. *Unbelievable.* I swiped the couch clean, while arranging the oversized table books of photography, fashion and travel on the coffee table. Organizing the Canon and tripod, I gave the couch and table another inspection and spotted the smudge of dry wine. *Setup check.*

I slipped into a pair of cotton black leggings and into an oversize black cashmere loose-neck sweater. Returning to the bathroom and the mirror I had previously ignored, there was the dilemma. My blowout still remained in decent shape, but my lips were stained burgundy while my mascara smudged under my right eye. Six minutes later, I was rejuvenated to the best of my ability. That was the beauty within my profession. What wasn't manageable would be corrected.

I grabbed my 50mm lens to compress the image and slim my face. *Focus with your eyes.* I reminded myself. This would draw Christoph into the picture. I positioned the tripod about five feet from where I would be seated and adjusted it a couple inches higher than my position to shoot at a downward angle. This would make my eyes appear larger and my face more delicate. Next, I set up the backlight beside the couch for added depth to my image. I attached the on-camera flash diffuser to soften any skin imperfections and replicate natural light.

Using a wireless remote shutter release, I shot various natural self-portraits, nervous with a fake smile. *Think of something funny.* Click. *Shit.* Click. *Dammit.* Click. Then I spotted just what I needed to relax me into my cross-legged seated pose. Placing my hands into the fold of my legs, I glanced slightly up and to the right, as if I were staring at someone in the room. I would explain to Christoph how the photo was taken at a recent gathering with girlfriends at my apartment. Click. I continued to stare at the one image that had traveled with me throughout the years. Pinned above my workstation was the Polaroid. *Click.* My *say cheese* moment gradually slipped out in a giant smile.

I composed a new e-mail to Christoph and attached the natural-looking shot. *If he only knew.*

Chapter 8

I had slept in hard as a result of the somersault routine with my pillow. My habit of never closing the blinds so I can wake to the sun screaming *Bright light and get up!* failed me during times of overcast. I struggled with being a morning person, and never understood the phrase since it was still dark outside. I ignored the guilt by staying in bed, lying there wondering what the weather and actual life was offering on the other side. I wished Christoph would just call and suggest we would have coffee today. I had reached my rejection quota for the year per Grayson Grates. Asking him wasn't an option. I didn't want to seem needy.

Gray skies had their upside for two reasons. First, I preferred the wardrobe selections, but most important, I did my finest thinking in these shades. Black and white was too extreme for creative thinking.

Today wasn't a shooting day, but a reflecting one. I needed to find my voice for the *Love Through Light* exhibit. It was a day to get lost in the shadows of the city. No matter how long I had lived there,

I always bumped into something or someone new. I could go from New Yorker to tourist in a snap. In a way, we were always visitors, as no matter how long you lived there, you couldn't do it all.

I searched my hangers one by one for a comfy outfit to also help relax my brooding mood.

Nope. Sloppy. Hmm . . .

I grabbed a collaboration of pages seven and twenty-two. A pair of matchstick denim jeans, a navy and white-checkered silk shirt complimented with a navy, ruffled cardigan. I adored how each silk petal was delicately sewn to the front of the merino sweater. I treasured details, even the tiniest ones.

Returning to Miami would be bittersweet since bumping into Grayson there clearly opened the gateways into the art world. Withdrawal from New York just for a bit would budge me outside the perimeters of my comfort zone. I acknowledged it was necessary to prove the curator wrong. *I was ready for this exhibit.*

Sharp focus is critical for impressive shots. A photographer doesn't want to hinge on the auto focus mode, since it doesn't know what you want to focus on, and usually focuses on whatever is closest to the camera. Just because it's closest to your lens doesn't make it the right subject or shot. I wondered if the same was true for the heart.

Unfortunately, when the person holding the camera was out of focus, it resulted in a mess. My other hardware, my heart, was entirely fixated on this void and I couldn't predict where Christoph and I might be moving since he wasn't physically near me at the moment—though his presence was within me.

My Blackberry alerted with a new text.

Kate was reminding me of our plans. *Meet me at 5:00 p.m. Tribeca Cinemas on Varick & Laight. We have a date with Holly*

Golightly! Kate was far from a romantic, but a giant fan of troubled souls.

She was a switchblade with the potential to cut quick and deep, and her latest coping mechanism to life was cruel sarcasm. She had been dumped by Ian, her boyfriend of five years and hoped to be soon fiancé.

They had met through Kickstarter.com, a website that helped fund creative projects. She was an eager entrepreneur with a dream of opening a natural food deli to sell her homemade raw recipes. He had been one of the many supporters who donated money to help her project to launch. His donation was accompanied by a message and her deli wasn't the only thing that got started. It went from PayPal to passion with a click. For the most part, their relationship seemed ordinary. They both worked hard, loved the dog, moved in together with no talk of marriage, but she began to sense his resentment towards her gluten-free cooking and Feng Shui flow.

When Kate went to retrieve Mr. George Washington's toy from under their bed, the dog's disappointment was equal to her surprise. The only bone was the one she had to pick with Ian and the sheer red thong that she pinched between her index finger and thumb. When she called and left a voicemail for him, inquiring about the delicate red item that he added to their bedroom, any Feng Shui expert would have been thrilled. This color resembled the *fire of energy* and was recommended for this specific room in the house.

Ian never returned her call. That evening when she returned home from work, Ian had left a note on what had been his pillow. Note was an overstatement. His message was scribbled on the back of a card that included one of her recipes. He had punched her twice in the heart since he had taken their dog with him and never gave her the chance to say goodbye. Kate was inconsolable.

We assumed he received the voicemail, feared for his life, collected his property, including the five-pound ex-president, and moved onto his Miss Thong, leaving Kate with an empty heart matching her apartment.

Even though her exterior resembled a strong and confident woman with her jet-black pixie cut and her naturally caramel-toned skin glowed, it contained her smashed spirit. We were waiting for the day she would again embrace her three favorite words, *Power of Choice* and drop the grudge against mankind and underwear.

"Kate!" I yelled from across the street, waving while I observed her lean yogi body. I wished she felt as fantastic as she looked.

"Right on time as always. I thought artists were flakey."

"Always in a rush to put people in a box," I poked.

"I have the tickets and snacks." She opened her bag for me to peek. "We're all set!"

"Snacks? Kate, I'm getting popcorn." I pushed her to go and get seats to avoid the poison lecture. I had no problem eating her mysterious natural trickery. How she mixed dates, nuts, coconut oil or cashew butter into recipes that tasted equal to familiar candy stumped the hell out of me. I reminded her how sweet and salty combined are the best. I would sprinkle her unprocessed bites into the bag of saturated fat, sodium-enriched kernels, shaking it to cause an ideal salt to sweet ratio per handful.

Her raw foods cafe was around the corner from my apartment. Her recipes were devilish and one evening I had a walnut-carob-cookie-eating contest, which I won, even though I was the only one competing.

Stephanie once shared with us that Kate's extreme ways were a result of her unhealthy past. She would actually steal cigarettes from her mother's purse and trade them to the lunch ladies for extra bacon, hot rolls, or cakes in high school. While most teenage girls wanted to be noticed with the boys, Kate became cozy with the cooks.

Yet, chubbiness hadn't led to her demise. Rather, it was the torture from extreme dentists. As a child her food choices had given Kate the Big C: cavities. She was that one percent where dental procedures turned out terribly wrong, from faulty fillings to root canals. She had demanded none of us marry or date dentists.

As Holly Golightly sipped her champagne and danced around the party in her cocktail attire, I waited for the *Timber!* scene to distract others, including Kate, to check my phone. I cautiously pulled out the intruding device while cupping my hand over the brightly lit screen, simultaneously maintaining the circus act of balancing my popcorn on my lap.

Finally!

I had missed his call and two text messages.

"Chloe, unless someone is drowning in a pool of their own blood and you need to dial 911, put the phone away." She was the actual distraction in the theater while heads peered our way.

"Sorry. Sorry! Can I have another piece of candy, please?"

"Southern hospitality my ass," she hissed. A couple seconds later, she said, "Here, take two pieces."

Even though she was frightening, sometimes lethal, you might slip past her guard.

Don't do it, Chloe.

In Tasmanian devil mode, I popped it out of my sweater and saw one new text message.

"Enough already. Give me your damn phone." Her nose wrinkled while she caught me with a sideways glance.

"I'm done!" I whispered, desperate to be tolerated. I switched to silent mode.

"You have no control, Chloe. You're missing Hepburn." She shook her head.

We both turned our attention back to the beautiful mess on the big screen.

None of us dared to speak to Kate about her ex, Ian. Even though the past ran deep, it always rested right under the surface of her skin. We accepted Kate's bittersweet attitude. She was resilient, yet fragile at the same time, although we allowed her to believe we were unaware of the latter. She thought she was convincing as the actress we watched on the big screen. As her friends, we never agreed if not confronting her did more damage than good. We were patiently waiting for the day where she would wake up and want to talk about it, him, or missing their dog. She did everything in her power to dump the wounded woman she felt forced to become in a trunk and throw it with the key to the bottom of the Hudson River.

We were greeted with darkness as we exited the theater while the wind scattered the autumn leaves throughout the streets. The air was cool and crisp.

"Wow," Kate said. "Inhale that air."

"This weather always makes me crave pumpkin pie," I moaned.

"Well, you're just in luck."

"You baked a pie?" I shrieked.

She rolled her eyes. "You'll see."

Entering her apartment for her to *cook*, I broke the silence. "What's on the menu tonight?"

"We'll be having . . ." Kate squinted while searching for my seriousness. She continued and pointed. "A ginger sunflower pate for cucumber dipping, a baby spinach salad with bosc pear and pecans and a spicy pumpkin soup." She lifted the pot's lid and inhaled the aroma. The zest of lemongrass crept into my nose while it wrapped around us.

"It's been simmering for a couple of hours," she noted.

"Pumpkin!" I cheered. I pressed my palms against the counter for a boost and a better look. "I hoped for something to dissect," I said, wondering if it was my comment or my search that annoyed her the most.

"You can be absolutely preoccupied with things, Chloe."

She served healthy portions onto plates and smiled. "How's the groundwork for the exhibit going?"

I couldn't admit Grayson Gates gave me a fat *F* for flop on my unimpressive proposal performance. "I've been . . . well . . . struggling with my theme."

"Well, you —"

"Jesus, its New York . . . there's inspiration everywhere!" I shrugged.

"Slow down . . .," Kate hissed. I stopped mid-bite until I realized she meant with freaking out.

"I'm finding it difficult to first define love and then understand it. I'm blocked!"

"You'll work it out. You have this chance because you're capable and talented, right?"

Her point pressed me to pause. "I've tried to conceptualize my feelings and thoughts to form a theme, but I don't make progress since the worrying to be inspired interrupts the entire process," I said. "Damn, this soup is fantastic."

Kate added another ladle serving to my bowl. "I know." She grinned. "Well, if you were to ask me about love in New York, I'd say we made Paris Hilton famous, we consider five hundred square foot mansion price-tag worthy, a woman can have a new face over lunch, and let's not forget that smart and chic mean the same thing here."

"What's not to love?" I joked.

"Don't get me started on New York City men." She took her own sizable breath and sighed. "Oh, and whores love red thongs."

"Hey, New York is one of the greatest cities in the world. What about—"

"Are we going to have one of your hopeless romantic reruns?" She moaned. "Everything isn't a *Harry Met Sally* or chocolate fudge sundaes at Serendipity, Chloe."

"What does that mean?" I didn't want to be defensive or remind her that Manhattan wasn't the man who broke her heart.

"Chloe, it was easier to break down the Berlin Wall than to remove the walls you've formed."

"Excuse me?" I asked.

"You're a closet soul mate searcher like Emma."

"Oh, come on." I rolled my eyes. "I'm not senseless."

"You're both out of your minds with being hopeless romantics, but at least she carries her crazy well. It's her perfect accessory," she laughed. "You're scared of rejection—I wonder if you'll ever allow yourself to completely fall in love."

I felt my blood boiling and it wasn't courteous since the chef didn't consume anything over ninety-two degrees. "According to you, that wouldn't be such a bad thing, right?" I asked.

"With people, you can't control the outcome, Chloe. This I know and that's all I'm saying."

I remained silent by slowly chewing a piece of pear. The food was gone and I wondered what I would grab for dinner. Her cooking instantly caused me to crave meat.

"What was up with you during the movie?" she asked.

I wasn't sure if I was ready to share Christoph. We hadn't met, but I felt it was fair to my rational hat that I listened to her rigid input. Her message was good, but her delivery sucked badly, the messenger would be killed without a doubt.

"All right, Kate," I said and extended my pinky finger. "I'll tell you, but this is just between us."

"What, are we eight? I swear on your success," she laughed.

"I—"

"Dammit, let me get the phone," she interrupted. I took it as a sign for me to shut up, as maybe telling her wasn't my brightest idea. *Was Christoph newsworthy, yet?*

"Chloe, it's Emma. She wants me to remind you of the book club tomorrow."

"But he has a husband?" I tried to wiggle my way out with logic. I had my own gorgeous straight host in our club for two. "Why does she still want to go?"

"You don't want to go now? You never quit anything?" Kate appeared puzzled. "Emma, she'll call you tomorrow. We're in the middle of dinner." She rolled her eyes. "Yes, Emma. I cooked. Jesus, it's called raw."

"What?" I wondered.

"Yes, I'll ask her if she started the book. Goodnight," Kate sighed.

Kate's hesitation triggered my spine to tingle.

"You were rude to me with your phone during the movie. You're being wishy-washy. Now you're going to flake on Emma? Is it the exhibit?"

"I met someone. Well, not technically in person," I said.

"Are you talking to a man online? Bullshit! They write these New York Times best-seller profiles to screw you. I mean—"

"Not online. I met him through a woman and we've been talking a lot."

"Woman? Who? You don't trust anyone but us—"

"Well, I haven't met her either. She actually saw me at the book club. I'm never in Brooklyn. Funny, right? She saw me. She contacted me. He contacted me. We talked for hours the other night. He's stimulating and insightful and I've never met a man this expressive."

"You're making me nauseous. First, you try to pinky swear and now you're rambling on like a teenager about a boy you've never met. Did you already friend each other on Facebook? Let me guess, you updated your relationship status didn't you?"

Her attitude at times was tasteless like her food.

"He's a diplomat and writing a book on the soul mate theory. We have a coffee or maybe wine date."

"You've talked on the phone, but never met?"

"Yeah," I answered.

"His friend found you in a book club?"

"Yep. We're reading his favorite book! It's weird and feels—"

"And he kept texting you in a movie? He sounds egotistical."

"You don't even know him." Feeling a heat wave flood my body. "You can't—"

"Earth to Chloe. You don't either! I swear, what is it with artists and their inner struggle? You have a gallery wall to pay attention to, your career is launching and you're acting like a juvenile."

"The exhibit's my priority. *Love Through Light* isn't my ambition, but figuring out love itself. I thought you'd be happy for me, since it's difficult for me to trust." I wondered if it was ever possible for us to speak the same language. "Heat just like love turns energy into the nutrients we need. Your raw food offers nourishment, just as I would say the heart creates love to sustain us."

"Seriously, Kassidy, that's your angle here? Love and food?"

"Let's agree we're what we eat and how we love. You eat raw and I want to experience this raw emotion," I joked, shoving a cucumber slice in my mouth.

"You should be a lawyer," she laughed. "Remember that you must process the picture to see its entirety. Just be careful and don't forget certain things must be 'real' first to be a 'REL-ationship.'"

I don't care if she doesn't understand.

"I'll never admit this to anyone—if it ever comes up—I'll know to kill you," she said. I nodded for confirmation as I got a glimpse of Sally Caudwell, the bully back in elementary.

"When I was grasping onto hope last year after Ian, I picked up some self-help books," she blushed. "It was the alternative to tequila."

I touched her arm.

"Anyway, several books mentioned a psychologist by the name of Robert Sternberg. He created some triangular theory of love."

"Go on," I said. "I need to learn everything I can about love at this point."

"The theory characterizes love by three components: intimacy, passion, and commitment. The amount of love one experiences determines the strength of these three components. Each of them explains a different stage in a relationship and the type of love depending on the different combinations of the three components."

"Okay, I'm following," I said.

"I was with Ian for five years. Slowly, time is revealing things about us I chose to ignore. Slapping a commitment label on an empty box doesn't do much good."

I imagined that Christoph might fill the empty chair beside me at brunch, our fingers intertwined during a stroll along a tree-lined street, toast over cocktails when I passed spots where the most romantic scenes were created.

I had never allowed myself to be hurt by someone. It was my main fear and I acted accordingly for it to remain that way. At the same time, I couldn't let her fears fuel mine. "Okay, I promise."

Chapter 9

It would be easier to blame parents and the childhood trips to the Magic Kingdom for leading women to their demise searching for Prince Charming, their own fairy tale, and their need to be treated like a princess. The eagerness to come across him could be dangerous. Disney World created this desire to live in a wonderland and be subjected to the idea of enchanted love. Growing up, my imagination gave me optimism for the future. Then adulthood came too fast, and I wished to sue Cinderella for creating this unfulfilled desire to chase after forever.

It's ironic that generations exploit these imaginary characters to teach us lessons, to set examples, and to guide us from kids into accountable adults. Mentors who are fictitious characters we'll never come to know. Being an adult, I still adored the tales while coming to know that's all that they were. Subconsciously at a responsible age, I found it hard not to compare all men to these ideals—thanks to my parents, Alice and Robert Kassidy.

Walt Disney gave birth to my expectations, but watching my mother's responses to love and the unfolding of her life was disheartening. I wondered if our trips to the *Greatest place on earth* were for me as much as an escape as it was for her. Although, my parents still remained married in my childhood home, it was impossible to miss my mother's attitude. Her past, present, and future were one and the same. She lived for a story, rather than relishing her own, no matter what the plot was or had the potential to become. Her bitterness from her life not becoming what she felt she was entitled to caused her to miss the love surrounding her. Her mind grew into a self-inflicted prison sentence where she allowed life to pass her by. She looked at life through the lens of *I deserve* and had expected the universe to offer free delivery. I wouldn't follow in her footsteps. I never wanted to make her mistake of not living a passionate life, while being high strung and ungrateful. My own drive was to make this our greatest difference. This unhealthy attitude proved to be her most significant motherly lesson. I wasn't looking forward to my trip home to Atlanta for Christmas.

From: Christoph Kostas
To: Chloe Kassidy
Subject: When I see her smile
Date: October 23, 3:16 p.m.

You're probably still working like mad on this Sunday afternoon, which probably means I won't hear from you till tomorrow. I decided to pass on a house party invitation, whose alcohol would probably cheer me up, yet, I'm still not 100% from this work week. I think I'll try and sink myself into words—words I need to write concerning my peace plan, words I need to listen to in songs, and even words I'm writing here, though to be honest, I'm not sure whether I'm writing this to you or myself.

Have you ever felt like you've been staring at your life from a distance and you're trying to decide which path to follow? I'm torn between making the world a better place and wondering whether I should just stop being an idealist and concentrate on the people who are here now? Writing a book is important to me.

My dad called me early this morning to tell me my grandpa was sick. I was speechless. Not literally. I comforted him. I'm trapped in this duality of distance and time difference. In fact, I haven't been part of their lives for years now. While I was building on my academic career, my professional experience, my international life, I was distancing myself from those who matter the most to me, those who created me, who protected me while I was a fragile infant and those who genuinely applaud my every success. I would fly home twice a year, and I felt great every single time, yet I haven't been part of home for years, and look at my grandpa now. Who knows how many more memories I would have had, how many more precious moments, how many silly fights, how many meaningful hugs, how many books-and-tea times.

I should stop writing. I'm not sure I'll manage to press 'send' if I go back and review this. You just texted me from the gallery and I'm trying to picture you working. I bet you look breathtaking. Enjoy your evening, beautiful. I hope we can schedule something this week.

Christoph

I love and hate stress equally. I read once it was a true characteristic of an Aquarian. I was heavy with guilt that morning for coming home last night and crashing without checking my emails. I wanted to be there for him, coping with his ill grandfather.

When I called from the gallery to check in and proposed a Sunday night drink at 7:30 p.m., I was happy he agreed. It sounded like we both needed one.

"I enjoy being alone, too. Sundays and winters are my best buddies. I almost deem Sundays were created for each person to experience them alone or with the one person who's pretty much themselves," he said.

"For me Sundays are a 'pause' mode, and I can create, shoot, take it in for as long as I want to, no rules or expectations attached," I shared. I was almost positive the world's greatest masterpiece, whether photographs, books, or paintings, had been created on Sundays. Yet, I wanted to share this day with him.

"Time is the greatest healer, but it doesn't mean one forgets . . . or one comes to peace when someone is sick and possibly dying." His voice quivered with a hint of defeat.

"Maybe, you just stop seeing your loved ones in everything you do, and you slowly learn how to baby step in this new reality without them. I don't know if we're ever ready to let go," I said.

"I don't think anyone truly is," he sighed.

I never imagined I would be staring at the ceiling that night, disappointed. I was expecting more of a butterfly effect for what was going to be my first meeting with Christoph, but the evening came and passed without him while he caught a late flight home to be by his grandfather's side.

From: Christoph Kostas
To: Chloe Kassidy
Subject: Hello from the airport
Date: October 23, 9:17 p.m.

I was flying out and I didn't want to because you were there. I believe our 'thingy,' is surreal, intense, inexplicable, irrational but . . . feels great, it confuses me, terrifies me, wants me to throw cold water on my face and get back to my senses one minute, and the next, it makes me smile, makes me warm inside and makes me to want to take every single moment in, as if to become one with this dream of mine.

Christoph

The phone startled me at 5:15 the next morning.

"I'm unbelievably tired," he sighed. "I arrived home about an hour and a half ago, had a long shower and now I'm sitting by the fireplace," he said softly, like he was fluctuating in between stages of sleep.

"How's your family? How are you?"

"My grandmother has asked me to spend time with her. She wants to make dinner for me, and so she's cooking while I'm sitting here looking around at this—"

"If you need to go, I—"

He choked up.

"At this beautiful house . . . browsing mentally through every memory . . . listening to sounds from these old wooden floors."

Our new connection was taking away from the exhibit, but it satisfied my thinking that matters of the heart might spark the necessary creativity for my themes. He was becoming my little muse.

My efforts to convert to a heart person had graduated from baby steps to leaping hurdles. My guarded rational self took a back seat, but at times I felt unnoticed by him. I reassured myself he was in a sensitized environment and a bit fragile, but I couldn't give him me all at once. I didn't want to do it all at once. I enjoyed getting to know him. I cherished our conversations. Maybe he was better at expressing his feelings through words. Perhaps, I did better through actions. I know he might not believe this, many people don't, but I'm an open person. He just can't have every part of me in thirty days.

From: Christoph Kostas
To: Chloe Kassidy
Subject: Update
Date: October 26, 1:14 p.m.

Grief is a circle of stages. I'm at the beginning, and something tells me I'll be at it for quite some time. I have to be the idealist and the believer. I can't be radical and I can't be too realistic. I may be able to see certain things about life way too early for my years. Sometimes it's about choosing not to and fooling yourself into believing what's easiest.

I wish you were here to see how my little cousins look at me. I'm this figure in the family their parents always talk about 'When you grow up, you should be like Christoph,' 'You should do this and you should do that, but you should be like Christoph,' 'When Christoph was your age, he did this at school, or he would do that.' My little cousins look at me like I'm God. They ask me questions and they take for granted my answers will be the best ones and the wisest ones in the world. My uncles and aunties, they always talk about me and to me like I'm perfect, as if I'm flawless, as if nothing can compare to me, and it's not true.

p.s. Okay, here's a serendipity sign for you. My mum walks in just now and says, 'I know how stubborn you are, and you'll stay at the hospital no matter what, so I brought you a book to read from the ones you have in your collection.' And guess which book she brought: *The Reader.*

From: Christoph Kostas
To: Chloe Kassidy
Subject: Update
Date: October 30, 3:14 p.m.

This morning we were told chances are getting worse by the day. I canceled my flight out tonight. I need to stay here and experience this. We have a continent that is now between us, but that's okay. When I close my eyes, you're everywhere.

From: Chloe Kassidy
To: Christoph Kostas
Subject: Re: Update
Date: October 30, 4:16 p.m.

I'm sorry about your grandfather. If it were up to me, we would climb under the covers, I would hold your hands and we would hide together from the world. Just for a bit, enough to rest your worries. I could use that right now myself.

From: Christoph Kostas
To: Chloe Kassidy
Subject: Re: Re: Update
Date: October 30, 6:30 p.m.

That is why this is hard for me right now. I want you here. I want you right here next to me. I don't want to talk about it. I don't want to explain, and I don't want to think or feel out loud. I just need you close to me with no words and no explanations. Given the circumstances, if I could have one thing, it would be you on the phone with no words. I just want to hear you breathe, close my eyes and pretend you're right there next to me. Do you think it's ever possible to start falling for someone you've never seen?
Christoph

Is this what people meant when they talked about *Love at first sight*? Maybe they were already feeling it before they even laid eyes on each other for the first time? *Hmm . . . possible theme?* Before I had a chance to respond, Switzerland called me.

"I'm not a stalker and I'm not lame. And I'm sorry I'm open about this. It's just bizarre. It's almost fiction material, if that makes any sense. I realize I don't make much sense right now. Please ignore this and never use it against me," he pleaded.

"Christoph, I wish I could be there for you. I wish an entire time zone didn't distance us."

"Chloe, I'm so, so sorry. I can't believe I just said that. You're probably putting on your running shoes by now."

"Listen, don't worry about me. Please take care of your family and let me know if there's anything I can do." I knew it was an empty offer.

"My mum is signaling for me. Sorry, sweetheart, let me call you later."

"Of course," I accepted. We lingered for a bit before ending the call. And then he was gone again. Cell phones weren't permitted in ICU.

If I had read this in a novel, I wouldn't believe you could honestly develop a bond with someone reading words from a screen or a voice through the phone. Then again, maybe by only having our words, we weren't distracted by sexual tension, that intensity causing frustration and awkwardness, especially since I was interested in the diplomat with benefits.

I meant to go into the gallery that evening, but didn't. What if he needed me to talk or listen? I sat in disbelief when my next thought troubled me. *Am I falling in love?*

I tossed and turned while trying to fall asleep over the thought *If love at first e-mail was possible.* The frustration fueled a loud scream inside my head while I spooned my pillow.

November

Chapter 10

"Morning, sleepyhead," he said. "I figured you must have fallen asleep on me again."

"What time is it?" I asked. Smiling was my new morning stretch. "It's five forty-three!"

He laughed. "It hit me yesterday—I've completely changed my perspective on my grandfather's condition. I headed to the clinic about two hours after you fell asleep this morning and harassed my grandmother and father into going to lunch to help them forget about things for a while . . . And then I spent a couple hours having coffee and catching up with my other favorite woman in the world."

"I'm hoping that would be your mom?" I joked to lighten the tone.

I had recalled his telling me once my birthday was probably the most insightful of signs, because his mother was his favorite woman in the entire world, the person he loved the most. I just happened to share her birthday.

"Dork . . ." he mumbled.

"I think you and your family needed to remind yourselves you're not alone in this scary process. You'll still have each other and no matter what, you'll deal with it with admiration."

"I also stopped by my grandpa's favorite bookstore, bought his favorite book and gave it to my grandmother. She wanted to read to him alone, so we left."

My guard softened from the possibility of us decades from now still having our book club.

"I think I'm ready to talk to what appears to be the 'fastest growing' second runner-up to the 'my favorite woman in the world' title, Miss Kassidy."

What a thought to begin the day.

It was November and I was grateful for having three months until opening night. I worked over time with shooting, retouching and balancing Milton Bright with Grayson Gates since they both were sticking pins and needles to me if I dropped the ball. The curator promised our careers would be cursed since his career comeback depended on the opening. He even swore on his own mother. Which rang odd since she had died several years ago.

As I put together my sailing ensemble, I glanced to the picture pinned above my workstation once more. *I'd come so far from the path I always wished for.* The familiar tone of my Blackberry sidetracked me. Thank God no one was around to slap the stupid smile off my face while I opened his e-mail.

From: Christoph Kostas

To: Chloe Kassidy

Subject: Invitation for the best chocolate!

Date: November 7, 6:10 a.m.

What about you coming here? I'm here. I'll pick you up. I'll show you around and if you can't put up with my charm, you'll have still seen Geneva.

Not bad for a first date, right?

From: Chloe Kassidy

To: Christoph Kostas

Subject: Re: Invitation for the best chocolate!

Date: November 7, 6:17 a.m.

Priceless! As much as I want to meet you and also see Switzerland, I'm not the girl who gets on a plane and flies around the world to a man I've developed this unexplainable bond with but have never placed my eyes on. Would make for a nice book!

From: Christoph Kostas

To: Chloe Kassidy

Subject: Re: Re: Invitation for the best chocolate!

Date: November 7, 7:13 a.m.

Your e-mail made me smile. I think a certain guarded girl has switched on her sugariness and is becoming sweeter by the second. Guess what? You can actually be sweet . . . who would have thought?

You're right. My major concern with our first date in Geneva is my entire family is here and I'm a private person, and also traditional. I don't do the 'bring the girl home' thing to avoid giving them reason to talk and ask questions. I wouldn't mind bringing you here, in fact, I'm anxious to show you my world, but how about we do that for our second date?

One of my aunts is a travel agent. She's actually on her way over. My grandma is hosting a grappa and cake get-together of the family to talk to us. I'll ask her to check for itineraries from NY to my absolute definition of romantic places. I'll get back to you. I need to warn you though: if we go, you'll never be able to say 'no' to me ever again. In fact, you'll probably end up becoming my stalker.

Seriously, since you're the New York local, I'm open to suggestions for our first date when I return. If it were completely up to me, being spontaneous and cute, I'd make you breakfast at my apartment while we sat on the terrace, but I know how that would freak you out.
p.s. What are you wearing?

From: Chloe Kassidy
To: Christoph Kostas
Subject: Re: Re: Re: Invitation for the best chocolate!
Date: November 7, 8:09 a.m.

Almost ready . . . dark denim skinny jeans, black leather ballet flats (a must for my feet), yellow (think banana) button-up shirt tucked in with sleeves rolled to mid forearm. Hair is messy. All in 20 minutes. I'm off to work! Talk to you later.
p.s. You're corrupting my mind. I actually hate you for this!

From: Christoph Kostas
To: Chloe Kassidy
Subject: Re: Re: Re: Re: Invitation for the best chocolate!
Date: November 7, 8:11 a.m.

Oh boy, this is where it's obvious Aquarians blow cold and blow hot without ever knowing what they want. You just told me that I corrupt your mind? Like I'm a criminal and you're the innocent girl who falls for it? Ha! Relax Miss Control Freak.
p.s. Hate isn't the opposite of love.

From: Mary Polt
To: Chloe Kassidy, Christoph Kostas
Subject: Conspiracy
Date: November 7, 8:44 a.m.

I connected you two and now I don't get to know what's cooking? You should both be ashamed. Miss Chloe, you've ruined this girly conspiracy by not giving me the inside details! I hope you both know without me you wouldn't be talking.
Shame on you both for leaving me in the dark!
Your Matchmaker

Mary's e-mail interfered with my bagel and lox routine while I walked into the office early to sign documents and show face, since I planned to sneak out at lunch. I was still uneasy communicating with Mary and with her involvement in this, although *this* wouldn't even exist without her, as she clearly pointed out. The matchmaker was a third wheel as far as I was concerned, and I didn't need training wheels to guide me through this experience. I needed Stephanie to hold my hand.

From: Christoph Kostas
To: Chloe Kassidy, Mary Polt
Subject: Re: Conspiracy
Date: November 7, 9:13 a.m.

Just ignore Miss Matchmaker. I explained to her you're not ignoring her, but just shy. Mary, sorry, but there is only room for two people in this boat! I think the dinners and drinks over the weekend paid back my debt for introducing me to the loveliest girl in the world. The rest is up to us!
Christoph

Trust is a delicate thing when it comes to matters of the heart. With my love for photography, it was solely a matter of trusting my instinct, my eye, and the direction of my inner compass. Add a man into the shot and I compromised control over the outcome, and upped the risk of being humiliated and broken through the crumbling of my concrete walls. In spite of this, what was the alternative? *Was true love worth the risk?* The question was gradually suffocating my insecurity and allowing interest to breathe.

Today was going to be an adventure like never before. At 12:30 p.m., I was scheduled to hop aboard a yacht and circle around the city I dearly loved, and would hopefully capture my theme. *I love New York* was tattooed on key chains, coffee mugs, T-shirts and hats for a reason. It was loved in the most unconditional way. We took the city's good with bad, cleanliness with the stench, whopping opportunities sacrificing living spaces. Surrounding this scene with my Canon had more meaning, since with a circle there is no beginning or end. It's constant. It's what unconditional, true love resembles. Today, I was going to make that happen.

My corner office at Bright Images, Inc. offered a panoramic view of the Hudson River. It was one of the perks that pushed me to accepting the job. Watching the river versus riding on it was a dreadfully different experience, mainly with the shadowy clouds lurking above. I looked forward to the first day of snow, only not today.

Milton entered my office unannounced. "I just received confirmation that you sent over the contracts," he said.

"Yes, everything was signed and sent over this morning," I nodded. I had found and signed a new client to Bright Images, Inc. I assumed this was his way of acknowledging a job well done.

"I haven't seen you wear anything new lately," he analyzed me from head to toe. "*Image* is part of our company name."

"I left the final campaign proofs on your desk. If you could approve them, we can get the ball rolling. The client approved them yesterday."

"I reviewed them. Go with it. They look great," he said and exited my office.

Resorting to Lamaze breathing to appease my nerves, I forwarded the approval to the printer and headed to the lobby to hail a taxi to the South Street Seaport. I checked the sky again, noticing the sunlight was struggling to spread out. I needed three hours for the tour and a steady focus-and-capture platform. Being on a boat in bitter November might be more work than I had anticipated.

By the sight of the black and white yacht with fire-engine-red writing, *Circle Line*, I had arrived at my destination. There were several companies to choose from, World Yacht and Classic Harbor to name the two runners-up. I chose Circle Line not because it was the most famous, but because of what the word *circle* meant to me.

A loop of rope in the form of a circle symbolized the eternal because it had no beginning and no end, according to the ancient Egyptian shen. The wedding ring is the symbol of eternity and synonymous with love. The Egyptians saw love as everlasting. The Egyptians designed a ring to wear around the finger perceived as a universal symbol of unity, wholeness, infinity, the goddess, female power, and the sun.

"Good Morning. You must be Chloe?" a mid-fortyish gentleman asked while he approached me, safeguarded in his camel-color overalls. His outwear clearly pointed out two details: I wasn't dressed appropriately, and I was going to freeze my ass off. He resembled Richard Gere. I reminded myself to not be a mindless girl, but the professional photographer I came here to be.

"That would be me. Thanks again for the private tour today."

"Of course. I have you set up on the stern side, but you're free to move around and about through the course of our trip."

"Okay," I agreed.

"Please just yell if you need me to slow down to capture whatever you're searching for." He clapped his hands once and quickly returned them to his jacket pockets.

"Damn, it's cold!" I shrieked. *Wait . . . stern?*

"By the way, has anyone told you—"

Wait, where is the stern? "I look like Natalie Portman, of—" "I was going to say that Miss Portman has a striking resemblance to you," he said with an adolescent grin.

Smiling, "Should we get this show on the road?" Flirting wasn't on the itinerary.

"Certainly. Today's trip isn't suitable to drop anchor."

I continued to nod foolishly.

"Also, if you're feeling sick—it can sneak up on you—I've got meds in the galley to fight off nausea."

Sick. Oh dear, and what the heck is a galley?

"All aboard!" he announced and I wondered if I was deserving of his enthusiasm.

"Wait! I don't speak boat." I blushed.

He rolled his eyes with a look of *how cute*.

"Where's the stern? What's a galley?"

"I apologize for the maritime terms. Go to the right side of the boat. If you get nauseous the meds are in the kitchen."

I reminded myself a vomit joke was more revolting than humorous. "Got it, Cap! All aboard!"

"That's my line," he interjected.

"Oh . . ."

"I'm kidding," he smiled.

Just like my love for photography, and my love for love, I was going to have to trust I would make it on a moving platform. *What is love without trust?* Well, the next three hours would depend on how much I trusted the Cap.

Choosing a position at the yacht's rear, I removed the Canon and secured it around my neck, taking the necessary precautions if I wanted it to return home with me and not overboard. I didn't want to imagine what swam or floated in the Hudson.

The cruise departed from the South Street Seaport, the southern tip of the island, while I viewed the oldest architecture in downtown through my screen. *Click. Click. Click.*

Checking to make sure my framed view was mirroring the beauty that moved before me proved a bit more difficult in mobility.

Bump . . . Whoa . . . Click.

The cruise began to circle around to head north along the Hudson River, brushing against Manhattan's body. To my left, the almost-6,000-foot and largest suspension bridge in the world, The Brooklyn Bridge, competed for space with the clouds. The manmade connector attached me to my new-found pen pal from a different world. *Click. Click. Click.* This art of steel remained, linking walks of life from around the world, and possibly connecting me to my soul mate. It makes for a nice story and was so *Bridges of Madison County. Well, so far without all the steamy sex.*

With the bridge behind me, we approached Governor's Island and made our way to Battery Park, Wall Street and the New York Stock Exchange with a bump, turn and a wave to one of the most famed skyscrapers, the Woolworth Building. This building was still recognized as one of the fifty tallest buildings in the world. It resembled a European Gothic cathedral with an exterior decoration cast in limestone-colored, glazed architectural terra-cotta panels. Manhattan's foundation was a little piece of every part of the world, a true example of a melting pot. *Click.* The boat picked up speed, causing me to eat my hair. Luckily, I'd remembered putting a hair band in my coat pocket.

While securing my hair back and without warning, the memory snuck up fast upon me. The hole in the sky prompted me to recall where the Twin Towers once stood. Like shiny ornaments decorating the skyline. Now, gracefully peeking into the sky was the completion of the first Freedom Tower. The tip of the cranes seemed to almost touch the clouds, right into heaven.

Loss was a four-letter word just like *love*. The words had the same length and height, but the weight felt heavier and the devastation of it paralyzed me. As much as I loved love, I was petrified of what loss would do to me.

I checked my Blackberry, while I had a solid minute before the boat approached my next shot calmly advancing along the city's silhouette.

Text from Christoph: *Good Day, Mate! I don't want to bother the artist. I just wanted to say hello. I should be concentrating on my family, but I think you're causing me to lose my head a bit!*

I didn't want to lose my balance and crush the Canon. I shuffled to a bench to respond. We had bypassed the Empire State Building, considering that it was too obvious. I wanted to capture my own New York love story. *Sleepless in Seattle* had Hanks and Ryan owning that.

Text from Chloe: *I'm being productive! No boat sickness yet and Captain Richard Gere is totally informative. I'm getting magnificent shots. A theme is another story.*

Text from Christoph: *The Captain is a Richard Gere's twin? He better just be trying to steer the ship! That's it? Want to tell me something a bit sweeter?*

"It's getting a bit rough. They're calling for a storm sooner than we expected. We need to head back," the captain shouted.

This isn't Perfect Storm, Chloe.

"We'll be approaching the Statue of Liberty and Ellis Island on your right before reaching the dock," he yelled out.

I could see land, so swimming for my life was an option.

Text from Chloe: *Have to get back to work. A storm is coming in!*

When I put my phone away and grabbed the Canon, I heard a beep indicating a new message, but ignored the signal. The clouds above had my undivided attention. I had to point, shoot, and get home, not only to process these images, but also to Christoph's *Losing my head* comment.

Ellis Island, the main entry for immigrants to New York, was in my frame. I wasn't an immigrant, but I understood the desire for more, to move to a place where dreams were born. New York was a whole new world of crowded streets flooding with foreigners, originality, and that one and only hustle and bustle.

The woman of copper, caused from chemical weathering, was now the sea green Goddess—The Statue of Liberty. I bowed my thanks to the people of France for flakey croissants and this stunning statue. The power of her presence was more remarkable from underneath. I recalled the tablet within the pedestal at the statue's base and the poem by Emma Lazarus. *Keep, ancient lands, your storied pomp!* Love was *pomp* to me.

This indeed wasn't only a sightseeing tour, but a heart-seeing one. There had to be something here to spark possible concepts for *Love Through Light*. The loop was complete and it was back on solid ground. It didn't require a healthy dose of imagination to realize a monsoon was pending and it was time for caffeine and cover, fast.

Chapter 11

I hailed a cab to the grocery store. I needed to buy coffee, and carbs, for the hours of processing ahead. I was eager to study the frames from this afternoon and hoping after five months of ownership, my Illy investment would make me a proud sipper of a foaming concoction. This purchase should have required an operating certificate, since this sophisticated European machinery wasn't a part of my southern hospitality upbringing.

I forgot about my decision to join Christoph's book club or return with Emma to Brooklyn. I craved Christoph reading to me, especially on a thunderous evening. It was difficult picking the one word to express the satisfying tone of his words while syllables slipped from his foreign lips. His voice was the flesh of his storytelling. It wasn't everyday that a gorgeous, witty, and charming guy read to me.

One thing for certain I couldn't deny, Christoph was the first person I wanted to share my day with. I couldn't explain my openness to him, with him. *Why was I letting a stranger inside my safe zone where proven tried and trusted solely had access?* For Christ sakes, he hadn't passed his own coffee test yet.

I arrived at my apartment safe, sound and not completely soaked when the sprinkles progressed to hammering. I dropped everything, stripped down and hopped into a steamy shower to rid the river. I considered if becoming shocked in the shower was possible from the electrified sensation running through me. I didn't want to miss Christoph's call and couldn't wait to download my shots.

Grabbing a towel, I did a 1-2-3 pat down and dove on the bed for my phone.

"Finally, I get to hear your voice today," Christoph muttered.

"It seems like forever," I admitted, slightly embarrassed. We had texted and emailed throughout the day. In today's world, emails and texts were approved methods of well-mannered communication. No one ever used the phone anymore, except for him. He favored speaking.

"Well, don't keep me waiting, Chloe . . . How did the shoot go?"

"It's coming along. I'll admit, shooting while traveling in a circle with the threat of a thunderstorm was a true test to my skills."

"You're passionate . . . I'm sure your technique is brilliant," he said.

I knew I wanted to do something passionate with artistic freedom, and drawing with light was the technique that came naturally to me.

"Send me a couple . . . I want to see!"

Show him my work?

"I will soon. I need to retouch first," I said.

He sighed. "Oh, come on. It's me!"

Sometimes my creative endeavors were more concerned with the need to create something, to entertain people, or express myself.

They were less about discovering the true meaning in life. I made something out of nothing at times, and it felt magnificent. Yet, I wasn't ready to share this piece of me with him.

"Maybe I'll bring samples for our coffee test. If you pass, you get a peek," I joked.

"Why do you want to wait until next week? I hate 'until thens'. . . It's such a squander of life."

Even with my hesitation, I continued my role in moving us forward.

"And did Mr. Gere hit on you? I'm sure he did—"

"No, of course not silly. He was busy steering the ship!" I laughed. "But . . ." Not sure if I should continue, "The resemblance was wild. He actually questioned my Natalie Portman look alike as well."

"There may be a resemblance, but you're more stunning. Your eyes carry something special, Chloe. I almost passed out that morning when I opened the attachment from your e-mail. I kept looking at it during a meeting at the UN, and lost myself while sitting around at table of suits scribbling in their Mont Blanc pens," he revealed.

Mont Blanc . . . I knew it!

"I'm sure Gere was bewildered as well. What are you wearing?" Christoph asked.

"Can I call you back in two seconds?" I was wearing only a towel.

"What's wrong?"

Giggling and stuttering to answer, "I actually—"

"You sound odd," he said.

"I just stepped out of the shower. Let me call you back!"

"Okay. I want to hear about your shoot," he said. "Hmm . . . I'm a bit distracted by you in a towel—my apologies!"

I threw on some clothes and proceeded into International territory, the kitchen. The fire engine red, Francis Francis X1 Illy espresso machine and I were at a standoff. *Please . . . Francis.* On the inside I was begging her to let me have my way, but I stood there confidently reminding myself I had a college degree. *You can do this.* A foamy cappuccino fit into my scenario of being home while talking to a diplomat and working on my dream, not a tablespoon of Folgers and two minutes in the microwave.

I gathered all necessary utensils and approached her. I gently pressed her button and she was turned on. Next, I placed the capsule containing freshly ground espresso into what resembled an ice cream scoop. After filling the machine with milk, I grabbed the steaming pitcher and approached the wand. Only sixty seconds to froth and *voila* I would have my cappuccino. *Gurgle. TSSSSS. Screech!* The hot liquid began to splatter while droplets sprayed hitting my neck. *Froth! Ouch! No!* I shoved the wand deeper into the metal pitcher, which lead to a horrible noise. *Ouch! Hot! Francis!* I stood against the kitchen wall rubbing my chest from the spray of boiling milk dots. *Thank God Canon was Chloe friendly*. I would never forgive Francis for this or the sales lady at Macy's. Just as I reached for the Folgers, the phone rang.

"Are you decent?" he asked.

"You're a comedian now?"

"I thought you were going to call me back. Is everything all right?"

"Yes, I made a cappuccino." I unplugged the machine.

"Tell me about today. How does ship shooting work?"

"You want to know?" I was curious if he was sincerely interested since he didn't seem like a man who made small talk.

"I'm beginning to adore every part of you Chloe Kassidy. The artist, the shy girl, your stubbornness . . . the 'head' person that's a hopeless romantic. Tell me please," he begged.

"Well, okay, but we can always talk about it during coffee." I needed to get to work and apply Aloe Vera on my battle wounds.

"Look at us. Do you honestly think we'll have a problem with topics to talk about?" he replied with a soft, adorable laugh.

"True. I guess our 'thingy' is going well." I bit my lip.

"The cruise around the city was motivating and I shot over three hundred images. I'm keeping everything crossed I captured a couple of usable frames." The pressure for Gates approval was thick and choked me by the permanent knot in my throat.

"Everything crossed?" he asked.

"Sorry, I forgot about the European slang barrier."

"Well, I forgot your American sarcasm is you trying to be funny and not cold."

"Fair," I responded.

"Like keeping your fingers crossed in luck then prosperity may come of your action," I explained. "For extra luck, I could cross my arms, legs, toes and eyes, but that would be a bit hard with a camera."

"Ahh. I see. Okay, go on . . ." he said sounding unimpressed.

Europeans, I swear.

I was interested in signs ever since the first time someone made the comment, "Oh you must be an Aquarius," and further enlightening me on Air being my element and Uranus my planet. I was relieved with the planet discussion, since I wasn't sure where *your anus* was going. I was comfortable living among Aquarian characteristics, as it felt natural. However, I would never understand why the water bearer pours electricity, it seemed risky. My sign had the *art of knowing* attitude, the aloofness, the stubbornness, and my sarcasm to hide any sensitivity. This designated sign placed upon me suited me well. I would have to work on my sarcasm with Christoph, deal with the uneasiness of change and not make him feel anything regarding us was a waste of time.

That was the thing with Aries, with the element of Fire, a ruling planet of Mars, and being the Ram. He had to be recognized since his need for attention is strong. I didn't know much else about the Aries, except the sign was compared to the Peter Pan theory . . . never wanting to grow up. My curiosity had gotten the best of me and I researched if the planets in charge considered this Swiss Lindt and the American Hershey combination compatible.

"Well, the first obstacle to overcome is shooting from an unstable platform. I'm clumsy, therefore, I'm a fan of high-quality tripods. When shooting landscape, it's crucial to shoot on solid ground, capturing multiple frames and wanting to have the ability to expand exposure range and depth of field—"

He interrupted, "You're clumsy? Women, I swear."

"Are you saying sharp shooting sounds easy?" I asked.

"Sharp shooting? What do you mean?"

"Most of my photography work was in studios and controlled environments. Not challenging conditions that require stabilization, fast lenses and expanded ISO capability . . . oh and fast shutter speeds!"

"Boats with Captain Gere?" he teased.

"Exactly," I replied, now questioning if he knew I exaggerated. I sounded mind numbing and explaining my process didn't offer as romantic an explanation as writing a book on soul mates connecting in a lifetime.

"I'm sure you mastered all this and have trophy winning shots?" he said.

I was intimidated by the diplomat title and this feeling that my own work was insignificant and not impressionable was unfamiliar to me. I couldn't return the favor on International Law, United Nations cases or why Mont Blanc pens were worth their sticker price.

"You know, photography is like love is it not?" he said.

"How do you mean?" I asked, waiting to be enlightened.

"Unstable platforms versus controlled solid grounds . . . controlling our exposure, perfect versus imperfect . . . changing your perspective and what about how we evaluate emotions?" Christoph continued. "The individual who can grasp this takes home the prize."

"The prize?"

"Yes, Chloe . . . true love. Goes back to my theory most people give up or run away from the feelings they cannot control or predict," he said. "It's scary knowing your heart will be leading the way. It's breathtaking knowing you no longer have control . . . you're no longer truly yours . . . you're his or hers. How many people can accept that? Not many. I believe, close to none."

I adore him.

"What made you want to become a diplomat?" I asked. I wasn't sure what it exactly meant or required.

"Representing the United Nations is an excellent way for me to use my rare talents to make a positive difference in the world. My studies are in international law and philosophy—"

"My friend Emma studied philosophy . . ." *I hope he isn't a nut job.*

"I started working in government jobs and then had an opportunity to work with Darfur. It's a tough life since it entails employment with embassies or consulates and an aptitude for foreign languages," he continued.

"I must say, it sounds extraordinary."

"I value communication with people from different backgrounds and political beliefs," he said.

"And are you content with your career choices?"

"I've always felt like I was sent here to serve a higher purpose, to perhaps sacrifice my own self for the sake of the whole. Sitting here trying to find a peace proposal for the ethnic groups of Darfur is what makes me content in knowing the world can be a better place. I'm bad at admitting I'm weak and fragile at times because . . . there are souls and kids and women out there who need me to be strong for them, who need me to be strong at all times, to almost be Superman."

"You're doing more than most people ever will." I wondered if he didn't have passion for writing, if he would even be interested in a creative person. "I hope you realize that," I said.

Naturally, I felt the desire to be his gravity. To pull him away from his doubts and reassure him of his causes. To return the favor as best as I could.

"Also, to think, if you married me, you would be exempt from sales tax," he joked.

Married?

Moving past the delicate subject, "You're exempt?"

"Yep, I have my little card here. Being a diplomat comes with benefits and I don't mean a Blackberry. I have diplomatic immunity and I'm given safe passage under host country laws."

"Well, I'm not one of those girls where the retail industry suffers if I go on vacation."

Although, one of my favorite things to do is read the *New York Times Sunday Style* section. My budget only allotted me creative accessories for my Canon. Thanks to J. Crew, the budget included a personal stylist. *Thank God for Jenna's picks.*

While we were both in the moment, my mind pulled me to my deadline.

"I should hit the keys."

"You can't go!" He seemed shocked that this thought even crossed my mind. "I have work to do as well, but I know I'll be distracted with thinking of you."

"It's a dilemma, but we have—"

"Let's do book club just for a bit and then we can both work," he suggested.

"Okay, but only for a little while," I agreed. I needed to be in two moments at once.

"Are you comfortable?" he asked.

"I'm ready."

His voice altered slightly to a deeper tone offering emotional warmth like a lingering hug. He began reading while the chapter took us on an intimate journey with these two characters Hanna and Michael from lovemaking to showering.

"Are you okay, Chloe?" he deliberately whispered, I suspect from his own shyness of the scene he just described.

"Yes." I wouldn't admit the timing of the chapter made me uneasy, like the pressure of one's first kiss.

After finishing Chapter 10, we had been on the phone for another forty-five minutes.

"I'm enjoying this novel," I said.

"And our book club?"

"I'm pleased with it," I admitted.

"I need to get to work," I said gawking at the time and my abandoned workstation.

"Okay, if you must."

I made another instant cup of coffee and positioned myself with Photoshop that had been patiently waiting for me to commence.

"What was that alarm?"

"What?"

"I heard beeping?"

"Oh, I made another cup of coffee," I responded and then cringed with embarrassment.

"Typical American—"

"What does that mean?" I asked.

"You just microwaved coffee? We need to get you an Illy!"

"I have one!" I admitted proudly and then cringed again.

It was going to be a tedious Tuesday, and I sent an e-mail to the office informing them I would be working from home today. Within seconds I received a message.

Text from Milton: *Changed my mind on proofs. See e-mail for revisions.*

I rushed over to my computer and logged into the printing company's ordering page. "Stop the press!" I yelled out as I typed the urgent message to cancel the order. I knew better than to send the files based on Milton's word and not his signature on the dotted line.

Walking into the kitchen, I glanced at Francis.

You won't put me in a bad mood.

I grabbed the instant coffee once again, scooping a heapful into my black *I Love NY* cup, adding water and placing it in the magic box until *ding*! Putting shame aside, I loathed myself for worrying how Christoph would be appalled, *Why on earth are you drinking the cleaning lady's coffee?*

I secured my hair back into a loose ponytail and opened the window to let the morning chill keep my fingertips at attention. Gently pressed into the smooth flat keys, I closed my eyes and opened my heart.

What is true love? Why do I love? New York is . . . Did I brush my teeth?

There is no city like New York in the world. It was an urban kaleidoscope of infinite textures and uniquely individual microcosms. It was still relatively un-homogenized, especially in the village. Mom and Pop grocery stores, pizza joints, and bakeries remained on the corners they were first created. You can wear couture on a Wednesday afternoon and fall in love with the shape of a shadow. The energy is rampant. You felt it the minute you came out of the subway. There was something for everyone, from art, education, nightlife, sports, Central Park, Penn to Grand Central Station. The movie *Bright Lights Big City* came to my mind. There was also JFK Airport, offering direct flights to destinations around the world. Manhattan had a vibe unlike any other city in the world. Why else would Frank Sinatra sing *New York, New York*? There was a mystery about walking alone in the midst of thousands. It sang, it danced . . . it was quiet with the roar of a lion. I couldn't forget about the beautiful men from around the world and the fact that people find their life's loves in this city. I loved New York for reasons I couldn't explain, but I felt it. It was there. I would never stop. *Wasn't that true love?*

Chapter 12

Startled by the ring, I was lead to consider I did have ADHD since almost two hours had vanished. Emma called, and I was disappointed when the screen didn't flash *private*.

"Good Morning, Emma," I answered with an extra dash of *happy to hear from you*. I knew her purpose for the call.

"You're coming tonight, right?" she sighed without even hearing my response.

"No how are you? Good Morning?"

"You're still coming, right?" she persisted.

"Yes, of course. I haven't completed the novel, I'm on Chapter—"

"Chloe! I can't believe you're reading it? I'm going to look lazy," she whined.

"It's a book club. A club where people read books and discuss them . . . I didn't realize you needed a memo on something you forced my participation." I refocused my efforts back to the task at hand.

"I'm not going for the stupid book. I can't believe you don't understand."

"You're right . . . I don't . . . You should explain it to me," I groaned, now completely annoyed and forcing myself not to give her a proverbial kick in the ass.

"I still think I've got a chance! There's a connection."

"Emma, he's gay. Seeing is believing, and I believe we both witnessed this critical detail last month. The only chance you have for him to be in your life is Lily having two new handsome uncles."

"What are you cranky about?" she asked in an absurd tone.

"Listen, I'm busy with my deadline."

"I'll pick you up at four o'clock . . . That'll give us plenty of time."

"Got it," I confirmed, annoyed that I'd picked up the curator's two word habit. "You should at least read the synopsis on the back, Emma. There's going to be a discussion tonight . . . Just an FYI."

"Super idea!" she cheered.

Within seconds of me returning to work, I received a message.

Text from Christoph: *I'm already missing talking to you and remembering you've got book club tonight. You should skip it and we will do our book club! p.s. What are you wearing?*

Text from Chloe: *Still have work to do between now and book club! Page four, page thirteen, page seventeen and suede black flats with hair in a ponytail.*

Text from Chloe: *p.s. Most recent J. Crew catalog. Do your homework! And you? xo.*

Text from Christoph: *Jeans, espresso V-neck cashmere sweater, dark brown shoes, three-button corduroy sport coat, collar's up.*

At 4:00 p.m. on the dot I was curbside, book in hand, waiting on my ride, while my mind was still upstairs attached to the image on my screen. Cabs were flashing by sending the effects of my blur tool to draw contrast as a mental image. This possibly was an out of body experience.

From: Christoph Kostas
To: Chloe Kassidy
Subject: Thoughts
Date: November 9, 4:01 p.m.

I know this will probably freak you out and trust me you have no idea how much it freaks me out, but it's amazing how right you feel even though I've never laid my eyes on you. It makes me scared, speechless, amazed, terrified, a little crazy, a bit uncomfortable, way out of my safety zone. I can go on for hours.

I don't consider you a stranger—I wonder if you've failed to notice we almost probably no longer are. Are you ready for someone with expectations and a crazily unique interpretation of life and people? The part that has no choice but to think of this perfect stranger while you're out with great friends, I'm dying to read to you tonight but who of course, will never admit it . . . only . . . he just did . . . look at her smile.
Christoph

> *Regroup Chloe.*
> An approaching cab had a wild arm waving outside the window.
> *Smile.*
> "Ready?" she screamed from inside.
> *Smile bigger.*

Heading towards DUMBO, I grew melancholy. I began counting the minutes I wouldn't be talking with him. I wouldn't be on my bed listening to the sound of his foreign pronunciation delivering passages to me. I had let my guard relax more than I would even admit to myself. I had exposed a tiny piece of me out into the open, ready at any moment to be pounded like a New York City cockroach. Even though it was bite sized, when it came to matters of the heart, it was enormous. It was a piece of my heart that made up a huge chunk of me. Except, what if destruction didn't occur? What if, just what if, this was my happily ever after? It was the beginning of something.

"How's work going? I know you'll be your charming and your impressive self," Emma said.

"Thank you for the vote of confidence," I said. My friend's support meant the world to me. "What's going on with you? How's Lily?" She was in a trance being seduced by her iPhone. "Hello!" I poked her knee.

"I posted on Facebook about the second night of the club," she responded.

"You should be careful," I warned. With all her soul mates, I was honestly surprised she didn't have a stalker.

"You're super paranoid," she rolled her eyes.

"You're missing this when you're typing away on that." I pointed out the window. "What about living in this moment right now instead of writing about it?"

"Everyone is doing it, Chloe."

"Do not check us in—it's stalker central," I said. "Never mind," I mumbled while leaning my head against the window. I watched the passersby get high off the city's energy. New York was a drug I never wanted to kick. It would be a habit for life.

We arrived early at book club and had our pick of seats. Of course, she chose close by the fetching husband, determined more than ever. Emma disregarded all facts and decided this called for keeping her competition closer.

The sign-in sheet moved around the room. I wondered if Mary would introduce herself. I didn't recognize anyone from the first meeting. When I looked through my lens, all experiences were more identifiable. I was next to last to sign in. I had seconds to scroll the list of attendees. There was no Mary Polt.

"Please make sure your phones are off. We'll begin in a couple minutes. I hope everyone brought their book and read it," the host studied our faces searching for hints of anxiety.

"Shit, I forgot my book!" Emma panicked.

"Wow, you're making an effort to turn him straight," I said.

"Chloe, give me yours . . . You don't care about him," Emma hissed.

"You mean the club?" I replied.

"You know what I mean, I—"

"Seriously, it's frightening but I don't," I replied, unsure of why I sat there when I wanted to be home behind closed doors and on the phone with *him.* "I need it back when you're done," and released my grip with her nod of confirmation.

Fumbling through my bag for my Blackberry, I wanted to double check for the third time if it was silenced. Just when I confirmed the vibrate mode, I saw his message.

From: Christoph Kostas
To: Chloe Kassidy
Subject: Dinner & Movie
Date: November 9, 5:06 p.m.

I know you're in book club. Sorry I didn't reach you before. I was still with my grandfather. I have an idea. On your way home tonight, grab sushi and call me when you're home. Try to enjoy our book. It won't be the same without me!

p.s. Stop smiling!

Christoph

I was smitten. I adored his determination to stay connected while he was in Geneva.

"What is a hopeless romantic?" Thomas asked. Emma shoved her hand up immediately. "It's open discussion, no need to ask permission to speak," he advised.

"Hopeless romantics believe in fairy tales and finding one true love," she said ambitiously.

"They're idealists, sentimental dreamers," another woman added.

"Loving love," I said. Emma shot me an evil eye.

"They're total stalkers and utilize the title to get away with being creepy," an early twenties looking girl shared.

"They allow feelings of love to override common sense," a man suggested.

"And what about the rationality of love. Is love irrational or, in fact, rational?" Thomas asked. "For instance in *The Reader*, look what love makes people do. Is that love?"

Thomas's self-assured husband entered the debate. "Something rational can be explained. Love can be defended. Irrationality cannot be defended." Emma's tense expression relaxed with his every word. He charmed the room and for a second I think she believed Thomas was one lucky guy. "True love requires two special ingredients, compromise and honesty," he continued.

He impressed me as well. He was a witty and tender man with a contagious smile.

"Love makes people do crazy things. Sometimes . . . questionable and other times adorable," a woman interrupted.

"Perhaps, love is rational irrationality," Thomas suggested. "Clyde and Susan Henrik developed six basic love styles. Eros is physical and emotional love. Ludus is known to be a love played in conquest. Affectionate love slowly developed from friendship is called Storge. Pragma is when your head controls your heart. Obsessive love that can be possessive with highs and lows is defined as Mania," he said. Holding up one last finger with the opposite hand for number six, "And saving the best for last is Agape, the selfless unconditional love."

"We convince ourselves to fight when it doesn't exist or for the sake of fighting because *The Notebook* movie says we should and that's love . . . Every great love story in the past has told us to do so," a man pointed out. "Give me a freakin break," he snarled while crossing his arms. I prayed Emma would keep cool since nobody messed with actor Ryan Gosling in her presence.

"Fighting for love is an industry. Couples who know they aren't suitable for each other want a taste of what it's like to feel any little emotion coming their way," a woman said.

Emma shot a glare at me and I signaled her to relax by slowly motioning a zipper action across my lips.

"If you ever have to question whether you should be with someone or not, chances are you shouldn't be," Emma said. "Ryan Gosling's character never questioned his love for her."

Who didn't want The Notebook? Then again, was it worth the risk of ending up naked in the fetal position on the apartment floor, clutching your phone in one hand and a bottle in the other, begging to know how life started resembling the A&E show, *Intervention*. Come to think of it, *Hoarders* was more appropriate. People could hoard heartbreak or even worse be compulsive soul mate collectors. I imagined Emma playing a leading role.

I had never heard of this word *Agape* and thought it sounded similar to a type of antioxidant. I couldn't risk being converted back to my strict rational thinking or reprogrammed to what love is by this group. Thomas's last question made me uncomfortable and I hadn't a clue for the reasoning.

"What type of love is your relationship?" he asked. I instantly began counting the tattoos on the man's arm seated directly across from me for distraction. The uncertainty sent Emma into frenzy, as Thomas showed no intentions of crossing over. We both were officially book club dropouts.

My phone rang the minute after we were dismissed. It was Christoph.

"I was about to text you!" I said.

"Well, good because I've been waiting. Are you on your way home?"

"Yes. What's with the sushi?" I asked.

"I thought we could spend the evening together. I'm walking to go get my favorite salmon and avocado roll and you do the same."

With the time difference, it was late for him to be having dinner, but I didn't ask. I looked forward to it.

"What's your favorite roll?" he continued. I adored his attention to my details.

"Shrimp tempura," I shared. I might have transplanted myself to NYC, but I would always be a Southern girl in need of her fried shrimp fix. If only rolling them in grits rather than rice was an option.

"All right, Miss Kassidy. I'll meet you at home in fifteen minutes. Principessa, get cozy and get ready for one of my favorite movies we can stream from Netflix."

"What's that?" I asked, knowing I would be impressed.

"*La vita e bella*," he said as every syllable rolled off his sensual tongue. I tried to imagine what his lips looked liked as they released each word and drew breath.

"I can't believe we're doing this! You'll be back soon."

That night while we each lay in our own beds with our preferred sushi choices, we watched a movie together on Netflix. Here were two strangers, two evenings, two dinners in one moment while on speakerphone.

He had confided in me about his writing. "I don't want to write a book to discover myself, Chloe. I want to write a book to make the world discover me." I couldn't help but to wonder what we were left with at the end of our lives. Probably, it was the love we've spread and the memories we've helped shape in other peoples' lives, minds and hearts. For a second, I judged whether his intentions with me were solely for his book and his character's voice. *His legacy to be remembered.* I quickly shut down my fancy imagination when doubt attempted to write the biography of Christoph Kostas.

His mind was what initially attracted me, but he probably thought it was his passion. I was excited by the way he challenged me with his traditional thinking. I listened carefully, observing his strengths and sense of frailties. I believed we both found comfort in knowing the other cared, even with the dramatic evidence we required for reassurance at times this early in the game.

From: Christoph Kostas
To: Chloe Kassidy
Subject: Nighty Night
Date: November 9, 11:53 p.m.

One last thing! I don't know if I believe in miracles; I was raised to believe life, success, relationships, friendships, they take hard work and nothing should be left to luck. Then again, I do believe in destiny and in occurrences happening for a reason. I just sometimes wish the reason(s) were more transparent, to give people the necessary strength, will and courage to keep going, to feel appreciated and taken care of, to feel . . . blessed by a Divine force one cannot see nor touch, but one can feel 101%.

Christoph

Chapter 13

I looked forward to having a pleasant lunch with the girls. Swallowing sushi and Luna bars in front of my blank wall grew dull.

In the unfriendly November temperatures, the air felt crisper, the designer heels louder, and the taxi horns sharper. I was hypersensitive and continuing to open myself up further each day, which was possibly a result of my new romance and Christoph's part in the removal of my rational hat.

He had a handful of nights remaining in Geneva and they were having a celebratory dinner for his grandfather's recovery and Christoph's departure back to America. A much needed evening dedicated to wine sipping, I imagined. I tried picturing him with his family and what he wore to complete my mental image.

He would ask me, "A penny for your thoughts?"

I would unquestionably respond, "How about a quarter?"

He would then respond, "Typical American."

The three of them were situated at a table when I walked into the jam-packed bistro swarming with suits.

"Hello," Emma addressed me with an English accent distracting my hungry friends. I hoped my tardiness would go unnoticed. Her accent was a clear sign she had ridden with Stephanie in her Range Rover. She had a habit of imitating the woman's accent on the navigation system suchlike to her ex British soul mate.

"Are you wearing a tool belt?" Kate stared.

Removing the other arm from my coat, I glanced down. "Oh . . . I forgot to take it off," I said. "I just came from the gallery." I reassured them while I unsnapped it.

"Speaking of gallery . . . can we get an update?" Stephanie asked. They rested their menus on the table and waited for my response.

"How was your lunch with Gates?" Emma asked.

"Let's just say it was more about Demi Moore than the discipline of my work, but I did get an important contact from him," I said.

"Who? Like a celebrity?" Emma continued.

"No." I laughed. "His name is Reed Scott," I better add *research RS* to my list. "Gates suggested I meet with him when I'm in Miami." I couldn't admit that the curator had shit on my soul and was unimpressed with my pitch.

"How old is the infamous curator anyway?" Kate asked.

"He claims to be forty-six," I answered skimming the menu.

"How many years ago?" Kate joked. "Fifteen, maybe?"

"There's no way he's that young with the amount of women he claims to have courted," Stephanie giggled. Grayson Gates decorated Page Six consistently denying the lies and lovers the *NY Post* created.

"I disagree. Justin Bieber is a total gigolo and isn't even twenty," I noted. "Wait—where's Lily?" I asked. Emma brought Lily everywhere, as New York City babysitters' were as lavish as hiring a driver for the day or that other type of escort.

"She had a sleepover with a friend since I had a date last night," she said confidently.

Stephanie choked on her water and kept her eyes focused on Emma. She desperately wanted to let go of her grudge and forgive Emma as soon as she settled into common sense.

"Tell us about him," Stephanie probed. Kate continued on with the menu selections. The subject was a broken record.

"We met at the salad bar in a grocery store near Tribeca and—"

Kate and Stephanie simultaneously, "What were you doing in Tribeca?"

"Will y'all not interrupt my story?" Emma pleaded. She went from British to Southern Belle in a flash. "I wanted to take Lily for a stroll alongside the West Side Highway. We were starving and stopped for a bite."

The waiter interrupted with our drinks. "Chloe, we ordered you an extra hot latte," Stephanie said.

"Perfect." I smiled then sipped. I had to order coffee extra hot from all my at home coffee microwaving. The temperature in restaurants didn't fulfill my bubbling standards.

Emma continued. "Anyway, when I was done getting Mac & Cheese for Lily, he stood beside me waiting his turn. I thought it was Kenny Rogers at first."

"The old country singer?" Kate wrinkled her nose.

"A younger version before the plastic surgery," Emma rolled her eyes. "We had lunch and then he asked for my number. When I made it home . . . he had left a sweet message saying 'If we were in high school, I would have asked you to prom, but how about dinner.' We had a lovely time at Mara's Homemade restaurant. They've got great barbecue."

"The redneck caviar version of a beautiful evening," Kate said. "Don't you think you need to get a grip on this soul mate saga?" She continued while returning to her menu. "I mean, think about your kid . . . It's not fair." We sat there in disbelief observing the tyrant. Kate went completely overboard with her ship sinking and still wouldn't shut up. "I mean, you're a smart girl. Didn't you go to college?" she continued.

"Yes . . . Oglethorpe, Kate. You know Chloe and I studied there," Emma replied while her lip quivered.

"Well, maybe you just went there to have lunch, because I don't see—"

"What's your problem?" I interrupted.

I refused to believe time expired with finding love. It's love and sometimes we search for it and sometimes it just finds you at the salad bar. Then it's the most beautiful collision the heart or mind could have ever imagined; something words cannot describe, because it's the weight of the feeling. The hold it has on you is gravity. It turns you inside out. *Christoph.*

"Whether you experience it just once in your life or everyday . . . the point is to love . . . not be a bitch," I said. "It's never too late." I shoved my nose into my menu.

"Geez, Chloe. I want a lick of your peach," Emma cried out, regaining her beam.

"Retract the claws, Chloe." Kate said.

"True love is metal," Stephanie sighed. The thought seemed to carry her off into a particular memory.

"Do you work for emotional intelligence now?" Kate asked. "Were you undercover this whole time, Chloe?" She was completely flustered and diverging any attention away from herself. "Are you sure you went to a book club or was it a soul mate support group?"

We reunited with laughter and buried our faces into our menus. Even though we pushed each other's buttons, we always ended on a higher note. Sometimes the voice of our fears did the talking, ignoring reasoning and with Kate, her manners.

"Let's change the subject. This is more suitable for tequila not my chai tea," Kate said. "You guys are bitchy when you're hungry," she laughed.

"Love can turn anything around," I added wanting to have the last word, being the control freak I was.

"Well, just make sure it's love and not reverse psychology," Kate said, getting the final word.

When I looked down, my finger traced the damp ring from my coffee, getting lost in the moment. Over and over, there was no ending to the beginning. No beginning to the ending. Love was a connection and Mr. Grayson Gates not embracing my circle theme was aggravating.

I wanted to tell them about Christoph. He flew out tonight and would touchdown tomorrow. How I felt forever in him like the moments I captured through my lens. You can capture a sparkle and make it last forever. I wanted to tell them how I found my small parenthesis, how he had opened me up to believing complete surrender is the absence of fear, and it was possible to find *home* in someone.

Tomorrow would be a month and a half since his first e-mail. Our book club, discussions of head versus heart, laughs, our voices, all with a person I hadn't met but had an unexplainable bond with. I didn't think it had to be explained. I had fallen for him. I had opened up to him with trust in my heart and confided in him, to him, and with him. I was on a roll. His voice soothed me, his love for words and passion for writing, his strengths in his silences, his love for his family, his sleepy sweetness, the way he wanted to learn about my photography, that we had erased *lame* from our vocabulary. *How was it possible to miss something you had never seen?* He said sometimes, "The greatest matters in life are the most challenging." I was excited, but my rational hat forced me to wonder if you had to see it to believe it.

While I walked home, I read his latest e-mail.

From: Christoph Kostas
To: Chloe Kassidy
Subject: Can't wait to meet you!
Date: November 13, 2:15 p.m.

When two people can talk through silences and not words, so long as they have their own codes, their own gestures, whispers, colorful shades, so long as they shine through each other, with each other, a bond has been already made and was already accepted without anyone realizing, approving or even witnessing. You make the rest of the world look . . . colorless, tasteless, odorless.
Christoph

My hair appointment had been booked for tomorrow morning for over a week now. I wanted the natural *I'm-put-together-without-trying* look. I was also in desperate need of a manicure, noticing chunks of polish missing when I threw my hands in the air to hail a taxi. The only prepping time I had was for shooting pictures not styling myself pretty.

From: Mary Polt

To: Chloe Kassidy, Christoph Kostas

Subject: Re: I'm home!

Date: November 14, 1:15 p.m.

Your cousin and I are already at the airport waiting for you! I just need one of those relaxing lunches, our afternoons with coffee and your company. And finally, I cannot wait to meet Chloe and see you happy together.

Mary

Was this seriously happening? With the distance from his travels, my protective walls were slightly back up, and I was hopeful the breakdown would resume after meeting him. I wasn't thrilled his sidekicks were a part of the welcome home wagon.

Eventually, the private number flashed across my Blackberry screen. "Chloe, it's me," he said. "How are you, baby?"

"I'm happy to hear from you!" I said with a breath of relief. "Just at the gallery with the curator and chaos as usual," I said while heading outside for privacy. "Welcome back!"

"I can hear you smiling."

"How are you?"

"I just picked up my coffee, raspberry scone, and walked into the UN for a couple of conferences. I would rather be spending time with you," he said. "Mary took me directly to the office since lunch would delay me leaving even later today."

"I take it you're good then? I asked how you were, not what you were doing, silly."

"Oh, I'm good. Mary is dying to know about us."

Us?

"I truly believe a relationship is between the two people in it and no one else," he said.

"That's a relief to hear. I'm uncomfortable talking with Mary," I admitted. This was my first rodeo in the love arena. Him in close proximity now panicked me.

I wanted to embrace this man entirely, but maybe he was too self-satisfied for my own good. This man so honest and expressive.

"Chloe, I'm starting to think we have one thing in common: we're reserved and hard-to-get, simply because once our guards are down, we're vulnerable and unprotected and God help us if we become the prey of thoughtless and insensitive people."

Feeling numb, I knew my next response wouldn't be rich enough, open enough, risking enough for him. "I'll say this . . . I have walls up . . . I'm not arguing. Not from ever being hurt, but of never wanting to be. My core fear, besides failing at the upcoming exhibit—"

"Why do you do that? This sarcasm, Chloe—"

Ignoring him, "My biggest fear is being at the mercy of another. To follow someone's heart that chooses not to follow me back . . . to be heartbroken would be devastating," I admitted. I need my heart wholeheartedly for my photography.

"I just wish you'd stop freaking out and start noticing somehow, someway we just both bumped into something beautiful," he said almost in a soft whisper.

His voice melts me.

"I need to head into my conferences . . . I'll call you when I'm done and we'll have to meet somewhere closer to Times Square or I can have a cab drop me off at the corner of your apartment."

"I'll be leaving from the gallery."

"Beautiful, I have to run. I'll call you by six o'clock," he confirmed.

"Sure . . . Have a great day, Mr. Kostas."

"You as well, Miss Kassidy. E-mail me when you think about me." He giggled.

"Will do," I said, feeling the weight of his request. He was serious.

Before my fingertips fully released my Blackberry, I received a text from him.

Text from Christoph*: Hey, it's crazy but it took the 'I'm very happy to hear from you, Mr. Kostas' line to make me smile for the first time today.*

Heading back inside I heard the curator screaming for me. "Over here, Mr. Gates!"

The anticipation killed me. I walked around the gallery trying to direct my attention to a new theme. *Do you need to see to love?* The idea appealed to me and I hadn't realized I was fixated on a blank wall. I switched to responding to imperative emails when I received a text.

Text from Christoph: *Let's meet at the Red Cat by you at 8:00 p.m.*

Text from Chloe: *Sounds great. See you there. xo.*

I grew worried when the clock struck 8:27 p.m. *Did he not understand me at all?* I was stunned with devastation considering I was five weeks in and yet the effects of this rejection and disappointment was more akin to the destruction of a one-year anniversary. *Tick. Tock. Cinderella.* The wound he left was fresh and deep. I had lived thirty years without him, but now I had to search for a way to survive him.

In this time, my world had flipped upside down and I lost track to which side was right. *Could love compare to the bends?* I wasn't familiar with scuba diving since I was terrified of swimming in waters where creatures considered me a happy meal. I had read about DCI, Decompression Illness. During a college trip to Mexico, I safely remained dry on the boat reading about the diving activity while my then boyfriend and tourists relished their vacation under me. We broke up soon after realizing we defined adventure differently.

The bends is the illness that results from nitrogen bubbles formed in the blood stream and tissues. It's caused by decreasing pressure too quickly after a period of increased pressure, such as ascending too quickly after a dive. It gets its name from the fact nitrogen bubbles may form in or near the joints, causing pain and causing the diver to *bend over*.

I knew my diminishing guard had caused me to fall for this Swiss diplomat rather quickly. It caused me aching in a place I'd always tried to guard from unknown waters with the same thought my soul would be seen like a mouthwatering dining experience.

I couldn't respond by e-mail or text. My fingers were aggravated from punching the wrong keys. My middles were ready to send their own emotional message. Instead, I dialed his cell immediately.

No answer.

"Are you sure I can't get you anything?" Looking up I hadn't noticed the bartender had returned, witnessing my meltdown. His gaze extended far across the bar with his eyebrows slightly pulled together in the middle.

I continued to stare at him while my fingers texted snappishly to Christoph. "Anything at all?" I returned my attention back to the bartender noticing his head now slightly tilted to the side with the corners of his full lips turned down with concern.

Shaking my head *No,* I grabbed my belongings and quickly headed out the door. I pressed my lips together tightly to keep my mouth closed, attempting to swallow the ball of tears. The pressure of my tongue protruding against the back of my front teeth beat my efforts and now I noticed the same look of pity from the passersby similar to the bartender.

Back at the gallery, I hid my tears and from the curator. My heartbeat was in my throat. *Don't you dare cry, Chloe.* I began to sweat and my vision slightly dimmed. *Did he stand me up?* I had to get out of here, but unsure where to head. Rushing towards the door I felt the room take its first spin and knew I had no control over Christoph, the exhibit outcome, and what was about to happen. Just when the sensation of the gallery floor rose to catch me, it turned dark.

"Chloe?" Hearing a faint familiar voice I detected the commotion around me.

"The moon was noisy," I mumbled. My eyes were stinging making it painful to even squint from the bright bluish illumination. "What's buzzing?" For a second, I thought I was on an operating table having my broken heart repaired, but my shoes were on. "Am I dead?" I asked while being pulled up with the rush of blood jetting to my feet. My toes secured me as miniature paperweights stabilizing me upright.

A panicked Grayson, "You fainted, dear. I thought you dropped dead on me. Never do that again!" he shouted. "Dammit, turn those spotlights off now or I'm firing someone!" he continued.

One of Mr. Gates personal assistants ran towards me with a miniature bottle of water. "Well, open it for her!" The rattling of his Tic Tacs was still heard over his screams. "Have my car pulled up to the front. We have to get her home. I can't afford anymore bad press."

His assistant made sure I was settled in my apartment before abandoning me. While I lay in bed, I accepted I wasn't on her job description. I couldn't erase the frantic Grayson Gates from my worries. Would he believe me to be unstable, not prepared, or even worse not cut out for this?

Text message from Chloe: *Well don't know what to say. Thanks for not getting back to me. This day keeps getting better and better. I can honestly say . . . I've seen into the light.*

Text message from Christoph: *In the absence of your apology for attacking me, only one word . . . Ridiculous! To ache and to feel unappreciated isn't worth it. Do you care to know what happened?*

My fingertips to text a reply were lifeless. I would hope after everything, I would be first priority on this journey. God knows I earned the miles to elite status with my patience.

I tried to avoid experiencing another episode of scuba disease with this decompression attack. I wasn't sure what was up or down, fact or fiction, but memory loss was definitely a symptom.

Once I answered his call, he was impossible to ignore. Once I heard his voice, I listened.

"Chloe, someone hurt Mary physically. If you cannot understand then I'm sorry to count on you forever," he said.

"Who is hurt?" I asked.

"Mary! I'm disappointed in you! I thought I could count on you always and for anything," he shouted, attempting to imply I was the bad guy here.

"You couldn't text or call?" I said. "Is she drowning in a pool of her own blood?" I knew Kate would smile for using her line.

"I was at the hospital! Do whatever you need to do," his ego replied dismissing me.

He was bipolar if he thought I would accept that I'm the jerk and he's the victim. His words pierced my eardrums. "You failed me and Mary today and that's how this was done."

I hung up on him. When the phone rang seconds later, I answered. I couldn't restrain myself. I had to hear more of the excuse. "I'm not a guy who's chasing after life. Life should be chasing after me—I know you're my fate—I'm not going to sit here and follow your lead into saying 'oh it's just not meant to be.' The Universe works for us, with us—even if we sometimes fail to realize it."

He had the audacity to talk about fate?

"Your attitude is what's tragic. Nothing else, Christoph," I screamed.

"You're a disgrace, Chloe."

I dug deep and let loose a gut twisting laugh.

"Chloe, I'm not a toy. You want us to make plans, then we need to talk to make them. This pushing and reacting and pulling and assuming and yelling isn't communicating according to my dictionary."

"Wow, this is seriously a fairy tale," I joked.

"I'm not Cinderella. I don't change forms, identity or life after midnight," he yelled with his voice breaking.

It was impossible to accept a witty and articulate man, one where I shared heart felt heart-opening conversations quickly turned using clever banter. He was charming, poetic, and wanted to save the world, but he didn't see his part in this. He rationalized his behavior more when I was shattered by his actions or lack thereof, and I resented my accusations and verbal punches towards him. He played this meaningful role helping others and to spread love. He was an expert in law, philosophy and a peacemaker, so why was it challenging for him to make peace with me?

Diplomat or not, don't our hearts follow the same rules? I removed my rational hat. I gave into my heart, which wasn't self-sacrifice, but a chance for love. He couldn't be in denial of how this hurt me. Was I overreacting only to blame him first rather then to wait and see if there was fault on my doing?

I curled into a ball under my covers, and snuggled with the vulnerability. It amazed me how living in one of the busiest cities running twenty fours hour a day, you can still experience loneliness. I let the rings pass while being enclosed in my goose down cocoon providing a required time out. Jack Johnson's song *Cocoon* and our favorite line floated through me. I took the corner of the blanket and wiped my tears from recalling our first phone conversation. If I could remain like this I would be isolated from it all. Figuring out how to escape the walls of my mind became unbearable. The phone rang again and I squeezed my eyes tighter. On the third attempt, I freed myself and hit ignore sending Christoph directly to voicemail. He didn't even deserve my standard greeting as far as I was concerned.

Waking up in the middle of the night to check on the little red flashing light was a bad habit I had developed from the Swiss. I would have preferred the chocolate rather than the man since a tummy ache couldn't compare to heartache. *There it was, flashing.*

Chapter 14

From: Christoph Kostas
To: Chloe Kassidy
Subject: Nothing to lose
Date: November 15, 9:13 a.m.

I think you're determined to label me the 'bad guy.' You're being ridiculous and paranoid.

I find my having to justify myself ridiculous. You are offending me again and again and I'm sitting here and explaining when I don't have to. If you want to sit there and make up scenarios in your head, scenarios will help you build your anti-me movement more easily, please go ahead. But Chloe, you'll have to stop and realize it's sad we've come to this, insulting each other. I'm the same guy who spent hours talking to you every night. You might be upset with me, but I'm still a person sharing this world with you. A little respect has never hurt anyone. It can make a world of difference, but instead we allow ourselves to be conquered by human passion and madness and we forget every great legacy commences with a tiny step.

You think I've the power to stay away from you, but the truth is, I don't have the power to ever let you go. That is exactly why I can't do a simple coffee knowing how you've reacted, knowing how strong you can be without me. Do you imagine how much more of a wreck I'd be right now? Do you care to know any of this? I don't even know that. I don't even know if you care to know I care. How ironic is that? I was confident in us and now, I don't know if we ever defined concepts in the same manner.

Christoph

From: Chloe Kassidy
To: Christoph Kostas
Subject: Everything to lose!
Date: November 15, 9:45 a.m.

I've never felt afraid of someone and consumed by them at the same time. I hate that I'm honest with you, this person who can't make the effort to even meet me. You are exhausting.

Chloe

From: Christoph Kostas
To: Chloe Kassidy
Subject: Re: Everything to lose!
Date: November 15, 9:59 a.m.

Listen to you. I mean really, is this what it comes down to? You sound like a crazy, little person now.

You don't have to ask me to meet you. You don't have to ask me to care for you. You don't have to ask me to allow myself to be consumed by you. What you do have to ask me is to believe in your feelings when they're followed by outbursts like this. What you do need to ask me is to believe if we go to coffee and something goes wrong and you decide to go out and meet guys again, I'll be able to rise and move on with my life. What you do have to ask me is to believe we share the same definition of forever in spite of your hurtful words, your offensive insults and your I-want-nothing-to-do-with-you stance. I'm new at this, but at least I'm not pretending to know and I'm not ashamed I don't know.

Christoph

When Stephanie called and asked me to Tea & Sympathy, I knew empathy was much needed with her. I missed her reference to the boutique restaurant. Instead, I recommended Argo Tea, since it was far from the West Village occupied by Christoph's favorite cafes and bookstores. I avoided the risk of bumping into him allowing the universe to have another laugh. I couldn't figure out why this man would devote such a ridiculous amount of time writing these messages, only to have bad intentions. I feared the time lost in these emails exchanges and not focusing on the gallery would cost me more than I realized.

When I exited Madison Square Park, I saw her inside, cozy at a table by the window. Argo Tea was popular among the tea enthusiasts offering such a vast selection that it required an entire afternoon to sample.

Upon entering the space, I felt stoned from the intense aroma of baked goods. I eyed an oversized lemon poppy seed muffin that definitely needed to be in my belly.

"One second," she whispered. She seemed to be Skyping on her iPad. I pointed to the counter and proceeded to place our order. Stephanie was addicted to the Bubble Tea, a milky iced tea with chewy pearls and their chocolate duet gluten-free cookies. At first, I assumed Kate had converted her over to the other side, but Stephanie admitted she considered them not real cookies. Gluten free meant guilt free.

"Can I help you?" the young woman behind the counter asked.

"I need—"

A piercing voice interrupted me. "Let your body move . . . hey, hey, hey," the barista belted out.

I returned by attention back to my order. "Is that *Vogue*?"

"She loves to sing," she rolled her eyes. "Order?"

"I'll take that muff—"

"Not just where you bump and grind it," the barista sang worthy of an American Idol rejection not Madonna.

I had to move fast. "That muffin . . . two gluten free cookies . . . a small Bubble Tea . . . and a small Sparkle Tea," I said and slammed a twenty on the counter.

"Sorry about that," Stephanie said while standing up to give me a hug. "You ordered the gluten free ones, right?" she asked peeking into the bag.

"Yes. Your timing couldn't be better. I needed to see you," I admitted taking a huge bite of my muffin before removing my coat.

"To be honest, I heard it in your voice."

"These unknowns are driving—"

"What? What's wrong?" she asked.

"Hold on . . . I just have to let this chick finish," I said.

"Vogue. Vogue. Vogue. Vogue," she continued with a higher pitch. The singing barista seemed to not have a care in the world and the patrons seemed to relish in her mood.

"These unknowns are driving me insane . . . I'm stuck," I admitted.

"Chloe, are we talking about the exhibit?" Stephanie asked.

"Do you want me to lie or really lie?" I joked. "This guy," I rolled my eyes.

"You must get a grip. In my opinion, you keep accepting his excuses, because you've convinced yourself things are happening for a reason," she paused to take a bite. I sipped my tea allowing her time to swallow. "Nothing has changed. This guy has remained the same," she said. "Want a bite?"

"No . . . come on, finish your point," I said.

"You're a smart cookie—" Her iPad rang and she hit ignore.

"Who were you chatting with?" I asked.

"My coworker is traveling alone in China . . . Walking The Great Wall, something on her bucket list. She Skyped me for some virtual companionship."

"Oh . . . I'm familiar with that," I said. "Christoph and I used it while he was in Geneva."

"Were you nervous?"

"Nervous?"

"The first time you see this guy you've bonded with is through a camera," she said. "I guess you're comfortable with looking through a lens, though." She laughed. "What's wrong?"

"We've never used the camera. I haven't seen him yet, except for jpegs we've emailed each other."

"Why? I don't understand."

"That makes two of us." I rolled my eyes. "He feels that would be unromantic for us to see each other for the first time through the computer."

"But your whole relationship is through technology!" Stephanie said. Her frustration seemed to be catching up with mine.

I took several deep breathes since I couldn't afford another fainting spell.

"What?" Stephanie jumped grabbing the table.

The frothing sound heated my patience even more. The thought of Francis infuriated me. I glanced at the menu displayed on the wall when I spotted the teapuccino. *Makes sense.*

"Maybe he's not where he says he is?" she suggested. We both went straight to sucking our teas. "The crappy thing is you haven't taken advantage of the video to see face to face. That would make you have some trust with him until you meet in person."

I stuffed a large piece of muffin into my mouth to avoid her question and acknowledge this ongoing global lesson I appeared to be learning.

"Even his cell number is managed by some VOIP networks," I said.

"Some what?"

"These static numbers or networks based on availability," I said. "I'm not even sure I understand—"

"Crap!" she screamed.

"Calm down . . . I'll—"

"Sorry . . . A bubble got stuck in my straw. Anyway, it kills me to see you consumed with this nonsense. It has to be hindering your creativity and especially your confidence. You need these things, ya know?"

"I'm confident I'll get my shots under any condition," I responded with complete uncertainty. The truth was I couldn't afford his lies.

"Just be aware of how your perspective is affected. Comparison is about perspective, something you were familiar with and had complete control over."

"Stephanie, confidence is a choice. I can handle Christoph," I reassured her while doubt weighed on my shoulders. "My problem is confidence only lasts by asking questions. That's how you learn and somehow along the way, I stopped asking him questions. I just don't want to fail at this."

She grabbed a piece of my muffin, from the bottom half, as she knew the top part with its chewier, well done texture was my favorite part. "Speaking of failing, we're taking in Alexander's mother's dog. His chewing is costing her a pretty penny."

"So . . . he's going to eat his way through your house?"

"I'm sure the dog can't be that rotten. I've told you his mother is outrageous. Her entire life is set to a military schedule. You know her social calendar is a full-time job."

"I'm sure . . . What kind of dog?"

"Don't laugh," Stephanie begged. "It's a Cockapoo," she whispered as saying *cock* was far outside her comfort zone while she hid her mouth behind her hand.

"Dear God, is Kate going to have fun with this. Well, what's your cock's name?"

"She named him Ninja!"

Tea and Stephanie are just what my cardiologist would have prescribed.

Chapter 15

After my dramatic performance at the gallery, from being caught in a spotlight to my fainting goat episode, I acknowledged that lunch with Kate and Emma was necessary. They would set me free at least for a couple of hours and gravitate me back to balance. Kate suggested we meet at the meat packing district location for One Lucky Duck, the takeaway version of Pure Food & Wine. We grabbed our preferred salads and unprocessed ice cream to spread out on a bench along the High Line, the designed one-mile linear park that now overlooked the Hudson River.

"Natalie Portman would sue you if she had a glimpse of this mess," Kate uttered and dug into her dessert first.

"I've been under a bit of stress lately. One word—"

"What's his name? Doesn't it start with a K?" Kate interrupted. "Well, not in a *Special*.

K kind of way," she mumbled.

"The word was *gallery*, guys. Not Kostas."

The chat grew annoying, but generated a mental note. Christoph wasn't fond of being called by his name. He preferred a reference more enduring like *Baby*.

Emma tapped Kate's forearm, "Oh hush, Kate. Chloe, is he your soul mate?"

I froze, realizing they both assumed we'd met.

Before taking my first bite, "Can we just enjoy the day without—"

"What? Talking?" Kate asked.

I took an enormous bite of my salad to buy silence.

"Chloe, what's his sign?" Emma asked.

"Aries, what now?" I moaned digging into the Taco section of my salad and shoveling in portions not appropriate for eating in public. The river sparkled under the sunshine and looked welcoming, unlike my yacht day.

"Allow him the time he needs to passionately go after his interests. He's a territorial creature, a standard birthright. He needs to know where his world begins and ends," Emma said while Kate switched her full attention to her spicy sesame salad. "He can irritate you with his self-centeredness, yet charm you by making you feel powerful and worthy," Emma continued.

"Spot on," I rewarded her and added my own British version of the Range Rover guide. "You don't need to worry about me." I smiled while they both looked away. "I'm overwhelmed with a life changing opportunity while under Grayson's thumb, and meeting this guy has . . . brought me out of my skin . . . But in a way has forced me to step out from behind my camera and—"

"And what, Chloe?" Emma leaned in closer.

"And experience—"

"Don't you dare say love," Kate interrupted.

"And experience life," I said.

The fact was, I wasn't ready to quit him and lose the chance of fighting for my one true love. I wouldn't know what to do if I had to spend the rest of my days with the thought of *what if* in every step and breath of my life. I was aware my personality was considered at times icy and aloof. I pulled the artist card for tolerance. My passion for art triggered me to often stop abruptly to focus on a subject of interest. Maybe I seemed easily bored or lacked appreciation with predictable scenarios and people. Maybe this is why I allowed patience to rule with him.

That was the connection with Christoph, he naturally responded to this and respected my individuality and need for freedom, yet never underestimated my wish to open up and be loved. Our understanding with each other gravitated us both towards a greater stability. Our connection had somehow pushed me from my limits of ordinary time and space to a heart opening one. Before the Swiss, I treasured my work, since it prevented me from living two days in a row the same way. Now, I wanted to be with him, and if each day were the same, I wouldn't mind.

Then again, with the growing distance between us, I felt like my power cord was being severed and my soul was slowly being pulled out of me. I couldn't believe to experience love you had to ache.

"The guy must be super hot for you to be this tolerant, Miss Kassidy." Kate yawned and stretched out, taking in the clear sky. The change of seasons in NYC was like fashion week, a spectacle and shouldn't be missed.

"He's beautiful," I assured them, but kept the fact I'd only seen him through the several jpegs we had exchanged. He was a decent photographer, I had admitted to him. He captured depth and meaning and I was mesmerized by how much he had documented his life experiences. He had several pictures of himself from leisure, work, and travel. His eyes first attracted me physically to him, but his writing, his words, and his passion for life is why I removed my rational hat. I absorbed him through the phone and he stuck.

Emma and I slid a spoonful of the cold sweet treat down our tongues.

"Interesting," Kate mumbled. "Your names are Chloe Kassidy and Christoph Kostas. CK + CK," she joked.

"Oh my, that's too cute!" Emma screamed while she sputtered ice cream.

"Actually, if you think about it, you stick with him and nothing will change. You remain the same—CK," Kate said for her closing argument. "Well, ladies I have to head to my colonic, flirting with the front desk guy relaxes me."

Through my peripheral view, Emma gawked, which prevented me from gasping. Kate not bashing the male species? To abruptly change the tone of our behavior would only have her retract back into her shell. Sarcastic and bitchy was the only way to support this woman, stabilizing her at this stage.

"Wow, you share everything," I interjected. "How could anyone flirt at an appointment when it involved *anal*?" I joked, taking my turn.

"Yep. Nothing to hide here," Kate took another jab.

I begged myself not to mention her past.

"This hot guy knows the schedule of your bowel movements? That's sexy," I said, now disgusted and no longer able to look at the natural mushy concoction resembling taco meat.

"Excuse me? You have this new guy we've never met and you want to talk about how I'm full of shit?"

"You can be exceptionally nasty, Kate," I said, turning my back to her and full attention to Emma.

"Just pointing out your gut is weak and needs some improvement," Kate said. She walked away leaving Emma and me alone with her last words. Jumping into the Hudson River was reckless, but offered the quickest escape if she returned for more.

Text from Christoph: *When could I take you for coffee?*

Text from Chloe: *I'm flying out to Miami tomorrow. It would be nice if we returned to our normal before I head out.*

Text from Christoph: *We are not normal. We can never be normal. We don't talk normal, fight normal, make up normal, write normal or live normal! And you know what? Had they all out there known what this felt like, I guarantee you everyone would kill to be abnormal.*

No matter how low this arguing moment, I knew walking away was impractical, since I didn't want to imagine tomorrow without him. I had joined his club. I wanted to get back to the two strangers who bumped into something beautiful. I didn't want to be angry. I wanted to be in love.

On my walk home, I thought about Kate getting under my skin. I pictured a man, maybe a grandfather, stout, patchy hair guy from Iowa misusing his son's identity to talk to young women. Although, I didn't think he masked an accent from Iowa. I'm not sure what that even sounds like.

While creating the image of my eighty-year old boyfriend, I received a Facebook friend request from none other than Christoph Kostas. His timing was impeccable and my fears subsided a tad. I didn't want to be his online friend when I had been coined his soul mate. This was an odd move for the Swiss philosopher. I was hesitant to accept his request and allow him even more into my world with access to my friends.

Nevertheless, with one *I confirm*, our relationship grew to a more official status. We were now Facebook friends. The tug of war was between two equally important sides. One, allowing him more into my world when I wasn't a thing in his, and two, making us more significant by being visible to the outside world. There he was, neatly organized with his name, city where he lives, 217 friendships and photos of places where he has traveled, including ones I had already saved to my desktop from our electronic conversations. Perhaps, my imagination had gotten the best of me.

It was his idea and with his guidance we created a Facebook business page and Twitter account for my *brand*, as he referred to it. *Brand* sounded formal and serious, but he reminded me, *Chloe, don't you realize how talented you are? You are a brand. Jesus, your debut is in one of Manhattan's top galleries. Your name is on a wall.* He wondered how I hadn't grasped the concept yet. *The Facebook and Twitter accounts can showcase your work, build a following, and allow your fans to see updates on your progress*, he had pointed out. *If you're brave, go public and do social media.*

I began posting, tweeting, and now allowing an entire world of invisible strangers a peek into my life. I couldn't help but wonder if his supportive idea was to permit him to keep tabs on me, but I couldn't dismiss his support for my success. I waited for him to push me to take us public, causing me even more social awkwardness. In return, we set up a Facebook page and Twitter account for the aspiring artist writing his debut novel, based on his soul mate theory.

His cell rang straight to voicemail and I begged myself not to leave a long monologue before the maddening beep prompted me.

"I'm leaving tomorrow morning for Miami and didn't hear from you about meeting up. I would like to fix us before I leave. Just choose a time to meet wherever you want. I can't e-mail anymore or do this phone thing. It's destroying everything about us."

Several minutes later he sent a text.

Text message from Christoph: *In meeting. I'm confused. Nothing I do is right and everything around me, inside of me is you. I'm bad at being mad at you but then again it looks like I'm bad at us in your eyes.*

Text message from Chloe: *Just make it simple. Choose a place and time now. Please, I'm giving you a fair chance. I leave for Miami tomorrow.*

Text message from Christoph: *You have given me nothing. I hate every corner of this city and every inch of me that belongs to you. I feel kind of miserable after your behavior.*

Rationality and control couldn't catch up with the fury running through my veins while my fingers furiously typed away, flushing the disappointment and anger out of me, resembling my soul version of colonic therapy. My typing was unstoppable. Maybe, Kate was right, my gut was weak.

Text message from Chloe: *I'll not give you one more day of my life. You chose to text rather than pick a bench.*

Text message from Christoph: *Thanks, but no thanks. You keep breaking my heart, so what's the point really?*

Text message from Christoph: *You always say expresso instead of espresso—I hadn't noticed early on but I wasn't sure if you'd be annoyed if I told you, until I felt nothing I'd do or say would make you adore me any less.*

I turned off my phone. *Chloe, you didn't fail. He doesn't exist.*

Chapter 16

I missed parts of the old Chloe. Sitting on the plane, seven rows to my left was a man whose profile fit that of Christoph Kostas. I found myself staring and adjusting my position to catch another glimpse of his features, his eyes, the twirls of hair brushing the corners of his eyelash, the sharpness of his nose. His features were haunting me. Christoph made me believe we were left up to serendipity now. *Was he coming to Miami to find me? Was I stalking an innocent passenger?*

Possibly, it wasn't about him and his soul. *Was he the one?* Imaginably it was about my soul and I should have been paying closer attention to how I felt than any sign keeping me waiting for him. I held onto this idea of *us,* as I desperately needed validation for my behavior in this. This wasn't about self-sacrifice or having to accept a bad hand I was dealt or up to fate. Love wasn't a game, and God only knows I had been playing a role on a bad reality show titled, *The Soul Mate Survivor*. Every word he gave me illustrated a scene and in the book he wrote with me playing his leading role. Christoph's writing was intense and focused on how people treated love, how far they would go for their soul mate, and what made people tick. The idea my life was merely research felt like a dirty scene, the ones where you yell at the actress, *You're better than this!*

Exiting the plane and heading towards ground transportation, I switched my phone on, unsure whether it would be a high or low flood of unanswered correspondences from him.

From: Mary Polt
To: Chloe Kassidy
Subject: Checking on you
Date: November 18, 12:56 p.m.

Dearest Chloe,

As I myself am caught in the midst of endless thoughts, I cannot help but reach out to you and ask why. I, from the very beginning of his unnecessary complicated ways around you, have been on your side and tried to pass on advice to you. I gave courage and insightfulness to your own thoughts, feelings and desires. This time around I'm puzzled, astounded, unwilling to justify your behavior towards Christoph. I'm not here to judge you in any way. I'm nevertheless surprised to see you turning your back to a man who has stood up for everything that makes him, unique as he is, as beautiful as ever.

If I can ask you only one thing and one thing only, it's for you to not blame him for my own problems and for my own decision to reach out to him and ask for his help. He did nothing wrong. In fact, he did everything right as always, and I hate to see him in pain now because you think he didn't care enough for you. If you've decided you no longer want to be in your relationship with Christoph, please let it not be because I asked for his help. That would be such a crime. Of yours as well as my own.

My best,

Mary

I stepped into the taxi line and disregarded the cramp twisting my side. I was thirsty. My level of staying power was near to the ground and I was tempted to stop, drop my shit, hurl my fists in the air and yell. Instead, I hit voicemail to retrieve his message.

"And here's my truth. I care for you. I do more than you'll ever know. More than anyone else ever will and you're asking me to let go, but the truth is, I can't let go of my beliefs, my heart, and myself. I'm sorry you no longer believe. I've the right to hope though one day you'll remember this is where you want to be . . . you're . . . wrong, Chloe. I'm the partner who'll make you happy. Even in silence I'm positive about us. You're the person who knows me the best. I don't care to make anyone else understand but you. Besides, we were brought here for a reason and we cannot escape it no matter what. Chloe, we need to talk, please."

Heading to Miami Beach, the phone rang and I hit ignore. I threw my arm up in the air and attempted to shake my phone to death. The terrified look on the cab driver's face almost forced me to switch to a fist pump motion, but the radio was off. The salty breeze smelled sweet caressing my skin with stickiness while the highway lured my thoughts into dropping my phone, spiraling it into shattered pieces matching my confidence. Instead, I called him back with it going straight to voicemail only to terminate my effort.

I licked my lips to separate them. I would check into the hotel, unwind and forget about all things Switzerland. I promised God first, then myself second.

He called and I pushed *ignore* immediately.

I punched *86 to listen to the lies.

"Why won't you answer, baby? The truth is you don't want to hear it because in your head you created this horrible scenario that gives you strength. There's no way you don't know who I am, how I am, and that I'm one of the most beautiful people you've ever encountered. We're not a tragedy, and this isn't a movie with a bad ending! We're two of the luckiest people in the world, for having found it, and having found it so early on. And we both know what 'it' stands for. Otherwise, we . . . we would have both given up weeks ago, like we did with previous relationships, like we would do with future ones!"

The gallery had taken the liberty of putting me up at the Delano Hotel in South Beach. It was divine. The smell of the salt-water pulled me into the hotel lobby reminiscent of the ocean's current I spotted from the patio where guests enjoyed lunch. I crossed the dark mahogany wood floors and walked through the Greek-like amphitheater beams, through a tunnel of sheer white drapes that hung from the high ceiling. *Heaven.* Walking towards the light landed me by a lovely sun-filled spot, picture-perfect for a bite and much needed cocktail to alleviate the bulk of this irrational stress.

This was my home for the next week, while making my rounds of meetings, seminars and dinners with the Art Basel committee. I looked forward to the one-on-one with Grayson Gates's referral,

Reed Scott. This introduction was a colossal peek into the elite art world. Any direction I acquired from him would ease my insecurity I had developed since being accepted as an emerging artist. I considered pitching my new theme idea to Reed. *Do you need to see to believe?*

After a light meal and two mojitos, I tucked myself into bed and hoped one day soon someone would be doing it with me. Here I was in Miami as an artist with a wall, meeting a major art committee, and staying in a chic hotel. Success was in fingers' reach and I was disappointed in my heart focusing on the lack of a man instead the abundance evolving in my life.

Christoph was an expert at pushing my buttons. Texting became too difficult with my white knuckles while the aggravation took control like an evil spirit. I knew better than to call, but the sin in my heart was wild like fire.

"Chloe?" he answered. "I've been staring at my phone screen again and again hoping you'll get out of your misery. Running when the phone rings, thinking it was you, only to realize it's just a family member, a friend or a phone operator running a survey."

"Christoph—"

"Maybe you'll then realize what it feels like blaming yourself again and again for not letting you know I wasn't avoiding you. Now, that I can tell you, will you grant me the right to talk?" he asked.

"Christoph, I've said before, I'm no longer scared of being vulnerable. Just like you, this is necessary to me, but I won't discuss us over the—"

"But . . .," he interrupted.

"If this was important to you, then why wouldn't you make an effort and say, 'Chloe, let's meet for coffee or a walk and talk?'. I know you're busy, but isn't this supposed to be us?" I continued.

"You've never, ever stopped to just reflect . . . To appreciate me, to acknowledge me, to defend me, not to everyone else, but to yourself. You've been the worst enemy of us. You've been the most unwilling listener, the most aggressive talker . . . and the most passive feeler," he said.

The view from my hotel room rescued me for a moment. The crystal water was now vintage black while the moon created a path of light into this abyss, seducing me. If you watched closely, you captured the silky waves slithering from the beach all the way out to the floating pearl high in the sky. Moon River was an actual river in Savannah, GA we took weekend trips to during my childhood. The exact river Audrey Hepburn sang in *Breakfast at Tiffany's* forced me to recall Kate's advice. "It must be real to be a rel–ationship."

"Are you listening, Chloe? You're probably going out and having fun! My girlfriend going out and having drinks with God knows who rather than wanting to talk. To fix us."

"Excuse me . . . Your what?" I asked.

He took a deep sigh and remained silent for a handful of seconds. "I'm a man who knows exactly what he wants, where he is in life and where he can be. I'm a person of high values and a genuine interest for humanity. I do care for you greatly, but I won't allow you to question me again and again, to doubt me continuously and to threaten me with your departures. To forget the bigger picture."

"The bigger picture, Christoph? I need clarifying at this point," I said.

"If you want to be done, the door is open for you to exit. I will not beg anyone including you to appreciate my specialness, my passion, my romanticism but most importantly my adoration for love and those things other people simply walk by without noticing. I'm enough of a mess as it is."

"I understand, but unfortunately I can't trust someone who stood me up knowing I'm out of my comfort zone. The other night was painful, Christoph. I cried continuously. I'm thirty and know exactly what I need," I admitted. I forced myself to catch a lungful breath. I couldn't afford to shed more tears. I needed to save face. The corners of my eyes were chapped. Photoshop didn't work in physical life. The lack of sleep and bawling had left me with puffy eyes and inflated cheeks.

"I'm sorry you cried. No one is worthy of your tears, sweetheart, not even me. Chloe," he sighed. "I want you to be my girlfriend. I only want to be with you."

I froze.

"Will you be with me?"

My heart was in my mouth and my head and gut were failing me miserably. *Tell me what to do!* I couldn't abandon them as what would I have left. I closed my eyes and proceeded with the first answer I heard. "Yes, Christoph." I wasn't sure where the whisper came from and if I should have listened to it. *What are you doing?*

"I don't understand how you can quickly turn. Baby, I'm home!" he reassured me. "Mary was rushed to the hospital alone and needed me. I'm sorry how this affected you."

"I'm still lying in bed feeling lonely and hurt. Who wins?" I asked, but he remained quiet. "I stopped being a head person, it was natural opening up with you. Everything about us has consumed my life and work. I'm insane," I laughed for the first time in days. Like it was a cheat day on my diet of drama, allowing a smile had the same effect of sweets. It made me giddy.

"Chloe, I promise you we will work out. Nothing that comes easy is truly worth fighting for. This is where we differ. I don't think love expires."

"I don't think love expires. I think our chance of becoming something will," I said.

"Why do you act like the clock is always about to run out for us?"

"The more time passes between us, the greater loss I feel with each passing day," I admitted.

"I'll keep trying. Not for you, but for me. To stand true to your feelings is living, but us meeting will dissolve your fears, doubts, and scenarios," he said.

Our talk that night comforted me by suppressing my aggressive doubts that lately had been chipping away at any peace of mind. I knew if we just met, it would disinfect the problem and put us back on a clean slate. Until then, I feared more words temporarily slapped a bandage on the wound. My fear of being heartbroken spread like an infection within me with the panic of rejection from him suffocating my creativity and my theme. The majority of the other artists had finalized theirs and moved to different stages of their preparation. My confidence slipped and I felt like I was losing it. I denied that Christoph Kostas was a bad guy, since a game would mean that my heart had failed me for trusting him. *What would that say for my work? What if following my heart had fucked up my focus and I failed?* This was the closest thing to crazy I've ever been. Being close to him was being crazy.

Text: from Christoph: *I just woke up and turned around to kiss you good morning. I'm losing it.*

I acknowledged love as a selfless act. It's an act that makes a suit-dressed guy buy a yoga mat. It's an act that makes a stubborn woman open up to possibilities.

As I headed out the door, he left me with one last text for the afternoon.

Text message from Christoph: *How romantic will it be if I gave you your French, Aristocratic promise ring?*

The change in scenery had been pleasant while I attempted to adopt the attitude of *Life is a Beach* rather than the alternative. One tall Swiss and one significant theme, and I couldn't get a grasp on either. I ignored his text messages and proceeded with my day.

Art Basel began in just a few weeks, running from December 6–9. After conquering my exhibit in New York, getting a bite of the Basel would be my next goal. The four day exhibit included roughly two hundred and sixty leading art galleries from around the globe and almost two thousand artists, emerging status included. The MCH Swiss Exhibition organized the spectacular event, a Switzerland based leading convention company. Looking back since my college days, it was ironic how much that country kept popping up in my path. The internship in Switzerland, being discovered at Art Basel last year by Grayson, and now the Swiss diplomat. *Signs?*

The seven-minute walk to the Miami Convention Center would allow time for me to mentally prep. This afternoon was an incredible occasion to see how this elite selection committee produced one of the most prestigious art shows in the world. The next several hours would be filled with observation.

Entering the building, I stepped into an adult fantasyland. *Breathe.* It was a version of the Magic Kingdom, except Disney characters were replaced with the world's elite art collectors and artists. Small teams of men were building exhibitions as far as my eyes could see. I walked through this evolving process for Art Basel, while observing the hundreds of galleries from every country.

"Can I help you?" An exotic fortyish year old woman approached me showing off her curves in a coral sundress that seemed she had been poured into.

"I'm Chloe. Grayson—"

"Wonderful to meet you, Miss Kassidy." Her demeanor brightened matching her wardrobe. "I'm Valencia, one of the coordinators for the convention center. Grayson's assistant phoned to say you would be stopping by today."

"Here I am."

"I'll let you do your thing," she said. "Congratulations on your exhibit acceptance with Curator Gates." Then she was gone.

I realized why Grayson Gates sent each of us here before the NYC gallery opening. It's to remind us that *Dreams do come true.*

I relaxed on a bench to pass the time until the gallery committee held a seminar on shooting RAW. The similarity in themes amused me as my hardware, my camera and heart were experiencing exposure, contrast and recovery. Basic adjustments can make up the backbone of your photography post-production. Almost every photograph can use even a little basic adjustment. Many work independently while others work best when treated together. A little goes a long way with exposure, something I had obviously forgotten with Christoph. The slider will help you recover pieces of the detail you lost, and I prayed recovery was still an option. With regards to contrast, the darker midtones become darker while the lighter midtones become lighter. My frames with Mr. Kostas were shifting even darker within me.

An unknown number popped on the screen. It was a Miami area code.

"This is Chloe," I answered. "Crap."

"Hello?" an unfamiliar voice asked.

I'm not sure what I did to upset the universe, for being shit on, literally. Lately, my days were challenged with keeping signs straight, from a man to my new friend a bird, now perched beside me on the bench while I cleaned up his mess.

"This is Reed. Reed Scott." I swear the bird froze as well.

"Oh! Hello, I'm sorry," I said.

Reed continued, "Are you all right?"

"Yes, I apologize for the disruption."

"Grayson had mentioned you were in Miami this week and I wanted to be sure I reached out to you."

"Thank you for calling," I said. "I appreciate you taking time to meet with me."

"Can you grab a drink tomorrow night?"

"Sounds great. I . . . appreciate your time." *Stop repeating yourself, Chloe!*

"No problem. Where are you staying?"

"The Delano," I said. I checked again to make sure I was poop free.

"Let's meet at The Setai hotel down the street. It's convenient and will give you a change in scenery. Will eight o'clock work?" he asked.

"Yes. Of course," I responded. Having a set time with the curator's referral was a relief. I had meant to reach out to him, but I wanted to have a grasp on a theme first.

Opening a copy of *Miami Magazine*, I immediately noticed RS Public Relations listed fourth from the top under *Sponsors & Supporters*. Grayson Gates or Reed Scott never mentioned his company was connected to Art Basel. Reed Scott was the CEO of the PR firm for one of the largest annual art events in the world.

Glancing back at my neighbor with flustered feathers, I felt my own wings of hope ruffle. His call spiked my courage enough to pull me back up on my heels and embrace this new day with another chance to get it right.

Chapter 17

It was 7:57 p.m. The results of my extensive internet research portrayed Reed Scott as smart, highly successful, pleasant to work with, and as one media source referred to as, *Offers invaluable understanding into the skill of photography*. I was eager to see the documentary his firm was producing for the New York City opening. I assumed Reed was in his late thirties, but from watching several YouTube videos, I sensed an old soul.

The content of his online interviews were made more favorable by his delivery. He had a presence about him when transporting his message with the perfect marriage of individuality and heart.

I recalled a conversation with Christoph on marriage. He had begun talking about what marriage meant to him while in Geneva, surrounded by his family. He expressed that he didn't believe in marriage before, and I hurried to put him in the *All men think this way* category. Maybe it was my maneuvering from staring at the floor, or one of those times when I chose to politely take a shortcut in a joking mode or maybe, it was just me, while staring into my closet trying to decide what to wear.

Christoph explained to me that he didn't believe in marriage the way it's *executed* nowadays; the huge guest lists, the rules, the procedure, the paper, the labels, the expected proposal, the expected dress and suit, the expected kiss at the *You may now kiss the bride*. He didn't believe in justifying the reasoning, the person, and the moment. He didn't believe in rationale when it comes to one's heart. And so, he didn't accept membership in the *All men think this way* category, for this modus vivendi e operandi, very scary and adventurous and very guarantees-free. Then, it suddenly struck me. *He was a scared man hiding behind strong words.*

The black leather motorcycle boots approaching suspended my current thought while I studied his dark jeans, black blazer and T-shirt. *I should have written my questions down.* His stout facial features contributed to his depth with his smooth dark hair, tranquilizing gray eyes, and striking 6'3" stature. He was different from the Wall Street suits that filled Manhattan and he carried a speck of All-American boy at his surface. His noticeable physical strength wasn't the reason I felt in safe hands with his presence, even though it stood in the Asian inspired lobby at The Setai hotel with us as its own crowd. His natural cologne was his sweet softness. Immediately, his caring demeanor in his face forced me to move from his eyes to his smile, and I guessed he had sisters or was incredibly close to his mother.

"Reed," I said raising my hand.

"I take it you're Chloe?" he extended his hand.

"Yes, nice to meet you." I realized it was now obvious I had looked him up before this introduction. *Dammit.*

"I have a table reserved for us outside, if that's okay?" he asked.

"Wonderful," I said and followed him. The hotel was a piece of Zen. Stepping outside to sit alfresco, I was in awe of the dimly lit serene surroundings. The layout was astonishing while the scene oozed seduction. The cushioned benches and cocktail tables were divided into four squares by a fountain the size of a small pond. It offered an abundance of tranquility for its size with palm trees strategically added for a taste of Miami. I took a seat while Reed sat across from me picking up the cocktail list. The scene was flawless as if the universe had arranged these elements by Feng Shui.

"Should we order something?" He handed me the menu. "The dumplings are a phenomenon," he grinned. "Really, we should order them."

"Maybe, two orders?" I responded taking note of my comfort level. "It's not everyday I experience a phenomenon." He laughed.

For the next two hours, Reed Scott helped me refocus throughout an assortment of steamed dumplings and cocktails. I couldn't resist the chili martini. I had to order a second one. He suggested I not allow the pressures of the exhibit to upset my view, but continue exercising the lens I trusted and put my faith in finding my way.

"It carried you here . . . You're doing something right," he said warmly.

We laughed at my idea of *Seeing is believing* and joked on how I would present my work. "It's genius!" I said taking a sipping break and placed my cocktail on the table. "What about showing three blank pieces and guests would have to create their own image of what light is through love?"

"Chloe, isn't it *Love through Light*?" We laughed again.

Reed Scott had a softer approach then Grayson Gates's method of tearing out your soul. "Do yourself a favor—ignore the bullshit. Be Chloe Kassidy," he said pointing out that my theme would come from my willingness to expose myself. "Do you trust yourself?" Reed asked.

I took a fresh breath and exhaled. "Sometimes."

Reed shrugged his shoulders. "Trust and love work together," he said. "Think about it."

"Trust was love and love was trust," I replied. It was an honest moment and I didn't worry for a second if it was good enough or impressive.

"Have you always wanted to be a photographer?"

I didn't have to think about it. Photography was the first crush that I connected with at first click. I couldn't imagine living my life without the style, colors, depth, and the reactions inspired by it all.

"Yes. Always. I think I even was one in a past life." I giggled.

"Really? You were reincarnated into the same person?"

"Oh . . . I was kid—"

He interrupted. "I know."

That grin.

"I had never thought I was a tree, a World War II nurse, or a bumblebee. I only knew and felt me as me. I have wondered if maybe I was a pilot in a former life," I said. I took another sip of my cocktail. "I'm actually serious this time." I smiled.

I found peace in airports. I was inspired in them. I saw the grace in the rhythm of it all. I did my best thinking and feeling at those platforms of coming and going. It was difficult to put into syllables this theory about *leaving something behind* or *coming towards it all*. I felt a bit deeper, clearer and ahead of myself more while surrounded by the chaos.

"So, I wondered if I were to believe in reincarnation, if I was a pilot. Yes, maybe in a past life."

"Tell me more," Reed said.

"About being a pilot?" I laughed.

"Come on." He placed his drink down and leaned back in his chair.

"Well, I'm neurotic about schedules, planning, and hypersensitive to time. Delays and tardiness made me a nervous mess. I loved the flow, even when it feels like I'm going around in circles rather than in a straight line from A to B and back to A."

"Does your theme feel like a straight line between theme and no theme?"

"Yes." I took another sip. I knew I could do this. I followed direction. I led. I searched for routes to carry me to my destination. I didn't shy away at the mere site of a crossroad or storm. From take off to landing, I found meaning in my life's routes. Whether I was grounded or up in the air, nothing was too outrageous for me to overcome. No matter how high or low I was, I would never see an obstacle taller than myself. The view matched. Any obstacle wasn't a problem, but a challenge, a challenge required digging deep down into our central control tower, our hearts, to find those solutions.

"Chloe, no matter how many storms you've encountered, you stayed focused, on course, and will find another route by any means. Sometimes flights are delayed and canceled because elements are not in place to support the success of the trip," he said. "Those elements are crucial for everything to happen. When elements are missing, no matter how determined a pilot can be, take off is grounded and the journey is unsuccessful. Whether it was a dream, a passion, a theme . . . flights are canceled for a reason."

"I know I'll create something this exhibit deserves. I'm meant to be a part of this opening," I admitted. The chili concoction was increasing my confidence.

"There you go, Chloe." He gently clapped. "Something to think about is the triangle of exposure? Have you heard of it?"

Intimacy, passion, and commitment was the same theory Kate explained from her self-help reading stint. "Yes, my friend Kate told me about it."

"What does Kate say?"

"It's a long story." I took another sip while making sure none of the chili speckles remained on my lips. "Another time," I blushed with my assumption there would be one.

He grinned. "You know the 'amount' of love one experiences depends on the absolute strength of those three components. The 'type' of love one experiences depends on their strengths relative to each other," he said. "Different stages and types of love can be explained as different combinations of intimacy, passion, and commitment."

"Love is madness," I rolled my eyes.

"Well, Miss Kassidy, there's always a little madness in life but then again there's always a lot of life in madness." There was that grin of his again. Reed Scott was a man of many things, but I couldn't find that one word that would describe him wholeheartedly.

I took Reed up on his offer to walk me the three blocks back to my hotel. He left me at the entrance and we promised to be in touch. His suggestions and this trip were suitable for a brilliant theme deserving a wall. I was relieved the cocktails didn't cause me to cut on the curator.

During the night, I jerked awake. I double-checked to make sure I was, in fact, still in my bed and hadn't landed on the floor. My speedy heartbeat pounded to the blink of my Blackberry. These days my heartbeat and that little light were both flashing red rapidly.

From: Christoph Kostas
To: Chloe Kassidy
Subject: Had a lot of wine for the both of us
Date: November 20, 1:07 a.m.

I'm hopelessly falling for you, Kassidy. Are you ready for a new relationship in your life? I mean honestly ready?

Things like this you are never ready for and from what I've been told, it's always when you least expect it. This isn't me. Being open and making myself vulnerable, I don't do this. I've never laid eyes on this woman at the other end . . . on the other side. What do I have to lose? Although, I cannot handle you freaking out on me one more time.
Christoph

I felt ashamed Christoph had easily opened me up. My rational hat was the only thing pressuring me at times to take it slow and wait for coffee, but I ran after my heart and prayed I would catch up and snatch control of it soon.

Then of course there were my friends. I could hear them now. Could they believe I would be falling for someone, a man who inspired me to open up and allowed me to let go of *what ifs* by embracing moments I just drew breath from, but suffocated my creativity.

Bravo reruns had become my lover, softly singing me to sleep. It seemed waking up to a pillow wall was my bedtime routine even when in a hotel. I lived in a dream with Christoph even though I was fully aware real months, days, hours, minutes and moments were spent waiting.

The phone rang around 2:30 a.m., once again interrupting my attempt of a deep sleep. Moments like these made me indebted to the talent gods that my work occurred behind the lens.

I had barely whispered, "Hello," and his trembling voice responded.

"I'm screwed, Kassidy, because there's something of you in everything in me." We laid there in silence listening to each other breathe. That was enough for him, but I struggled with stillness. I no longer felt the satisfaction we just wanted to be there with each other as close as possible without our eyes on each other, the exchange of our scent, the touch of our lips. While blank minutes passed, I pleaded to know why this happened. I couldn't believe this man, the man who would lay there for hours each night wasn't dying to hold me, kiss me, not live a second without me knowing the vulnerability on my end. Yet, his dark and twisted scent of irrationality put a spell on me.

There was a hold on me, really tight at times I couldn't handle its influence and it fluctuated from an extreme need for him to a pain of suffocation leisurely killing me. I knew that was him as well.

I broke our silence. "Listen. I'm scared I've told you too many things about myself, my life!" I wanted to steal back the details, descriptions and memories of my friends I had given him without their permission.

"It's your right to regret telling me specifics about your life, but it's also my right to acknowledge things when I see them and the truth is whether you like it or not, the universe wants us to be together, crashing our heads eternally."

I hated to accept it, but I pictured our image.

"You know how other people picture themselves growing old together, holding hands, and taking Central Park strolls?"

"Yes," he answered with hesitation.

"Our image would be a little different—"

"We'd be in bed trying to fall asleep and you'd have one of your photography-inspired long monologues 'and this happened today' and 'didn't happen' and 'I can't believe Grayson Gates did this' and 'I can't believe Kate said that' and I would be turning on the other side to turn out the light while whispering 'will you just shut up so we can finally go to sleep, woman!'"

"But—"

"Sweetheart, you found me and I found you and that should make your heart melt," he said.

"Yes, but—"

"Okay, yes, I've handled us wrong, I know it, and I admitted it and I apologized for it. When are you going to stop punishing me for it? You ought to realize, Chloe, that I'm not a bad person," he pleaded.

A few days ago I'd admitted to myself I was screwed. Even when he hurt me with his roughness I couldn't wait to crawl into bed, close my eyes for a few seconds before falling asleep to think of him.

While I wanted my old self to step in and burst out *Let's please let go of each other*, I couldn't risk that he would respond *Okay*. He had promised me if another pointless month passed without us meeting then he would walk away. We had a deal. I was too terrified to exploit it as a threat although I swore he wanted me more than I wanted him. It was like, for once, the double sided coin that kept landing with tails would call heads when I least expected it.

"I want to do something special for you. How about I throw a party to welcome you home from Miami? We can invite our friends and officially introduce each other into our lives," he suggested enthusiastically. "My apartment can accommodate everyone."

"That's sweet of you. It's just . . . I want to meet you first and not at a party. We've happened backwards and I want to reverse our actions and move forward." I hoped my rejection wasn't a set back.

"I understand. You see I'm uniquely adorable and romantic. You need to keep in mind before thinking you know it all, Miss Aristotelian."

"Seeing you will tell me much more than words could ever prove. Almost like I need to see what I believe, if there is any reasoning to my own rhymes," I said, chewing the right inner side of my thumb. Christoph and I were two characters fulfilling roles, separate from our realties.

"I'll e-mail you points that should make you comfortable for now," he offered. The peacemaker was unable to comprehend the required action, not a surplus of words. He needed to show himself not send an e-mail about him.

The warmth and softness of the duvet bedding this time seduced me to sleep.

My sophisticated pen pal was a teenager every now and again. The next morning, I found myself reading a list of his dietary habits. This was a substitute for his typical expressive self.

Why can't he just speak to me directly and not through a dialogue of emails? Perhaps, fairy tales have no clear definition, no boundaries, no explainable reasons for the *hows* and *whys.* The struggle between my heart and rational hat left me with a knot in my throat. This love game resembled an obstacle course full of challenging mental and physical hurdles. As I navigated my way through by climbing, crawling and jumping, I reassured myself that it was necessary for two souls to find each other. I reached my limit. Instead of team Kassidy and Kostas, I competed alone and knew his words wouldn't hoist me up the rope and over the wall. I couldn't do it alone. The pain in my chest weakened my upper body strength. I needed him to grip my feet and steady me. Our first date failures were distracting, but it was time to refocus and regain my confidence back somehow. I clenched the thick, twisted line and prayed to pull myself up without rope burn while getting closer to answers.

My time in the magic city was limited to hours allowing me a lunch along the shoreline and silence to process Reed Scott's tips. I wandered the sun-bathed beaches, assessing the light, reflection and shades.

A hotel cabana boy set me up under a navy umbrella, lounge chair, and with a menu on the fluffy white sand at the shore's edge. Ordering the seafood ceviche and lemonade, I removed my black tunic sheer cover up, exposing my black string bikini. Lying on the lounge chair, while my legs dangled, the ocean raised softly kissing the tips of my toes. There I faced, the Earth's mouth, which at any time might swallow me whole or a creature swimming in it. I couldn't remember the last time I had walked into an ocean past my knees. I had to have been really young, that fearless age, before doubt and what-ifs had weighed in on judgment. The unknown terrified me.

Don't think. Just do it. Stop thinking. Go, Chloe.

Fighting tears, I took a bottomless breath and marched forward into what appeared like a gigantic aquamarine diamond. The unfriendly temperature caused goose bumps as the surface quickly reached my shins, knees, lower thighs, and now chest. With each new section of myself submerged, the familiar sound effects of *Jaws* hummed in my head. I stopped while the water tickled the cap of my shoulders and stared out into the abyss.

Just Breathe. You're fine. Nothing will eat you!

I put up a solid fight for exactly twenty-three seconds before I let the shark attack scene play into my head. *Is that a fin?* I flipped around to check the distance to my chair. *Swim!* I swore I sensed a mass move underneath me brushing the tip of my big toe. *Where was the Coast Guard when I needed them?*

Alternating clumsy methods of running, swimming, and swallowing salt water, I succeeded to safety with the beaches' full attention, creating an absolute spectacle of myself. There watching me was the panicked server who had situated the tray of food on my chair. I plopped down and sucked the sugary sweet substance to rid the salt from my mouth. *I did it!*

I sat in airport staring onto the runway while the planes zigged and zagged as I waited for my gratis first class seat to be called. I was on a whirlwind. I was part of an upcoming new artist exhibition, working with the infamous Grayson Gates, creating a name for myself by hanging my heart on the wall, and I had to make money from sales that evening. The opportunity for people to purchase my work, to think it was worthy for a price tag, and a hefty one at that, reassured me my passion was no longer a hobby. Miami allowed me to peek behind the stage curtain to observe how these components were supporting my dreams more than ever before. It proved the most vital piece was heart, and it was up to me to put it in whole. This desire from me was at a cellular level. If only my doubts would remain in airplane mode until the opening to maintain absolute concentration.

Maybe I was a pilot since the aim in my life was direction. I appreciated and acknowledged the journey and realized I had much more to learn and offer the world. Maybe I was a pilot since I liked to shoot for the sky, chase after stars, always landing safely on my two feet. The problem was my fear of crash and burn.

Any storm I faced, I realized, from ground level or from high above, was the same size. I realized while looking through my small window seat that my problems were essentially tiny. When I landed, they were the exact same size. It was just how I viewed them. Unlike my photography, I couldn't control life. I still wanted to find my true co-pilot.

Landing in New York at night is one of the most romantic experiences, coming out of the darkness and slowly descending on top of the twinkling lights there to welcome both residents and tourists. It didn't matter who you were or where you were from, the view was captivating every time. With the plane gracefully arriving on the runway, the Empire State Building officially welcomed us to the Big Apple. In honor of Thanksgiving, the multi-colored landmark, reflected orange and yellow tones.

Greeted by the mountain of *New York Post*s on my *Welcome* mat, I collected them to stack in the tiny spot that my real estate broker convinced me was a foyer. The word was out and on the front page. The exclusive opening from none other than Grayson Gates and, of course, drama between him and his exotic model friend, Penelope with no last name, covered the headline. She resembled a Miss Hawaii contestant. The press never printed her last name, similar to Madonna or Rihanna with only a one-name introduction. Twitter, Facebook, Gawker, artist online communities and message boards were blowing up on the opening. The *New York Post* Page Six presented teasers. *Who would be privileged enough to receive a personal invite from Mr. Gates to the private opening?* Those chosen ones would be allowed to pass the door guards fully equipped with their bicep guns, and have first pick of the art for sale. That was the beautiful thing about being a semi-struggling artist in NYC. Slap the word *private*, *exclusive*, *VIP*, and we were pretty much handed the magic money marker to price our work. The higher the more extraordinary.

Part Two

Chapter 18

Reed Scott was genuine. I was capable of digging deeper than *Do you need to see to love*? I looked forward to my one-on-one appointment at the Apple Store downtown to resolve issues with my RAW image files.

An impatient man offered entertainment to the small crowd waiting for the store to open. It was nearly 9:00 a.m., and the one-man-show amused us while we patiently waited. When he pressed his nose against the sizeable glass entrance door, it opened immediately, giving him the satisfaction it was his efforts. He chose to be upset, which was senseless since I spotted the oversized guard in his black suit and tie attire guarding the electronic jewels behind him. He was easily dressed to attend the funeral of the man he might kill at any second. The aggravated man's overreaction prompted me to let go of this discontent while I hurried past his scene.

I entered technology heaven. A place to have your life created, downloaded, saved and organized with step-by-step instructions. I contemplated asking my tutor for his thoughts on communication with my mystery man since the process was foreign to me. Maybe he could shed light on following signs or coincidences or if it was tragically too late to play hard to get. I was open to hear any survival strategies on how to move forward.

I took a seat by the window, watching the cabs shooting downtown as I waited my turn. The sessions were informative as I listened to a huddled group in the corner and the discussion on the triangle of exposure. Perfect exposure has three ingredients: aperture, shutter speed and ISO. Photography required the unlikable subject of geometry in order to grasp it. Perfect exposure can be thought of as a perfect triangle. All angles are equal and all sides are equal. If you change one side it's no longer perfect. You must change another point and maybe another, trying to make it perfect again. Just like me, I kept changing to make this be my ideal fairy tale. The elements were Chloe, Christoph and coffee. I had to anticipate the exposure and how one affects the other. I needed the *hows* and *whys* from Christoph to understand how to achieve my goal. To meet him.

Text from Emma: *Kate and I are meeting at Pinkberry in 40 minutes. Free?*

Text from Chloe: *I'm in the neighborhood. See you there. xo.*

I was relieved to see Kate and Emma spending time together. I still believed in my words. With love, it's not too late. It's love and sometimes we search for it and sometimes it just finds you through a friend at a book club. Or maybe you bump into it at the salad bar.

"You two little piggies couldn't wait for me, I see," I said spotting them inside at a table. In return, their only possible reply was swollen cheeks filled with the frozen treat.

"Welcome to Pinkberry," the popular looking teen greeted me from behind the counter. I assumed this was a trendy spot for kids to work in Manhattan as he looked like an Abercrombie & Fitch model with a high-ranking position on his high school football team. "What flavor would you like?"

"Original."

"Toppings?" he asked.

"I'll do a dash of all the chocolate ones."

"I don't understand?" He squinted and then turned to his coworker for direction. "All of them?"

"What's to understand?" I laughed. "It's chocolate," I pointed. This was a *Men are from Mars* scenario. His muscular build was more suitable serving protein shakes. He clearly lacked true passion for Pinkberry.

When he took my money, I noticed the inside of my right thumb had healed. I sat in the lime green acrylic chair against the window, the sunlight shined through warming me.

"Did you just get toppings?" Emma asked. Her eyes began digging through my assorted candies just seconds before her spoon took a dig. *Clearly we had no boundaries.*

"It's bits of simple sugar. Absolute poison," Kate added. She looked unsatisfied with her naked green tea flavored treat.

The raw guru ate Pinkberry, but I wouldn't tease since when her taste buds did get a break it was an orgasmic experience.

"Yum . . .," Kate moaned.

Her seductive sounds conjured up an instance from months earlier. I blushed.

"Chloe, you're going to choke," Emma warned. "Slow down," she demonstrated a chewing motion like she often did with Lily.

"Sorry . . .," I said. I stuck another spoonful in my mouth. We had been eating sushi when Kate sipped on miso soup and ate single slices of ginger as an entrée. Her dinner that night had a happy ending. That was my first time witnessing someone moan over miso, and the flashback of her flavorgasm made me nervous in public.

"You're awfully bubbly today, Miss Kassidy," Kate said. She focused on my eyes forcing me to stare at the floor.

"I agree," Emma added. "You're rather peaceful, more than usual, to be under extreme pressure."

"Besides devouring these M&M's and making my deadline, I'm just happy to spend time with you guys." I skipped the part about the other chocolate treat. *The Swiss.*

"How was Miami?" Emma asked. "I haven't been there since Lily was born. Where did you stay? Did you meet any hot men?" She moved towards the edge of her seat with each question.

"Did you ever meet that guy?" Kate asked while she savored the last spoonful. *Please don't moan.*

"Tell us about him," Emma said, scraping the sides of the cup and spoon signaling mine closer for a bite.

"It was an incredible meeting. He made me feel . . . capable," I smiled. "I unquestionably owe Grayson Gates for that setup."

Emma gasped, putting her hand on her mouth to prevent spitting on me again. "See there are signs everywhere," she shrieked. "You would never have met this guy if it wasn't for Miami last year, bumping into Grayson, and your acceptance into the exhibit." She was now on her soul mate high horse.

"Wait a second," Kate said. "I thought Emma dragged you to book club and this girl . . . how does the curator know the diplomat?"

"Wait. What?" Emma giggled. "I'm lost."

"I'm talking about Grayson Gates associate, Reed Scott, who helped me get my theme out of the gutter," I said intervening their soap opera while the other Pinkberry patrons witnessed our candy high.

"I meant the diplomat," Kate said while Emma simultaneously confirmed, "Oh my—I'm still right on Reed Scott."

"The diplomat and I met through his friend from book club. He's from Geneva, speaks French, is working on his first book, and super passionate about peace while saving the world," I said ignoring Emma. "He's extraordinarily handsome, too sexy, with blue eyes and . . . he's twenty-eight." I waited for their round of applause. *Bravo, Chloe, you met your match.*

"God, I love those Swiss Lindt chocolates!" Emma shouted. "Those would be delicious with Pinkberry."

"Robbing the cradle, I see," Kate joked. "Although, I'm not sure a twenty-eight year old can handle you."

"His dedication to help others inspires me to concentrate on my work at a deeper level. He's adding this . . .," not being able to find the best word, "to my life in a way," I said. I wanted a positive word to reveal my thought, but the word *chaos* reached my tongue first.

"Does he have diplomatic immunity?" Kate asked.

"I think—" Emma took another bite. I wondered how many of those little candies she consumed. She was cracked out on cocoa. "If you guys get married, you won't have to pay taxes on anything, Chloe! Think of all those savings for your J.Crew shopping!" Emma almost snapping her plastic chair when leaning back.

"Girls, this conversation is absurd," I pointed out.

"What's in the right upper corner of your apartment?" Emma continued.

"You both have lost your mind . . . My office is set up there."

"Well . . . lovely," Kate interrupted. "When he kidnaps you and sells you to a human trafficking organization, he'll have legal immunity and one of us is going to have to call Alice."

"Oh dear," I said. My friends were aware of my mother's always the victim routine.

"All right, let's be nice ladies," Emma said.

"You're right," Kate said. She pointed at me and shook her finger. "It's Chloe's fault. How could you do that to your mother?"

"You must go home a.s.a.p. and put a plant or something alive," Emma demanded. "According to Feng Shui, it's your love corner. You cannot stay married to your work, can you?"

"How have you both been?" Attempting to redirect our chat away from Christoph.

"Well . . . the salad bar guy," she slumped and sighed. "He was a disaster."

"Which one was he?" Kate asked. It was hard keeping up with Emma's passion patrol.

"Kenny Rogers before surgery," I confirmed.

"There are no men in this city for me," Emma said. "Just bad luck," she winced, sitting up in her chair while she rested her elbows on the table and clasped her hands. "I hope you'll support me in my decision."

Kate and I nodded our heads simultaneously and adjusted our posture to match Emma's in order to brace ourselves.

"What is it, Sweetie?" I returned to chewing the healed spot on my thumb.

"Chloe, stop!" Kate demanded. "Flesh and yogurt?" She secured my hand away from my mouth.

"Lily and I are moving back to Georgia," she uttered quickly. Taking advantage of the silence, she revealed more of the whopping verdict. "My landlord found another renter, we're moving at Christmas."

"That's like a month," I said. Emma was always spontaneous, but this timing was absolutely wild.

"I know, but why prolong it? It's what I need to do . . . The sooner the better," Emma said.

"Chloe, aren't you going to your parents then?" Kate asked.

"Yes. I'll help you in anyway I can," I said. Only seconds passed until it hit me. "I have an idea!"

"Damn, Chloe!" Kate screamed. "You scared me!"

"Sorry!"

"Well . . . what is it?" Kate pushed.

"What about a move date of December twenty-third?" I asked. I attempted to analyze their reactions. "I'm going to cash in my flight my dad sent me and we can make it a road trip—what do you think?"

"That sounds fun, but I'm moving. Our furniture won't fit into the trunk of a car," Emma smiled at my efforts.

"I'll exchange the funds from my flight and rent us a U-Haul!" I suggested while picturing us on the road. My Miami whirlwind caused me to be a bit impulsive, but it was a potential option.

"Let's do it!" Emma agreed and we hugged on it while Kate remained dumbstruck, not with Emma's ultimate choice, but with me steering a box truck over multiple state lines.

I woke up on the optimistic side of the bed this morning and feeling *It's going to be the best day of the rest of my life* attitude with the gallery, Christoph, and love itself. We were meeting tonight at Cafe Orlin around the corner from my apartment. I needed my coffee fix and it had nothing to do with caffeine.

I scrambled for my phone lost in the pyramid of pillows to call him. Stopping the search, I noted my reading chair by the window. The pillows would have to go there once the right side of the bed was taken. It was the only available space in my studio for storage.

I dialed his number.

"Hi. How's my better half?" he asked.

"Good Morning!"

"I can hear a smile," he said in a manner where I detected no need for reassurance. "I'm about to walk into my meeting. I need to play my usual role, the UN-er."

"I wanted to confirm tonight." I prayed for no excuses.

"I adore you, Chloe. See you tonight at eight."

At 7:30 p.m., Grayson Gates called while I added the final swipe of mascara. Answering would waste the minutes I had for changing outfits a third time. It was almost two months until the exhibit and I anticipated complete madness to occur when several artists were involved in one project. Creative people were irrational.

"This is Chloe," I said while the endless possibilities of what he wanted tickled my brain.

"It's Grayson Gates. I need you to be at the gallery in thirty minutes. It's an emergency meeting. Got it?"

"Yes, Mr. Gates. I'll—"

He immediately hung up.

Text from Chloe: *Sorry! Gates is claiming 911. I need to head into the gallery for a quick meeting. Will be a little late. Say 8:30 p.m.?*

Text from Christoph: *I'm having to escort an official to drop off documents at the embassy. I'll stick with a bunch of bureaucrats until then.*

The gallery was unusually quiet while artists were taking seats on the floor in the main room's center. The panicked and exhausted look of Grayson's three assistances pacing, texting, and praying had everyone on edge. We sat, waiting and watching their every move attempting to decipher their whispers and body language.

The Tic Tac shuffle fiercely approached from behind announcing the curator's arrival. The air became stale forcing me to hold my breath.

"My phony friends, or I should say sabotagers, created bad press," he informed us.

This wasn't anything new since Grayson Gates graced the newspapers on a regular basis.

"The emergency is . . . I've lost investors. It's outrageous and affects all of you sitting here. I'm counting on this exhibit to re-establish my reputation as the best goddamn curator in this city and to fund my new gallery in Paris. If I can't get these startled simpletons back on board . . . your dreams are dead. Got it?"

The meeting continued with Grayson turning his frustrations onto his assistances, frantically texting, and yelling into one of his many phones. I waited for a game of duck duck goose to break out any moment and for him to punch one of us in the head, "You're out!"

It was 9:23 p.m. I was late and I couldn't dream up a polite way to step out and call Christoph. The risk of sending a text to let him know was unthinkable. I imagined Grayson Gates stoning me to death with his breath freshening mints if I was caught. At this point, we were prisoners of his war.

Text from Chloe: *Heading there now! Sorry!*

I was in a cab heading to the restaurant. There was a missed call from Christoph, but I received only silence from him now.

Text from Chloe: *Are you there?*
Text from Chloe: *I'm sorry I'm late! Couldn't text you.*

I was numb. I sat alone with a glass of red wine. I was exposed as the brick wall I leaned against and thankful the restaurant was dark and mainly lit by flickering candles hoping my tears weren't more noticeable. I studied couples holding each other across the table, arm in arm, embraced in each other's words, feeding each other from their plates. Of course *Love is a Losing Game* by Amy Winehouse began playing. Purely a coincidence, as it would make for a preposterous sign.

My waiter snapped me back to the current moment leading me further into letdown.

"Are you ready to order?"

"Yes." I was tempted to ask if the kitchen might create a tall, dark and handsome diplomat with Swiss. "Just the check." Forcing a smile I detected his tough luck expression. I picked up my full glass, toasted to the votive candleholder, "To *Love Through Light*," and decanted the wine into me before my tears poured.

Chapter 19

Watching the sunrise from my bed the next morning, I was uneasy
to make the call. I slept squeezing my cell as the warm companion
it had become lately. Today was Thanksgiving and I would soon be
heading out to the Hampton's for Stephanie and Alexander's holiday
feast. We had to resolve this and move on. Christoph had to let me
explain it was Grayson Gate's fault not mine.

"Good Morning," he answered with the least greeting tone.

"What happened to you last night?" I asked. "You wouldn't let
me explain and just left me confused about your intentions."

"It sucks how you're back to 'I don't know about us,' Chloe. It
hurts and I don't deserve this."

"I'm—"

"I'm tired of you taking one step forward and five backwards,"
he interrupted. "Did you stand me up last night to get even with me?"

"What? No! I'm sorry about last night. Grayson Gates called
an emergency meeting . . . I couldn't sneak out to call you," I said.

"I rushed to the restaurant and sat there alone having a drink by myself . . . Why didn't you respond?"

"Yes, let's drink to the jerk," he mumbled. "You stood me up in a restaurant and you didn't let me know what was going on."

"Seriously, Christoph?" I asked. "You want to talk about being stood up?"

"Am I that scary? I don't deserve someone who doesn't know what she wants. I don't deserve someone who doesn't willingly fight for me, with me."

"This wasn't about that," I yelled. "I was stuck in a meeting," I repeated pushing my palm into my forehead hoping to relieve the migraine.

"I'm an asshole for many reasons," he said.

"You won't hear me disagree."

"But you're wrong on this one—I don't expect the world to revolve around my life. I was raised in a family that taught me to have my life revolve around the world, for the world. And that's what I did wrong. It took this to make me realize 'the world' could be just . . . one person."

"Why wouldn't you at least respond to my calls or texts?"

"I'm going to say this one last time," he said. "I don't play games. If by now you don't know I'm a person of substance and high morals . . . you probably never will."

"Listen—"

"I will not settle for this behavior. I want us to matter enough for you to be willing to give a shot at the things you haven't done before."

"I deserve—"

"Chloe, I don't deserve someone who, just because things are happening a bit backwards between us, forgets to notice she has never had this. I don't deserve someone who doesn't notice in the grand scheme of things, finding your person means that from that point onwards, everything changes—including who you've been and how you've been up until then."

"It's Thanksgiving and I don't want to spend this day arguing with you or with a headache," I said.

"I simply adore you, but I also happen to be an imperfect human being who happens to make mistakes! I accept I've done the same to you."

"Yes, Christoph, but—"

"Let's just move past this," he suggested.

"Fine. I'll call you when I'm back in the city," I said.

Thanksgiving morning melted the snow to slush. This walking city's shape became messy and fast. The turkey feast was in East Hampton, where the weather wouldn't be a bother since the sun gave us more than a fair share of being full with gratitude. This was key for The Cudneys' unique dining experience on a traditional day and in November. Stephanie and Alexander loathed the harsh winters in New York City and the infamous five foot igloo shaped mounds each morning as a result of the snow trucks creating clear paths for life to resume. The Hamptons was a year-round escape for them, with their essential industrial sized (not sold for individual use) heat lamps that adorned the outdoor patio of their second home.

It was funny, and fitting for The Cudneys, and the reason Kate would most likely be bitchy today. Her mentality that *Everything works out for the happy couple,* would present its sarcastic side sometime between the slicing of the bird and passing of the gallon of gravy. Dining outside in the winter, stuffed as the glazed mountain of meat centered before us and bundled up in our winter wear, sipping drinks under a heated ceiling was outrageous, and Stephanie made it gracefully work, not unlike one of her ballet recitals.

The ninety-minute drive would be effortless with Brad the Dad. The risk of me not coming out, especially with the weight of the exhibit boulder balancing on my brain, Alexander and Stephanie would send their driver to pick me up and deliver me equal to a fragile package. Brad was more than a driver. He was a trusted part of their family, a second father to both Stephanie and Alexander.

They weren't only appreciated for their unique holiday hosted events, but also for giving us a sense of home when we couldn't make it back to our families for the holidays.

As usual, we pulled up to the *Town & Country* full page spread. The house and lawn were still groomed to perfection under a layer of snow and accompanied by the scent of freshly baked goods with faint sounds of a cocktail shaker like machine gun. Their home was always dressed to the nines, with arranged fresh flowers on every table, flickering vanilla votive candles, decorated food spreads, and filled crystal pitchers of water with slices of thick cucumber and lemons. It was magical and Stephanie somehow pulled it off without us witnessing her efforts. I once saw a cockroach on the patio with leopard print wings and even it had manners. I wouldn't be surprised if the Bravo crew showed up to shoot, *Household with Heart starring The Cudneys*, proving money and class were able to coexist.

As I entered, the house was vacant and beautified entirely in a frosty white decor. It was whimsical as I walked around in search of human life. Passing the charcuterie spread of meats, terrines, pâté and cheese, I detected muffled chatter from outside. Before sliding the glass door open, I took in my circle of friends sitting toasty, poolside, and each sipping their preferred holiday cocktail. It was going to be another remarkable afternoon with Emma & baby Lily, Stephanie & Alexander, and Kate, but I had to admit, the lack of Christoph communication aggravated me.

"Everyone seems to be in their place," I announced almost causing a disaster by walking through the screen door.

"Look who arrived safe and sound," Alexander raised his glass toasting my arrival as a celebration itself. He made the effort for each of us to feel special.

"Yes, of course Alexander Cudney," I teased with the formality of a full name basis. "Thank you for sending Mr. Brad. I'm here in one piece," I smiled. He appreciated recognition for his overboard thoughtfulness, especially since the estrogen outnumbered him.

"Chloe!" Stephanie hopped up for a hug. "Let me get you something to nibble on. You must be starving. What would you like to drink? Red, White, Champagne or—"

Indulgence. At the moment's end, I would return to my blank wall, rapidly eating something that required no utensils and minimal chewing. Stephanie and Alexander were fashioned entertainers. "Red would be great."

"I need a refill, please," Emma whispered. She extended her arm to the sky with the empty wine glass dangling for my taking. "Well, since I'm up," I joked.

"Shh . . .," she gestured with her lips while her arms wrapped Lily sleeping serenely across her chest.

It was an impressive afternoon, sitting poolside in winter, as the breeze orchestrated the naked branches into a musical of bare bones. "Emma, hold this pose and let me grab my camera."

Just as I reached the door to go back inside, Stephanie and Alexander screamed, "Emma!"

Flipping around I watched the oversized umbrella pushed over by a sudden burst of wind, but stopped by the stainless steel lamp's beam to prevent them from being crushed.

Each grabbing a piece of the umbrella to lift it up, we were relieved to see Lily remain asleep while her pursed mouth mommy sat drenched in wine.

"The Barolo is everywhere!" Alexander shouted. He always brought out something from his family's collection for special occasions.

We turned our attention towards him in disbelief of his frantic tone on the bottle rather than the baby.

"Stephanie, you two having kids soon?" Kate asked, triggering the rest of us to want to crawl under the umbrella.

"Honey, please—" Stephanie hissed. "No need to cry over spilled—"

"Wine," Kate and I teased.

The memorable moment had passed. I grabbed a slice of cheese and removed my boots to soak my feet into the heated pool. "The wine is quite sophisticated, Alexander. Thank you guys for having us out here," I said.

"Chloe, I hope you stay the night," Stephanie said.

"What? You might leave?" Kate interrupted.

"We're going to have a superb dinner, a midnight swim and light up the ball of fire," Stephanie said attempting to sell me on sleeping over. "Brad the Dad can take you home first thing in the morning."

The ball of fire was an outdoor encaged metal fire pit on the patio.

"What about the S'mores kit?" Alexander asked. "Come on! It's the holidays."

"None of us are on diets this week, Mr. Cudney," I laughed. "S'mores it is."

"The surfer who digs S'mores . . . give me a break," Kate poked.

"With dark chocolate though, right?" Stephanie asked.

"Dinner and S'mores, please tell me the garbage pail breakfast is on the menu tomorrow morning?" Emma asked.

"Do you have anything uncooked or with fruit or vegetables?" Kate interrupted.

Let the bitching begin.

The breakfast title sounded intimidating and for a fair reason. The recipe was a secret, but we all agreed it wasn't for the faint heart. The brie alone could kill you. The garbage pail required a team approach of scrambling eggs, chopping potatoes, sausage, peppers, onions and stirring in the cream. Each layered lined with slices of cheese in a pan and baked.

"It's barbaric," Kate said.

"Well, you say that now Kate, but you most likely will need it tomorrow morning," Alexander interrupted.

"What do you mean?" I asked.

"Didn't you know she does magic tricks? She's an extremely talented magician," Alexander said.

"Really? Lily loves magic tricks," Emma naively responded.

"Emma, Lily is two," Kate said. "Please go on. Will you need your tiny magic wand?" She glanced at Alexander's crouch.

"Kate!" Emma shouted. She directed her attention to the baby. "No hot dogs references around Lily."

"Me want doggie! Mommy, me want doggie!" Lily screamed sending Alexander into a blush.

He placed his freshly shaken, but not stirred, martini in front of Kate. "Watch closely, everyone," as he waved his invisible wand over her head. "Pay attention—it will disappear before you know it—Poof!"

She did fancy her cocktails.

That was the thing about Alexander. As reserved and conservative the county club going guy was, he humored us with his jokes and his random facts, such as *Did you know Hawaii every year moves six inches towards the U.S.?* or *A human being in their lifetime will swallow thirty spiders while sleeping.* We never admitted to him, but we knew he stole his material from the neighborhood movie theater bathroom walls. He plagiarized his jokes. No one was perfect.

"Don't worry. We picked up raw falafel and quinoa with tofu from the store on our way in from the city," Stephanie reassured her grouchy guest.

Alexander interrupted, "Wait, I almost forgot. Who wants to go splitsville on some Reuben action while we cook?" *Action* was his second favorite word besides *Stephanie*. It was always something action i.e. gym action, dinner action, and action action.

"Speaking of martinis . . . is it too early for a second?" Kate asked. Simultaneously we glanced at the once full cocktail placed before her and it had disappeared within minutes.

"Poof!" he announced once again while we gave him a round of applause amusing Lily.

"More. Mommy, more!" Lily screamed.

I swiftly pulled out my phone to see if Christoph had contacted me while checking the time for her. "It's one thirty-four," I responded.

"Hmm . . .," Kate contemplated, but waited for one of us to make it for her.

Rather than leaving her hanging, I interrupted, "Hey, it's happy hour in Switzerland." My answer landed me peculiar looks and not the laugh I expected. "It's the holidays!" I said trying to save myself.

I quickly opened the unread while they created their cocktails.

Text from Christoph: *Did you get there safe? I'm thinking of you, baby.*

This indeed had become a guilty pleasure. I didn't want to take for granted this Hampton time. I mean, no one had their iPads out. I had to respond. I wanted to respond. I missed a man I had never laid eyes on.

Text from Chloe: *Hi there, stranger. Yep. Safe and poolside.*

Text from Christoph: *It's November! Your friends are crazy. Too bad you're there. You should meet Mary and me for drinks.*

"What are you smiling about?" Stephanie asked causing all attention on me.

"It's just an e-mail regarding the opening," I said.

"Really? You have the same stupid expression you did at the movies," Kate said.

"What look?" Alexander asked.

Stephanie intervened, "Enough, guys. Chloe has loads of pressure on her, let's stop the teasing."

I realized Kate's emotional instability was heart-blocking her friendship skills. Confiding in her would have to be on a case by case basis and required a *Noodle against the wall* test to see if her discretion stuck.

"Chloe, what's with the secrets? You should know better than keeping stuff from us. That's a bad—very bad—sign," Alexander said. He took it upon himself proudly to share his wife's mentoring me, as the band around his finger bound this automatic duty to him.

"I haven't met him yet," I blurted. "It's a long story, but I'll tell you about him after we meet for coffee," I said wishing to rapidly pull in the string of words.

"Coffee? He's totally gay," Alexander said while waiting for confirmation from one of the women surrounding him.

"Cut it out," Stephanie intervened.

"He's romantic," I demanded.

"Oh my, what are you going to wear?" Emma startled Lily.

"Something light and tight. Then you'll know if he plays for the opposite team or not," Alexander added sticking out his pec muscles with a stern wink.

"Thanks for the seal the deal advice," I said rolling my eyes. "Stephanie, can you give your husband a time out or something?" I asked while pointing to the corner on the other side of the pool with no heat lamp.

Unexpectedly, Lily started bawling. "What's wrong with her? Is she okay?" I asked.

"It's probably just a post traumatic reflex of the umbrella falling on top of her," Alexander suggested. I wondered if he had ever suffered from any sort of trauma from years of surfing the ocean waves. I believe I did from my recent imaginary shark attack.

"She's happy as a clam, just fussy," Emma reassured us.

"Charlie bit me, mommy," Lily cried. Her face distorted in a way that was unbelievable that a delicate little girl could express that.

"Who the hell is Charlie?" Kate asked.

"Charlie is her imaginary friend," Emma confirmed. "Did he sweet pea? You tell Charlie to play nice."

"I'm going to head upstairs and unpack," I said.

"You're staying!" Stephanie cheered.

I went directly to my designated room, tossed my bag on the bed and placed my camera on the top shelf away from sticky fingers. They might get trigger-happy this evening from cocktail confidence.

"Just checking on you," Kate said. She flashed a quick look of concern before snooping from the doorway. "You're tense and not your lively self."

"I wanted to unpack and respond to a couple emails."

"Work emails on Thanksgiving?" She studied my face.

"Yep . . . If only you could experience a front row seat to the Grayson Gates circus act," I added.

"What are we chatting about?" Emma poked her head in the doorway.

Stephanie intervened. "Are you trying to give Chloe a nervous breakdown before her debut?"

"Can we get some zip it action, ladies, and more cooking action," Alexander pleaded when he reached the top of the steps joining them. Five people in this gigantic house and my bedroom turned into a cluster fuck. "Chop. Chat. Chew. Please ladies to the kitchen," he begged while we remained still and staring at each other.

"Has he sent you flowers?" Emma continued.

"I surprise my wife with a single flower left in random places all the time," Alexander smiled.

Emma, Kate, and I fell for Alexander even more. "He's a keeper. I must admit," Kate said dropping her guard.

"It's sweet—" Stephanie shared before being interrupted by the gurgling sounds of her starving better half. "Didn't you just eat a Reuben?" she asked.

"What? I was a little dizzy and needed something. You ladies make me nervous with your drama," he said while heading back downstairs. "Chicks—I swear," he mumbled.

"I've told him to lay off the soy vanilla lattes. I think it has tapped into his estrogen or something," Stephanie teased giving us a good laugh and back to the same side.

Chapter 20

Alexander prepared the ball of fire, while rechecking the turbo heat lamps by the pool since the evening loomed. He lit the floating candles as the late night swim always followed the dessert course. Pushing up the sleeve of his fleece jacket, he dipped his hand into the water, "The temperature is on point!"

While he tackled the setup outside, we started to prepare dinner. I proceeded to chop, Emma started to set, Kate maneuvered the open wine and sipped, of course, while Stephanie jumped into her strategically planned *Food Network* episode.

"Chloe, please cut the vine ripened tomatoes, not the cherry," Stephanie directed with an unidentifiable stirring utensil.

"No can do," I said while securing my lime green apron around my waist. "We go over this every single time, people. I don't chop vine tomatoes. They're messy and make my salad look dreadful. Cherry takes one slit and I end up with two equal halves. No goop."

I was thankful my kitchen duties were limited. Stephanie banned both Alexander and me from clean up as she didn't approve of our bachelor wash methods of rinse and wipe.

"Fire in the hole!" Alexander screamed as he entered the kitchen sneaking up behind his wife and kissing a spot below her ballerina bun. Any moment, I anticipated the sportsman to gracefully elevate her above his shoulders, then into a spin and leap across the kitchen. The Cudneys were a flawless duo.

"What are you ladies chatting about in here? A little MPN?" Alexander asked.

It must be difficult for him to be the only man with his wife's circle of friends constantly around. Especially with us acting as each other's security blankets.

"MPN?" I hesitantly asked while not breaking concentration on creating precise halves.

"Pinch me as I can't wait for an explanation," Kate paused mid pour.

"Who is MPN?" Emma asked.

"You know . . . MPN. Makeup, perfume, nails." He snickered shaking his fingers in a drying motion.

"Do you guys smell something burning?" I asked. Sheer panic quickly overpowered the turkey aroma. I was spectacular under pressure, but hopeless when it came to any situation involving threat or emergencies. We were convinced I lacked a chromosome as those fainting goats. They definitely do exist. I Googled it.

A chorus of "Oh my Gods" traveled throughout the room only a church choir could deliver as we scrambled around the kitchen. The house wasn't burning to the ground.

"It must be the ball of fire!" I yelled.

Running outside we immediately checked the pit and it was fine.

Alexander ran to the opposite side of the pool; two of the candles had floated into the pump and began melting the linoleum.

"Well, I never thought I would say this, guys —the pool is on fire," I said.

"Looks like you're CDAR," Kate directed to Alexander. "Can't Do Anything Right!" she laughed.

After the cooking episode came to a wrap, we were thankful for the holiday spread and Kate's course for one. Cuddled around the table, secure in our winter apparel appropriate for dining outdoors, we pulled back the fingertips on our gloves to eat. The towering heat lamps were on high, roasting us as the turkey centered before us. The risk of hypothermia was greater than hypoglycemia.

"Who is going to do the toast?" I asked.

"I will," Alexander replied.

Stephanie popped up, "I think we've had enough entertainment from the CDAR," she instigated a melody of laughter. "Sit down, Mr. Renaissance man." She put her hand on Alexander's shoulder and gently gave it a polite tap. "Thank you for being in our lives," she paused, raising her glass an inch higher. "For being a part of our home. We love you. Bon Appetito!"

Eating dimmed our voices with the tranquil ambience of the candle lit pool, music and the Hampton breeze under the stars.

"Are you okay, Chloe? Is something wrong with the food?" Stephanie peered at my plate.

"I'm . . . totally fine," I said. "Pass the sweet potatoes, please."

I was ashamed for getting this motivated by a man I'd never met. I occasionally glanced at Alexander, observing his choices and habits. *Did Christoph have unique tendencies like never combining food with contradicting tastes?* Alexander, under no circumstances, got his Thanksgiving turkey near the cranberry dressing. He wanted salty to be salty and sweet to be sweet. *What did Christoph put on his salads? Snack on during a road trip? Did he eat insane amounts of White Swiss chocolate since he was Swiss?* Knowing these things is what would make someone their special person.

"You killed it!" Kate said, hysterical.

I sprung up onto my chair. "Holy shit, where is it?" I screamed.

"What?" Kate yelled.

"Is there a bug?" I panicked.

"Sit down, you sissy!" Kate continued. "Even if it was, I think the leopard cockroaches walking around this house won't bite."

"They do exist," I said, but still waited to receive confirmation from Stephanie.

"Someone killed the falafel! Was this microwaved?" Kate asked.

"I'm sorry . . . I wasn't supposed to?" I asked. I knew better to not go beyond the cutting board.

Kate dropped the chickpea shaped ball back onto her plate with starvation showing on her face. It was Thanksgiving and past 8:00 p.m. Stores were closed. New options were out.

I bit my lip. "I was just trying to help." The nut was now dinnerless and landed me on the chopping block.

"We can give it to Ninja. I'll mix it in with her turkey," Stephanie said.

We sat tongue-tied pretending that Stephanie's concern for the dog's holiday meal didn't overshadow the human guest next to her. I could see Ninja inside with his face inside his bowl.

"How come the dog gets to eat inside?" Kate continued.

"Would you like an ice-cream sandwich? I bought a package of Skinny Cow," Emma suggested.

"Really Emma?" Kate asked.

"What's wrong with that?" Alexander asked.

"I'm sitting outside in November and you want to know if I would like ice cream?" Kate continued.

"Cool it," I said staring her bitchiness back.

"Skinny Cow? God, talk about toying with the woman fighting to stay on the health wagon," Kate said. Her blood pressure elevated with each breath while she eyed the juicy sliced meat on my plate. Her face flushed matching the cranberry sauce.

I could only imagine the restraint it took her. To be disciplined everyday, the hard work sacrificed by one slip of temptation. I did kill her food. I imagined the effort as being in labor for twenty hours only to be told you need an emergency C-section and robbed of the natural birth title.

After dinner Alexander suggested a late night swim, ignoring Emma's *We should wait thirty minutes,* suggestion by turning the music up louder. Emma still maintained her sweetness from her childhood. She still believed everything her mother told her, *If you play with frogs you will get warts,* or *You'll go blind if you sit too close to the TV,* and *If you don't close the bag, the air evaporates your cotton candy.* Until a couple years ago, after her and I took Lily to the circus, I had to demonstrate that the candy goes stale. The only way it disappeared was by her mother eating it when she went to bed.

"Come on! The pool temperature is perfect—Who's in?" Alexander asked.

Alexander had this zest for living in the moment and from loving his woman. He gave us hope Disney wasn't complete deception.

I, however, was ready to go to sleep and make a goodnight call.

"I'm calling it a night," I said while pushing in my chair. The benefit on wearing puffy coats during a holiday meal is that it hid our food babies.

"What? Come on, we can race to the other side," Alexander pouted.

"What are we chickens?" I poked.

Emma supported Lily in the water, teaching her to float. I watched the warm subtle water caress her fragile body and thought how love connected to floating. Sometimes it's not natural, but must be learned. It sometimes means sinking several times. Maybe the heart must break to know what it's capable of. It's all a part of swimming or living, I would think, or from what I saw through my lens. You attempt it. You try it. You trust the other to stay afloat and even then sometimes we sink. We believe our teachers will also be our partners, helping keep our head above water. We can only hope they are honest and genuine, to share the balance of the experience and not allow the water to swallow us. I didn't want to drown. Staring at the deep end of the pool, I questioned if had the chance, if I could tread back safely to the shallow end to stand.

Once under my covers, I thought of Christoph's voice. It used to feel as aromatherapy with scents of sandalwood, Cyprus and a hint of vanilla. I'd absorbed him instantly. I missed this and how it was the last thing I wanted to hear before falling asleep.

Now, Chloe Kassidy plus Christoph Kostas seemed cursed. It's like a CIA device, that

self-destructs . . . 10 . . . 9 . . . 8 . . . 7 . . . 6 . . . 5 . . . 4 . . . 3 . . . 2 . . .

While Brad the Dad and I returned to the city, I took advantage of being the passenger. With having two months to go until the opening, I began flipping through images hoping to spark theme ideas. Just as I inserted my earphones, the phone rang.

"Tell me how much you missed me yesterday!" I detected a trace of animation in Christoph's tone. "Baby, I'm sitting here writing with your picture on my screen," he continued.

"How was your Thanksgiving?" I asked realizing he probably didn't celebrate it.

"You chose a turkey over me," he said. Within seconds he pulled a reverse on me while my excitement increased with his good mood intentions, he slipped in another rain check. Christoph informed me he was heading to La Chaux-de-Fonds for three weeks. La Chaux-de-Fonds is a Swiss city resided in the Jura Mountains where he would be completing a project. The town was known for its watch making industry, which was ironic for someone who lacked respect for time. A respect he attempted to beautify with his tongue of superfluous words while he delicately broke the news of his upcoming trip.

"Moments like this reaffirm my duty in this world to spread love among people, to make them see how much more they can achieve by loving each other, than by killing each other's daughters, sons, wives, husbands, friends, mothers or fathers."

"When will you be back from this trip?" I asked trying not to sound unappreciative of the killings.

"Right before Christmas, I'm told. Tell your friends you're marrying me, getting the Swiss citizenship and moving to the elitist Europe!" he joked.

Was this a prank?

Maybe this was a self-deserved curse by believing in *Once upon a time* and *Happily ever after*. Mary was a wicked fairy who placed this curse upon me. Although, it wasn't a finger prick, one appeared to be involved. I wanted this guy to recognize the heart I opened and the love within it.

"I want the fairy tale," I whispered. I wanted my god damn *Pretty Woman* moment, hooker or not.

"Wait, you're leaving now?" I screamed in panic causing Brad to flip around to assess the situation in his back seat. Mouthing the five letter word slowly, "Sorry," I realized my unpredictability might lead to an interstate accident.

"They called me at six-thirty this morning . . . I'm sorry," he said. "My schedule is killing you, I know it."

"Are you free today before you fly out?" I asked. I thought at least we could say hi and bye with a quick coffee. "I'm on my way back to Manhattan as we speak."

"I'm preparing politicians to go live on Euronews. I'm in the CNN studios waiting to witness the fall of a person who thinks he's best when he only speaks through the words of others. The UN week sessions are finished but the PR continues."

"I just don't understand . . .," I said.

"My field of work is of a certain nature that requires people to trust me—when I can't tell them certain things or explain any further . . . even when nothing makes sense, Chloe. You'll have to learn to trust me."

"When will you be back?"

"I promise I'll be home before Christmas."

"Emma and I leave for Atlanta on the twenty-third," I reminded him.

"If I have to take an official escort in the ambassadorial car to get back to you, I will. Anyway, I've planned the perfect date on December twenty-first! Chef Erik Roberts said yes."

"Yes?"

"At the end of December, for five hours on a Sunday, it's you, me and Chef Roberts for a private cooking demonstration and dinner at restaurant Le Banc."

"That sounds nice," I responded trying to mask any disappointment. When the heart cries, it feels three times its weight and the pumping shakes the entire body like an earthquake. It's completely opposite of an orgasm. The pumps felt forced with each breath, my heart cramped, unable to fully contract, stuck and stinging in my chest with no energy for tears. It was numbing and left me emotionless. I felt Brad checking on me through the rearview mirror, but pretended I hadn't noticed. "Can we Skype while you're away at least?" I asked.

"The area I'm going to is a secure government site and they enforce strict rules and have absurd limitations," he explained.

"A tremendous amount of privacy comes with your position," I poked. I hoped his next words would shine light on this cryptic character.

"I work for Intelligence and that means working with a sort of mystery with regard to your job and identity. It's critical for diplomats to avoid overexposure on the Internet for political reasons as well. Listen—I didn't choose for us to happen. I didn't choose for you or me to happen for that matter," he reminded me.

When did diplomats work for Intelligence? He didn't choose for us to happen?

"I'll be back, please wait for me," he begged.

Perhaps, he had a point with me. I blew hot then cold in a matter of seconds. My heart said, *I'm scared.* My gut asked, *Will he show?* My head said, *Call Stephanie!*

Three rings. Four rings. "Does someone already miss me?" Stephanie answered.

"Stephanie! Thank the stars you picked up," I said frantically. His truth saddened me along with his distance. Catching him in this manipulation would be more rewarding than if he rang my doorbell. He had disappointed me more than I wanted to admit. *If our fairy tale began tomorrow, would I always accuse him, doubt him, or think he might disappear any second?*

"What's wrong?" she asked.

I was now involving someone else in my web of diplomatic deception.

"I know you're close with Erik Roberts's wife," I pointed out.

"I saw her at a fundraiser last week," she said. "Why?"

"I overheard someone at the gallery mention Mr. Roberts—"

"Erik, yes . . .," she continued.

"Erik offers private dinners at Le Banc?" I spit it out quickly, then held my breath hoping it wouldn't be long to get the truth, to know something was false or fact. At this point, I pretended Brad the Dad wasn't an arm length away. He didn't exist or bear witness to this humiliating scene.

"Private classes? You mean with the *Top Chef* show?" she asked, confused like me. "Oh, Chloe, my grocery delivery just arrived. I'll have to call you back in a bit . . . I'll ask Erik about private classes, but it may be a bit before I receive a response. He's with his family traveling through France."

"You think they will spend Christmas in New York?"

"I can find out when they are planning to return," she answered. "I gotta run."

Chapter 21

"Shopping!" Emma screamed with the opening of my apartment door.

"Good Morning, Miss Photographer!" Stephanie screeched. They pushed through the door simultaneously.

This would be a treat for both Emma and me, but Stephanie's spending enthusiasm was backbreaking considering most people joined gyms for exercise.

"Chloe, this is going to be an adventure. I have our agenda mapped out," Stephanie said. She pulled out her Ulysee anise green leather Hermes notebook to review our itinerary.

I wouldn't lie. I was excited to venture outside my Jenna's picks. I wanted a remarkable outfit to christen me into this new life. It was comparable to Holy Communion, Sweet 16, prom, college graduation, but lower than the monumental *I do to your Boo* day. I wanted to be confirmed and accepted as an artist, which meant saving months from my Bright Images, Inc. pay stubs to afford me just that.

"Emma, we're shopping for shoes, not serendipity," I joked.

Delicately wetting her index finger on the tip of her tongue, Stephanie flipped the page to today's place. "Here we are, November 30. We'll grab a bite at Fred's in Barneys, then head to Intermix on Madison, and then stop at Bergdorfs for shoes and accessories."

"But if we're eating at Fred's, why don't we look for a dress there?" Emma questioned.

If it was written in the Hermes, it happened. At $280 a pop, Stephanie's sacred planner contained pages where revisions couldn't be justified. It was our Holy Grail this afternoon and we were going to obey it.

"Intermix is where her outfit's at. They received new pieces from Furstenberg, Rodriguez and Lang." Stephanie pointed to the list with her pen as if she forgot to dot one of her 'i's. "My contact there will give Chloe forty-percent off."

I intervened before we battled on Bergdorfs. I adored entering this 5th Avenue monument, housed in the Vanderbilt mansion only to glide up the escalators to the department of soles. When I first arrived as a New York transplant, I would spend hours walking in circles, trying on, browsing and trying on again, never finding one fitting. Not because of the size, but because of the price tag. It was still fun to play dress up.

Once at Fred's we ordered three rounds of Estelle's chicken soup, grandma's recipe to cure colds and not bloat, and Fred's chopped chicken salad, which replaced the majority of conversation as we were devouring every bite for fuel. I knew they would have me slipping in and out of options like superwoman.

"I would like to toast our artist. Here's to successful spending," Stephanie smiled, raising her flute of champagne towards ours. I missed Kate not experiencing the afternoon with us. Shopping was one thing she hated more than men. If it wasn't activewear or Tom's shoes she gave it no consideration.

"Chloe . . . when do we finally meet the anonymous man pocketing your time?" Emma asked.

"I'm not sure where we stand right now," I whispered before Stephanie moved to a friendlier topic. Ignoring the issue didn't change the truth.

"You'll find your way, Chloe." Stephanie said.

"Might be a bad sign if you don't know where things are headed?" Emma added while she signaled for the dessert menu, which she always perused, but never ordered from. She liked knowing her options.

"No signs and soul mate facts today, okay?" I begged adjusting my face to a more cheerful position.

"I'm concerned," Stephanie admitted. She signaled for another round of cocktails while shooing away the server with Emma's previous request.

"What is it with these signs? Maybe some things lead to the truth and some things lead to nothing," I said.

"Why? What is this man's Zodiac?" Stephanie persisted while the server delivered the fresh flutes.

"I was referring to signs not being coincidences, but Christoph is an Aries," I answered taking a sip, causing a chain reaction of bottoms up, before Emma's input continued.

"Your astrological sun rules your heart. Him, he will be in touch with his feelings and openly communicates, I assume," she said.

"Yeah, he's a talker," I confirmed. *But . . . not a walker.*

Emma continued, "Aries can be impatient, a live wire in relationships, they fear boredom, their favorite words are 'I am,' and often attracted to active and assertive individuals like an Aquarius . . . like you, Chloe."

"Do all women suffer from this planet contribution?" I asked. "It's like PMS, it only causes pain and problems," I said feeling equally fragile as the delicate stem between my fingertips containing the fizzy venting potion.

Stephanie pretended to be more focused on sipping than sharing her opinion. As a mentor, I knew she wanted me to take a *self* approach.

"But you paint the picture quite well. He's causing me mental agony by provoking me to express myself only to disappointment me, which results in my retaliating with accusations," I said, finishing my flute. His need for attention was immature and I hoped he would be embarrassed by his twenty-twenty hindsight. I shared details that didn't shine a charming light on Christoph. The light I wanted him to be in. I closed my eyes shutting out the truth to avoid admitting what wasn't happening. Him being a visible man whose actions matched his promises.

Stephanie finished her second glass, which was rare. She was a one-drink kind of girl. Daintily tapping the corners of her mouth with her napkin, she tucked her hair behind her ears and with a deep gaze, "I hate to say this, but he's fucking outrageous." Stephanie was a one-curse word a day kind of girl as well. In my opinion, lunchtime was way too early to meet your *F* quota. "Love isn't painful," she aggressively poked the air almost like she popped the bubble I was in. "Please remember that," she said.

I desperately needed another sip, but with the no sales return policy at Intermix, I couldn't risk my judgment being blocked by bubbly.

Arriving at Intermix, they pushed me into a fitting room and told me to stay put and get naked. I stared back at my tipsy self, studying the signs of stress. While I smiled, frowned and made fish lips to accentuate my cheekbones, I waved to Natalie Portman reflecting back at me. *What would Portman do?* I bet she would make lemonade. If life brought me lemons, I would throw them at Swiss jerks, then pick up the fruit and make myself a cocktail. I'm sure concentrating on a moving target would make me thirsty.

I behaved pathetically with continually responding and accepting his weightless words. He claimed he couldn't be without me, yet he couldn't be with me. Everything that was first sweet was now sour. It was a Sour Patch Kid addiction. I took the black fine point Sharpie from my purse and with my left hand scribbled on my other palm, the one responsible for my replies. The promise of the *permanent* marker would be temporarily offering enough time for my senses to sharpen. I began with *P* for my thought of *Prick*, but continued to pen *Perspective*. This was a wiser choice then the mustache I contemplated first.

Without warning the curtain flew open and I faced two tipsy women ready to tango me into an outfit.

"Who are you talking to?" they asked.

"I'm drunk." I squeezed my hand into a fist to protect my secret word.

December

Chapter 22

The month of December signifies birth, salvation, reflection and living. It's the year's end in preparation for a new beginning.

I revisited Central Park to watch strangers while they strolled by absorbing the city. Their appreciation made me honored to be a New Yorker. The city was this masterpiece, a gem affecting each resident or visitor in a rare way. That's how truly intense the energy was here. Central Park was my kryptonite.

The solid, now rare, oak trees connected me to home. Georgia was a scenery filled with native trees through a variety of spreading, vase-shaped, rounded, and my favorite, weeping. They stood tall and long lasting identical to New York City's skyscrapers and historical monuments. These oversized plants enclosed in their bark shell, protecting their circles, traced the ancestry roots, bloodline and lineage belonging specifically to them. The thought of what a tree bears witness to and endures only to remain standing still was quixotic.

From: Christoph Kostas
To: Chloe Kassidy
Subject: Problemo
Date: December 1, 5:12 p.m.

I flew into Geneva and then came to this program right away, I didn't have the time to go to my Swiss phone company and sign for a cell contract. Instead, once I arrived here, I bought a temporary pay card number from a kiosk and I put minutes/credit on it by buying occasional cards. Seeing as I'm stuck 8kms outside the city in a cottage in a technologically underdeveloped area, the kiosk has run out of big-bucks cards, and only has 5 and 8 euro ones. That will allow us a talking time of . . . 3-4 minutes. Go on Skype, and using your credit card, buy a $10 credit. And then call my cell from your computer, using the microphone you have on your computer. That should give us at least 1-2 hours.

You know I'm a gentleman and I would never have asked this if this weren't my situation, but unfortunately I'm stuck in the middle of nowhere, and I do miss your voice. If not, then we'll stick to emailing and I'll have to go in the city tomorrow. This sounds out of a war movie.
Christoph

    1-2-3 and Skype connected me to a place I'd never imagined traveling to, but sounded fabulous, foreign, and closer from the sounds of his voice.

    "Baby . . . can you hear me?" he asked in a shy tone. Not wanting to launch a new argument, I focused on his voice and not the fact that most people who Skyped took advantage of the camera feature. He was against the unromantic idea for the first way our eyes would meet each other, and, on this specific occasion, a bad connection.

"You're my life, my world, my baby," he sighed and I detected an unusual tone of stress in his voice, but remained quiet. I wanted to hear him speak without giving him any ammunition to turn things back on me. "I never, ever want to be without you, and I know these days this is a hard argument to support. But . . . I'm confident in the way we're in perfect harmony with the world, with our very selves, when we're sharing body, mind and soul with no one else."

He continued to confide in me, he was in love with us. Everything we were, everything we wanted to be, and everything we could be. I couldn't deny he was truly an artist with words. And when he said, "Chloe, I'm in love with the way I feel when I'm thinking of you." He made my gut tingle.

"I know the time difference and my job are killing you with the way things are. I think you're weaker with our distance and I don't want to lose you while discovering my work and myself. This . . . isn't how it's supposed to work."

Watching this admission from a face on my screen would be more romantic than listening to noise from a speaker. "I agree. It wasn't supposed to be like this from the beginning," I said while placing a Post-It over the tiny camera as a precaution.

"Want to travel here and relax a little bit? We can go back together?" he asked.

I declined since it was impossible with the upcoming exhibit and because, as much as I smiled at the gist, I felt it was another empty promise.

"I don't know why, but I have this knot in my stomach. I miss you and New York . . . Was coming here a mistake?"

"A mistake?" He was going to have to be a bit more specific.

"I'm thinking when I return I'll work on my book. The sooner, the better," he said confidently.

"Are you drinking, Kostas?"

"I'll stop drinking something called Zivania. It's forty-five percent alcohol . . . and rude to decline it!" He laughed and I followed, as he was contagious and intoxicated from top to bottom on the gift from his Greek coworkers.

"What's in it exactly?"

"It's produced from the pomace of grapes that are pressed during the winemaking process and combined with local dry wines from the island of Cyprus . . . It's colorless with a gentle aroma of raisins."

The Zivania kept him talking, and for once he had skipped the *Kassidy, you're an iceberg* lecture.

"I told them I needed to catch up on emails and contact my girlfriend. I started talking about you to the guys here. I hope you don't mind."

I didn't respond because I wasn't sure how.

"They said I look extremely goofy and happy when I'm talking about you. Well . . .

I am—" I heard his lips slightly smack to swallow when he sipped the happy juice. "You know what I miss the most from New York?" he asked.

"What's that?" I was curious to know if I made the cut.

"The parks, the Wi-Fi, Starbucks, my Whole Foods's salmon sushi, my own space . . . YOU. This is about you. I miss you. I love you."

He loves me? Even with the tone and strength of his words, I searched for a deeper understanding on how he loved me without ever meeting me.

That evening, I met a different side to Christoph Kostas. He had insecurities and doubts, not with us, but with his calling in the world and the expectations sitting solid on his shoulders. He struggled with where his family wanted him to live, his career and how to make it work. An inner revelation transpired on where to take root. He always considered Europe to be home so he could participate in the making of civilization and culture. But now, he insinuated having lived in New York, knowing I was there, knowing of the opportunities for excellence, distinction and recognition, he wondered if it was worth battling against the old-school mentality, of trying to operate in Switzerland, just so he could be next to his family.

"Can I put my life on hold for a year? Should I put my life on hold for a year? Should I finish my book? Should I help build this program or leave the UN? What should I do? And where does that leave us, Chloe?"

Everything about him and us made me fulfilled and empty at the same time. I could no longer reassure myself where my tears came from. *Were they sadness or relief that I didn't believe him?*

"I can't because putting myself last means putting you last and I can't do that. I don't want to do that. I love you . . . and . . . us more than I can ever say. You're my world, Chloe Kassidy, and believe me I don't just say words to say them."

"Christoph, I should go—" I said uncomfortable with the weight of our conversation. I had to see him to believe him.

"I want to grow old with you," he interrupted. "Just be a little patient. I'm working on getting back. I promise."

The week continued with his alphabetical exchanges consuming my inbox.

From: Christoph Kostas
To: Chloe Kassidy
Subject: Good Morning, Beautiful!
Date: December 3, 8:31 a.m.

I don't know why, but all I can think about is Serendipity's frozen drinks today! Argh. I miss New York! I'd settle for a cappuccino and a chocolate-dipped cannoli at Veniero's! I'll stop with the desserts I could mention. Rao's for instance, that's Italian yumminess! I'm in physical anxiety over Manhattan! Can't wait to be home.

Also, I swear to God, I'm buying you a ring tomorrow. What's your size? And don't be stubborn in not telling me because I'll buy it and I won't be able to return it. No more fooling around. You're taken. Get used to it. Chloe and Christoph or C-square!

By the way, baby, it looks like I'll be coming on December 23rd. I need to take care of this before coming back, and need to stay for two additional days. I don't want you to get caught up in the middle of this drama.

The issues I've discovered here are politically and legally wrong and I don't want to get you involved in any way, even by confiding in you. I need to be especially careful in order to avoid creating enemies. I want you out of this until I figure it out. Just promise me you'll be a little more patient. It's three weeks . . . (think of it in weeks not days) and we will be together. I swear to God, if I come back only to have you break up with me the first night, I'm going to kill you.

I'm off to meet with the ambassador and the consulate.

p.s. I thought if it's okay with you, I would like to speak with Stephanie.

Christoph

I'm going to kill you?

I had my reservations, but sent him her e-mail address to see what actions would follow. Stephanie could handle anyone. Not because of a mean mouth, tough ego or biceps, but she had this street sense that made her loyal with no problem defending her friends. An international diplomat would need all the extra protection he could muster.

From: Christoph Kostas

To: Stephanie Cudney, Chloe Kassidy

Subject: Greetings

Date: December 7, 2:18 p.m.

Hey Stephanie,

My being nervous isn't and shouldn't be interpreted as a pitfall in this heartfelt communication of ours. If anything, I would be more nervous, had I not been a little nervous, whilst conversing for the first time with Chloe's best friend.

I'm not a virtual person. I oftentimes wish my complicated and over analytical nature were virtual but those, too, are real. I would have said 'unfortunately real' but the truth is, who I am and who I am not, is exactly the product of those spiritual, empirical, cognitive and philosophical debates and interactions, and so long as a person is true to his search for his human conscience, to his call for inner peace, he won't but end up in a beautiful place.

Life is simple, when we frame it as such. It's not to say that in simplicity there does not lay a miracle. People need to believe in miracles to go through the unexpected things in life. Yet, they ought to also believe in impossible possibilities, in extreme potential, in inhumane power to achieve, create and be reborn. In the midst of walking the corridors of my soul and engaging in a journey of truthful self-discovery, I bumped into one of your most precious gifts in life. For the first time ever, I started being unable not to notice my journey had just started, not throughout the finding of new landscapes, but in acquiring a new set of eyes. Unexpected, unprovoked and unpredicted, she, one way or another, has managed to pause me enough to make me realize maybe the world's greatest miracle might be happening, not miles away from my footsteps. Just round the corner from where I would have least expected it—inside of me.

We have both hurt each other, as much as comforted each other. Laughed with one another and cried because of the other.

I don't have the textbook to help me guarantee you, her or myself for that matter, that I'll never again make her upset, sad or desperate. Stephanie, if there's one thing, I can tell you with all the nobleness and humbleness of my being, I do love this gift of yours.

The idea this love, admiration and devotion isn't complete, due to the lack of physical intimacy and simple, everyday occurrences that make a relationship real and solid, makes me choke a little bit. It is scary to know a single person possesses the power, the gift, the right and even the charisma to paint your life's portrait in a way everything is colorful when they are around, and black and white when they are not.

Best,

Christoph

From: Stephanie Cudney

To: Christoph Kostas, Chloe Kassidy

Subject: Re: Greetings

Date: December 7, 3:36 p.m.

Hi Christoph,

Now from the protective and watchful friend over one of my most precious gifts in life . . . I get a connection with the famous Christoph. You seem to have a vision, drive and inner spirit that will take you many beautiful places in life. The new set of eyes we're given by the experiences and people we meet are truly gifts. I'm happy to hear Chloe was one of those people for you.

I always said if anyone could see her heart like we do, they would never be able to stop staring at her, and, as back breaking as I'm sure it can be, make her their constant in life.

Stephanie

From: Christoph Kostas

To: Stephanie Cudney, Chloe Kassidy

Subject: Re: Re: Greetings

Date: December 7, 4:02 p.m.

Dear Stephanie,

I can be a handful at times, and yes, I'm not the world's most easy-going person, but sometimes simplicity comes with a little bit of an uphill road in life, and unfortunately it took me a while to realize the fear of pain is worse than the pain itself.

Thanks for taking the time to actually share your thoughts, feelings and love for a truly remarkable individual. Love is instinctively protective and watchful, love is honest and expressive, love is kind enough to be wishing a dreamer such as myself all the favor needed in the quest to winning her heart. After all, finding one's self is the pursuit of life . . .

Christoph

From: Stephanie Cudney
To: Christoph Kostas, Chloe Kassidy
Subject: Re: Re: Re: Greetings
Date: December 7, 4:36 p.m.

Aside from the obvious reasons for brow raising expressions, I'm anxious to hear from Chloe that the 'in person' Christoph is even more impressive, interesting, respectful, beautiful, and saturated with integrity than the 'virtual' Christoph.

With that out of the way, I understand sometimes simplicity can be made muddy by the waters of life, but oftentimes it's us who are doing all the stirring. I hope I'm reading what you're saying correctly in that you're going to stand still long enough to let simplicity take hold and enjoy the fabulous and gracious gift that is in front of you.

It is simple, life that is. God, love and loyalty to family and friends with a giving spirit, that's about it, don't you think? When we can remember to live, regardless of our circumstance, life is lived with more joy and less suffering.

I wish all the favor needed in winning Chloe's heart, a feat that has never been done outside her family and friends. Once it's captured though, look out! I can't wait to see and watch her happiness blossom more than she ever imagined.

Stephanie

After reading her reply to him, I was relieved to have someone outside of us acknowledge how this exhausting emotional rollercoaster could weaken anyone. It made me sick to think how much time had passed waiting for coffee. It hadn't crossed my mind to invite him to the opening. Our virtual relationship never crossed into reality. The phone rang and the timing of it had to be either Mr. Invisible with more words or Mrs. Mentor with direction.

"Hey, Stephanie."

"It's hard to believe he's out there saving the world and manages to write such lengthy emails," she joked.

"What do you think?" I asked, wondering if she was impressed.

"He sounds great, Chloe. Mature and passionate and well—"

"Well, what?" I asked trying to control my tone and protecting my thumb in my pocket.

"I'm worried about you. You're either too stressed out, too emotional and skeptical about your exhibit, or —"

"Stephanie . . ."

"Do you genuinely trust this guy?"

"I've been living in this state of confusion . . . I mean his actions never catch up to his words, but then—"

"I know I shouldn't be putting more pressure on you to answer such a question, but I had no idea the extent of . . . I should have checked in on your more," she sighed. "I know this is a rough period of time for you, with these decisions confronting you. You get stressed out, putting yourself in an emotional and physical uphill marathon before you see the big picture, breathe and realize you can achieve it all."

"I know you're concerned," I admitted.

"It's been my experience with you that just as you think you're going to break, you burst out into a great place. Everyone from time to time—just needs to be reminded—everything does not have to be perfect to be right."

This was a hard concept for me to grasp. Sometimes the people in my life have to breathe for me until I come around.

"Just be careful, is all I'm suggesting. I pray it's him you're having a relationship with. Months have passed and—"

"Stephanie, I know where you're going with this. I—"

"Are you sure?"

"We have spent a lot of time together, how could he have bad intentions? What would he be getting out of this? I mean—there's been no identity theft or bank scam." I laughed and stopped when I realized I was the only one. "This is the first time I've opened up—I go from hot to cold to—"

"Wait a minute," she demanded. "You being wishy washy should not be taken as you not knowing how to love or care for someone. Any girl would be when you don't know who someone truly is. I mean he's a ghost at this point."

"I can't believe I'm failing at this."

"You can't hold on or force something to be true, just because you don't want to be wrong. I want you to consider something. Okay?" She asked.

"Of course, I know you always have my best interests at heart." And she did. She always did, like the unconditional love between sisters.

"Think of it as this . . . you've received a huge present in a huge box with a huge bow and opened it to riffle through huge amounts of tissue paper sprinkled with glitter only to find a tiny little key as the present. Well, the perception is exciting, but a key to nowhere is pretty useless," she pointed out.

Perspective.

There were days I wanted to march into the United Nations building to put my eyes on him. Of course, security would be tight, but how harmful would it be to approach the information desk and ask for Christoph Kostas? I didn't take control for two reasons. First, I didn't want to force our meeting. It's not how I envisioned our beginning unfolding. Not with these doubts, accusations and failed attempts splattered across the pages of our story. Second, I was terrified of hearing, "There's no diplomat by that name employed here with the United Nations." *What would that say about following my heart?* Standing on the edge of vulnerability and opening the secret door to my soul only to fall flat on my face.

Chapter 23

I had exactly fifty-four days until the opening. Tracking time was my new hobby between the exhibit and the overwhelming stretch of time that had passed since my introduction to the diplomat. Well, the lack of a proper introduction. My relationship with Christoph in the real world, outside of Mary and Stephanie, was as discreet as a Canon operating in silent shooting.

Lately, my rapid heartbeat was bursting similarly to the continuous shooting of rapid fire, think Paparazzi. I typically switched the mode to silent, since the quick machine gun clicks were disruptive. Working with the camera was a ceremonial routine, like a bride and groom in their first dance. After removing the lens cap, I held the body of my Canon by wrapping my hand around its right side, gripping tightly. The body was designed to seamlessly fit into your hand making it possible to naturally hold it with one. The index finger extended around the side to gently rest on the shutter button. Taking my other hand to support under the camera's body.

The connection was flawless. The only thing left was to move and shoot.

Capturing New York in the winter was one of my favorites. Bare trees displayed their unique features with their individualities exposed, letting you peek into the tree's soul and how it responds to the environmental changes throughout its lifetime. With the city glazed over in white and a gray sky backdrop, shooting in the wintertime naturally offered colorless photography. The frames were black and white and cold like the temperature. The bareness of it all showed the forte of whatever supported the snow, be it a tree branch, struggling not to bend or break. I tried to balance love in it all.

I favored the silence and rawness in these varying shades of gray rather than the Rockefeller Center crowds hosting muffled voices with a halo lit sky set off by thousands of lights. The energy itself was a high definition experience. To warm my monochrome shots, I would add a sepia touch.

From: Christoph Kostas
To: Chloe Kassidy
Subject: One true love can turn you around
Date: December 14, 8:03 a.m.

Good morning/afternoon,
I thought about you during the night and everything going through your mind, your heart. These heavy decisions of the exhibit and whether to believe in us are weighing on your shoulders. Just breathe, baby, and take it a day, a call, and a step at a time. Your heart will tell you everything. I have no doubt when the time comes, your worries, questions and opportunities will fall into order. Your life is filled with great passion and for this—everyone is proud of you.

From: Mary Polt
To: Chloe Kassidy, Christoph Kostas
Subject: Meant to be
Date: December 14, 9:14 a.m.

I wake up this morning and I'm greeted by a cute little package. I think to myself what better way to feel special than a gift! I open it up only to find carefully wrapped items and a note to say 'drop this off to Chloe.' Seriously now, Christoph, I mean, I know I owe you because of you know why but you want me to give this to Chloe?

From: Christoph Kostas
To: Mary Polt, Chloe Kassidy
Subject: Re: Meant to be
Date: December 14, 9:30 a.m.

Listen woman! You just happened to be the connector in this story. I want you to connect us for the last time. It's pretty simple! I want you to go give Miss Kassidy her package. You're my one and only secretary! I can't recruit anyone else because we started this because of you. You know you'll give in eventually. I'm away for nine more days! Please?
Christoph

   Nothing was ever simple with Christoph The Great.
   The fact I was to have a first date with his *secretary*, but still no date with him after months, sparked new doubts, but also relieved me he didn't have bad intentions just a grueling work schedule. I was meeting his dear friend today. I took a cab and headed to Rockefeller Plaza, the ice skating rink to be exact. I looked for a tall, blonde,

normal built girl with a bag of items for me, items only Christoph and I would understand, according to him. They were things belonging to us since they were in our language.

She found me first and I was grateful since I wouldn't have picked her by his description and I didn't recall her at the first book club gathering. She was average height, light brown messy hair, extremely pale, and not curvy, but unfit which caused me to question his taste in women since he described her as attractive and failed to mention she was a tomboy. I took her to coffee and we sat in Bryant Park away from the crowds. It was sunny, but a windy afternoon that filled our silent pauses by securing our hair, holding onto our cups, and adjusting our coats. She wanted to know our romantic details, but I didn't share. I was a complete stranger and prior to us sitting, the only thing she knew about me was my e-mail address and I read *The Reader.*

"How many guys do you know who would wrap one, two, three, four items in matching shades of blue and even perfume them or something? He's Christoph! He isn't supposed to be doing these things! I don't recognize him anymore," Mary claimed.

I smiled as she finally let go of the gift bag.

"I hope it didn't take this for you to realize what you bumped into, Chloe. I wish someone would do that for me."

While I removed the items from the bag, my fingertips revealed what each individually wrapped item was before removing the tissue. Three new books for our book club and a leather journal that contained his poems.

"Chloe, I'm yours to ask whatever you want," she said interrupting my moment. I forgot she was there. "What do you want to know about him?" I wasn't sure which she enjoyed more, her drink or her self-proclaimed importance in her friend's upsetting behavior.

"Questions? All I have are words," I said. "I don't need answers. I need action," I smiled.

"Seriously, what do you want to know? Ask me anything."

When I wouldn't budge, we sat sipping in silence until we both hit cup bottom.

"He'll be back from Europe in a couple days and I hope you two can just work it out and be together," she said, almost pleading. "You two have something rare, something I would die for. I can't watch you both stubbornly give it up. It's just foolish," she fumed turning her body completely towards me while grabbing my shoulder. "Now the distance will be over and you two can make it work. How can you not fight for each other? He's your soul mate."

My heart was clouded. Hearing her speak about him and the effort he had made, maybe I was paranoid about his intentions. Yet, I couldn't shake the feeling that this was the first time she had seen me by the way she inspected me. She stared at my clothes, jewelry, and my nervous raw spot, and I swear even the breakout on my chin, barely blinking. I had a hunch that it wasn't because she was a fan of Natalie Portman.

From: Christoph Kostas
To: Chloe Kassidy
Subject: Finding forever
Date: December 14, 3:37 p.m.

I talked to her. She said you have a contagious smile, freckles on your face, large brown eyes, you knew the books before you opened them, and she couldn't get a romantic word out of your mouth. She explained you talked about me similar to a good friend. 'He's such a sweet guy,' which she found cute and I don't obviously want to be your friend.

Reiner, one of my coworkers here said, 'This girl has turned you from the leader of adventure to the leader of settling down, from the master of the world to the master of your home with her. Is the gang losing its master king?' Why does everyone say you've changed me? Do I sound different?

I'm good nighting my company. Grab wine and you can talk to me from the tub. I promise I'll keep my eyes and imagination shut. I have to say something and please don't get me wrong. We are both shy when it comes to certain topics but the way I feel about you, about us, the degree to which I'm confident of this feeling and I'll admit that making love to you would just be a natural consequence. Are you ready for a marathon phone call tonight?

Christoph

I took advantage of our time difference and him not calling by spending the afternoon reviewing images I had previously pulled for another process of elimination.

Eventually I received an instant message from him.

Baby . . . too much champagne sucks. Sorry, I didn't call. I fell asleep.

Returning to retouching, I was interrupted again, by an unexpected knock at the door. The doorman always notified me first with a visitor.

"You just show up at my apartment? What a surprise!"

"I was in the neighborhood," Stephanie stepped inside.

"I stopped by earlier, but the doorman said you were out and you weren't answering your phone." She walked inside while studying the disaster on my desk and a blank computer screen. "I guess you're too busy for your best friend?" Her obvious sarcasm didn't go unnoticed.

I wouldn't tell her about my date with Mary. I knew she would lecture me on how the secretary wasn't a substitute. "I had errands to run for the gallery," I lied.

"Well, I'm here to take you for a surprise," she said showing her teeth, hoping I wouldn't put up a struggle.

"For what?" I asked.

"Do you need the definition of a surprise?"

"No, but—"

"I insist, Chloe," she pushed.

"Is this an intervention?" I joked. Living in one room made the front door accessible and I considered making a run for it. I knew she would remain in my apartment until I returned to face the reason I had taken a spontaneous run.

We walked to Tribeca, arm in arm, chatting and sipping our foamy cappuccinos. Stephanie's source of light, her heart, created a beauty about her parallel to photography. The girl I had met almost ten years ago, the Minnesotan, was a true one of a kind. That afternoon, her love bared the woman she was and would always be. She taught me unconditional love, something I'd always hoped my mother would learn, since she didn't exhibit it naturally within her maternal role.

"When you take a picture you're exposing it to light. All photography is captured light. Without the light, there is no picture," I explained while we crossed the street. "We don't see things, we see the light reflected off things." My throat was sore from inhaling the numbing air brought by December. Or, maybe it was yelling at Switzerland.

"The camera is your heart," she said.

"Yep. If only I could keep the shutter closed," I admitted causing us to both spit coffee.

"The shutter closes and opens quickly when you're taking a picture?" she gestured the movement with her free hand.

"It's like a curtain that covers the eye of the camera," I continued. "The lens stands in front of the shutter and is the key to seeing it all. When I press the button on my camera, or open my heart," I said while demonstrating, "my camera takes a picture exposing the frame to light, sort of like exposing myself to the outside."

"It's all fascinating. Your passion makes me miss my ballerina days," she frowned. "Well, with the exception of my instructor, Olga." Stephanie once told me how the Russian trainer taught class, even demonstrated technique, with a coffee in one hand and a lit cigarette in the other. Olga could extend her toned leg over her head without a drop of ash hitting the floor.

"The shutter opens exposing the film to light, my heart opens to expose myself to love and, with a blink of an eye, it records whatever is in front of the camera. This sensitivity is the strength that records the experience," I said.

Even though the heart is delicate, its power captures the love reflected from within. These frames with Christoph, I began to believe my shutter was pulling the curtain over my eyes.

She abruptly stopped walking. "Surprise!"

There we were staring into the Swedish design store that contained the frames I desperately wanted to afford for my gallery pieces.

"I know you've had your eye on those frames. I—"

"Stephanie Cudney! What did you do?"

"I called in a favor and the owner is going to lend you three frames to showcase your pieces!"

Stephanie didn't come from money, and as much as The Cudneys were worth, she didn't cringe at the thought of ever returning to what she came from. The converted Manhattanite with a home in the Hampton's and a collection of Hermes Birkin bags the color of a rainbow, never forgot where she came from. She remained humble with everything she now came into. If you looked up the word *humble* in the dictionary, there Stephanie would be holding her Birkin blushingly.

Chapter 24

I stared at my white ceiling from bed, smiling from seeing color while tucked under my covers being it was only 6:13 a.m. This long distance relationship had created a morning person out of me.

"Two and a half months into it?" I asked Christoph noticing my abandoned workstation housing images desperately needing my full attention. I pulled the covers over my head shutting out the world to be in this one moment with him. Although, I still heard the Mac screaming *Get your ass over here!*

"Completely. Wholeheartedly. Yes . . . Any regrets yet, Miss Kassidy?" he asked.

Before I could answer, he spoke again. "I found my forever and I never ever want to let go—Chloe Kassidy, I truly, madly, deeply love you. I wish I knew of something more original to say, but the truth is, there isn't something more original than the true and loyal adaptation of the most meaningful of traditions," he lowered his voice to his seductive whisper.

Sheer panic silenced me.

"I'm truly sorry this makes you question whether or not it's 'normal' or 'rational' to feel this way about someone you've never seen, touched or tasted before, but the truth is, love can be neither normal nor rational. Nothing about us is normal or rational and that's exactly what makes us incredibly unique and special," he persisted.

"Christoph, I think it would be more appropriate to discuss ideas like this in face to face. Can't you understand that?" I asked.

"Ideas?" he laughed. "I'm a writer and a feeler and you should know by now that my words and my writings are who I am . . . my giving you a line, or two or three or five, is like if I stood naked in front of you; no safety nets, no back-ups, just me; unprotected, unpretentious, as real and as close to you as ever," he said.

It was only a matter of seconds, we sat there speechless, but I swear it felt like watching an ice cube melt while waiting for his next words. It brought flashbacks from when I was a kid competing against my cousins to see who stayed underwater the longest. When I sensed hyperventilation, my legs began kicking and arms pushing the water in an upward movement attempting to buy more time. I instantly pushed the duvet off me.

"And you know what? It sucks you choose not to talk about it. It sucks because it took a lot of guts for me to share in the first place, and it sucks how even though you should be more concerned with making me believe it's okay to share, you were more scared about saying too much and so you end up saying too little," he ranted. "Of all people—I would have thought," he sighed. "I would have thought you would understand exactly how vulnerable one feels when sharing his heart."

"I see what you're saying. I know vulnerability can make one fragile and that's why I worry about being badly hurt—that I might lose a part of myself," I said. "And maybe never get it back. To feel incomplete is suffering," I admitted. "I do understand," I continued, knowing this answer wasn't profound enough for him.

"I have—" he whispered. "I haven't contradicted who I am or my principles in any way. Never having said the phrase 'I love you' doesn't mean that I cannot acknowledge my soul starting to fall in love with the substance, truthfulness and quality of the heart and existence of another person."

"Christoph, the L-word terrifies me and I—"

"Who refers to love as an L-word?" he snarled. "Because the L-word is exactly what this world needs to start working on becoming better," he pointed out. The frustration caused his breathing to sound serious as he spit his words. "You know, Chloe, the L-word is so unique, so personal, so 'yours and yours alone' that if you don't have it inside of you, no one can judge you, no one can blame you, and no one should expect that from you."

My brain switched to bodyguard mode working to draw together my best comebacks, however, Christoph stole my turn.

"My L-word is also mine, and just mine. I cannot have any sort of expectations from you—I have all sorts of expectations from myself," he said. "While you don't know, I do, and maybe sometimes knowing means being strong and kind-hearted enough to let go simply because, I do want you to experience this great, crazy feeling those books talk about, and if you haven't gotten a glimpse of it in my whispers and the variations of my European voice, then you should probably keep looking and keep allowing yourself to explore the dimensions of this mysterious land, called, life."

Woah!

"A life lived without a plan . . . usually the most beautiful of things come unexpectedly," he spoke softly.

"Don't be upset with me," I begged.

"Why is falling in love conceived by you as an act of self-sacrifice? You don't fall in love to please someone else or satisfy their ego, as a matter of fact, we don't have a choice as to how, for who, when or why we fall in love and that's why it's an inexplicably amazing feeling. Jesus, I love you, Chloe!"

"Chr—"

"And for the record, there is risk to every part of love," he said. Then he was gone.

From: Christoph Kostas

To: Chloe Kassidy, Mum

Subject: Mum meet Chloe.

Date: December 17, 11:03 a.m.

Hi Mum,

I know you're probably sleeping. I wish this happened differently because it's a moment I'll always cherish, but I don't want to wait any longer, and if these are the circumstances I have, I'll be an engineer of life and I'll work with what I have. Mum, this is Chloe, my Chloe. The first woman I have ever talked to you about, the first woman who's made me cry out of despair, and made me laugh out of unbearable joy, the woman who I know without a doubt that I'll love forever. I've hurt her already in the brevity of our lifetime together, but I've also guided her, I've disappointed her to the extent that she at times doubted my feelings for her, but I've also inspired her. I've made her cry, but I've also made her smile genuinely and deeply. And Mum, I absolutely adore her to the extent that I'm incapable, weak, incompetent and lifeless without her.

Chloe, this is my mum. She's the reason I'm who I am, I can dream the way I dream and love the way I love. She's the world's most selfless and giving individual. She's my rock, my sanity, my shelter, and my world. I want nothing more than for my mum to see how much you mean to me, and for you, Chloe, to show my mum that her boy has found his buddy who'll always be by his side, no matter what. I'm sorry I'm putting you on the spot. I'm allowing my mum to get a glimpse of us, but I need her blessing.

Mum, thank you for teaching me love heals everything and love is all there is. By loving, one isn't less of a person for giving his heart away, but more of a person for being courageous enough to do it.
Love,
Christoph

The mention of his mother made me panic-stricken. This relationship wasn't 100% part of my world in a physical sense, and the fact he was invisible, the fact that Stephanie, Mary and now his mom were tangled up in this fairy tale that wasn't even in full swing caused me to punch my couch. *Get a grip.* Here was this audience now reading our story when I wasn't ready to write the next chapter until I met the main character. I had lost complete control of this convoluted connection. He created multiple strings attached to us that pulled me away from what truly needed my attention. His words dropped me to my knees while they squeezed through these tiny holes in my heart like a chunk of Swiss cheese. All the pieces of me so internally compartmentalized bled together. My brain was in my throat, my voice in my stomach, and the toxic souvenirs in my heart hemorrhaged throughout me. Nothing was protected. The words that made me want him also weakened me. A place where the dark shadows of myself grew stronger and my fear, the authority, sending out soldiers of insecurity to lose the battle against my most required life sustaining organ.

Christoph had spent the last two weeks in La Chaux-de-Fonds in a State Department Youth Program that brought together the world's future leaders. As a Peace Studies scholar and a practitioner in the field, they had brought him in to teach the conflict resolution curriculum.

I admired him for knowing with hard work, dedication, and a genuine spirit we can achieve little miracles. I soon hoped we would be strolling along a tree lined street, holding his arm and thinking *Yes, it's possible*, of smiling and feeling that today is a new day, a day that has the potential of being the best day ever, of loving and knowing that by loving someone you disarm them, not because they're scared of you, but exactly because they are not.

Today was going to be a remarkable day. There were fifty-one days remaining to opening night. Christoph would be back in my time zone within a week.

Chapter 25

The phone alarmed me during the middle of the night, "Good morning, beautiful," his unmistakable voice said.

"You better be calling to say you're on a flight home," I mumbled sluggishly.

"I'm meeting up with the ambassador tomorrow afternoon to negotiate. He said he wants to close this deal before I leave on the twenty-third. My flight is on the twenty-second and lands around five o'clock that next morning."

"That's cutting it close!"

"It will work out fine," he assured me. "We can go for breakfast and I can send you off safely. By the way, it would be nice if we had a summer house here as it's breathtaking."

"What?" I asked. I was now awake. "Christoph, you're not back to secure a coffee date and you're speaking of summer homes in Europe? Please let's not be complicated. Let's be simple until then," I begged.

"Great . . . Do your friends know we're together?"

Here we go.

"Don't you think you're putting the cart before the horse?" I sighed.

"What horse?" he asked.

"You want me to be an open book about us and let the world read our story like a free Kindle download," I said.

"I'm pissed off with your rudeness to me. You need to stop with this behavior," he yelled. His voice now carried hints of a threatening tone.

"I'm just . . . sensitive when I open up and get no clear answer from you whatsoever," I said. "I'm not sure we are ever going to happen?"

"I know we're too much alike. That's what makes us extremely intense chemistry-wise, as well as arguing-wise," he poked. "But, Chloe . . . I'm the idiot who puts himself out there, who makes plans out loud, who calls you his wife between a joke and seriousness . . . and you're the smart one who never commits, who doesn't make important statements, who holds back because she knows better," he said.

"You're the most dramatic coffee date I've ever not been on a date with," I said, realizing the absurdity while gently massaging my temples. I noticed traces of my scribbled reminder on my palm while it moved in a circular soothing motion. *Perspective.*

His romantic stance annoyed me. Our issues were a consequence of one distinct cause that could be resolved by a direct solution.

"I want to Skype now and with the camera!"

"We can if you must do this," he sighed. "Now that my constant travel schedule is ending, please don't make Skype the first time we see each other. How unromantic and insincere that would be, although I thought our separate lives are already pretty prosaic."

"I need you to ensure me that I'm communicating with a real person, then perhaps I wouldn't get upset with the obstacles that constantly interrupt our plans," I continued.

Even with his love, there was a clear line that divided us— fantasy and reality.

I didn't want to be the one who gave up on love, this *beautiful thing we bumped into*. He pointed out the distance, time, and never meeting wasn't in vain, but might be a great test of the strength of our connection.

"If we can't be better and stronger than not talking eight hours per day, then maybe we're not as magical as we both thought ourselves to be," he proposed. "Separation makes me love you more, makes me crave for you more, makes me miss you."

He sometimes cornered me with his tendency to argue, like I fought against this universal fate, something working for both of us when we lost hope in destiny.

"Chloe, can't you see that no matter what you do to distract yourself, trying to escape me and the thought of me, that I'm still going to be there?"

"Part of the reason I can't escape is that you've become a controversial topic of conversation and a growing conflict among my friends."

"Why do they care about me anyways? They barely even know me. You don't talk about me because you're private. You're still claiming to be single because you're too uncomfortable with explaining the situation to anyone. You're happy about your new career. You have your art fans. I don't understand why they care."

"Why is it difficult for you to understand that my friends love me? That I value their opinion?"

It wasn't about loving someone who's safer, less intense, who doesn't drive me crazy. For him not being worthy of my time or energy. It was about him deserving first place in my heart.

"I'm just a horrible person who has always wanted to hurt you and play with you."

"Those are your words, Christoph." I wanted him to be this person I believed him to be. I knew I'd fought for this and us against his excuses and people. I was done with running in circles only to stop, be hurt and then start running again. "We've both been hurt," I reminded him.

"I told you many times in the past, as much as I love you, I'll never try to convince you to love me, to be thinking of me, to be crazy about me and us. That's one thing—the only thing—that should be happening naturally. It is the one thing—the only thing—that distinguishes relationships from 'relationships,' love from lust and habit, partnership from plain co-existence, growth from aging, us from everyone else."

"Listen, I have to wake up each morning and make the best out of every good or bad decision, every good or bad moment, every good or bad occurrence. February seventh is my moment of do or die. I've been waiting for this opportunity since my delivery room debut thirty years ago," I said.

"I understand you. Although, you need to understand that, as much as I understand you, I'm still me, and I do still possess the reasoning that I do, for better or worse. I don't have the right to ask you to sit there and wait, be sad or frustrated, be intense vis-a-vis me," he said.

"I . . . want you to do what feels fit for you, what makes you smile, because you do have a wonderful smile."

That was exactly the kind of wording I couldn't handle while he traveled. I needed him to park his butt in a chair with two coffees.

"You don't have to respond to this . . . I don't want either one of us to feel stupid for opening up, for investing in us, for daydreaming, for believing in soul mates. If I never have another thing, I would still have everything for loving you," Christoph declared.

I didn't want to get hurt. I didn't want to be love's fool. I didn't want to make a mistake thinking of him to be something he isn't just because I want to find that person desperately.

"Chloe, but I know. And you know how? Because your faults are such that I love you still the better for them," he continued.

Emma's soul mate theories on how the signs Aquarius and Aries relate to each other possibly may hold weight in this matter. Christoph Kostas, Mr. Aries, didn't ask permission or approval from the world to feel, act or create. He set the standards of his own life. If everyone else understood, that's great, if not, he felt that's why people are designed to create little circles: those include only the people who get it. All the rest cannot understand, by nature and virtue. If they did, that would upset the balance and order of the world and good society. It would play into his *Everything happens for a reason* theory.

I was Atlanta bound in two days. We would be two ladies and a baby U-hauling our way to Southern Exposure. Emma was a bit fragile with her life changing decision and I wanted to support her with driving by her side.

We decided Central Park was the most suitable for a going away gathering before heading to Emma's apartment to help pack up the remaining boxes into the truck. We settled on a picnic table under the sun-filled sky with hints of a possible storm. It was unusually warm for December. We took turns teasing Emma about how a sane person would never leave New York City. I began taking pictures capturing natural shots and recording memories for not only Emma, but also Lily while reminding Alexander to stop posing. I imagined her heading to college and her mother sharing stories of her Big Apple adventures with her extra aunts and uncles.

Click. Click. Click.

"Because 'fuck' is intrinsic to our local dialect," Kate pointed out.

"Because there's a Starbucks on every block," Stephanie followed.

"Because New Yorkers drink at lunch," Kate added. She raised her plastic cup and sipped competing with Stephanie.

"Because of the restaurants! The food is a phenomena," Stephanie announced.

This reason transported me back to that peaceful evening with Reed eating dumplings. I took a sip of my wine and hoped for a taste of chili martini.

"Because city kids have been there and done that before they reach five," Alexander added.

"Because we worship high fashion in collapsible tents. Fashion forward, hello? Enough said," Stephanie winked.

"Depending on the neighborhood, you can spend your afternoon or evening in Paris, Italy, Russia, in the park with a hotdog or at a quaint table street side," Kate added. Her fact was worthy of a brow raise since she would never eat a hotdog.

"Because there are plenty of great men who are looking for women like you," Alexander said. Before Kate could interrupt him. "Just don't close your eyes when you open your heart. You're going to miss him walking right by."

I wanted to change the subject. "Best damn manicures in less than ten minutes, and making your own coffee will be a burden you placed on yourself willingly," I said.

Emma added, "Because you don't have to drive." Only we understood that being from Atlanta. Interstate 400 was a sure way of receiving an early checkout on life by a Ford F150. Whatever genius created seven lanes of car chaos obviously didn't live in a driving city.

Hesitant to answer Christoph's call, I knew this would be our final long distance chat before his touchdown in New York. The closeness made me nervous, but I couldn't deal with another delay. "Sorry, guys, I need to take this call," I shivered and walked to put distance between us.

"Hi, Beautiful."

"Hey there," I responded. I wondered if Stephanie had confirmed Chef Roberts travel schedule for the holidays.

"Speaking of beautiful things, tomorrow one of my many, many cousins is getting married and everyone's eagerly anticipating the festivities. There's a huge car parade from the bride and groom's house respectively to the church. All cars drive in line and all drivers press the horn repeatedly to announce a wedding to the city."

"A wedding in Geneva sounds dreamy. Who's your date?" I teased.

"Not funny, Kassidy," he said. "My Dad asked me if I had brought a tux because I just found out about the nuptials yesterday."

Who travels around with a tux?

Immediately, I recalled a picture he had emailed me from a diplomatic dinner dressed in a black suit, collar up and hair messy. I blushed at the thought of him in the monochrome jpeg flashing a devilish grin. Even a black and white image, his eyes were accentuated. A spirit that glittered and seemed it might explode from his delicate soul any moment. His constant need for reassurance and insecure behavior rang odd for a man who was too gorgeous to be a UN official and more suitable for a European heartthrob. Enrique Iglesias didn't have a thing on him, mole or not.

"Imagine the poor couple, standing there and smiling for about a thousand guests," Christoph said.

"Send me pictures. I would love to see a Switzerland wedding," I said. "I love to watch when love is put into action." I didn't have a thing to lose at this point except for this pleasant conversation. "Sometimes, I fear you only know how to love in theory," I admitted.

His whisper quickly turned into a matter-of-fact tone, "I only know how to love in theory? Even if that were true, Chloe, then you should sit and realize how I was able to give you more love in theory than anyone ever has," he said. Perhaps, European men were blessed with charm, sophistication and a sex-receiving accent because, as I learned, they could be arrogant.

His words had become dark alleys and I couldn't find my way out. His words pained me as I had never met anyone to match him. I looked for him to shut up and show up for me.

"You're my soul mate. You just suck when you act on your own, Chloe."

"I need to go," I sobbed while the tears formed teams for another emotional tournament. "I'm with my friends."

"Are you testing my theory? You're my dream come true. Jesus, Chloe."

"Please—I have to go, Christoph," I begged.

"If you were my soul mate, according to my theory, you'd be crying now. If you're not, then my theory is either mistaken, or you're just not my other half," he trembled.

"I'm upset because I've been an idiot," I cried. I was an emotional basket case that felt stuck in a constant state of PMS with severe bouts of crying, pain and irritability.

"How could I ever write about love before experiencing it? And how would I find it this early on when people have died without ever bumping into it?" he asked.

"Stop being a lawyer, Christoph. I'm not on trial for your behavior."

"Should I forget about the dreams I've made about us, Chloe? Let go and leave you alone? Just forget about you and never contact you again?" he asked.

"You're unfair. How can you not understand my feelings? How your actions are hurting me?"

"I'm hurting you? Wow . . ." he mumbled. "My heart isn't a shop to which you can walk in and out, Miss Kassidy."

I hated him, then I wanted him, then I hated him, then I craved him again. My only option was to hang up, which would land me in diplomat detention.

Chapter 26

My parents weren't thrilled anymore than I was about my driving the white and orange box truck. I prepared by taking a couple of days to study the operating instructions before our trip and had 1-800-GO-UHAUL programmed into my phone for emergencies.

While he passed through the clouds, I prayed our meeting would go as intended. For this planned date, I didn't bother to tell my friends. I knew they would throw a fit and forbid it. Emma and I were Atlanta bound at 8:00 p.m. to escape traffic. Hitting the highway before morning rush hour was impossible if Emma would make it out of the truck alive. Caffeine, a full stomach, or the anticipation of a trip, couldn't shake my grogginess before sunrise.

I received an update from Christoph and fell numb.

Landed in NYC. Stuck at customs. Visa issue. Can't use phone. Call soon.

I wasn't sure if I was calm because I expected something to occur or that it didn't matter with my nine day Christmas trip ahead.

Since I wouldn't be waiting on him to return, I felt less pathetic and less eager to throw accusations.

I cursed the thought of having a glass half full attitude. I believed most would say the glass was empty and advise me to throw it at him. I imagined Kate, "Aim for his balls!"

I would focus on the bittersweet moment for all of us with Emma moving home to Atlanta. Emma decided that Manhattan single life and searching for her soul mate wasn't her main priority and that maybe her true love would find her wherever she was in the world.

With fifteen minutes until our departure, I frantically finished up sanitizing the steering wheel and seatbelt while Emma studied herself in the oversized vanity side mirror.

"A little help, please?" I teased.

"These seats aren't that comfortable," Emma complained. She fidgeted around in the static ninety degree captain chair. "Can you believe these seats don't recline?"

"What about Lily's comfort?" I asked causing us to both stare at the large space between our chairs where her car seat would be situated. Emma's nervous expression sent me straight into sending a prayer request. *Please let her sleep.*

"She loves road trips!" Emma continued as she lifted Lily up into the captain chair and secured her in the car seat. "I have plenty of toys, snacks and a movie set up on my iPad."

I pulled myself up into the driver seat and snapped my belt into the buckle. Alexander tapped on my window and signaled to roll it down.

"Chloe, remember that you have about two additional inches of width on each side," he said and pointed to the back of the truck while I observed in my review mirror.

"Need moving help?" Kate sang. "We've got your back! It's not too late! At your destination?"

I realized she was reading the side of the truck.

"Also, be careful around semi trucks. They'll flash their break lights to pass and that's to say 'thank you' . . . Okay?" Alexander asked.

"Did you get that tip from the movie theater wall?" I joked.

"Nope. Brad the Dad," he said. "And avoid truck stops," he continued. "Stop at well-lit places that are crowded. It will be safer."

Christoph should have been the man standing outside my truck window teaching me these safety tips. He should have been the one caring and making me better prepared. I felt dumb for believing in us.

While we pulled away from the curb waving our arms out the window at Kate, Stephanie and Alexander, a camera flash caught my eye. Kate documented this and I knew it wasn't Emma's departure she was focused on, but me steering a truck. Either way, this was one photo I didn't mind being on the other side of the lens. I pushed the horn and with the squeaky honk we were twenty-five seconds into our sixteen and half hour journey. Holding the wheel, I repositioned my grip and wondered what other journeys had taken place in this exact truck.

"Wow . . . it sort of feels like we're sitting on top a washing machine, right?" Emma laughed.

Oh dear.

We sang the lyrics to *Take me Home* and *On the Road Again*. Emma claimed my singing was more *Acrapella* and that I should stick with photography.

"Maybe it's not looking for love, but love finding you. Love works for itself and no one else," she said. "Your soul mate isn't about the other person—but your own soul," she shared. She stared out the window, distracted by another thought. Maybe, there was more to this story for moving home than she admitted. I wouldn't push. I was guilty of keeping secrets.

This lesson came from a collection of obstacles and choices she was blessed to see and learn from. It was tricky to grasp, but Emma's soul mate saga connected her to herself, and that's what is required to attract her one true love. Maybe I had been conceiving this wrong. I had forgotten about me in the process, my own soul in the search. Rather than feeling unlucky in love, maybe I asked myself the wrong questions. Instead of asking, *Why is he doing this?* I should be asking, *What can I learn from Christoph?* and move on like she did from her disastrous dating record. I put my heart into it and I could take it back out. Christoph was right, perhaps, there wasn't a choice when it came to true love. The heart only knows and feels what it does. That might be absolutely true, but that doesn't give him permission to hurt me.

"I think we all get a little blinded by the fairy tale," I admitted.

"I'm not sure what you mean?" Emma tried to fake a puzzled expression, but she couldn't help but laugh with me.

We had judged Emma for her mistakes. She wasn't senseless, but she wasn't making the best choices either, and she knew it. The look in her eyes occasionally during the drive that night sent a wave of shame through me. *Who was I to judge her?* She wanted a partner to share her life. In the end, we all wanted to be loved. *But, how far would I go to be with my soul mate? Did signs and coincidences determine who that was?* I knew there had to be more than an attractive list that charmed me from paper. Life might be full of coincidences and luck, or what she referred to as *manifested intentions* and desires, but the bottom line was you had to choose well. Love wasn't a hard choice. It was a natural one.

The wide road opened further offering a sense of freedom. The further we drove, the lighter I became. We had reached North Carolina and decided it was time for another pee break.

Christoph's last text read, *Call me please!*

"Hey," he sighed. "Are you still driving?"

"We have four hours left," I said waiting for an explanation.

"I'm sorry we missed each other. I can't believe this, honestly," he said. "It was horrible getting through customs. This bizarre issue with my Visa."

"I'm fed up with your fancy stories!" I screamed. "Just be honest, Christoph! Just be straightforward with me."

"Why does Stephanie, or you for that matter, hope me to be this honest man? Don't you know by now what kind of person I am? Don't you know my deepest dreams, my biggest fears, what makes me laugh, what makes me mad, what makes me hopeless," he said. "You know me inside out!"

He always knew the words that would take my heart hostage. It's what I desperately wanted to believe in. My gut and heart were at war and I wondered when my rational hat would call surrender. The e-mail tennis grew tiresome. If only the ball boy would stop the back and forth and force a truce.

"And you don't know what my smile looks like or that I tend to gaze into the horizon when something is bothering me. You don't know how I walk or what my touch feels like, what I smell like. Those things, though, the ones you don't know of, are not things that make a person, but rather things that make someone visible socially," Christoph continued.

I would believe he graduated at the top of his law class. He argued you to exhaustion and turned your thinking cap backwards causing you to point the finger at yourself.

I signaled to Emma for one minute while she hoisted Lily and herself into the truck. I still couldn't believe I drove the vehicle that was now filling up at pump number four. Her life packed and bubble wrapped entirely in my hands. *Christ.* Look how I handled my own.

"Why do you still hope for me to be this person, when you know I am?" he asked.

"Know who you are?" I laughed. "Everything you say you are, your actions prove otherwise."

"Why do you still hope for me to be this person when you're supposed to love this person already?"

It was my turn to the stand. "How am I the one not making sense?" I argued, offended by his cross-examination.

"Because you're asking me to prove myself, you're asking me to help you see that I'm the person you're supposed to know and love already no matter what. This is new to you—you hate losing control. It's like you hate being the girl in a relationship, and you don't trust yourself during this 'loving mode.'"

He often referred to this *loving mode* and how it was unfamiliar territory for me. Once he admitted without a doubt, that, "You've never, never loved before, Chloe." From the beginning he hesitated on whether I would be able to fall in love. Whether my love would be stronger than my desire to always be powerful and in control. I started to see that this was how he forced my guard down further. I worked to prove I could fall in love, but this only proved how powerful and in control he was.

After everything, was it too much to ask him to pick up the damn phone and scream, "I'm here! Meet me here!"

"This drama is going to be over just like I told you, Chloe."

"I need to get us back on the road. It's been a long trip and I can't do this now. It's Christmas and I need to be with my family and Emma."

"Okay, if that's what you need."

"I'll call you when I'm back in New York. Perhaps, then we can finally put all these questions behind us and have that coffee." The truth was I didn't know if I would give him another chance.

"Okay, honey. Please drive safe," he said.

As we ventured onto the seven lane interstate, Emma set up my coffee and secured the lid tab back. "What? No wine?" I joked.

"Two Splenda and a splash of half and half," she smiled. She reached into the paper bag, "I also thought you could use these," she said pulling out a bag of Bits of Honey candy. "You've been pensive. I know how these cheer you up."

"Even better!" I gushed. We both unwrapped the sticky candy and began to chew.

"You know . . . love and wine are sort of the same. To fully enjoy it, you gotta open your heart—" She quickly caught a drip of drool interrupting her moment.

"Gross!" I screamed.

"This rubbish is impossible to eat," she said, spitting it into a napkin. "To fully enjoy love, you gotta open your heart and let it breathe," she continued.

Friendship had many wonderful parts and her knowing my favorite possessions no matter how small and trivial, meant the world to me. The obsessions that only people close to you could know. Ironically, Christoph didn't know how I loved these hard to chew candies and how they immediately redirected my worries to the tension in my teeth, giving my mind and thumb a break. Christoph was unaware of my candy codependency. I think he thought he was my answer to everything.

While I stared out into the stretched highway before us, I realized that I never thought to buy him a Christmas present.

We crossed state lines into Georgia, and I embraced the warmth of the winter season here and not the never-ending drive. I estimated our arrival time at 11:00 a.m. "Toto—" I paused, realizing we were home for Emma. That was the point of the U-Haul soon to pull into my parent's driveway.

"Are you looking forward to seeing your parents?" Emma asked.

"Yes, of course." With the realization that Manhattan was 748 miles away I abruptly ached to whip this thing around and double time it back to the North. "I have the exhibit to diffuse any awkward moments between them or convincing my mother snapping pictures is my passion when she breaks into her scenarios of how I'm not understanding one of her many meltdowns."

"I remember how she would leave those article clippings for you," Emma said. "Your personal letter box would be stuffed when we would visit from college. Why wouldn't she just mail them to you?" Emma puzzled.

In the kitchen of my parent's home was a shelf divided into three boxes where my mother would deliver her daily tips to my father and me. Her box remained empty as my father and I never participated in her clipping chaos. As I grew older, so did the subjects of the articles. When I turned twenty-six, my box became superfluous with pieces covering the *Death of fertile eggs* and my risk of *Infertility on the rise* according to *Redbook* and *Ladies Home Journal* magazine. When I turned twenty-nine, she grew overwhelmingly concerned that my relationship status was stuck on single. The now inappropriate clippings such as *Ten ways to turn him on* filled my designated mailbox. I cringed at the image of my father getting his own mail and seeing words like *clitoris* with his morning coffee or *blowjob* while he ate breakfast.

I guided the truck onto the Sandy Springs exit, with only nine miles remaining until our final destination, my parents. Entering into the neighborhood lined with Southern style homes splashed with Christmas cheer, we saw mine, the sixth house on the right. My mother's holiday decorating added splashes of color to the modest white house with black shutters. I gradually pulled into the driveway, careful not to get too close to my father's new SUV or the row of shimmering candy canes that lined the path. Our first road trip seemed a success as I had steered clear of any complications. I wanted to end the journey on a high note. Not with a dent or adding further damage to my mother's decorating. The house remained unchanged with its approachable relaxing and traditional porch that wrapped around the front displaying the wicker seating area. There were many childhood memories of late night cookouts with neighbors, sleepovers, a pyramid of bikes in the driveway, Sunday mornings filled with my friends eating pancakes, and afternoons on the porch with popsicles. Yes, it resembled a picture perfect home that passersby and visitors might wish they lived in. Yet, my retouching skills couldn't enhance the brightness of my family's problematic interior. Oddly, the only smiles of my parents I remember were the ones that were simultaneously practiced and hung along the staircase hallway. *Say cheese.*

I felt my heels click 1-2-3 against the brake wondering if I could pull a Dorothy and be back in New York. "Girls!" my mother yelled, waving from the front porch.

"Hi, Alice!" Emma waved energetically. My mother's ink black hair was twisted up in her signature bun accentuating her jewel framed reading glasses. Her lips pressed together while her gaze that studied the truck let me know she wondered how I had accomplished this mission. She was rather tan for winter.

As we unloaded ourselves to solid ground, my father joined us in the driveway. "Finally, you're home," he said with a tone that I'd come to my senses and moved out of a crime and drug environment. Almost a year had passed since my last visit when I noticed my father's chestnut brown hair turning silver gray with thinning sides. His recent crew cut and freshly shaven face exposed his bright smile further. My genes resembled a fair balance between my parents.

We exchanged hugs. "Now Dad, Emma is moving back. I'm only here for nine days," I reminded him.

"What are you going to do with all these boxes once you're done?" he asked. He loathed wasting anything. This characteristic could be picked up on from eating a meal with him, to his toothpaste tube, to the condiment bottles turned upside down in the refrigerator.

"I can't believe you drove all the way here," my mother yelled. She remained on the porch with my memories, waiting like a well-trained dog that never left her routine. The sight saddened me since she talked her whole life of seeing the world, but she never traveled further than the conversation.

"It was an adventure for Lily," I responded. I noticed Emma's face tense like she was the cause for a negative experience that my mother had invented in her mind. The comment caused Emma to pause as she unbuckled Lily from the car seat.

We followed my father up the steps as he brought in our luggage, complimenting the garland with lights and a decorated chalkboard that displayed *Happy Holidays* as we crossed the *Welcome* mat. The smoky smell of burning wood pulled us into the living room. My mother went heavy on the garland this year, and I imagined my father waking up extra early to clean out Home Depot's holiday supply. The over decorated, lit tree was covered with various sized and shaped red, green and gold ornaments, while a thick red velvet ribbon waved in and out of every crevice. Every inch was covered and every space filled. The tree was ready to burst.

We gathered in the kitchen. The large poinsettias were strategically placed while several candles from Yankee Candle burned with scents of gingerbread. Emma and I both spotted the unidentifiable fruit pie arranged along with holiday tableware decorated with words like *Joy* and *Peace*.

I could only hope.

"It's peach cobbler," my mother pointed out. "Where shall we grab lunch, Chloe? I hope you'll be joining us, Emma?" slathering more lipstick over the already fresh application. My mother was a teacher who always had her hair blown out, a heaping scoop of blush across her cheeks, and completely over dressed for every single occasion. She flipped her hair while she turned to us for a response. "Emma, you'll join us won't you? We haven't seen Lily—"

"What?" I asked wondering why she paused.

"Lily!" Emma said and jumped up to grab one of the plastic candy canes out of her mouth that had lined the driveway. "Sorry, Alice."

"It's fine," I interrupted. "She didn't hurt anything."

"I was saying that we haven't seen Lily since she was born," my mother continued while she pinched Lily's cheek. I tried to measure her sincerity.

Checking my emails, I received an International update, but promised myself I would only open with no reply. I was home and would make the most of it by not spending day after day face down into this device.

"Chloe, put that thing away and decide on a restaurant," my father interrupted.

"Sorry, Mrs. Kassidy, little Lily needs to go for a nap," Emma responded while giving Lily a glare to almost hypnotize her to misbehave since it had been a full ten minutes with my mother, but I wasn't counting. Eating with Alice was dinner theater, but she made sure she was the center of attention. The show was always a rerun from her past and it exhausted everyone.

"My parent's are coming to pick us up," Emma continued. My dad is going to drive the truck to my new apartment. We have to unload the truck, but thank you for the invitation," Emma said.

"I'll come by tomorrow and help you get settled into your new place," I said.

"It's the least you could do," Emma winked. "It's Christmas." We laughed. "You guys should try that new sushi spot down the street," Emma suggested.

"Sushi sounds great." I said.

My mother followed with a million questions, "Sushi? Why? I read this new article on mercury and—"

"Sushi it is," my Dad interrupted. He ignored my mother's high maintenance huffs and puffs. "She just drove through the night." He shot me a wink.

He was a man of few words since being a numbers guy left him a bit antisocial. Don't get me wrong, he loved people. He loved reading about them and responding to them when in a group situation, but he preferred the quality of his friends rather than the quantity of a social club. He preferred numbers since they were silent.

Over my life, I'd witnessed my parent's marriage lose life with each passing year. Yet, they had stuck together. When my mother spoke of loving my father, it was always a story from the past that caused her to smile. At the age of seventeen, my father had shown up at my mother's house when she was sixteen, with a new royal blue bicycle, sparkly streamers dangling from the handlebars and a daisy basket for the final touch. It was a gift for her birthday. My fathers' determination to win my mother's heart had been the frame of my parents' marriage my mother held, the gift that made her feel desired.

With photography, the scene was my focus. The lens and scene played tug of war. It's emotionless until the frame is provoked, comparable to the heart and head until love comes along. I slowly scanned the scenery until I found the one thing that made it deem authentic. I favored serene over chaotic. Like love, sometimes our hearts are pulled towards it, exposed and we can only choose to see one frame versus the entire album. We choose the ones that present a more pleasant experience to remember.

There are many layers to photography. So much occurs within the tiny frame that a photographer must get into that lens, that depth. I decided the final outcome, what I chose to create for the final print. It was whatever I desired, and others would only see what I wanted them to, not the entirety of what I had been exposed to. I scanned for something that made it bear truth. Whether it was chaotic or serene, my heart and my hardware were my guides. Just like the blue bicycle for my mother and the truth in their marriage.

The depth of field is when we look at an image, there's a part that's in absolute focus and then there are parts that begin to be out of focus. You can have a small depth of field where only your subject is in focus, or you can have a deep depth of field where everything is in focus. Somehow, my life choices lately created both my surroundings and myself out of focus.

Chapter 27

Sometimes, when I woke up, I wondered if Christoph would be lying beside me. That this was all a nightmare. I would turn over and there would be his sleeping foreign features creating contrast with his unshaven cheeks against my sheets. His smell and scratchy throat from talking all night like teenagers under the covers. His broad shoulders, the long crease in his chest and fingers marked with ink from his book writing, there for me to pinch, to grab and never let go. To lie next to each other with our bodies bent, not knowing where mine would end and his would begin. He would say, "Good morning, baby," in his soft sleepy voice. *Yes. When I open my eyes, he will be there. He was always there.*

My body woke up extra early seeing that my internal clock buzzed with Christmas spirit. At thirty years old the magical feeling of *Tis the season* still fluttered in my chest. The story of Santa was one of those tales that, at the appropriate age, we eventually come to understand he's nothing but another man in a fancy suit. *I swear I will never lie to my kids.* Even with the truth and at my age, Christmas Day was still enchanting. I might not celebrate the make believe Santa, but it was enough to still believe in the kind and generous idea of him.

The aroma of coffee pulled me downstairs to the kitchen where I found my parents. It didn't represent a Folgers's commercial one bit. My mother sat at the island eating small bites of muffin while grading papers. My father hid behind the newspaper, occasionally swallowing his brown, flakey scrambled eggs. My mother didn't know how to cook eggs without serving the burnt film from the excessive nonstick spray. I would bet that his eggs were extra brown from yesterday's sushi recommendation.

"How did you sleep?" she asked while pushing back her reading glasses to the top of her head.

"Good," I said while stretching out my neck. I realized first hand that a U-Haul didn't do a body good.

"You sleep late," she said. Her acrylic French painted nails clicked the counter with each crumb as she pressed to pick them up. "I woke up at five-thirty and tried to be quiet not to wake you."

"Didn't hear a thing," I said searching the refrigerator. "What time is it?" I asked. Her competitiveness didn't take holidays off.

"It's eight fifty-three," my father answered. He folded the paper and returned to his breakfast. "Want some?" he grinned.

"I had a dream about pie," I said. I cut and slid a large triangle onto a plate and poured a cup of coffee. *The best part of waking up, is . . .*

"Yes, please help your father eat it. I don't eat sugar," she said.

"Anymore?" I teased.

"I make sure he has a fresh one each week." She rolled her eyes. "He loves his junk food."

The golden brown crust resembled a perfectly knit sweater, a bit fancy for my mother's baking skill level. "You baked this?" I knew she didn't.

"Well, no . . . I . . ." She looked at her overflowing paper pile. "I have to make a trip to the store."

I wanted to savor each bite, but I couldn't with my mouth full of words. I almost choked without taking the first bite. "What's wrong with you?" I asked putting down my fork. My father continued with his eggs and focused his attention towards the window.

"I've had a hard week, Chloe. I think I'm getting sick. Don't pick on me," my mother returned her efforts back to the chicken scratch from her second graders.

"Why are you . . . I don't know, just miserable all the time?" I continued while picking up where I left off with my pie. My Dad remained quiet. He was supportive of my inquiry, but how these two seriously stayed together twisted my serenity in a knot.

They were different, but yet the same. My father was relaxed, quiet, simple and never complained. My mother was tense, pretentious, and whined. She carried baggage, causing situations to end in ways she needn't have. This Christmas morning included. My mother didn't realize she was the victim of her own frustration.

"You don't understand how hard I work. I'm tired . . . I get up at five-thirty every morning, I've been sick, I have these school projects, and—"

"Mom, it's Christmas. This week is a vacation. Why are you working this morning? Why don't you rest and enjoy your—"

"I don't have a week. I have to go into my classroom and remove the Christmas decorations and prepare my lesson plans for January. You don't understand how hard my job is," she continued. "You take pictures!"

At this point, I was at least waiting for my father to intervene since he worked longer hours and didn't have the summer off. He remained quiet. For Christ sakes, he had to deal with tax season. It was easier to let her delusion continue and not rock the boat. His tense expression signaled me to stop. This was his full-time life and just a short visit for me. The fact was they were equal. Insecurity was a tricky trait and a characteristic in both of them. My father strived for comfortable by laying low and just wanting to get by. My mother fought hard to overcompensate for everything she lacked and played each hand with the victim card for any attention. Neither of them knew balance.

"You will get it one day," while she collected her papers and neatly stacked them in the corner. "Everyday isn't some adventure, filled with these 'Aww . . .' moments. Of course life seems the best in the beginning, but reality happens . . . That's a fact." She walked passed me and placed her cup in the sink.

"Bitterness can be expensive, Mom," I said. "Depending on how much time you let it cost you."

"What are you wearing?" she studied me. I guess my mysterious wardrobe of black cotton leggings and wrap didn't suit her holiday dress code while she headed upstairs in her floral print skirt, silk blouse, and chunky jewelry decorated with tiny sunflowers.

No one should have their best moments at the beginning of their lives. I couldn't help but see the similarities in my relationship with Christoph. Maybe I was stuck in a perspective and unable to see anything outside of it.

The touch of my father's hand on my shoulder brought me back to the present moment. "I'm glad you're home honey. We have a great restaurant booked for Christmas dinner," he smiled. "Our reservation is for seven-thirty at Canoe. It's that restaurant tucked away along the banks of the Chattahoochee River," he explained and headed outside to putt golf balls.

Visiting home was the thing to do, even though I preferred a snowy holiday rather than the sunny fifty-four degrees this morning.

The countdown to opening was fast approaching with one month and thirteen days until lights, camera, and an evening of action.

The house became quiet and I was thrilled my Dad had booked a restaurant. Sitting at home made the time pass slower inside my head leaving me in a trance.

I took in the view of the running river while the brightly lit sign, *Canoe*, sparkled in the reflection. I explored the menu options with my taste buds leaping back and forth between the grilled salmon with a squash and carrot sauté or the lamb Bolognese. Looking for my dad's input, "What do you—" and without warning, I saw him at the bar. *What was he doing here?*

"What's that, Chloe?" my Dad asked attempting to trigger my previous train of thought. "They raised their prices," he continued.

"I was . . . I'm . . . what do you think of the salmon?" I continued refocusing my attention to food. *What should I do?*

"Are you okay?" my mother interrupted. "Why are you fidgety?"

"I think I'm going for . . .," I glanced back to the bar and he was gone.

"Good Evening, Miss Kassidy." Practically slapping myself in the chest, he startled me. No surprise disguised his voice. He stood beside me. His soul-piercing eyes caused me to lose my appetite.

"Hello . . . Merry Christmas." I smiled. "This is Reed Scott." I couldn't believe I was introducing him to my parents.

"It's a pleasure to meet you both," Reed said. "You must be very proud of your daughter."

The last thing I needed was my mother on her *She better not quit her real job!* rampage.

"What brings you to Atlanta?" I interrupted.

"My best friend just had a baby. I'm spending the holidays with his family," Reed said. "What a nice surprise bumping into you like this," he smiled. "I don't want to disturb your dinner. Just wanted to say hello and Merry Chris—"

"How nice of you," my mother interrupted while flipping her hair.

"My friends and I will have drinks on the patio if you and your parents," he looked at my father, "would like to join us after dinner."

"Thank you . . . It was nice seeing you," I said.

He touched my shoulder and with one last smile left me with that moment. "Always a pleasure, Miss Kassidy."

"I'm ordering the salmon. What about you guys?" My parents seemed more interested in the man they just met.

"How do you know him?" my father asked.

"He's fond of you," my mother added.

"It's not like that. He's a business contact—I met through the curator."

"The menu isn't expensive," she responded to my father's previous comment.

"He's a business contact," I repeated.

"Whatever you say," my mother muttered.

When the server decanted our wine, it reminded me to breathe myself. *Just breathe, Chloe.*

Reed Scott's gift was his aura, his capacity to convince people and make them confident in what he said, with his advice in Miami I believed in myself again. I prayed my gift was photography.

I placed the red envelope on the table between my parents, "Merry Christmas."

"You can do the honors," my father said to my mother.

"Thank you, honey," she said and tore the seal with one of her acrylic tips. "This is wonderful!" my mother squealed.

"Chloe, that is too expensive. You don't need to spend your money on us," my father interrupted.

I had purchased two Broadway show tickets to *Wicked* for them to attend while in New York City for my exhibit. "It's a spectacular show," I said. "Dad, I wanted to do this."

"I'm thrilled!" My mother said as she secured the tickets in the envelope and placed it in her purse. "I've read the reviews in a magazine. I heard tickets were impossible to get . . . I can't believe we're seeing this show," she continued.

I disregarded my mother's sudden burst of excitement for their February visit.

"That's wonderful, Chloe," my father said. "Now your mother and I get to attend two incredible shows during our trip."

"Thanks, Dad." We smiled while my mother sipped her wine.

My father handed me an envelope decorated with a candy cane pattern.

"Merry Christmas," my parents spoke simultaneously.

I already knew my gift, but each year I opened the envelope with surprise. "How did you know?" I gushed. It was a gift certificate to J. Crew. "Thank you, I love it!"

After dinner I said goodbye to Reed and passed on his invitation for cocktails even though I wished to join him. My visit home was limited and I didn't want my parents to feel neglected or to expose our professional relationship to my mother. We promised each other we would be in touch if we didn't bump into each other again first.

While my father drove us home, I opened Christoph's e-mail. *Don't respond, Chloe.* He had ignored my request not to talk until I returned to New York.

From: Christoph Kostas
To: Chloe Kassidy
Subject: Our holiday tradition.
Date: December 25, 10:17 p.m.

Here are the details in case you want to make it! The pie, it's sweet, made with milk, flour, eggs, sugar, and cinnamon, called in literal translation 'the Santa's pie.' On top, it's decorated with nuts forming the shape of the current calendar year. Supposedly, the third piece, after God and Virgin Mary, is for Santa, then for the family members. Santa's piece is served on a plate and placed on the dining table along with cookies, milk or wine and the family's wallet. The tradition says that when Santa comes in through the fireplace to bring the gifts he will need to rest a little bit, grab a bite and put a blessing on the wallet for a wealthy year.

My heart is yours. It might be a stupid heart but it's still a heart.

Merry Christmas,

Christoph

Chapter 28

The minute Christmas day expired Milton worked on managing the remainder of my holiday vacation. The absence of his employees drove him crazy like a caged animal. Opening the folder on my computer marked *Bright Images*, I scrolled through documents searching for his latest request.

Once again, the phone rang, but this time it wasn't my boss. "Chloe?" Christoph said.

"I thought the plan was that I'd call when I returned home?"

"Yes, but I can't be with someone who ditches me when she feels that I'm not honoring her! You continuing to be like this when you know I'm hurting is unacceptable."

"You're the master of turning everything around. You talk and make plans and then you come up with little ways for it to fall apart. And it always falls apart," I laughed. "You talk and talk and plan and plan . . ." I panted from my vocal marathon. "But not one time can I say you kept your word or followed through! What kind of partner could you ever be?"

"Chloe, you're crazy," he said.

"And you're a liar!" I screamed into the one-pound sleek device, my only weapon for mass destruction, as it carried my voice across his line of defense. He couldn't hide in the trenches. The holes wouldn't be deep enough to protect him. I didn't have my eyes, a dirty look, or a door to slam in his face.

"No I'm not, woman! This isn't fair and stop making me yell. I'm surrounded by colleagues . . . this is completely unprofessional and I will not tolerate this disrespectful, trashy behavior."

"If it's unprofessional, Mr. Fancy Pants, then why the hell did you call me?" I hung up. A peace treaty between Geneva and New York was impossible. This was war.

The phone rang and I answered immediately. I had lost control. "I don't understand why you're keeping in contact with me when we both know you'll never be here," I admitted. *Ouch.*

"Maybe, you'll then get a clue of what it feels like to know you love her, but to doubt she ever loved you back," he responded then he was gone. This was the first time the diplomat had ever hung up on me.

Text message from Christoph: *I don't want to spend the rest of my life wondering what you're up to. You're not an accessory. You're the flesh and bones that brings us together.*

Text message from Christoph: *I don't play games.*

Text message from Christoph: *I don't want to get married and have kids and spend the rest of my life with someone. I want to get married and have kids and spend the rest of my life with you and because of you.*

Text message from Christoph: *I'm not a philosopher. Words are just the mere reflection of my soul and my soul is yours truly.*

Text message from Chloe: *What's this bullshit list of confessions?*

Text message from Christoph: *It's not groceries. It's what my heart wants.*

Text message from Chloe: *You took me for granted.*

Text message from Chloe: *You walked away from me by never walking to me. You are writing your story, make the most of it, both for your life and your book, Christoph.*

How ironic that immediately, I received an e-mail from his biggest fan.

From: Mary Polt
To: Chloe Kassidy
Subject: Please
Date: December 26, 11:47 a.m.

Dear Chloe,
Don't do this now if you can. You both need to stop fighting this, because it's this constant fighting that causes the tension and the reaction.

If you could do without each other, then you would have both done already. You're just too oversensitive to take his gesture for what it really was. He adores you, Chloe. You brought him back to life, and if anything, he feels he owes you everything. Don't misjudge him. You're exhausted, I know, and if you need out then be out. You are the only one who knows what you need. I think I know, but you know best. We should meet if you want to. Maybe that will make you so much more relieved.

My best,

Mary

I was shocked that I had feeling left in my fingertips. Any words left unsaid or unused, I couldn't think of them. Composing an e-mail, my next task was to fire the secretary.

The faint ringing came from somewhere. After Christoph insinuated my behavior was crazy and he dumped me by dial tone, my phone had landed itself in a tight spot. Crawling across the bed I slid in between the wall and mattress hanging by my torso.

"Chloe . . .," he sighed.

I remained hanging since I had neither the energy to respond to him or to pull myself up. The pressure began to build inside my head at the same time as the blood rushed. It comforted me to know my head still existed, considering it had been neglected.

"Why do we always accept as real what makes us safe but refuse to accept as real what makes us scared? Everything that is bigger than us . . . is what's real," he said.

He knew I was there by my heavy breath. I was exhausted by his habit of saying a lot of nothing. "I can't do this. Safe or scared—I want to talk to a man not a ghost."

"It wasn't a fairy tale, Chloe. Fairy tales are just fabricated stories. It was real. It will always be real," he continued.

"If you ever did love me . . . let me go and just be," I begged.

"I'm not a ghost and I'm not hiding. I hid from life until you came along, and all I wanted to do ever since . . . was live it with you. Love isn't an excuse," he said.

"I'm not spending the day doing this again. My family is downstairs. I'm done talking."

"I've made a series of mistakes. Yes . . . I'm to be blamed for getting us here. Yes . . . I'm human—"

"I won't argue with you."

"I didn't know how to handle my life and work decisions. I didn't know how to handle my heart, and I didn't know how to love, but—"

"That's my fear. Stephanie thinks you're just a key to nowhere," I said wanting to hurt him.

"What?"

"Yep—a huge box full of tissue paper," I cried. "Oh—and with glitter."

"Your friends win," he laughed. "I'm done. I just can't do this anymore. I can't be punished indefinitely for something I'm already punching myself for daily."

"You can't cope with what I'm doing?" I screamed.

"I'm not strong enough to cope with your bitterness, your tough sentences, and your cruelty—"

"Christoph—"

"I gave three months for you to not stick around for the last meters of this road . . . I'm shocked at your friends' impact on you. You're thirty years old," he said.

"Their impact? It's called caring—"

"Well, I also know that there's some of Chloe I've seen, and they never will."

Again, I found myself participating in this banter. "Why don't you grow a set and meet a girl for coffee?" I yelled. "Are you familiar with that expression, Mr. Switzerland?"

"You—"

"I've gotta go," I said and hung up.

"What's going on in here?" my mother's voice had entered my room. "Who are you screaming at?"

I remained silent while still hung over the side of my bed.

I could hear my father's footsteps entering the room. "Chloe, you okay? Are you stuck?"

"I'm fine," I moaned. "I just need some privacy."

"Okay, honey," my father responded and then I heard the door close.

From: Christoph Kostas
To: Chloe Kassidy
Subject: Waiting for you
Date: December 26, 12:32 p.m.

I just finished nostalgically reading a few of our first emails. Gosh, it's amazing to see that there was so much chemistry between us from the beginning. It almost felt like we'd known each other forever.

Your friends are giving you a hard time. They don't understand your need to be here with me. You hate losing control. You hate not being the put-together strong one. You hate your friends witnessing this new side of you. I love you and I hate you so much at the same time. I love you for everything you are and I hate you for not realizing just how much I love you.
Christoph

When the phone rang again, I boosted up.

"Stop calling me!" I screamed.

"What's with the attitude? Geez . . . I'm sure Santa sent you a lump of coal," Emma said.

"I'm sorry," I said. "I thought—"

"Well, think while you drive your butt over here. You're late!"

I had completely lost track of time and my promise to help Emma get settled into her new place.

"I've opened a beer, but I'm not touching a box until you get here," she continued. "It's boring and I need you here to suffer through it with me."

"I'm on my way!"

Chapter 29

I became better not responding to his weightless words, but sometimes that strength turned on me making me weaker to make up for lost time. He hit me hard with e-mail after e-mail and a text in between. The phone rang and although I hesitated, I knew it would take handcuffs to keep me from answering.

"Let me repeat this . . . I want YOU AND ME to do something fun together when you're back," he said.

"The keyword is *together*. Not over the phone or through e-mail or text, correct?" I asked.

"When will you realize that the day we met has changed our lives forever? You're never alone anymore, no matter what. I'm always with you—in you, Chloe. We don't have a voice when our hearts make the choices!"

"We don't have a choice? I won't let you tell me it's not your choice when you don't show up." I held my ground.

"We always come back to each other. Wake up! We've found each other, Chloe. We found it . . . deal with it and accept it."

"Christoph, I'm confident the moment I look into your eyes I'll know your true feelings."

"And yes . . . if we end up a complete disaster, if we end up never meeting, if we end up never being able to see eye to eye and not make each other happy . . . I'll have no regrets. I love loving you," he continued.

"That's sweet, but it's a mess because you're not seeing the bigger picture."

"Sweetheart, tell me a few things I am to you and which terrify you. I'll help you see the bigger picture. I love this about us," he said. "I've never had this with anyone . . . and realized it that night after your lunch with the curator."

"Why?"

"When I'm stressed, you manage to calm me, and when you freak out, I manage to make you see from a different perspective . . . It's like we're each other's only remedy."

Did I have anything else to lose? I enlightened him hoping to get him to finally meet me. "You're my frustrations. You're my emails. You're my texts. You're my biggest headache—"

"Funny," he said.

"It's all quite romantic," I poked.

While he talked, I collected my thoughts to neatly fold and put away the coming tears.

"And that's exactly what makes us rare—the fact that we feel so intensely about each other . . . without those necessities that make every other person in this world attracted to another person and form a relationship," he continued. "Do you realize how much easier and natural our life is going to be with those things?"

"I want to speak to you in person. I want to see you happy. I want to see you mad with your odd European expressions. I want to see you sleepy. I want to see if you and Francis get along."

He giggled. "You're the most rational person we both know, and yet, you adore me without reason."

"I was rational," I admitted.

He was either too romantic or too emotional for me, or, I was too practical and too rational for him. He was either defining those three words, *I love you*, enormously differently than I was, or, I wasn't in love.

"And that reason is beyond you or me to understand. We'll never know why we feel the way we do. We'll always know, though, that we do. And no one else has to get it," he said.

It was a romantic thought, but it had to make some sense to others. I considered that Manson, Jeffery Dahmer and Snooki had similar rationalizing to Christoph's remark.

"No one else has to comprehend it. It's ours and if anyone else understood this . . . then it wouldn't be true love's mystery," he said.

Whether it was the beginning or end, I found myself in a circle of confusion.

"I need you to know I love you . . . I just don't know how to love you perfectly."

Emma once explained to me the theory of sign mates and how I should be careful with an Aries, since I felt lost.

"If he lacks a sense of direction, something is absolutely wrong," she informed me. "Chloe, he will run in circles in panic only causing you to feel as lost as him." Her conclusion to this theory was that my Aquarianess would respond to him by rejecting the disoriented feeling. Emma sounded convincing, but her equation needed to include him being a ghost since at this point he remained invisible.

"What do you think of an equation that includes you, me and forever?"

Forever.

I wondered if he was just toying with me, or was I bipolar? *Did Britney Spears ever see it coming?* Running my fingers through my hair, I confirmed I hadn't reached the breaking point with losing my locks over love.

"Are you even sorry for standing me up again before Christmas?" I asked.

"Baby, how can we ever move on and not look back?" he whispered. "Don't do this, Chloe," he sighed. "What was I supposed to do? It's my work!"

"Trust me. I get it," I said, now clenching my teeth. The pain released from the sides of my neck and shot to my chest. It was a heart punch. "Listen . . .," I said while taking one deep breath, hoping to let go of him in one last breath. "I don't think you're a horrible man. I deserve more than three months of you being a no show . . . your excuses . . . this complicated nonsense . . . and lack of effort. I deserve someone who wants to be with me." My last words wounded me. "This just makes you—not the man for me," I said. "Love might be a process and always changing, but not in this direction."

"Don't act like I did this alone or if it was even my choice. You think I don't love you? This is just crazily ironic," he replied while we both allowed a time out for several seconds.

"Welcome to the world of consequences. Don't act surprised, Christoph."

"You think I was making fake plans? You're wrong, Chloe!" he screamed.

"I don't know if I can give you another chance!" I admitted and hung up the phone.

I felt guilty for hanging up, but reminded myself of his lack of remorse for standing me up multiple dates. For feeding me empty promises only for me to end up starving for fulfillment. My soul was emaciated at this point. I didn't understand what he wanted from me. I couldn't shake the feeling he avoided us meeting.

None of it made sense. *Why on earth was he here when it came to calling and emailing me, but then full of excuses when it came down to facing me?* The effort to create fake plans only to invent more lies to support them infuriated me. I was fuming.

I wished he would make use of his manners and help me understand. He always grew defensive when I put him on the spot only to come back with a trivial question or speech about believing in something extraordinary to rebuild his destruction. I was scared of him, but I was terrified of me at this point.

Christoph Kostas consumed my inbox. We had reached almost 3,500 emails since October.

Text message from Christoph: *Honey . . . can I fix this? I'll wait for your call and won't bother you again.*

Perhaps, it wasn't the universe responsible for those signs, but him creating them. I was sick to my stomach with his words without him truly giving me anything. I needed comfort food and forced myself to make tomato soup and a pimento grilled cheese with sliced tomato. Telling Stephanie about his behavior sickened me and I couldn't tolerate Emma's soul mate signs with this nausea. I placed my comfort onto a tray and tucked myself into bed. *Seinfeld* reruns would pull my mind to a better place. I was fine until I noticed my tears were splattering my soup everywhere.

Heavy thunderstorms and pouring rain happened on my last day in Atlanta. I found myself studying his pictures, listening to his music and reading our emails. While manipulating the images of love on my screen for theme ideas, I thought about the possibility he was actively manipulating me. I knew I couldn't trust myself. He had hypnotized me through the phone. I would delete his number like a junkie would a dealer. I had no control and just wanted to be sober from his toxicity. I had become blinded by the fairy tale.

Christoph's lengthy biblical emails stopped after my *I don't know if I can give you another chance!* comment a couple days ago.

Today, this rational photographer that was lazy, put on her detective cap. Rather than spend a rainy afternoon with Emma watching the *Time Traveler's Wife*, I researched Christoph Kostas the diplomat from Geneva. In all honesty, the last thing I needed was to watch a love story where two people destined for each other struggled to be together and featured a super-hot soul mate in his disappearing routines. My imagination was on lock down with no visitation rights whatsoever.

It was hard to accept that Christoph remained unseen from Google as well. I was sure there was an iPhone App developed for this entire procedure.

Google was still no help. I needed more than signs and his new Facebook profile and growing friends list. For someone who was on social networking sites, he was pretty antisocial. He had plenty of connections but rarely any communication. There were no results for a diplomat named Christoph Kostas or anything remotely close to his name. Nothing came up in my searches for the United Nations, Switzerland, D.C. or New York. A banner for a people search website popped on the screen. For $3.99 it offered a US search, a small price to pay for three months of my life. When I broke down the cost per day, the frustration, tears, and time waiting weren't worth one penny. My accounting of the situation would have made my father proud, but my continuous investing with such a horrible return, not so much.

The website confirmed that there were three Christoph Kostas in the U.S. The monthly fee displayed the city, marital status, income, zodiac sign, political party, occupation and more. None of the information matched the man I'd shared my life.

IM from Christoph: *I miss you terribly and I love you.*

IM from Christoph: *You don't have to have any answers for me or for you . . . you're all my answers. This is up to you and what makes you more comfortable, but if it were up to me I'd rather have you on the stupid phone than not have you at all.*

I ignored him. Next, I searched with the reverse phone number look up. His numbers were related to a landline in Queens from the map displayed on my screen. Facebook and Twitter were the only two accounts that confirmed his identity. He had written a lengthy biography, but one adjective he couldn't claim was to ever have been a gentleman.

The search results made me dizzy. I took my tears to the tub. I had the energy to take a bath and soak my sorrows in bubbles.

"Chloe?" My mother said through the door.

"Yeah," I responded.

"Your father will be home shortly. Dinner will be ready in about thirty minutes."

"I'll be down in a bit."

I slowly submerged myself to my shoulders and stared at the cracks, the peeling and chipping away of the ceiling's lavender paint that went unnoticed along with specks of rust. Looking down, my childhood bathroom appeared spotless, but looking up I gained a different view. *How many of the couples out there have perfect circumstances, yet an imperfect sync between them?* I wondered if the smashing majority of relationships exist, breathe and grow in exactly this equation: perfect wrapping—imperfect content. The fear of this had landed me not in front of a prince or in a fairy tale, but a cyber-jerk writing a book.

The thought that someone had imposed pain and didn't give a damn was unbearable. While my tears leaked, adding to the body of water that held me, I soaked while drowning in my troubles. I needed to pull the plug to let it all swirl away. Yanking out the rubber stopper, the water slowly lowered revealing my prune like fingers and toes. I lay bare in an empty tub and for a second wished my soul would turn as cold and hard, better to handle any further attack. At least the feeling was real compared to the false ones that had instigated me floating in this mess. A chill was the only thing present to keep me company in that moment.

After a long dinner with my parents that included my father sharing stories on some of the outrageous write offs his clients pull each tax season and my mother panicking with preparing her classroom after the holiday break, I headed to bed. I tried to sleep, ignoring the foggy sounds of the TV in my parents' room. That's what the inside of my head felt like, a kaleidoscope of noise. The man caused me to jump in heart first, only for him to collect these *first place* trophies. He had beaten me at this love game.

The red light flashed. Though it couldn't be heard, I somehow sensed his messages even when I slept.

From: Christoph Kostas
To: Chloe Kassidy
Subject: Please baby
Date: December 30, 11:11 p.m.

There's just one thing I need to say and I'll try and use as few words as possible. I want to see you because they're things I need to say and do. You can choose a time and place soon, later, yesterday, today, tomorrow, some day, any day, it doesn't matter when. I just need to see you in this lifetime. It doesn't matter if you show up with your friends, your family, or a squat team. I don't care. I need to do this for me. I cannot carry on cheating myself believing I'm doing just fine without you when I'm clearly not. I don't expect you to promise me forever. All I want is to have you look me in the eyes and realize it's me. It doesn't matter if you love me or not. It doesn't matter if you hate me or not. Want me or not. Believe me or not. Have anything to say or not. I'm not asking you to get out of your comfort zone and meet me midway. Maybe I'm not all you've been looking for. It still doesn't matter. I have absolutely nothing to lose, Chloe.

I told Mary everything and you know what? Maybe you're right. Maybe it's me. Maybe I've been busy trying to make it perfect, thinking that it can only be perfect if it happens one and only way when everything else outside us was perfect that I ended up hurting you and myself in the process. I let my job, my fears, and my weaknesses get the better of me. And now that I'm a tabula rasa, I don't have the one thing I truly care about. I wanted to live it with you and dedicate myself to my writing. I thought I'd forget you because I'd be busy, but everywhere I go, there's a song, a line someone will say, a product, a landscape, a movie, a wind, a sunshine, that will remind me of you and give me a knot in my stomach, a weight on my chest. I can't pretend you're not everywhere, in everything. I can't pretend I'll go out there and find someone else to spend my life with. I want to be real. To myself. To you. To what we both deserve.

Christoph

While I deleted his latest e-mail, the phone rang.

"Did I wake you?" she asked in her recognizable motherly tone. It was genuine and sweet and couldn't be mistaken for anyone other than Stephanie.

"Nope. I miss you guys," I said.

"Emma called a little while ago and sounded worried about you. She mentioned you seemed extremely frustrated."

Before I could blame it on my mother, Milton, or my theme meltdown, "How much longer are you going to hold on?" she continued.

That was the precious thing about my dearest friend. Stephanie listened to my cries and snotty snorts, letting me know I wasn't alone. I didn't respond and she never said another word.

The only flight available to New York was on New Years Eve. Emma returned the favor by driving me twenty minutes to the airport. She pulled curbside and grabbed my suitcase from the trunk with her baby carrying biceps.

"I'm going to miss you." She dropped my suitcase right on my foot. "I can only imagine what you're feeling," she joked.

I hugged her and squeezed again to gain a few seconds. "Sometimes the hardest decisions are the best ones, and I think you're now following your heart," I said.

"I think we're going to be happy here. I guess getting closer to the truth sometimes requires facing your uncertainties," she said. "The fact is I have the love of my life, Lily. Meeting someone will just be an addition to us."

Facing my fears offered more than I bargained for, but I moved closer to the truth and to understanding my mother more. She had taught me, unknowingly, that perspective was a choice. Choosing happiness was always an option.

"Don't cry, Chloe."

We exchanged one last goodbye and reminded each other in four and a half weeks she would be in New York for the opening.

With the one hour and fifty minute flight time, I would be entering the New Year when I touched New York State. When the year approached, the flight attendants scurried throughout the aisles serving cups of a cheap brut with twenty-three minutes until midnight to toast 30,000 feet in the air.

10. 9. 8. 7. 6. 5. 4. 3. 2. 1 . . . Happy New Year, Chloe.

January

Chapter 30

It's a new year for new possibilities, I reminded myself with my early birthday present in hand, a gift to me from me. B&H, the New York superstore covered 34th street and Ninth Avenue, and was equivalent to a socialite's trip to Barneys or Bergdorf Goodman. Though, the designer shoes didn't motivate me like the kiosks of technology ready to sample. I kept my cameras as souvenirs. Each piece of hardware had provided me an experience, a learning curve leaving me more advanced than the years before. I loved through technology, my heart was my lens and I learned the better quality the lens, the more control you had over the outcome. You couldn't force true love where it didn't exist just like you couldn't force beauty. *Truth was beauty.*

The exhibit launch was nearly one month away while I attempted to calmly explore themes. Entering Bright Images, Inc. the casual wearing crowd was anything but relaxed. The familiar aroma of popcorn had been replaced with coffee breath and sweat. The ping-pong table was abandoned while bodies bounced in and out of the meeting room.

"He's in the elevator. Get to the meeting room!" A panicky account executive had said. We took seats and switched off our phones when the room silenced abruptly. Milton had arrived. He welcomed each year with his grueling annual sales meeting and account reviews. The nerves in the room generated an abundance of energy, enough to power the presentation itself. *Christ.* My week was a thick sludge of deadlines with Grayson Gates, themes, and finding time for love. It was now Milton Bright's turn with the ladle to give it a swirl.

Milton entered the room and the air was instantly sucked out like a vacuum when the door closed. "Are we ready to kick ass this month?" he yelled.

I did a quick sideways glance and everyone seemed to be playing along with his attempt to pump us up. I was sure it was due to the caffeine and Red Bull most of them had chugged prior to the meeting.

"Last year was a fantastic year . . . But I think we can do greater things. It's all up to each and every one of you," he continued. Milton Bright was famous for his compliment sandwiches. Weaken us with a compliment. Followed by his actual point. Finish with another compliment to leave a bit of spirit in us so that we will rush back to our offices and dive into our accounts. "However, many of you are dropping the ball. You're screwing it up for the rest of us," he said. "We're not going to accept that, are we? You know who you are and you better shape up or I will sink your ship!" He walked over to the chalkboard and began to create a list. "I believe in all of you! I want to make you successfully rich!"

After the meeting, I returned to my office to make the call. I hadn't spoke to Christoph since Atlanta. With our schedules continuing to mismatch, and his last no show, both Christoph and my own frustrations had reached the boiling point. I couldn't ignore a slight distaste in my mouth that he was avoiding me. Milton and this weren't helping my creativity one bit.

I dialed Christoph's number and locked my office door.

"Good morning, Honey. Are you back in New York?"

"Hi there," I said. "Yes, I returned last night. I'm already at the office."

"I've missed you. It was hard to accept us not talking the past few days. How was your visit?"

"Everything was nice. Emma is settled and I ate a lot of pie," I said. "How's work?"

"This week is heavily focused on European affairs in the United States. My schedule is punishing me with open houses during which the European Union embassies and the EU commission in the US are open."

"I wondered what caused all the traffic in the city this morning."

"It's going to be those weeks of six-thirty in the morning days straight through late into the evenings . . . I even have to work on Friday night," he said. "It would be with sixty fifteen-year olds and, while inspired and honored as I am, I promise I will find a way for us to meet."

After hearing about the EU while he walked and talked with the city as our soundtrack, I'd assumed the traditional Swiss romantic intentionally didn't mention that private lesson with Chef Roberts at Le Banc. His duty was to save the world, but even coffee seemed to be overwhelming. He had created a collection of possible first dates, and it seemed long ago that I was daydreaming of jetting off to Switzerland, us holding hands, taking pictures and wrapped up with each other on a bench talking like we had done on the phone.

He cleared his throat. "Baby, are you there?"

"Yeah. Where are you?"

"I'm heading to the French embassy to drop off documents to the ambassador—he'll have plenty of time to review and sign. I don't have to do it, but he appreciates the courtesy."

He thought it was his duty to make time for me to have coffee, but I had a theme to finalize, a deadline, a curator, and a job. I clenched so hard I swore I tasted blood. To allow him to think this was his call, I would just be showing off my substandard values yet again.

"Actually, this week won't work for me," I said. "I need to dedicate all my time on the exhibit and making the deadline. With the new year, it's a bit crazy at the office with Milton as well."

"Okay," he sounded surprised. "Maybe, next weekend?"

"It's hard to say. The next couple weeks will—"

"Chloe! I need to see you," Milton's screams through the speakerphone interrupted me.

"What was that?" Christoph asked.

"I need to run," I said.

"Yes, Milton. I'm coming," I screamed.

Chapter 31

The thirty-one day countdown commenced to opening night. Perspective became a focused thought taking up prime real estate in my head. The deadline for framing and hanging wasn't until the night before the launch. Organizing my workspace and brewing a fresh single cup of coffee, I lit up the room by pulling up the blinds and cracking the windows for the winter air to keep me alert. The tedious effort of retouching would distract my mind from trailing out into the black hole of Christoph's endless excuses and unanswered questions. Photoshop would prove to be more productive if I didn't give into the temptation of detective searches. My stomach rumbled as my reminder that skipping lunch couldn't continue. Super busy would have felt like a breeze compared to the time I had to cut from eating, sleeping, and at times showering to gain minutes for thinking, retouching and revising. I convinced myself to think of the remaining days to 744 hours or 44,640 minutes to make it seem the deadline was forever away.

The southern exposed views of Manhattan offered an abundance of sunlight and made my five hundred square foot box more tolerable. My view took my breath away at times. Securing my hair back and strengthening my posture, I viewed shots from the most recent shoots and prayed to Jesus I would find something wall worthy. While I searched, my fingers fumbled into one of those unknown shortcut functions.

Whatever I did, it opened up an old folder titled, *The Beginning*. The beginning was the start of my new life as a knowledgeable New Yorker. The file included shots from exploring the city, through tree-lined streets, high-energy underground subways, major tourist attractions and the zigzag of people from around the world crisscrossing paths. I had been an official New Yorker for less than twenty-four hours. It had been love at first frame. My very own New York City fairy tale.

This was my exhibit and my heart told me I could handle it on my own. I didn't need Christoph to teach me about love. I had been supportive of his work and schedule until he continually stood me up. I had been by the phone or on e-mail throughout these months whenever he needed me no matter the time of day or time difference. I was a team player patiently waiting on his work schedule, traveling, family visits and hardships that he experienced. I wasn't a supportive partner, but a pathetic pushover. That was my up-to-date perspective on these universal signs and bridge connection.

My calendar alarm notified me of this evening's engagement. Grayson Gates was in Miami to secure additional investors from the latest damaging publicity giving his emerging artists a break.

Tonight, we were gathering to celebrate our hard work at the KGB bar on 4th street and Bowery at 8:00 p.m. The dive bar was a bit of a New York City institution for artists.

I hopped into the shower, working a mint hydration mask into my scalp while the tingling sensation turned my thoughts to mush. I was interrupted sixty seconds into the five-minute penetration period. My cell rang. *Dammit*. One minute later, I was jerked out of my soothing moment again. I quickly rinsed my hair, wrapped a towel around me while I tip toed to the phone. This week offered a swing of potential emergencies from Milton to Grayson to Emma in Atlanta. An issue with tonight would mean showering was a waste of time and I could return to my image search.

It was Christoph. "What?" I answered eyeing the puddle of water that quickly formed where I was standing. I couldn't afford to lose my security deposit by a warped situation.

"What are you doing, Baby?"

"I was in the shower." Feeling my hair, the immediate silkiness was impressive.

"Perfect timing! I called to suggest we be spontaneous. Let's meet now!"

"What? I can't! I'm meeting the gallery group tonight, remember?" I was sure I mentioned it. Confiding in Christoph had become a daily part of my routine and the excitement when I found out Grayson Gates would be more than one hundred miles outside my radius, was definitely news worthy. I stepped out of the small puddle of water only to create another one.

"That's not being spontaneous, now is it?" His eagerness was quickly replaced with cynicism. "Can't you skip it? I want to take you out for drinks. What are we waiting for?"

"I couldn't agree more, Christoph—"

"Why do you call me by my name? Can't you be sweeter?"

"I would love to just run out the door, hop in a cab, and meet you . . . But I've been down that road."

"What's the problem?" he asked.

"I can't miss tonight. I promised I would be there. We've planned—"

"What about our promises?" There he was actually creating his defense and I didn't have time to be put on trial and sit through his lengthy closing argument. I was naked, wet, and my hair became curly with air dry. This wasn't up for discussion. I didn't need an approval from corporate. I had enough to deal with from Bright Images Inc., Gates, and Alice Kassidy.

"Listen . . . I needed to meet you immediately, like ninety days ago, but—"

"You surprise me. You're focused on the 'continuing to hurt,' what about the 'continuing to love' part, Chloe. You liked me extremely, but you never loved me in that poetic kind of way."

Checking the time, I had thirty-six minutes to get to the bar.

"Why are you doing this?" My frustrations were crossing the border into fighting territory. "I'm going to be late, I can't cancel on them."

"You care about me, but I've never inspired you, never caused you to lose your sleep and daydream, never made you expressive without control, never made you choke while trying to say goodbye. You've always—always—kept your cool, and you've always—always—made sure to maintain a power reserve just in case." His trial was in full swing.

"What we could have had by now if only—"

"What we could have had!" he yelled. "This sadly reaffirms my conclusion," he uttered now in a full on pout. "You're a disgrace.

Seriously, I'm disgusted." I detected the elitist tone like I was an enemy disturbing the efforts of the United Nations.

"If love is forgiving . . . if love is something you cannot deny even when you might want to, if love is never tired of waiting, if love has no pride and no opinion for itself, if love isn't emulous of others, then . . . you probably never loved me," he sighed. "If you have the power to choose between two roads and then act upon the one that takes you away from me, then you never loved me."

"This is about me choosing the gallery over you?" I was in shock that a sophisticated aristocratic behaved as a selfish boy with a new toy. *Had he already forgotten his countless work obligations these past months while standing me up?*

"Do what you need to, Chloe. This conversation has given birth to serious doubts if you're even deserving of my heart," he said. "You're clueless," he laughed.

"Excuse me?"

"I hate when you act like this New York City girl with your weightless western values. You're freaking unstable."

"You're treating me like this stranger. Like someone you don't even know," I uttered.

He laughed like I was this amusing joke that flew over my head. "You were never the person I believed you to be," he continued.

Crying made me powerless and he used my tears as a catalyst to get a greater reaction. I hung up the phone. *Screw him.*

I continued getting ready when he called back. I knew not to answer, but I did anyway. I didn't have the energy to talk with him. Though, I knew the battle would be greater if he was ignored.

"I don't understand why you keep thinking we're two individuals each stuck with his selfishness, wanting something entirely different," he said with the release of a deep breath that sounded as exhausted as I felt. "I want you and I can only hope you want me. Why can't you ever just choose me? Why do I need to ask you to do that?"

I knew better than to say what I was about to say. "I've always chosen you, Christoph. I have month after month, even after you didn't show up. Even after you not choosing me over everything," I said, now clenching my teeth. Without a doubt, I would be late.

"Can I give you an example of how you didn't choose me, and you're just like me, although you constantly complain about how I am?" he asked.

"I have to—"

"You'd hang up, hop in a cab, and call me to say 'let's do this Christoph,'" he said.

His example was weak. "The past few days, I've been super busy. I can't cancel on my fellow peers." What I wanted to say was that in his version of 'equal,' there was only 'u.'

"When I asked you on a date recently and again just now you didn't choose me. We should talk more, open up more, and share more, especially to avoid miscommunications?"

"Didn't choose you? When my curator calls me into an emergency meeting, I don't have a choice . . . Tonight my choice is to join my peers. I agreed to this planned date. Obviously, something you don't understand."

He cleared his throat, "It hurts knowing you still don't trust me enough or, should I say, don't love me enough? I really don't know what to say . . . I don't want to argue . . . I'm aching, Chloe."

The tone of his voice when he said *aching* broke my heart.

"When will you ever choose me? When will you ever fully entrust me with you?" he asked.

"When you look me in the eye, I'll know we're real," I said while swallowing my tears since red eyes would ruin my chance of making me less late.

"You have my heart. You have conquered my thoughts. I know I'm not the simplest person in the world, especially when it comes to my romanticism, but this isn't something new. This is who I've always been and if you haven't learned to love me even for that by now, you never will. For that I cannot be mad at you—I have to be loved—for my lowest low as well as my highest high," he wished.

"Unfortunately, I'm stubborn and terrified that unless you help me to move forward, I won't," I said. I hung up once again.

Tonight as artists, we had the opportunity to embrace this humbling experience since overnight success happened in a flash. Today, we were emerging artists, but from February 7 we daydreamed on who we might wake up to be. Life was too short to be compromising my heart into something that's not as magical as I had hoped it to be. My heart was an instrument that I needed working at 100%. I needed it to write my stories with light. My heart and my Canon were essential elements, both required beyond this one opening night.

Ten minutes later, the red flashing beckoned me. He wasn't done. I understood what being a slave to your Blackberry truly meant.

From: Christoph Kostas
To: Chloe Kassidy
Subject: Here's a little more:
Date: January 7, 7:49 p.m.

I can blame you for the thoughts you say and do, for your accusations, for your insults, for your hurtful comments, for allowing your frustration to make you forget, to make you deliberately ignore, to make you put aside. Your fears can be dissolved in a few seconds once you see me and touch me. But my fears are touching something deeper than that, my fears are related to your ability to be the partner I need, the partner who's going to be there for me, believe in me when the odds are against me, stand up for me when everyone is putting me down, be willing to go the line with me even when we've no guarantees of success, love me like crazy no matter what.

Christoph

Immediately, the phone rang.

"Hello?" I answered. Even God knew it was him calling.

"Baby, how can I explain anything to you? You have built concrete walls and all you've been doing is throwing attacks at me with insults, anger, and frustration. You're not listening to me."

"But . . .," I said, making my defense.

"And I'm not a stupid person. I know how to detect when speaking is completely useless."

Now he claimed to be a communications expert?

"Christoph! I need to go!"

"If there's one thing I've learned with you—is to shut up and let you do the yelling—and give it time. When you're over the initial craziness . . . you might actually sit and hear me out," he said.

"Are you serious?" I asked. My body became heated like the conversation.

"Like when I'm calm and you're yelling and I swear at any point if I wasn't hurt I would start laughing . . . You're yelling but are saying 'I'm not mad!'"

"I'm fully aware that I can be impossible at times," I admitted.

"I can deal with you being a handful, but when it's a handful that spits out accusations and impoliteness, it's against my classy standards to even respond," he said.

Needing a clear moment, I closed my eyes, inhaled a deep breath and threw invisible punches. "Responding to you and accepting your reasoning is a sign of disrespecting myself," I protested. "I can't say this enough—I'm over the fear of falling for you—It's not meeting that's upsetting," I said. "How can you prove to me any of your feelings if you're never around, Christoph?" Feeling satisfied with my closing argument, I wondered if the photographer could defeat the International official.

"And this is perhaps the only time I'm asking you to be the strong one and help me see the world. You call me selfish because I overanalyze and I'm blinded by my fears and don't take you into account, but what you don't realize is that again we're equal, even in this. Because, in my eyes . . . you're the selfish one, the one who grew scared that she failed to see that she left me alone fighting against my own questions. You just want me to do what you want me to do."

So meeting was all for me?

"I wish you would stop analyzing and start living a little more," I expressed, while another night passed with me locked in my apartment, alone with my invisible boyfriend.

"I'm not asking you to explain the whole thing to me over the phone. I'm not asking you to be in a relationship like this. I'm not asking you to make me any promises. I'm not asking you to wait for me. I'm not asking for anything. I just miss you," he said. "I miss this person I'd spend my entire day with not thinking, not worrying, not overanalyzing. I miss us, Chloe."

When we were good, even through the phone, it was the loveliest feeling in the world. That was before his no shows. That was before my doubts gave birth to my investigations.

"Your reactions these days, your hurtful words, your overall 'screw you Christoph' conduct, the feeling that I'm talking to an iceberg—I can't deal with. My field of work is of a certain nature that requires my people to trust me even when I can't tell them certain things. You will have to learn to trust me and know the way I function," he said.

He knew I had somewhere to be and sabotaged my effort to attend a deserved celebration. "I have to leave—I'm late," I said in a panic. "And I haven't decided if I can give you another chance!" and hung up. If only I could rewind and make him work for my attention.

Hoping I didn't resemble the mess that I felt, the mirror was as unkind as him. I was beyond a quick repair of a mascara touch up. After squeezing Visine drops into each eye to soothe the redness, I opened his two unopened emails.

From: Christoph Kostas
To: Chloe Kassidy
Subject: I'm the only one going through this!
Date: January 7, 7:59 p.m.

We're done. I've put myself out there, admitting my mistakes and willing to show you I love you. You just want me to pay for the rest of my flipping life for my schedule. Well, sorry but I'm not putting up with this quietly. This is no longer you attacking my heart. This is you attacking EVERYTHING I STAND FOR. Enjoy your city, your friends (the ones I kept you from), the moments I made you waste, and the awfully boring days and nights I forced you to spend talking to me. You must be the happiest girl in the world now to be freed from such a miserable, aggressive, insensitive, egocentric jerk. I'm the most awful human being you could ever encounter, but hey, you made it through and even out. That's an achievement. My applauds.

Unless, you have something else to add to this conversation, I'm done talking. I'm done making plans. I'm done putting my heart on the line. I'm done trying to cheer you up. I'm done trying to understand you taking it out on me. I'm done trying to comfort you and making stupid jokes just to cheer you up, only for you to make me the world's biggest fool for thinking you would listen to me, trust me, to love and miss me.

In any case, a relationship consists of two people who are both devoted to it, no matter what. I honestly believe that you don't deserve my words, my dreams, my ambitions, or my plans. You will still have it. I don't have a choice on that one, but what I do have a choice about is to not let you know. You're starting a new career, new schedule, new life . . . and a new relationship since this one never started.
Christoph

He wanted me to lose my rational hat, to remove it completely, hoping that while I chased my heart all reasoning would be left behind.

The most complicated man in the world can't even be this complicated.

I was forty minutes late and shadowed with shame for standing up my peers. My eyes were still swollen and not subsiding. Sending a group text, I apologized for being a no show last minute, and used a migraine attack for my excuse. I gave my own needs the cold shoulder, refusing to acknowledge these were more moments missed by turning out the light and calling it a night.

Chapter 32

Weeks passed without scheduling coffee with Christoph. I suffocated under my theme and the deadline rapidly approaching. How could I not wonder if he ever loved me? How could I not wonder why the same person, who called me his life, can go a day without meeting me, without feeling the need to see me, to share his moments with me, to come to me?

Eventually that night, he sent an e-mail and I chose to not respond, but only reread it over and over like a gloomy country song stuck on repeat.

From: Christoph Kostas
To: Chloe Kassidy
Subject: Not cool!
Date: January 12, 8:27 p.m.

Let me make it simpler: at the end of the day, are you happier having me even through a stupid e-mail, or without me at all? That is what you need to figure out, because your voice says 'so long' but you're monstrous behavior says you love me.

If there are questions in you, I'm afraid no one can answer them but you—especially these sorts of questions. I know what I want, what I need, what I care for. I also know I'm terribly good at it just as you are, regardless of low moments, because those moments only prove the extremity, intensity and rareness of the feelings accompanying this bond, this connection, this mental, emotional and physical chemistry that dances on the verge of pure intoxication. I'm one of the two components that can create this chemical reaction, you being the other. Christoph

My stupid heart ached like there was something I hadn't done today or yesterday or the day before. I couldn't quite put my finger on it. I had become absent from my own exciting life. I didn't know why I was doing this to myself. I should just let go. I should just turn the page and forget he ever existed. I just missed my friend, the one I spent hours with talking under my covers, and the one who made me smile and made me want to trust outside my circle, the one who had a special reading voice just for me.

No amount of work, music, movies or wine silenced the party happening in my head so I could concentrate. I desperately needed to eject myself, but my schedule didn't permit much flexibility. A subway ride uptown might do the trick.

I followed the twisted concrete setting deep into Central Park searching for the entrance to Woolman Rink. I wanted to be alone with New York. The air of January bit my face and even my fingers through my gloves. Growing up in the South didn't permit for this outdoor skating experience. This was another thing I wanted to be the only one to bear witness to.

Comparable to the Brooklyn Bridge, the ice rink was another landmark I undeniably couldn't continue to ignore. The fear of falling was painless considering the recent rejection. Maybe, I was letting my doubt get the best of me and I should believe in him. I should believe in us.

Balance.

Patience.

Damn, my skates are tight.

I moved into the pace of the other skaters. Skating in circles and taking in the skyline that peaked through the naked trees. Their winter break offered skaters a whole view of the city. I pushed hard to glide, wanting the full experience while the great New York tunes of Billy Joel and Frank Sinatra broadcasted overhead. I became lost in the circle and the sounds of the ice peeling away as my blades cut through its surface. Hours passed unnoticed practically dark and yet only 4:30 p.m. When I tip toed onto solid ground, I felt a wave of intoxication. I was lightheaded and the lights of the city resembled star trails in the black skyline. I was high off ice.

Accepting that falling in love is never a defeat, proved to be more difficult. It is one's ability to take in all that life teaches and turn it into art. Christoph Kostas helped me open up to the possibilities of love, but without trust. As long as I was 100% confident about my feelings, I wouldn't worry about what other people thought, so much so that I was assured in my capability to convince others around me if I had to.

Oftentimes, I felt my heart knew, but wouldn't allow me to completely say it out loud. Even when I had thought to say *I love you* to him, I never could initiate it myself. I knew love wasn't just a response, it's our soul's natural reflex. The gene to love and be loved exists in each and every one of us, but my hardware was unfamiliar when it came to externalizing it, to embracing it, to building on it, to completely giving into it. Love lies in every moment, in every defining instance, in every nuance of what I wanted to create with a man—us.

I couldn't get a grasp on clarity. My head and heart had turned my feelings, thoughts, and common sense into clutter. My tools were disorganized and filed into the wrong compartments. Common sense was in my *feelings* folder with feelings filed in my *head* folder. I was unable to trust any of it. For the first time in my life, I couldn't trust myself. This wasn't a winning characteristic for an artist.

I composed a new e-mail.

From: Chloe Kassidy
To: Christoph Kostas
Subject: Realization
Date: January 13, 5:37 p.m.

I'm not dropping my deadline and dreams to conveniently fit into your life. I know what I deserve and it's more than a voice and words on my computer screen. Why should I give you another chance?

From: Christoph Kostas
To: Chloe Kassidy
Subject: Breathless
Date: January 13, 5:54 p.m.

I've never touched you, smelled you, seen you, or tasted you. I've only listened to you and because of this absence of any other sense,

I've developed that sense so well that I can actually know you inside out by a simple, "Hey."

Moreover, I've learned to love, a sort of love that I guarantee wouldn't have occurred if I could see you. I'd be too shy to tell you all that I'm telling you, and too terrified to know that you could have every single thing you wanted just by looking at me in the eyes and saying, "Pretty please with sugar on top".

You don't have a thing to lose by taking chances. Chloe, you have a huge heart that even if you lost a little bit of it, you'd still have the world's biggest.

I want to be the best in your eyes. I need to be the best in your eyes. I have to be the best in your heart and you have to not have a say in that . . . that's how one knows. I don't expect you to stick around and just sit there and wait for me. That would be too unfair and selfish on my part. You're not to be taken for a granted. I fully acknowledge that.

I know I haven't been around, but that doesn't mean I don't exist or don't want to be around. It only proves how unfortunate my year has been so far. One can look at life's misfortunes in both a negative or a positive manner and I refuse to allow them to dissolve me or to dishonor all that I am and all that I am not.

One can never be too optimistic when it comes to love. After all, true love is usually much more painful than a mediocre feeling. Great pain has always been the main element in creating great miracles. Christoph

His words made my accusations of him never intending to be here doubt they entirely made sense. Was he this sentimental fool and not a game player? Losing me would have just been part of the game. The week continued with no wiggle room for me to waste on my diplomatic investigation or being stood up. I became wrapped up in this drama that I worked double time to make the exhibit deadline.

Without calling, Stephanie stopped by my apartment when she couldn't find me at the gallery.

"You seem to be unreachable by phone lately," she said. She stood in the doorway like she stood by her theory that the Swiss was hiding something and I might be research for his book. We had joked that if that was the case, I damn well better be part of the dedication.

"Stop being silly. Come in." Her expression caused me to cringe. "Oh, please excuse the mess."

My workstation was overwhelmed. I waited for the explosion of Post-It notes and candy wrappers to suck me up and swallow me whole. There were two weeks until opening and I hadn't submitted my theme to the curator. *How could this be happening?* I had never played with time like I did now. I continued to explore *Perspective* as my theme and labored with incorporating it into love and struggled to find three images that could showcase it. I pushed my keyboard aside and folded my arms to form a new black hole that I could hide in.

Stephanie began to sound like Kate. "Chloe, he has to be here first to have this relationship."

She knew I was in chaos and it was coming from him. They both had a valid point. *How could I love someone who treated me like this?* I wanted to love him, though, and it made me bitter to the core. Here I lived a complicated life, day after day, with this invisible man. I was being anti-social with my friends. I wanted to be home behind closed doors with him even if it was through a piece of technology. I became paranoid that he would just show up and surprise me one day, so anywhere I went, I attempted to look first-date ready. What if Stephanie was right, that he wasn't who he said he was? That finding nothing on him through my searches was a sign I should follow. He could be the guy at the gym on a nearby treadmill watching me behave foolishly while texting away.

"How's the theme coming along?" she asked.

"I'm not done," I admitted. "Can you believe this?"

"Well, sort of. You haven't been yourself lately."

"Don't worry about me, I'm—"

"Do you think you could accept the possibility that you've eaten his lies like a pre-theater, prix fixe menu, so quickly because of time and not to miss the show . . . that you're not realizing you haven't been getting much for your money?"

I didn't have an answer. She believed Christoph was a brilliant storyteller and I behaved naïvely chasing after his fairy tale, a version that prevented mine from coming true.

I would never forget one of our first conversations. It was an unnatural subject to be talking about so soon, yet one of the most natural times in my life talking about true love. I was proud of myself for opening up and letting him in that evening, but I was more in awe of this stern, soft-spoken man in just his late twenties to be passionate about love. He wasn't trying to take me out, get me tipsy and into bed. He wanted to know about my life, my dreams, and my thoughts on love and what I would do if I found the authentic thing.

I sat next to her on the couch. "You know, Christoph always says that true love is never logical. That nothing that is too great is logical," I said.

"Well, there you go," Stephanie said. "Just skip to the last page. He figured it out . . . Watch out Romeo for noble Christoph." We laughed.

"I've been doing some investigative research on him. It's like he doesn't exist."

"What kind of research?"

"Well, nothing CSI or anything," I joked. "Searches on Google, social media and some online company that does background checks. Christoph Kostas doesn't seem to match with an address, phone number—"

"Wait a minute," she interrupted. "He works with the United Nations. How could there not be any search results with news updates, missions, or whatever diplomats do?"

"Maybe it's a security thing? His social media pages add up with who he says he is," I said.

"What did he say when you told him about your search results?"

I remained silent.

"You haven't asked him?"

"Christoph never lets my defense mechanism take us too far away from his thoughts."

"What do you mean, Chloe?"

"He always says he is too confused to figure out my over-analytical mind without my help. That . . . I need to help him. That's all he's been asking me to do. Help him come to me and feel confident enough in my feelings." I was unfamiliar with a man admitting his weakness, especially one who embraced his sensitivity and philosophical side.

"Chloe, where is all this effort behind these heartfelt words of his?"

"Stephanie, I just need him to meet with me and prove me wrong, to stop being difficult, and say he will do whatever it takes to fix us!"

"You need to understand that just because you wanted to find true love and trusted this man, doesn't make your wanting to find love silly or that you were wrong to believe you deserve happiness."

We both sat there in silence and absorbed the truth in her words. Maybe she was right. I didn't want to be wrong after all these years of protecting myself from love. I didn't want to accept that I needed to quit him after being stood up at the Red Cat and my fainting spell.

"Listen, stop this. Look at your desk," she demanded. "Your dream is right there in arm's reach. If he is meant to be, he can wait a couple more weeks. You've waited almost four months." She stood up and pulled me to my feet. "Now, get to work Kassidy. You're worth this." Stephanie hugged me then headed to the door. "I'll call you tonight."

Photography was drawing with light, but I was dark. How could I do this when my thoughts, my heart, my theme was opaque. I had a complete creative block. My mind couldn't hold on long enough to trace a complete idea. I was blank. Blank just like my wall.

Burying my head deeper into my desk, I concentrated on my breath. *Inhale. Exhale. Inhale. Reed Scott.* Reed had reminded me to give myself an honest shot. *The hero is in the trying, Chloe.* Reed had a breathtaking persuasiveness that set him apart from others. *Give yourself an honest shot. What happened to love making me a better person? The butterflies?* I had to fill these holes with light. The light would push out the darkness.

Christoph had explained his upbringing and the differences between his father and mother. He had explained his theories on the great love stories like *Romeo and Juliet*. If love needed to be complicated for him to appreciate it, then maybe I wasn't enough for him. I wanted him to see that the struggle is finding the person and truly appreciating what that means. And when you find that person, that isn't enough. They still needed to behave like a partner. The guy wasn't called Prince Charming for nothing.

He had rejected my comments when I was rational. "Fuck it, Kassidy. You call me selfish? Because I need you to tell me you love me and mean it? Because I need to know you cannot be as strong as you seem to be without me? Fuck it, yes."

Two hours passed with me forcing myself to have a positive frame of mind. My wrists became cramped like my fingers from the excessive retouching. The sore spot on the inside of my thumb had been replaced with the lady like habit of cracking my knuckles. I could see my mother cringe with each sharp popping sound. *"What man wants to marry a woman with fat fingers?"*

The phone rang while I poured myself a glass of wine. It was Christoph.

The saying is that curiosity killed the cat and I can believe that. It was killing me—slowly. I couldn't confirm what caused the greatest weakness today. His new Facebook profile picture gave me hope he was real, or when I popped into a bookstore the other day, only to see *The Reader* displayed with the Bestsellers.

"Hello?" I answered.

"I'm just half empty without us, honey. Please, let's figure this out. Please," he cried.

Even though I knew better, I stayed on the phone. He was like a Nazi dressed in a Jesus costume and I awarded him a martyr status, when in reality he was murdering my soul.

"Why do you just care to continue this charade of yours?" I asked.

Full of shame, I sat in silence being a stupid little person with a stupid little heart. A heart that he would break then let me pick up the pieces before breaking them into smaller pieces. I could hear Dr. Phil now. "Chloe, what are you getting from this? It sure this hell isn't happiness." And just like the Swiss man, the Texas Ranger would point his finger at me.

"What are you doing, Chloe?"

"Thinking," I admitted. "Your name could be Donald. You could create a Facebook profile with false information and use any e-mail address. Hell, I could be Snow White at Gmail.com."

"You should be a detective!" He laughed.

If he only knew.

This is what our conversations had become. I remembered months ago when he asked me, "How do you know when you've found true love?" I wasn't 100 % sure on how the heart confirmed the exact definition of love. *Really, how did you know?* I wondered how much of a choice we had when it came to true love, especially when we began to put the search for our soul mate before our own happiness. *Screw you Dr. Phil.*

"I'm not perfect. Every time I try to talk, you cut me off. Can't we just put the bitterness behind us? We could have a great conversation, laughing and being completely consumed by the moment—if you would only not conclude with bitter and sarcastic remarks," he said.

I remained quiet. Opening my mouth landed me nowhere. Speaking exhausted me. I missed moments of absolute silence behind my lens. *Seeing was believing.*

"I've learned to be with you without you because, unfortunately, I can never let go of you. I'm my own person but at the same time, you bring me to a sort of life I never thought existed, Chloe. You're the only thing that makes sense. Nothing needs to be definite except for us, sweetheart."

Even if this was in focus, it wasn't sharp. If an image is out of focus, you can't make it focus by simply sharpening. You end up with nothing but a sharp, out of focus picture.

My heart was sensitive to the exposure. In photography, there is ISO, the film's sensitivity to light. The higher the sensitivity the less time or the less amount of light needed to correct exposure. The downside of a higher ISO is that it increases the noise or grain in the images. This can sometimes make the image look terrible that it becomes unstable. The photographer's objective is to use the lowest ISO possible, but balancing that with what they want to achieve whether it's overexposure or underexposure. The artist can let their artistic eye lead the way when needed. *What way was I going?*

"Miss Love of my Life, I can't sleep. I wish you were here . . . I could at least watch you sleeping."

I remained quiet.

"I'm concerned that you can control your feelings for me way too much. I ended up being the girl here!" Christoph said.

That night while I drifted into sleep, the loud ambulance siren roared through my apartment. It was Grayson Gates calling. I made a note to return his special tone to the standard ring since the risk of him knowing about it would indeed lead to me needing medical attention.

He called and gave me a brilliant speech about how these blank walls would be ours soon. To ignore the tabloids. "And Chloe, please sign the confidentiality agreement my assistant is sending to you now. It's just a technicality. Whatever happens within the gallery stays within those walls. Got it?"

"Of course, Mr. Gates. Will—"

"Get to work." He shut down my inquiry once again. The great curator had trouble curing his issues with the media. Grayson Gates was extraordinary when it came to the art world and his shows, but incapable of learning from his own mistakes.

It was almost 2:00 a.m. and for the first time in awhile I ignored all outside requests, except Stephanie's and chose sleep. *Yes, I'm worth it.*

Chapter 33

"You told me once that the best gift would be to spend your birthday on a bench with a book and me. I thought we could start celebrating a bit early. My plan was to bring you to me, a place leading to the bench. You'll see for yourself," his voicemail said.

Do I give him one last chance? I didn't want to feel excitement, but I wondered if Christoph would do something extra special to make up for lost time and my birthday. The timing couldn't be more ideal. We would finally meet, confirm our connection, celebrate my birthday with introducing him to my friends and even have him attend the opening. I had to believe it would work out. That these events would unfold like everything was meant to be.

About an hour later, on a lovely Sunday morning, the intercom system rang from the doorman station.

"Good morning, Miss Kassidy. There's a package for you here."

I grabbed my keys and headed straight for the elevator. *Package?* Poking the button and getting no action, I double-timed it down three flights of steps.

"Excuse me," I said to the doorman, humiliated since I had run down the steps and was panting.

"Yes, Miss Kassidy. It was dropped off this morning," he noted.

"By whom?"

He took his white glove covered fingertip and graciously slid it through the list.

"Hmm—there's no signature. A young woman delivered it. I told her we required signature and I.D., but she said you were expecting it and ran out," he said.

"What did she look like?" I asked wondering why nothing could be clear-cut.

"She had on a baseball cap. Probably your age, dark blonde hair, a bit heavy," he described.

Mary?

I grabbed the delivery, and took the elevator trying to catch my breath while I hugged the 8 x 10 manila envelope marked *Principessa.*

Dialing Stephanie immediately from behind my kitchen wall, I studied the bulky envelope like a bomb that required deactivation. I cursed myself for living in a studio.

"Help!" I screamed as soon as she answered.

"Are you okay?" Stephanie panicked. "What's wrong?"

"He's in my apartment," I said while taking another peek to see if it moved.

"What? Who? The diplomat?" She was more freaked out than me.

"No. No. No. I mean this envelope. A girl left it with my doorman," I clarified. "It's on my bed," I whispered.

"Chloe, why are you whispering?" she laughed. "Open it, but slowly!"

Out of the envelope I slid an unfolded handwritten letter along with ten smaller envelopes each labeled with a number from one to ten.

"Wait!" she shrieked. "How does he know where you live?"

I honestly couldn't recall how he knew this detail or if I had mentioned it to him.

"There's a letter—I'm going to read it."

Dearest Chloe,

Living requires heart, and my heart has been more alive while talking to you through a phone rather than being in a room full of people.

Living isn't counting the time you spent apart, and tagging 'I waited for months.' Love is waiting a lifetime if you have to, for you cannot truly live without him. Living love is even when there are no guarantees, no tangibility, and no reason, but the feeling itself.

Life is finding your heart and doing everything within your power to connect it with his, because it'd be half-complete otherwise.

And Chloe, can't you see that life all of a sudden has so much meaning because I'm in it? Ever since we first talked I've been in it, honey. I wasn't there living it with you physically, but I've always been there emotionally. You are never alone. You are everywhere with me, because I'm right there inside of you.

I'm here, Chloe, with my flaws, my imperfections, my complications, my over analytical spirit, but also with my goofiness, my romanticism, writing, and my special voice when I'm sleepy. The question is . . . are you? Are you ready to accept that you'll not be fine for the rest of your life whenever we're not okay? This IS love.

My legacy, the thing that I shall be remembered for forever will be for introducing you to love, and for loving you like nothing and no one else.

I may have wounded us, but please don't rip us apart.

Happy Birthday.
Christoph

He had created a treasure hunt for me to complete with clues throughout Manhattan.

"It's *P.S. I Love You*," Stephanie said. "Well, except he's not dead."

"He's a ghost!" We laughed.

"He certainly has put thought into all these details," Stephanie sighed. "But, his legacy? Chloe, please know that his behavior is not love. Maybe, today that will all change, but you chose to step outside of your fear and give this a shot."

I promised I would call her with an update. I ran to my closet, ripping tags off my latest delivery from Jenna's picks, swiped on blush and gloss and ran down the street, calling and begging for a blowout appointment at the neighborhood salon. I sank into the swivel chair and requested a natural style that looked like I had ran effortlessly out my door, no retouching involved.

Even though I wasn't supposed to open all of them at once, the anticipation killed me. I had to pass the time in the salon chair somehow. Each envelope contained hints through a quote, movie scene, or a favorite place we had shared with each other. These clues matched with a meeting place that meant something to us.

I reopened the first envelope and proceeded. The first letter read:

Without you, my circle would be void. This place connected us by 'The Passage' and proves love doesn't know what time it is. Love doesn't expire. Go back to our start.

I cabbed it up to 14th and Union Square. A circle of void would be the Metronome, a large public art installation located along the south end of Union Square. It showcased a round circular void from which puffs of white steam throughout the day were released. To the left of this is a display of fifteen large LED digits, called *The Passage*, which gives the time in a 24-hour format. Directly across the street is the Union Square Barnes & Noble that would contain *The Reader*.

Pushing through the rotating door, I quickly checked the tables on the lobby floor for a copy. Without luck, I headed up to the third floor to fiction. Slowly approaching the aisle, I studied the faces surrounding me. *Would he surprise me here?*

I continued with the next envelope nervous not knowing where the bench with him would be. At each spot I opened another letter giving me the next clue and another paper cut since my excitement made me sloppy. The clues determined the next location, if I guessed right. The scavenger hunt led me to Everyman Espresso for one of their famous heart shaped foamy concoctions, to 42nd street and United Nations for a glimpse of the blue and white flag waving the official UN emblem, Brooklyn Bridge, the Rockefeller ice skating rink, Lindt of Switzerland chocolate shop, the Hudson River Park to view Lady Liberty, my gallery wall, and even Lincoln Center to make a wish at the fountain.

He had faith in me with deciphering riddles. The tenth letter read:

'Following the light of the sun . . .'
Chloe, you complete my circle. You're my beginning and end.
Go to this last destination and wait for me there. p.s. Look for the matchbox.

This was a piece of cake. I hadn't an inkling what it meant or the source. I did what any savvy individual would do. I did a Google search. The quote showed Christopher Columbus was the reference. The *complete my circle* could only be one place, Columbus Circle. *Gotcha!*

The last destination was within walking distance from my current position at the fountain. I applied my plumping lip-gloss three times too many, feeling the chemical reaction like tiny red ants biting my lips while I walked. Once I arrived, I watched traffic circling the statue from across the street, waiting for permission to cross. I stood at the front of the statue and face to face with Christopher Columbus. The two Time Warner Center skyscrapers with their mirrored paneling stood over us reflecting Central Park and a never-ending blanket of clouds. The sun was blinding.

Making my way to the statue's base, I walked up the three short steps to read the inscription. My eyes followed up the column covered sporadically with the bronzed reliefs representing his ships. There, Columbus stood confidently, hands on his hips, with his left leg popped forward where the intricate details of his robe hung. I had successfully accomplished each clue and stood at his final destination.

The matchbox.

The stone seating connected in semicircles around me. I walked along them until I spotted the gray and black striped matchbox near the base leg of one of the benches. Glancing around with no one watching, I picked it up and took a seat. People and cars were busied, moving around me, while I sat still with this paper box in my lap. The note said to wait here for him. It didn't say not to open it.

Sliding out the base, the silver and gold intertwined band was revealed. My heart and rational hat were fighting for first place. I put the ring in the palm of my hand and squeezed it tightly.

I wasn't sure how much longer I could remain calm with waiting while the cold stone numbed my ass. *Would he call me? Text me? Simply tap me on the shoulder?* An hour passed and the previous warmth and brightness from the sun faded. The light changed on the statue with the sky's darkness forming shadows.

I looked for a man that resembled the jpegs my inbox had collected from the past four months. No one resembled Christoph Kostas. I was sweating. My pulse was ready to pop. I tried to swallow, but my throat was sandpaper.

I dialed his cell and after four painful rings, I left a voicemail. "Hey, it's Chloe. I'm here." I didn't know whether my voice shook because of the low temperature or the drop in my self-confidence, or maybe a combination of both.

Immediately, I was disgusted with myself for sitting here. Here I was in a fishbowl while this stranger was probably examining my movements and emotions. I spotted a Barnes & Noble across the street. I ran in and away from the windows.

There was still no response from him. Blown out and balling my eyes out, I stomped towards the entrance of the bookstore, waited for a getaway car to approach, not believing I was about to highjack a cab from a tourist. I think it was a New Yorker's right in case of an emergency. When the store attendant grabbed the cab handle, I ran for it and dove in. "Sorry. Excuse me!" Slamming the door, I begged, "Please go. Please please go!" I screamed and held my heart with one hand and my throbbing knee with the other. *Ouch.*

He hadn't called or replied. He hadn't showed. I had sat on a bench, living two lies, the ones he had fed me and the one I had told myself. Humiliated and crying, I forced my address clear enough for the driver to understand.

At the corner of 5th Avenue and 46th street, we were stopped at the traffic light and I was repulsed with the thought of the flashing red one that would be blowing up my phone soon with another excuse. Resting my head against the cold window for relief, I watched groups of kids through the Build a Bear store's window creating their personalized security blankets. Now, that I was a grown up, I worked on the adult version, a man. A small group of children stood with amazement in front of the machine while a tube of fluff began bringing their bears to life, followed by the signing of its birth certificate. The machine stuffed the limp animal shell until the skin resembled a soft and cuddly friend. The toy that would protect them from the boogieman under the bed when light fell too dark. I wondered if they made bears for adults. It was embarrassing to realize these kids had graduated to teddy bear level and I was stuck in the imaginary friend phase.

Text message from Chloe: *Why?*

No response.

I was overly acquainted with the cruelty of his failures. A cramp ached in my chest causing a catalyst with tightness shooting from my heart into my throat. It was impossible to catch a full breath. Slowly breathing in through my nose and out my mouth, I realized this was one of those times when a paper bag might be necessary. It was a panic attack. It was loss. It was pain. It was that I hated him. I didn't understand why he would do that to me. It was another heart punch. My eyes bled tears all the way home. I cried in pure shame.

My life belonged to me. Holding the ring, I promised myself, he would never take any of it away again. Looking at the circle, I realized maybe everything isn't connected. Maybe certain things lead to the truth and others lead to nothing. There was no wrong side to any circle. Circles don't have sides. This circle didn't exist, because the man I thought had given it to me hadn't. I couldn't even title him as someone I knew. *Who was he?*

While the taxi approached my building, I took one last look at the ring in the matchbox before leaving it on the seat and shutting the door. Who knows where it would end up, but certainly not with me. I chose to let the idea of this man go. Even if it meant I lost control, that someone had hurt me. When the taxi pulled away, I knew that would be the final time he or anything belonging to him would stand me up.

I sat on my couch staring at my reflection in the TV. There I was, a talented and inspired woman with an upcoming exhibition, Jenna-fied, alone in my apartment that was as empty as me. I wasn't fulfilled like the bears in the store that day. He wasn't a soul mate, but toxic as ingesting large quantities of sulfate. He wasn't a soul mate, but a cyber-stalker. Today marked his official expiration date.

Immediately, I called Stephanie.

Chapter 34

Understanding the depth of field helps bring your scene into focus. The real world is three-dimensional. The light from your lens comes from non-flat surfaces. A lens can only achieve perfect focus on a single plane at a time. When objects get further away from that plane, whether closer to or further from the camera, they get progressively more out of focus. The degree of blurriness is so miniscule that it can't be detected by the naked eye. What you end up with is a range in which these occurrences appear to be in focus, although technically only one point is actually in perfect focus. That one point never included the diplomat.

My heart, the principal part of me, that piece of hardware that kept me together in all aspects of my life, was blurred. The camera chip, a lightproof box, worked together with the frame, while the shutter, controlled the light's travel to its destination. Fine-tuning the amount of light allowed in brought the image into or out of focus. There was no in between, just like his actions. He wasn't a handsome prince but a bastard dragon that had swallowed my hopes whole.

The next morning he sent a text: *I was around the corner walking up and down. How could I ever abandon anyone? I'm scared of you and life without you. You just don't get it.*

From: Chloe Kassidy
To: Christoph Kostas
Subject: Putting pen to paper
Date: January 28, 8:47 a.m.

You need to listen to me very carefully. We don't exist. You're a fraud. Maybe it felt good to do what you've done. So be it. I know this experience will only make me stronger as I move on with my life. I know who I am and what I deserve. I have a life full of love to return to. Game Over.

From: Christoph Kostas
To: Chloe Kassidy
Subject: I . . .
Date: January 28, 9:07 a.m.

Talk about making a man feel like he's a shirt you're no longer interested in wearing. Chloe, I love you. If we did end, then we never really started for you. My intentions are serious. They are clear, they are upfront, and they are direct. I didn't hypnotize you into being here for God's sake. I'm not an Internet game. I'm not a guy who is miles away having a separate life and spending time emailing you. I'm the guy who's in love with you and will be true to you in good days and bad, in laughter and in tears, in sickness and in health. Didn't we fall in love with each other? It is throughout the pain that greatness arises if you stick around long enough to notice and appreciate.

You're sitting there implying that I've invented my entire lifeline so I can participate in a four month game that would leave me heartbroken, alone and completely disconnected from the woman I've shared everything with except for my body? That's an interesting theorem. I know you care. Don't think for one minute I believe you don't.

I'm not a storyteller. I'm not a prince. I'm not ordinary. Sometimes I have a bad sense of humor. I'm just a boy who fell in love for the first time in his life with his princess who coincidentally became his best friend as well. I love you with every fiber of my being even if you don't love me back, even if you never will. It's unconditional. And that's love.

And here's one more tip of information for you—even if I had a wife, a girlfriend, or whatever you think in your head, I would end it because my heart is yours. The truth is much simpler. As complicated as it may sound, it's actually simple.

p.s. Are you wearing my ring?

Christoph

To break this ongoing chain letter I had to change my number, block his emails and wholeheartedly accept he was a man with bad intentions. This chain didn't bring love or luck. I would ignore these emotionally manipulative stories and the exploitation of superstition that supposedly threatened me if I snubbed the conditions set out in a chain letter.

I had allowed this stranger to control my fate. His recklessness with my love was nothing compared to my own reckless behavior with my life. With one click, I blocked his e-mail account.

His feelings were always more important to him than mine. I wanted nothing more than this guy to disappear, especially from my inbox. I replied for the final time with a text: *Do not contact me again. Here's a clue for you to follow. Two words . . . Restraining Order.*

Text message from Christoph: *Are you serious? It has come down to a lawyer between us?*

Today, I witnessed the fall of a person who doesn't know truth. He only knows how to speak through the words of others. His quotes, false theories, and empty promises came from anyone, but him. The photography I would hang on my wall was *writing with light*, and it told a story with a newly discovered perspective.

My theme was clear, but I was still muddled. My ego had taken control only to influence my actions pleasing it instead of what was best for me. Processing the details that had developed, this story was hard to digest. This stranger's legacy wasn't love. It was lies. I was grateful the package was only meaningless words and a pile of paper rather than an envelope full of Anthrax. The threat was possible, since he adored tragedies.

I had taught him how to hurt me. Replacing my own thought process with his poetic pretty new one had caused me to lose all rationality. It was brainwashing at its best. His lavish flattery of how talented and special I was and his fabricated tales of saving the world while writing his way through it, never lead to anything, but me being here only to be stood up. My desperateness to find *Love Through Light* had given birth to this heartbreak. I had to kill the infection, before my heart grew toxic and bitterness attacked love. I was too young for heart disease.

My lack of effort to figure him out months ago was unsettling and unlike my control freak habits. *Why didn't I wait at the airport for his flight to arrive? Show up at the United Nations? Follow Mary after one of our dates? Question the dead ends from the Google research on his history, diplomacy and UN credits? E-mail his friends on Facebook or Twitter? Were they like me? A friend connection only because of a request?* Come to think of it, he was always alone. I never heard anyone in the background of our conversations, not one family member.

I switched off my phone and threw my thoughts into my theme. The images blurred while I quickly scrolled until my eye caught image #108. I double clicked the image and my heart stopped for the second time today. My iCloud software had backed up my photos from this afternoon. I knew it with every fiber of my being that this was the one. That one image that said it all to me, this circle of confusion, Columbus Circle. My gut and my head agreed this was worthy of a wall.

It was remarkable how focal length in photography affects images. You can have the same shot, but by selecting different focal lengths, you can reshape the aesthetics of your image. Zooming in and out on the same subject, whether you're distant or near, greatly changes the way in which a subject relates to background and the perceived distance between the two. It was the difference between the extremes, the lightest and darkest parts of photography, that self-exposure existed. *Call Reed Scott!*

I needed to stop blaming my autofocus for the lack of understanding of love on my part. It wasn't my heart's fault. I had never followed it before. This was a clear case of simple user error.

"Hi, Chloe," Reed answered.

"How are you?"

"I'm doing well . . . What do I owe the pleasure of your call today?"

"I don't want to disturb your weekend, but I had to call and tell you—I found the image!"

"That's great, Chloe."

"I wanted to see if you're around this week to discuss the details." I knew Reed would be honest with me. Even with this vulnerability, that is when I knew I could trust him even more.

"Well, I just poured a fresh cup of coffee and sat out on my terrace. I've got the ocean in front of me . . . and an artist having a moment. I'm ready when you are?"

In that moment, I imagined his one of a kind grin. He made me smile.

Reed's feedback sent me straight to work for hours without any disruption.

My body began to call for backup. I stood up to stretch and make coffee, when a new e-mail alert popped up on my screen obstructing me from my work.

From: Mary Polt
To: Chloe Kassidy
Subject: You said?
Date: January 28, 5:13 p.m.

Dear Chloe,

Christoph has specifically asked me to abstain from connecting with you and I respect that. Regrettably so, ever since you mentioned a lawyer coming between you two, he himself wishes to never hear of you again. I cannot express how dejected and shocked I am on your decision, but you shouldn't be preoccupied because we don't plan on bothering you.

I wanted to bring closure to our separate communication by sharing a few photos with you. He is a real trooper. I don't expect or even inquire for an answer from you. Can you honestly claim that he'd harm anyone? I've been asked to trash several books, handwritten letters, a few diaries, and a sealed box of items you shared together. I can't do it. I would hand them to you, mail them, what may. However, I would never forgive myself if the soul and writings of my friend were to become the stockpile on a lawyer's desk.

I extend my sincerest wishes to you for a fulfilling life. I'm sorry it has come to this. I sincerely thought things would be different.
Mary

I didn't owe her a response and immediately deleted her note. *God, they were both dramatic.* Before stripping out of the last *stood up* ensemble, I headed out to change my number. This would be the last time I would lose a phone number and my head. My new year was less than eight hours away with the countdown to my birthday tomorrow.

Working late at the gallery wasn't my ideal way of celebrating, but the opportunity was the gift and I was blessed. Photography put me in the mood for love and where there was love there was no real sacrifice. It was fifteen minutes until midnight with the first image framed and hung.

The other artists had finished, packed up, and were headed home. While I chased a stalker, they had worked on their walls. I couldn't go just yet, back home, where the breaking and entering into my heart unfolded. My apartment contained evidence of the crime scene.

I fought hard to ignore my bed's gravity pulling at my body. I remained devoted to my designated space. The echoes and the little white spotlights kept me company while I stared at the single image that decorated my wall ignoring my mind as it tried to think about his little white lies.

Rather than feeling anger, I was consumed by an abnormal sense of fear. I knew I wasn't alone, but I couldn't manage to turn around to see who was behind me. I remained calm and contemplated whether or not playing dead only worked on grizzly bears or if playing dumb would be more effective. The shuffling shoe sounds on the granite floor moved closer. It was only seconds before I sensed the closeness of this presence behind me. When I turned around, he rushed up to me with full force and grabbed each shoulder to pin me against my wall.

"You're hurting me," I began to tear up. Christoph remained silent, emotionless, and stared deep into my eyes like the rules of life didn't apply to him. I refused to be manipulated by his power, the power I gave him to create this hold over me.

Slowly raising my hands, I gently grabbed his wrists, never once breaking eye contact. To witness his body language, his breathing, his scent and touch was new to me even though I had fought with this man for four months. Real actions had replaced his voice and he never uttered one word while we stood face to face and I inhaled him.

I was no longer confused by his intentions or filled with frustration since it was replaced with being powerless and isolated in the gallery. Knowing his truth now didn't make him so gorgeous. I shockingly found his sent jpegs unattractive. His eyes offered nothing familiar to me. There was no love, flattery, or a man that would fight to be with me.

He gently released my arms and stood back, staring at me, resembling a piece of art on the wall while slowly analyzing me inch by inch. Taking a couple steps, I approached the man whose eyes were flooded with insecurity and vulnerability. I touched his face.

"It's okay," I whispered. He lowered his face in my hands. For a moment, I felt pity for him. I was torn between comforting his pain and kicking him in the balls and making a run for it.

I'm not sure why he came to the gallery. Maybe he wanted to see the truth in my reaction since I had craved action in his efforts while struggling with his deceit. He stood there, and I accepted that perhaps it symbolized his own acceptance in failing to gain my true admiration, respect and love.

I rejected the idea of fearing him, heartbreak, or love anymore. He stood in front of me and I just wanted him out of my space and away from my life. Coming towards me again, he reached into his jacket pocket with one last thing to do. I stood paralyzed only able to cover my eyes and scream to drown out any pain I was about to encounter.

"Hello?" A voice echoed. "Chloe . . . it's Stephanie." Her heels clicked across the gallery floor. "Are you okay?"

"What time is it?" I asked. *It was just a dream.*

"It's almost one-thirty in the morning," she responded with a concerned tone. "We've been trying to call you since midnight to wish you happy birthday."

"I must have fallen asleep. I wanted to get my first piece on the wall." I stood up and double-checked my surroundings. *It was just a dream.*

"Come on—let's get you in a cab."

While heading home, I observed the handful of strangers walking along the streets, thankful that it was a nightmare. The feeling of wanting nothing to do with him stuck with me. Finally, when your heart, head and gut are aligned, you know where you're meant to be. My heart kept me waiting on Christoph, since I wanted that love story. I didn't want to fail my first shot outside my lens. My head and gut had been alerting me that something wasn't right.

My life and belief in true love still existed after this error in judgment. Through his love fraud, I discovered there was no reason to fear heartbreak or the abyss of unknowns. The best thing I could do for myself was to forgive and forget Christoph. Immediately, I thought of one person—my mother.

Part Three

Chapter 35

It was the morning of my thirty-first birthday and the last thing I wanted to do was head into Bright Images, Inc., but I had to finalize a pending project. Thankfully, I scheduled months ago to take the first week of February off and concentrate on the exhibit's final preparations. My theme was confirmed and it was more than I ever imagined from my pitch to Grayson Gates months earlier.

The ringtone of my new phone still took getting accustomed to as did the relief that when it rang, it wasn't the devil's breath trying to suck me back in.

"Happy birthday, old lady!" Kate screamed.

"I'm still a year younger than you," I joked.

"Do you want me to stop by and pick you up? We can head to Stephanie's together." Tonight was my birthday dinner hosted by Stephanie and Alexander at their apartment. "Why, what's wrong?" I asked. My office was on the West side and the subway would shoot her straight up to their place.

"It's your day—I don't want to bog you down with drama," she said.

"I'm sure I can handle it, trust me."

"Stephanie is driving me crazy. I honestly can't stand her at the moment, and I'm only going tonight because of you."

"Kate—" I sighed. "Listen, I know you'll probably respond to this by saying something rude, but please don't."

"What is it?"

"You need to deal with this ex baggage," I said.

"That has nothing—"

"Listen . . . you and Stephanie not being one hundred percent is childish, especially over petty issues. She hasn't done anything to you but be a great friend."

"Jesus, Chloe —"

"There's no reason to be rude and unkind to anyone, especially your friends," I continued. "What your ex did is completely unrelated to anyone else. He was a bad egg," I said hoping I didn't go too far when I thought I heard her cry. "I'm sorry. I just don't want you to punish people who love and care for you just because of him. You're only alienating yourself."

She remained silent for several seconds then sniffled. "Okay," she muttered. "My behavior with her has been horrible. I'm hurt. I hate feeling lonely more than I hate what Ian did to me."

"Hey, why don't you still swing by and pick me up. That'll be nice."

With the call ending, I agreed I needed to take my own advice. *Just one bad egg.*

The Hudson River was tranquil today offering a sense of peacefulness to my office. "Chloe!" Milton's voice pierced from the speakerphone. *I spoke too soon.*

"Yes," I responded not caring what he wanted. He didn't have a purpose for being in the office but to create disorder.

"I've changed my mind on the upcoming shoot. Let's move it up a week and find a prettier model!"

"That's a huge problem. You signed the contract last week, remember?" My face heated since the month long negotiation to secure and setup the shoot next week was now crumbling. "I already faxed the contract over."

"I don't care! Fix it!"

Immediately, I walked out of my office to his door with his faint screams still pouring out of my speakerphone. "Knock. Knock." I moved towards his desk. He looked up and quickly tried to hide his shocked expression.

"This model is fat!" he screamed. "And . . . schedule a meeting with the photographer for tomorrow morning . . . The three of us can review the set."

"Milton, I'm not available this week—"

"Well, make yourself available."

"Milton, I'm not available. I've had this time blocked off my schedule—the gallery exhibit."

"Oh—that thing," he said unimpressed. "Speaking of that, I should attend. I heard it might be a cool party. Get me tickets," he demanded. Within the gallery walls, I was a debut artist, not his *do-girl*.

His manipulation and mind tricks didn't work on me. I didn't care how many self-help business books the moron had read. I was fed up with selfish and socially awkward men. "It's an invitation only event," I said with pleasure. "I'm sure you understand why it's tightly controlled. It's a VIP thing."

"Chloe, your lack of attendance on this project next week is disruptive. In fact, I question your dedication—"

"Milton . . . sorry to interrupt. Just so we're clear and you don't waste your time. My dedication is to the exhibit and my photography career. Not Bright Images." My throat clenched with shock. I hadn't planned on airing the words that had lived in my mind all these years.

"Well, Chloe, I believe this timing—"

"Sorry to interrupt you again. I believe this timing couldn't be more appropriate—"

"Appropriate for what exactly, Miss Kassidy?"

"To inform you of my resignation," I responded confidently. Immediately I pictured my mother's face. I was sick of working for a man who believed his employees' worth rested with him. That he had any significance outside of the Bright Images, Inc. oversized double glass doors. His power only remained inside this corporate office unless we let his manipulation make our reality his. The cause of his behavior had to be the result of his own realization that he was a man with daddy issues.

"I'll get to work on that letter for you and don't worry—I'll make sure someone reschedules your shoot and finds a model closer to a negative two size. Will that be all?" I asked. I imagined him scrambling for a response in one of his books, as I closed his office door behind me.

Needing fresh air and a snack break, I found a bench by the river. Taking the first bite of my granola bar, my phone beeped with a new message.

I forgot to block her.

From: Mary Polt

To: Chloe Kassidy

Subject: Please

Date: January 29, 1:17 p.m.

Dearest Chloe,

I hate to see this negativity amongst you two when there are more serious problems facing the world.

I will, for now, leave you with his words. You're a hurt woman in love. We have all been there. The difference with your case is that you're not just in love. Those kinds of true love are always with us.

His note he shared with me for you:

'I've always known that I'm a handful. Ever since I was a little kid and my parents discovered my extraordinary intelligence, I've always gotten the 'you'll be unhappy in your life' and I thought they were bullshitting me. I'd win chess competitions, IQ tournaments, treasure hunts, memory championships, and I was far away from being unhappy. When I started growing older, I lost friends because they didn't get me or I didn't get them. Friendships fade away. They have different priorities. I was still okay until you came along. I know my words don't matter to you, but I love you, Chloe, more than I love myself. The great loves in my books were great because they were incomplete, because they were difficult to get. And I'm so bad at you. I'm so bad at this. It's making me so sad.'

Happy Birthday.

Mary

From: Chloe Kassidy
To: Mary Polt
Subject: Re: Please
Date: January 29, 1:31 p.m.

Mary,
Thanks for the birthday wishes. Oh, and you're fired. Stop fucking emailing me. Get a life of your own.
All the best,
Chloe Kassidy

I blocked her e-mail and took a bite of my bar while returning to my moment of still processing the stand off with Milton Bright and the past four months with Christoph Kostas. I was back in control.

Kate and I headed uptown in a taxi. We remained unusually quiet for our own reasons. Seeing Kate after her breakdown on the phone with her own heartbroken experience ripped the Band-Aid slowly off my own wound. This was the first year I didn't want to celebrate my birthday. I was humiliated and hoped none of them would bring up his name. I hadn't mentioned a plus one to this dinner. If only canceling tonight was an option.

"What's wrong, Chloe?" she asked leaning her head towards me and lifting it with a nod.

I directed my attention to the passing traffic. "I'm just tired."

"You seem like you're hurting?"

I was heavyhearted, but the tears in my eyes were torrential. I hugged my knees to hide my face. Tonight I had to tell all my friends the truth. It was the only way to completely set myself free. "I'll explain later," I cried. I had just enough energy to go through this one last time. Telling them everything would be a relief.

"Happy Birthday!" they screamed when their apartment door swung open only to be struck with their own sniffling and snotty surprise.

"I'm sorry," I cried. "I don't want to ruin my dinner."

"Kate, what's wrong with her?" Alexander asked while he pulled me inside.

"Get her a strong drink," Kate demanded. "Actually, make that two."

We gathered on the couch while Alexander poured us each a scotch. "I can't drink this," I said.

"Do it, Chloe," Alexander pushed. "Take a deep breath and suck it down."

Getting a whiff, "If it burns my nose, what will swallowing it do to me?"

"Do it," Kate pushed. She threw her glass back.

After gulping the drink that left my mouth with a dirty fireplace taste, I confessed. Maybe it was just the fix for rejection.

While Stephanie remained silent, I waited for Alexander or Kate with suggestions.

"How could he be that involved in your life and us not be aware of it?" Kate asked.

"Why would you agree to be his girlfriend?" Alexander puzzled looking at Stephanie for clarification.

"I should have stopped you from going on that treasure hunt," Stephanie said.

"Chloe, how many emails have you exchanged with this man?" Alexander pried.

"A little over four thousand," I admitted. I was humiliated and I couldn't even get drunken immunity, since this wasn't a one-time incident.

"Chloe!" Stephanie panicked covering her mouth with one hand while grabbing Alexander's elbow with the other. I knew she now recalled her e-mail exchanges with him.

The truth was that I opened up to a man I had never laid my eyes on. I thought if things became too easy, too casual, too predictable, too planned, it'd go away, just like it happened to my parents and many other couples. *It was pseudo-intellectual bullshit!* He hid behind his computer screen boosting his undeserved ego.

"Come with me into the den," Alexander demanded. "Immediately!"

He pulled two chairs up to his architecture style table and instructed me to log into my

e-mail while Stephanie and Kate peered at the screen. I was embarrassed by what they would see next and knew that any time you had to keep secrets from your loved ones, it was wrong.

I clicked on the folder marked *Private*.

"Now what?" I asked.

"We're going to track him by his IP address. I want you to randomly pick ten emails. Choose various ones from the different places he claimed to be traveling and let's track the location and see if it matches," Alexander said.

"You can do that?" I asked. I wasn't sure if I rooted for Christoph or myself when either way resembled a naive dipshit or a super desperate naive dipshit.

I chose emails from the beginning, middle and end of our story. From dates when he lived in New York, his grandfather's illness in Geneva, the night Grayson Gates called an emergency meeting and I stood him up, when working in Le Chaux, my meeting with Mary, and the final day with the scavenger hunt while I hit the pavements in search of him, but instead learned the truth.

One by one, Alexander copied and pasted the small header into a tiny rectangle on the tracking site. This small text box would to uncover the truth. Stephanie steadied me from my complexion turning a faint combination of yellow and green. I slumped over, covering my eyes.

Alexander broke the silence by continuing, "Chloe, he's not a soul mate. He is a psychopath. These IP addresses are in Mountain View, California."

"He was never going to be here," I admitted while Alexander entered IPs from Mary's emails into the search field. "I can't explain it well, it's like sometimes I wanted to be with him and sometimes I wasn't sure because something happens or someone says something about him and all of a sudden we didn't make sense," I admitted.

"Two of her emails show the Vinegar Hill area in Brooklyn," Alexander continued. "The rest of the emails were sent from Maryland."

"Mary never mentioned Maryland. She lives in New York," I said. "I met her in the city once for coffee."

They gasped.

"Maybe Mary wasn't emailing you?" Stephanie said.

"You mean the guy pretended to be Mary?" Kate asked.

Looking back, the tone and manner of her emails didn't match the girl I met or her introductory e-mail. "I think he wrote from her e-mail account to talk me away from my doubts," I confessed. "The timing of her emails was always during our fights and to promote his goodness and intentions."

"He talked about himself as Mary, but he was himself?" Kate attempted to make sense of it all.

"I've done a Google search on both Mary Polt and Christoph Kostas and there are no results," he confirmed.

"Those weren't their real names, I assume. Christoph wasn't this internationally

well-traveled diplomat, with a dying grandfather, a New York City office at the United Nations, or life threatening missions in Darfur." I broke out into a hysterical laugh.

"She's having a nervous breakdown," Alexander said.

"This isn't funny, Chloe," Kate panicked. The fear in my friend's face put me in my place. "There was no cyber-sex, right?" she pried.

"Of course not!" I screamed. "He had my stories, my feelings, my fears and my dreams as tiny souvenirs in exchange for his fabricated fairy tales—that's all!"

"Or everything," Stephanie pointed out. "You need to move immediately . . . He knows where she lives!"

"This guy is screwed up. To invent an identity, a job, travel and stories to be a part of your life." Alexander wanted to be sure I wasn't having any doubt. I couldn't blame him.

"I bet my life that if I were to say Mountain View, California he would have an excuse to why. 'I use a program that most diplomats around the world utilize.'"

"What's in Mountain View?" Kate asked.

Alexander, on a roll, searched the city and state. "Nothing is there but Google and a naval airport. Wait a minute . . . Gmail accounts always link to this California IP address," he noted.

"He might be anywhere." I hid my face with my hands while the shame continued to surface.

"I wonder if he's been watching you?" Stephanie asked.

"You know that New York City has the highest sales of telescopes and Celestron binoculars? And I'm sure it's not to see Canada—just sayin," Alexander said. "Yep. Gmail automatically hides the IP addresses to protect the privacy of the e-mail account. That's probably why he preferred their service."

"If I questioned his occupation, he was confident. He would try to convince me otherwise that I was crazy. 'Chloe, I've worked for the Embassy. And you're right, with a simple Google search you'd see.'"

"Honey, what are you doing now?" Stephanie asked Alexander.

"It seems when the IP address is not available, you can determine the sender's approximate location from the time-zone of the originating computer," he said while he clicked on the *Gmail Labs* page and enabled the *Sender Time Zone* feature.

"Try one of his emails from Geneva," Kate suggested.

Alexander opened the e-mail from Christoph when he was at the hospital by his grandfather's side. I nervously watched as the mouse cursor moved to click *Show Details* to display the current time in the sender's time zone.

I was stunned. "The time zones are identical," I gasped.

"He didn't send those emails from Geneva," Alexander said.

"How he conducted himself as a United Nations diplomat is beyond me," Kate added.

"I knew it was like this, a research experiment for his book or a creepy infatuation," I muffled without tears. I had cried too many times.

Stephanie rushed to the phone immediately while Alexander, Kate, and I observed. There was no telling what any of our next moves would be.

She dialed a number and impatiently let the rings pass. "It's me. Yes, I know it's late, but we have an emergency. I need your help for my best friend. We need to find her a new apartment immediately. Yes. Yes. See you tomorrow," she said and hung up the phone. "This real estate broker owes us a favor—don't worry, there's no fee."

Kate walked to Stephanie and slowly hugged her. "Thank you for being there always, Stephanie."

"Why are you crying?" Stephanie was apprehensive with Kate's display of emotions. When she realized it was authentic, she wrapped her arms around her returning the affection.

"I'm sorry for being impolite," Kate said. She turned towards Alexander and me while she wiped away her tears. "I'm sorry for taking it out on you guys. Being dumped . . . I haven't been a decent friend to any of you. Jesus, I didn't even realize Chloe had an invisible boyfriend!" We laughed.

That was love.

After dinner and the largest piece of birthday cake I could fit into my belly, they drove me to my apartment to pack a bag while Kate headed home and prepared for me to sleep on her couch. I declined Stephanie's offer to stay in the second bedroom since staying with Kate would be good for the both of us. Although, I knew the comfort food situations would pretty much suck in the raw foodist's fridge. As an artist with a wall in one of the New Year's most exclusive openings, I never imagined I would be homeless and crashing on a friend's couch. *How could you be so stupid?*

I thought about the ferry ride in November and how the dark clouds and sun were competing for sky that day. The light was as real as the dark. My feelings had been genuine, yet it wasn't love, but the idea of being in love. The exhibit approaching and the pressure to understand love, I had *scam me* across my forehead as one of Emma's suitors with *soul mate*. I accepted that I had held on this long because I feared his rejection.

Snow fell at a rate that I was sure the city would be covered with a fresh blanket in hours. Tomorrow also offered a fresh start. I could live without him. My ego would just have to get over itself. There was one thing that still haunted me. *Who did I feel so close to?* Closing my eyes, I slowly took a breath and with a deep exhale pushed any thoughts of him out.

As I lay staring out the window from my couch bed into the darkness, I recalled a time back in college, heading out into the night to capture the beauty and stillness of the stars under the southern atmosphere. The stars didn't align perfectly, but my love of catching them standing still fueled my aim to be the artist I hoped to be. The night sky was an undreamed-of phenomenon. I stared at the star-filled sky in hopes of gaining clarity. The anticipation filled me with the same awe and wonder to the same degree of the length and mass of stars on display and the enormity of space above me. While lying there, I realized that life through a lens would offer a lifetime of observations and a chance to capture moments that might be easily missed.

The hurricane-like storms that year were hitting unusually hard and hindered the clearness of the night with cloud cover. That particular evening, an opportunity presented itself. It required a piece of equipment to express a clear, focused shot of stars. The earth's rotation makes it difficult to capture them in a still shot and without their apparent movement. They are called star trails. With a click of a button, I could hold the night sky, but the stars would still be gracefully moving, resulting in a trail-like effect. During a professor's explanation of setting my aperture to as wide as possible and putting the focus to infinity, I became fascinated with darkness. I came to understand the importance of pointing my camera towards the North Star, since it remains stationary while the other stars circle it. The North Star, the star of direction, accompanied references of true love. When your heart stood still, while the world around you kept moving. Hearing its name, struck the delicate void that rested in the thin shell that lined my heart.

These memories inspired me to not only see through my lens, but made me curious about stepping out from behind it and putting my heart on the line. I didn't want to just see and shoot. I wanted to practice love and not just through my camera. I wanted to believe wholeheartedly in my theme and image rather than manipulate it to simply tell a story for others to believe in. I wanted my exhibit to ignite emotion in the same way as the greatest love stories ever told.

"Chloe? You awake?" Kat appeared in the living room.

"Yeah."

She walked over and sat on my feet. "Cookie?"

We sat there in silence and nibbled away as we watched the snow float downward to the ground.

The next morning, I snuck out of Kate's apartment, not wanting to wake her. I had six days until the gallery opening. My appointment with the broker was at 10:30 a.m. I had hours to relish Central Park.

Like love that required essentials including honesty, trust, and compromise for a successful relationship, photography had its own requirements. Photographers could be technical or artistic with good vision. Artists vary in their approach and execution and their own self-exposure.

My heart had more in common with my Canon than I ever realized. Auto focus was a feature that gave my lens a hand, the help my heart needed.

With my shooting essentials in arm, I walked along the cement paths through Central Park. I snapped Turtle Pond and the Bethesda Fountain even though I had done so a million times before. That was the unexpected beauty of New York City. Nothing was the same twice. New York City never repeated itself.

Scenes filmed in this romantic borough included *When Harry Met Sally, Six Degrees of Separation, Kate & Leopold,* and the classic *Breakfast at Tiffany's*. I had almost forgotten until there it was stretched out in front of me while the boats paddled by, the famous bridge that revealed the truth in *You've Got Mail*. How ironic that my bridge scene connected me to something entirely different where everything was far from the truth.

Click. Click. Click.

The frames of this bridge were now darker since my *I've got mail* experience with a psycho pen pal.

Exiting the arched platform, I spotted a place to sit. Sliding my tall green rain boots out in front of me, I pulled my fur-lined hood over my head to cushion against the bench. I recalled my college professor teaching me, "Adjust your eyepiece or diopter. You must be able to see sharply through your eyepiece to know your subject is in good focus." I needed to adjust my view without any outside direction. I closed one eye and viewed the open sky and changed eyes for the lines of naked branches. Back and forth from eye to eye, I sharpened my focus.

Anything that has contrast will help the automatic focus work better and faster. It was the contrast between Christoph and me that attracted my attention to him.

I knew better than to depend on my *all focus point* mode. The mode doesn't know what you want to emphasize, and usually focuses on whatever is closest to the camera. My heart felt his sincere and unique presence with his voice through the phone. The little dreams when we first started, all those pretty little things I fell in love with. I didn't fall in love with a man. I fell for the idea of finding true love and being able to *Love Through Light* for the exhibit. The fairy tales and Shakespearian-like stories he often referred to helped keep me there. Waiting. Wondering. Wrecked. *To know love, to be love, you don't need to be pained.* Believing in that was a self-inflicted type of madness. Love wasn't dark.

Shooting frames in the dark was unproductive. A beautiful image with a story was produced from the light reflecting off an object. This had helped create my three *lighthearted pieces* for my wall.

Upon exiting Central Park, I saw the top of the statue through leafless trees. Christopher Columbus was still there. In fact, the circle had been there all along, right there in front of me. I had to create my own sense of love. This was about my soul's self-exploration and what I might discover.

February

Chapter 36

Several days later, Stephanie's broker found a new renter for my old apartment, while I signed the lease and scheduled movers for my new one. The pile of boxes and cardboard stench consumed my new studio apartment in Gramercy Park. This modern space brought a chance for fresh memories. I no longer saw my old self situated on my sofa, that insecure girl cuddling with doubt, empty promises, and waiting for an invisible psychopath to show up and murder her. It felt nice to laugh at myself.

"Knock! Knock!" Kate said as she peeked her head inside the already ajar front door.

"Who's there?" I joked.

"It's your back up team," Alexander answered. Stephanie walked in last wearing a serious expression and holding her recognizable green notebook that contained her itineraries.

"You're walking into a mess," I said. "Who wants coffee?"

"Where do we start?" Kate asked. We turned our attention to Stephanie.

She smiled. "Alexander is on bedroom setup and mounting the TV. Kate's on kitchen. Chloe's on office. I'm unpacking the closets."

"Aye Aye, Captain!" We scurried away like mice to our designated duties.

I had never considered living in this neighborhood, but I couldn't resist the key that accompanied my signed lease. The renter of the apartment had access to the private and quaint two-acre park surrounded by townhomes and condos. Having a key provided me easy access to an escape with a new set of benches along with the Edwin Booth statue situated in the park's center. He was a famous nineteenth century American actor recognized for his Shakespearian performances. It's said that some remembered him as one of the greatest American actors and unfortunately by others as the brother of John Wilkes Booth, the man who assassinated President Abraham Lincoln.

Another example of a bad egg.

The gallery opening wouldn't be spoiled or include anything rotten. My life had changed a great deal in these past few months. I had left the scared, controlling, and failure fearing girl curbside with the trash I had thrown out when I moved that morning.

I gave myself a last once-over since it took me hours to pick out my ensemble of a black leather pleated mini skirt with a pressed white button up tuxedo ruffle blouse accompanied by my black leather knee boots. It was sexier than I was accustomed to, but playing outside my comfort zone had become a new habit.

A significant crowd gathered in the once empty space that had carved a pit in my stomach. Those previously peculiar feeling of mixed emotions, each fighting for center stage within me, no longer existed. My awareness might not have been operating at its full potential, but tonight, I was on point.

My parents had flown in with Emma the night before and were meeting up with the rest of the group to attend together. I knew they would arrive at 7:00 p.m. sharp. I turned up an hour earlier to have my own moment. This was the debut I had imagined since I was that ten-year-old girl snapping shots of fairy tales.

I recalled the chilling October day last year, when I signed the foggy window with my finger. Tonight, the five thousand square foot street level space looked more intimidating with its entire floor to ceiling glass front interrupted only by the metal doorframes to enter and exit the gallery. The atmosphere was full of hustle and bustle staging the pristine maze-like space divided by cylindrical and rectangular walls.

This time it wasn't hard to miss. My signature was scribbled in the lovely Garamond font on the first right wall upon entering. There was my theme, *Love Through Light*, in the three

16 x 20 glossy prints that ran horizontally along the wall directly under it.

One last deep breath in and with exhale, I pushed in the door.

The opening at one of the top five galleries in Manhattan began shortly for the invitation only guests. A fresh coat of white paint had been applied days before so the aroma would clear before tonight. The modern white walls were full of love with our hearts strung across them. The décor was minimal with large square slate stone floors illuminated by the stainless steel lights that hung above. The space was bare with the sole purpose to flaunt our work by laying naked, seducing potential buyers.

"There's my future! I was just telling Penelope about your genius theme," Grayson Gates shouted with his candy soundtrack following him and his other candy on his arm. "Penelope, meet one of tonight's emerging artists, Chloe Kassidy." His personality had taken a 360 and the politeness caught me off guard.

I smiled when our hands clasped, "It's a pleasure to meet you," I said while gently trying to force life into our shake.

"She does look like Natalie Portman," she said.

I approached my wall embracing it with one huge mental hug. I was now a professional photographer and my job was my dream, but it was also meaningful because the past four months hadn't occurred in vain. My vulnerability had allowed me to create my theme. Without that experience, I recognized I wouldn't have been able to connect the dots and form that circle. I had no idea the strength of a circle until I experienced a true state of heart.

My heart was more than a hard–working organ that delivered blood to both my thickest and tiniest arteries. My heart did more than keep up the life support we call our circulatory system. My heart was more than my body's lifeline. By acquiring specific life tools, putting my heart into life and possessing strength, I had found the frame of mind within me to love. My heart would hold no space for this man with regrets. That would only leave less room for real love.

My theme had taken on an unexpected twist. The photographers that night would be presenting three images under their theme. After receiving permission from the curator, I would be presenting only one image demonstrated in three different perspectives. The image was an aerial shot of Columbus Circle shot from the fourth floor of the Time Warner Center. I had randomly chosen the fourth floor from the fifty-five story skyscraper to represent the four elements in my work–The two towers, Columbus Circle, and me. The image displayed Christopher Columbus in the center of the circle while three sidewalks permitted entrance to his statue. Traffic continuously circled the statue symbolizing love was art in motion.

While a group of attendees formed a crescent moon shape in front of my wall, I saw my father's arm waving three rows back while my mother struggled to secure it to a less noticeable place. She was already lecturing him. I introduced myself causing the crowd to turn silent.

"Good evening. My name is Chloe Kassidy. I would like to thank our curator, Mr. Grayson Gates, for this opportunity." Taking a clean breath, and moistening my lips, I heard muffles of *Natalie* and *Portman* among the crowd. "Tonight, I present to you my version on *Love Through Light*."

I followed with a brief pause while the gentle applause filled the air as oxygen, making it easier to breathe.

"Thank you," I smiled. Their support was the biggest compliment. "Perspective can be thought as the 'ability to see something.' My three pieces this evening present one shot in three different perspectives as a result of the various ranges of focal length I applied. The effect on looking at the same image, but with different perspectives, reshapes the scene. I think we can agree that seeing love from different perspectives reshapes the relationship in and of itself. With love, following a sign or labeling it a coincidence gives you what you want to see. Perhaps, perspective allows you to see what you need to see. The reality of what is occurring."

Grayson politely interrupted, "This is real, Chloe. Please continue."

"Each piece represents a different stage of love. These are intimacy, passion, and commitment." Taking a small pause, I noticed an older man, maybe ten years my senior, standing away from the crowd and staring at me before turning my attention back to Grayson. Perhaps, he was an art dealer or potential customer with questions. *Chloe, you can do this.*

"Experimenting with these various focal lengths is a powerful part of your creative process, we can see. Could you offer a more detailed breakdown between photograph one and three?" Grayson asked.

"Photograph one is the widest perspective. You can see the perspective is exaggerated. This ultra wide perspective also increased the depth of field so you get the entire scene since everything is in focus," I finished, acknowledging the nods of understanding and a look to go on. "This represents the commitment stage since the shot shows the entirety of the image details and hence their relationship," I paused. "With photograph three, you can see how the subject and background compression is in full effect and the scenery appears to be close compared to photograph one. You can see the statue is isolated in relation to the background scene. This image represents the passion stage since passion is a deeper emotion. So, two shots of the same image, but through different perspectives, offering two scenarios," I continued. "The remaining photograph in between these two images represents intimacy, that close interpersonal relationship, but not fully an encompassing emotion like passion."

"And the two buildings behind the statue?" a voice asked.

"Those would be the two Time Warner Center skyscrapers towering in the background. You can see they're connected at the base of the building and located at the intersection of 8th Avenue, Broadway, Central Park South, and Central Park West," I said.

"Chloe, of all the unique and historical fixtures in this city, why choose this one?" Grayson Gates interrupted.

"Interestingly enough, this landmark is the point from which all official distances from New York City are measured. The heart, equal to this 70-foot granite column, is the landmark we use to measure love. Coming to learn how we love is a journey, and much like Columbus, sometimes you never know what you might discover."

"And this incorporation of perspective applies to love how?" Grayson Gates asked.

"I was inspired by what love teaches us if we're willing to learn it. Sometimes love is a circle of confusion between two individuals. Love is a lot of things—I believe true love always wins. True love wins all." Turning to look at my wall, "I admired these two-mirrored towers standing tall while reflecting each other. They are two soul mates, those twin souls," I shared.

"Bravo, Miss Kassidy. We can't miss the fact that a piece of your heart is the art on that wall," Grayson replied, followed by the crowd clapping and dispersing on to the next artist.

Chapter 37

Rejoining my friends and family, I was relieved it was over, although my career was just beginning. "You were awesome!" Emma said squeezing me almost to death. It was hard to believe it had only been a month since I'd seen her. "Here, this is for you." Emma handed me a sealed envelope with no address.

"What is this?" I asked. "A present?"

"I have no idea. While you were speaking, this man came up to me and asked if I would give it to you," she explained.

"Which man?"

"He was over—" Emma pointed to where the stocky older man I caught staring at me stood. She searched the room seeing if she could spot him.

"I'm sure he was a potential buyer or maybe even press, if you're lucky," she smiled. "He did seem quite scruffy to attend this party though."

While I started to open the envelope, "You were amazing!" my dad interrupted approaching me with open arms. We hugged as Kate and Stephanie waited their turn. I noticed my mother people watching, probably still trying to understand how my picture-taking hobby landed me here.

"Darling, Chloe," Grayson said beckoning for my attention and pulling me away. "I need you to meet a couple of interested dealers."

The evening was more than I had anticipated. With a whirlwind round of handshakes, hugs, cheek-to-cheek intros, I found myself back and embraced by my loved ones.

"Darling, Chloe," I knew it was Grayson Gates approaching me again from behind. While I downed the rest of my champagne, I noticed my friends staring in amazement like those kids building their bears and watching their creations come to life. "I wanted to bring over Reed Scott. I believe you two have met?" he continued.

His eyes. There was something in his eyes, the way he looked at me and the way I felt my posture confidently react with them on me. He tilted his head slightly with a subtle grin of pride. The moment had swallowed me. I knew his grin was for me. The exhibit felt far-gone into the past and we both stared into something familiar.

"Congratulations, Miss Kassidy," Reed said.

Turning back around to make a formal introduction, my parents and friends were beaming with embarrassing expressions. I knew right then, they had witnessed the connection too.

Towards the end of the evening after the reception, Reed and I found ourselves standing back in the same circle.

"Can I take you for a celebratory drink?" he asked.

I sensed Stephanie's eyes on us immediately.

"That sounds nice," I said, knowing it was late enough that my parents and Emma would be heading to the hotel for bed. "What time is it?"

He looked at his watch, "It's ten thirty-three."

"I could leave soon. When will you be ready?"

"How about ten thirty-four," he said teasing me again with his captivating smile.

I blushed when I noticed Alexander gave me a thumbs up while Stephanie made a *hooray* movement identical to a cheerleader. Before The Cudneys could be more obvious, I started my round of goodbyes.

While watching the traffic easing by us, Reed turned toward me.

"A little birdy told me that your birthday was last week," he said while reaching out and squeezing my pinky finger. "I think you deserve more than a drink. I know just the place to celebrate all things Chloe," he winked.

"I think you're right," I said. "Where?"

"It's a surprise . . . Many talented people have created memorable moments there." Reed threw up his arm and hailed a cab.

I felt my gravity pulling towards his.

We walked into P.J Clarkes, the box cart shaped institution full of history, ambiance, and an intense inviting smell that gave birth to hunger pangs that I hadn't noticed a minute before. Sinatra's song, *L-O-V-E* was on the jukebox competing with the banter of patrons. I recalled the evening of skating to Sinatra in search of clarity. I had been so confused that it was hard to recognize that part of me this evening.

We pushed our way through the crowd. "Do you mind eating at the bar? This experience requires front row seats."

"I want the full experience," I said. He pulled out a high top stool for me, took my purse, and hung it on the hook under the bar in front of me. I brushed my fingertips along the bar ledge feeling the grooves from the wear and tear of the patrons. I wondered who had sat on my stool before me and over all the years. I wanted to make history and leave my own mark.

A fortyish looking man approached us with his white sleeves rolled up, black suspenders and tie tucked behind the middle shirt button. "Well, look at this good looking couple," he greeted us.

I stared at the sensitive spot on my inner thumb at the word *couple* and Reed glanced over at me with that grin.

"Hey, man. I'm Reed. This is Chloe."

"I'm Drew. Pleasure to meet you guys."

"I need to feed this beautiful woman. She has never had the best sliders in town," Reed said.

Drew turned his attention to the bar back. "Set'em up!" he yelled and flashed two fingers while he poured a glass of champagne for me, a Macallan 12 for my company, and placed one menu in front of us to share.

A Billie Holiday song came on while we studied the food items. This was a joint, a real old school New York spot where, for a hundred years, people reunited, made acquaintances and from the pictures hanging on the wall, created long lasting memories. I realized why Reed adored this place. It was busy with old souls just like him. I noticed, centered among the various chalkboards scribbled with wine lists and beer options, two framed pictures that hung above the bar. There was President JFK and President Abraham Lincoln next to him. Lincoln's image reminded me of my new neighborhood and how so much had evolved these past few months. Nothing about tonight was planned or provoked. It was genuine.

Reed was a good egg.

Drew returned. "What can I do for you guys?"

"Definitely the sliders," Reed responded.

"How do you want them?" Drew asked.

"Medium rare," we both said at once. Reed looked at me relieved, "Thank God. I once had a bad experience with a 'well done' girl."

"Cheese, pickle, sliced onion?" Drew confirmed.

Reed glanced at me for the answer.

"Yep. Yep. Yep," I said, completely effortless.

We couldn't just tell each other how happy we were to put eyes on each other again. Too easy. It would never sell tickets like the show tonight. The energy had to come from us thinking that we were starring in a movie until I was convinced that he was a supporting role in mine. I had to admit (never to him) that I looked forward to us rewriting my script . . . often. *Light.* That was the one word I searched for that night in Miami to describe Reed wholeheartedly. He was this *light* who helped me along the way understand *love* for my theme.

When the bite sized burgers arrived, we each took one of the buttery toasted buns dripping with juice and raised them to each other, but there was nothing messy about us.

"Cheers."

I sensed our first fight. Immediately after the first bite, we both eyed the third slider sitting solo on the plate. The hard part to explain is that his handsomeness wouldn't even make the first page of his resume with his charm. While we ate, we talked through our silences and not words, but our own gestures, and whispers. In his presence, I felt myself light-hearted.

I headed into the restroom to freshen up and apply lip-gloss when I saw the envelope Emma had handed me in my bag.

Dear Chloe,

I haven't been completely honest with you. I'm not married. I don't have kids. I'm not an Internet stalker. I might be relieved if any of the above were true, because then I would have a starting point to explain why I'm acting the way that I've been. You weren't a book project or any sort of project for that matter. I'm not a writer. I don't work with the United Nations.

Chloe, the first time I laid eyes on you, I was breathless. I never knew that such beauty could exist. I caught a glimpse of the beautiful soul behind your huge brown eyes. It was as if I was created in that exact second of time. It was as if my previous forty years had never existed or mattered at that point. You gave me life.

It was fate that I visited Mary in Brooklyn, her wonderful new city as she started her American life. I passed the time away in Barnes & Noble when I saw you holding The Reader. You left so fast following the bookstore employee to check out. I overheard you talking about book club, giving him your e-mail address and I couldn't ignore my desire to contact you.

And as my supportive secretary goes, Mary is my sister, who helped me connect with you. By meeting you, I know she helped me out of her own unconditional love for her brother. We only had each other left since our younger brother's death and somehow felt responsible for each other's happiness. A distraction from our own grief and loss, I suppose. Perhaps, our brother Christoph is your soul mate.

God, do I miss him. He was exceptionally talented with his music and book writing. I think he would have fallen in love with you the moment he laid eyes on you, just like I did. I question how God took him away. I question why he was the one who was born with a loving heart, yet toxic blood that pumped through it. I question why I'm not the one who passed away from Hodgkin's disease at twenty-eight years of age. I question how I could abuse his eyes, his words, his language and his heart to win my beautiful Chloe. But, we were brothers, so isn't he a part of me? Perhaps, you'll connect in another lifetime, but Chloe you were mine in this one.

Losing him meant I was left with nothing, and somehow with your belief in me, your encouragement, your sincere words and efforts, you made me feel . . . good about who I am, about what I have to offer, about what I can do with myself and life. You became my daily buddy, the person I confided in, and the person I knew would never hurt me or not help me.

The realization that I was living true love with finding you, I think it takes that instant for a man like me to feel that he's holding the entire world in that little square matchbox and for that I'll be grateful to you eternally. Chloe, you deserve the best man that there is, the prince who will bend down on his knee and make you the princess of his heart and his life forever.

Please know I sincerely apologize for every bad hour I may have caused you. I lost my way and I had no right to be selfish, to want you there with me, as much as I may have loved you, and even though I thought that love conquers all. I'll always be your greatest fan. I'll always smile at the thought of your successes. I will not bother you again. I'm sorry.

Eternally yours,
Phillip

Phillip? Taking a deep breath, I folded the letter into the envelope and dropped it in the trash. I made my own signs, my own fate. I had to determine my own path. There was only one constant in all of those past muffled up thoughts with this stranger and that was me. I was more powerful and more worthy than any of this, and I knew my heart would reign undoubtedly, no matter what it experienced. Life was certainly more interesting when you open yourself up to living without fear. I had learned to overcome fear and grow as a woman and an artist without it being my driving force.

Reed hailed a cab for me. When he grabbed the handle, he paused. "I would love to see you again, Chloe."

"Me too."

"I'll be back in New York on February eleventh, if that works for you."

"Well, I'm quite busy being an accomplished photographer and all," I smiled.

"You did sell all three of your pieces tonight."

I couldn't comprehend the price paid for my photographs. Grayson Gates's publicist had approached me after my presentation, informing me of the press interviews and project she secured me immediately after my last photograph sold. My dreams had now become full-time.

"It's a date," I said and gave him a hug with a small kiss on his cheek before letting go. Somehow Reed Scott's proposal of a second date felt already made and accepted before he even asked me. Without either of us approving or even witnessing, we had already connected before biting into the beef tonight.

The thought of chasing fairy tales that had been repeated through generation after generation amused me. The greatest love story ever told would be my very own. I realized this now. That my perspective on true love was for internal use only.

I took a mental snap shot of the handsome gentleman standing right there in front of me. I thought if Reed Scott hadn't existed, it'd be the exact same man I would have invented.

While the cab pulled away, I raised my hand to wave one last time.

Keep in touch with Cari at www.carikamm.com. You can also connect with her on Facebook at (www.facebook.com/CariKamm. Author) and Twitter (@CariKamm) for the latest news on events, giveaways, and her next book release.

18974465R00236

Made in the USA
Charleston, SC
30 April 2013